Praise for John Lutz

"Brilliant . . . a very scary and suspenseful read."
— *Booklist* on *In for the Kill*

"Lutz has a thorough command of plot and character, making this another enthralling page-turner."
—*Publishers Weekly* on *In for the Kill*

"Lutz can deliver a hard-boiled p.i. novel or a bloody thriller with equal ease. . . . The ingenuity of the plot shows that Lutz is in rare form."
—*The New York Times Book Review* on *Chill of Night*

"Lutz keeps the suspense high and populates his story with a collection of unique characters . . . an ideal beach read."
—*Publishers Weekly* on *Chill of Night*

"John Lutz knows how to make you shiver."
—Harlan Coben

"John Lutz is one of the masters of the police novel."
—Ridley Pearson

"A major talent."
—John Lescroart

"I've been a fan for years."
—T. Jefferson Parker

"John Lutz just keeps getting better and better."
—Tony Hillerman

"A gripping thriller . . . extremely taut scenes, great descriptions, nicely depicted supporting players . . . Lutz is good with characterization."
—*reviewingtheevidence.com* on *The Night Watcher*

"For a good scare and a well-paced story, Lutz delivers."
—*San Antonio Express News*

"Lutz knows how to seize and hold the reader's imagination."
—*Cleveland Plain Dealer*

"*SWF Seeks Same* is a complex, riveting, and chilling portrayal of urban terror, as well as a wonderful novel of New York City. Echoes of *Rosemary's Baby*, but this one's scarier because it could happen." —Jonathan Kellerman

"Lutz is a fine craftsman." —*Booklist* on *The Ex*

"A psychological thriller that few readers will be able to put down." —*Publishers Weekly* on *SWF Seeks Same*

"Tense and relentless." —*Publishers Weekly* on *The Torch*

"The author has the ability to capture his readers with fear, and has compiled a myriad of frightful chapters that captures and holds until the final sentence."
—*New Orleans Times-Picayune* on *Bonegrinder*

"Likable protagonists in a complex thriller."
—*Booklist* on *Final Seconds*

"Lutz is rapidly bleeding critics dry of superlatives."
—*St. Louis Post-Dispatch*

"It's easy to see why he's won an Edgar and two Shamuses."
—*Publishers Weekly*

NIGHT KILLS

JOHN LUTZ

PINNACLE BOOKS
KENSINGTON PUBLISHING CORP.
www.kensingtonbooks.com

Women and birds are able to see without turning
their heads,
and that is indeed a necessary provision, for they are
both surrounded by enemies.

—James Stephens, *The Demi-Gods*

1

Madeline was on the run.

She should have known better. She really should have.

An insect—a large bee or wasp—whizzed past close to her ear as she skidded around a corner, her right foot almost slipping out of her low-cut sneaker. An instant later came a flat *Blam!* She knew he was shooting at her.

No doubt now as to what he'd had in mind in the car.

He's trying to kill me!

Why? What did I do?

She was gasping for breath now, beginning to stumble from exhaustion as she ran down the dark street. Even late as it was, even in this neighborhood, *somebody* must be awake who would help her. *Anyone!*

Terror propelled her. Terror and the steady, relentless pounding of his footsteps behind her.

What caused this?

What's this about?

If he gets close enough to take another shot . . .

Her right side was aching now. The pain was an enemy trying to bend her body forward so she could no longer run, no longer live. Her legs weren't merely tired. They were becoming so numb that she could hardly feel any contact with the sidewalk.

Madeline was ready to surrender to the inevitable, and then she saw a shifting of shadow and a brightening at the next dark intersection.

A car's coming!

Behind her, closer, the gun fired again. It sounded like the flat of one huge palm slapping against another. There was a finality to the sharp report.

It signaled the end of something.

2

Retired homicide detective Frank Quinn was having strong black coffee after his breakfast at the Lotus Diner on Amsterdam when a saggy-jowled man who looked like a well-tailored bloodhound sat down opposite him.

"I know I'm late," the bloodhound growled.

"How so?" Quinn asked, sipping his coffee.

"If it were up to you, I'd have been here much sooner."

Quinn didn't answer. Overconfident people bored him.

The two men were almost exact opposites. The bloodhound, who was New York Police Commissioner Harley Renz, was not only saggy jowled but saggy bodied. He'd put on about forty pounds in the past few years, and the expensive chalk-stripe blue suit didn't disguise it as workable muscle. All vertical stripes did for Renz was zigzag.

Quinn, on the other hand, was tall and rangy, with a firm jaw, a nose broken once too often, and disconcerting flat green eyes. His straight, gray-flecked dark hair was cut short, and recently, but, as always, looked as if a barber should shape it to suit a human head. If Renz was the bloodhound, there was something of the wolf in Quinn.

"You're glad to see me," Renz went on, "because you don't like rotting in retirement at the age of fifty-five."

Thel the waitress came over and Quinn said, "A coffee for my antagonist."

"I haven't had breakfast," Renz said. "I'll have a waffle, too. Diet syrup."

"Stuff tastes like tree sap," Thel said. She was a dumpy, middle-aged woman who'd never been pretty, so substituted being frank. It worked pretty well for her.

"The real stuff, then," Renz said, grateful to be nudged off his diet.

Quinn listened for a moment to Upper West Side traffic flowing past on Amsterdam. Somebody just outside shouted an obscenity. Somebody leaned on a car horn and shouted back. New York.

"I'm rotting fast," he said. "Why don't you get to the point?"

"Sure. I need you and your team again."

Quinn and the two detectives Renz had assigned to him on his last case had become media darlings by tracking down a serial killer aptly called the Butcher. Their success had also resulted in Renz's swift climb up the promotional ladder to commissioner. He was, in fact, one of the most popular commissioners the city had ever known. In New York that meant he could do just about as he pleased, including yanking three detectives temporarily back into the NYPD as long as they were willing. He knew Quinn would be willing. And if Quinn was willing, so would be his two detectives. Like Renz, Quinn was a hard man to refuse.

"Why do you need us?"

Renz smiled. Still looked like a bloodhound. "In this city, Quinn, you're Mister Serial Killer."

"I'm not sure I like the way you put that."

"You know what I mean."

"Last time we went to work for you, you got promoted all the way to commissioner."

"And you got your good name back and became a big hero. There's something in this for both of us, Quinn. This for that. Tit for tat. That's how the world works."

"Your world."

"Well, that's the one I live in."

"What's next for you, Harley, mayor?"

Renz shrugged. "Who knows?" He seemed serious. Quinn couldn't see Harley as mayor. But then he hadn't been able to see him as police commissioner, and there he sat. Police commissioner.

"What are the terms?" Quinn asked.

"Work for hire. It won't interfere with your settlement or interrupt your retirement pay."

Quinn wasn't worried about the pay. Soon after the Night Prowler case, he'd gotten a large settlement from the city after having been falsely accused of raping a fourteen-year-old girl. Another cop had done it, and Quinn proved it. There was noplace Quinn could go to get his reputation back, so he settled for enough money to pay his attorneys and support himself comfortably with or without his pension.

"If I'm going to do it," he said, "it's got to interest me."

"Oh, it will."

Thel came over with Renz's coffee and waffle, and maple syrup in a container that looked like one of those little liquor bottles the airlines give you.

"This," Thel said, tapping the bottle's cap with a chipped, red-enameled nail, "is good stuff. Straight from the tree."

"I believe you, sweetheart," Renz said.

When she'd walked away, he slathered his waffle with butter, then poured the little bottle's entire contents over it.

"We've got us a serial killer," he said to Quinn, "but the media's not onto it yet. Except for Cindy Sellers, who's sitting on it."

"How many victims?"

"Two women."

"Doesn't sound like enough to make a serial killer."

"They were both killed in identical, distinctive ways."

"Then you have the bodies."

It wasn't a question. Renz picked up knife and fork and attacked his breakfast. "Parts of them," he said. "Well, that's not quite accurate," he amended through a mouthful of waffle. "We've got just their torsos."

He swallowed, then smacked his lips together in appreciation. "This stuff is yummy."

Which seemed a strange thing for a bloodhound to say, especially one who was police commissioner, but there it was.

Thel sashayed over with some more coffee immediately when Renz had forked in his last bite of waffle, probably because he'd called her sweetheart.

She returned to behind the counter.

"Shot with the same gun," Renz said, pushing away his empty plate. He dipped a finger into the residue of syrup and licked, then took a sip of coffee. Not in a rush. Relishing his tale. "Twenty-two-caliber hollow point, through the heart."

"Small gun."

"Big enough. The M.E. says the wounds were fatal, but the victims might have taken a while to die. Could be they were finished off with shots to the head. Not having the heads, we wouldn't know."

"Professional?"

"Nah. Pro wouldn't go to all the trouble of dismembering the bodies."

Quinn figured that was true. Then he cautioned himself not to come to any conclusions so soon.

"The other thing," Renz said, "is that both women were sexually violated by a long, sharply pointed instrument. Not a knife, more like a stake."

"Tell me that happened after they died," Quinn said.

"It did according to Nift." Nift was Dr. Julius Nift, a skillful but verbally brutal medical examiner. "Nift seemed disappointed by this glimmer of mercy in the killer."

"More like convenience," Quinn said. "Easier to bring down a victim with a bullet before going to work with a sharp instrument."

"That's why you the man," Renz said. "You can slip right into the minds of these sick creeps."

"Into yours, too."

"You figure he does that thing with the sharp stake or whatever 'cause he can't get it up?"

"There you go."

Renz licked some more syrup off a finger and smiled at Quinn. "So whaddya say?"

"We're on," Quinn said. "I'll call Feds and Pearl."

Feds was retired homicide detective Larry Fedderman.

Pearl was . . . well, Pearl.

And that could be a problem.

3

Pearl was short and curvaceous, buxom, and even in her gray uniform looked almost too vivid to be real. Perfect pale complexion. Black, black hair and eyes. White, white perfectly even large teeth. And there was a kind of energy about her that seemed as if it might attract paper clips if she got close to them.

She watched the man over at the table where the deposit and withdrawal slips were filled out. He seemed to be taking a long time filling out whichever he'd chosen, and he kept glancing around the bank.

Sixth National Bank was an older institution and boasted lots of marble, walnut paneling, and polished brass. Behind the long row of tellers' cages the great vault's open door was visible, like the entrance to the nineteenth century. This was the kind of bank where if anything changed it was with the slowness of molasses dripping on a cold day, and you just knew your money was safe.

Pearl liked being a bank guard at Sixth National. It was like a relaxed version of being a cop. The uniform might be gray instead of blue, but it was a uniform. You spent a lot of time on your feet, and many of the required skills were the same. If only the pay were better. But she wasn't complaining. She'd probably never remove the gun on her hip from its holster. Even if one of these days somebody like the dork at the walnut writing table really was casing the bank, or about to present a teller with a note informing him or her of a stickup.

And if it ever did happen, hell, Pearl was ready.

The guy who'd been writing so laboriously, a skinny dude with a sleeveless shirt and lots of tattoos—the washed-out blue kind they got in prison—finally left the table and sauntered over to one of the tellers. He handed the teller what looked like a deposit slip and some cash.

Pearl relaxed and moved back to stand against the wall, out of the way of the customers. She did keep a wary eye on Mr. Tattoos, though.

Her cell phone, on a belt clip near her nine millimeter, buzzed and vibrated. She tucked in her chin and glanced down at it, holding it at an angle so she could see the display.

Quinn's number.

She unclipped the phone and flipped up the lid so she could speak.

"Hello, Quinn," she said simply.

"I've got a proposition," said the voice on the phone.

"Been there, done that," Pearl said.

Her gaze returned to the tattooed guy and the teller, a woman named Judy. Judy was twentyish and chubby and had a round, pretty face that usually didn't display much emotion except at lunchtime. She was frowning now at Mr. Tats. Were they arguing?

"What kind of proposition?" Pearl asked, trying to hurry this along.

"Renz came by to see me. Seems there's a serial killer operating in the city. The news hasn't reached the media yet, but it's about to pop. Cindy Sellers of *City Beat* is sitting on it and about to release it."

Pearl remembered Cindy Sellers, a hard-ass little brunette who tended to move fast in straight lines.

Well, maybe the same could be said of Pearl.

"A serial killer could be harmful to Renz's career," Pearl said.

"Not if he's responsible for nailing the killer. Or seems to be. Then his career gets a major boost. He wants me to reassemble the team and try to achieve that result."

"He's already police commissioner. What more does he want?"

"Long term, I don't think we want to know. Whatever his motivation, he wants us on the hunt again."

Throughout the conversation, Pearl had kept watching Mr. Tattoo and Judy. They *were* arguing. Judy's round face was pale and she looked uncharacteristically furious, obviously trying to keep her cool. The guy with the tats was leaning toward her doing most of the talking.

"Pearl?"

"Yeah," she said, angling over and beginning to move toward Judy and the skinny guy with the tattooed arms. Dozens of tattoos, kind of connected, what they called full sleeve. "Serial killer. Sounds interesting."

"All the good guys have to work with are the victims' torsos. He also sexually mutilates the women with a sharply pointed object like a stake. I haven't called Feds yet. You in?"

"Just their torsos, you say?"

"Right. Both women shot through the heart, and with the same gun."

"Damn," Pearl said.

Mr. Tattoo said something that made Judy flinch, then he wheeled and made for the door at a fast walk.

Pearl looked at Judy.

Judy looked at Pearl.

Judy looked at Mr. Tattoo and silently mouthed, *"Stop him!"*

"You in, Pearl?"

Pearl took two long strides, shoved a woman in a teller's line aside, and made for the tattooed guy. "You," she said softly but firmly, so as not to cause instant bedlam. "Stop right where you are."

"What's that, Pearl? What's going on?"

She slipped the cell phone into a side pocket of her gray uniform pants and caught up with the tattooed guy. He glanced at her and broke into a run. Pearl tackled him and brought him down on the hard marble floor, bumping her elbow hard enough that her right arm went numb. Customers were moving fast, like dancing shadows, on the periphery of her vision. A woman screamed.

"Hey, you bitch!" yelled the tattooed guy, scrambling to get up.

Pearl kicked his legs out from under him.

"Hey!" he yelled again and scooted backward out of her reach. Didn't try to get up, though.

She fumbled for her gun and couldn't get it out of its holster. Hell with it. She crawled over and turned Mr. Tats on his belly and reached around for her handcuffs. He wasn't resisting. The kick in the legs she'd given him might have sprung one of his knees.

"Miss Kasner!" a woman's voice was saying. "Miss Kasner, don't hurt him! Please!"

Pearl looked up to see Judy standing over her. Behind Judy, all around the lobby, the bank's customers were frozen by fear. Some of them were on the floor like Pearl and the tattooed guy.

"You asked me to stop him," Pearl said to Judy. "Didn't he try to rob the bank?"

"No. He just robbed me by refusing to give me my child support money. He's my ex-husband, is all, not a bank robber."

Pearl struggled to her feet, furious. The pain in her elbow flared. "Why the hell did you ask me to stop him?"

"I dunno. I just did." Judy began to cry.

"I'm gonna goddamn sue you!" snarled the tattooed guy, sitting up now and glaring at Pearl.

"*Sue* me? You're lucky I didn't—"

"Miss Kasner."

Another voice. That of Copperthwaite, the bank manager. "When Judy calms down I'd like to see both of you in my office."

"I-I'm okay." Judy sniffled and used the back of her wrist to wipe her eyes, which were blackened by running mascara, making her look like a distraught raccoon. She kneeled low and brushed a lock of hair from Mr. Tats's forehead.

"Jesus H. Christ!" Pearl swore, dusting herself off and rubbing her sore elbow.

"Pearl . . . ?"

Yet another voice. Very faint. Familiar.

Oh, yeah. Quinn.

Pearl fished the cell phone out of her pocket and held it to her ear.

"I'm in," she said.

Fedderman wondered if he'd retired too soon. He was the youngest of the golf foursome from the Coral Castle condo project on Florida's serene and scenic southwest coast. It was like paradise here except for hurricane season, and Fedderman knew he should be happy despite the fact that his wife, Blanche, had left him . . . what, a year ago now. It seemed much shorter. All he had to do in life was collect his pension and lie around the condo or play golf. Being retired, he was supposed to like just lying around. He was supposed to like golf.

He was supposed to like fishing, too, but frankly some of the things he'd caught in the ocean while deep-sea fishing scared him. Not to mention the seasickness.

"Hit the damned ball, Larry!" Chet, one of his foursome, shouted.

Fedderman looked back at him and waved. His drive had taken him off the fairway and into the rough, which was to say high saw grass that would cut your hand if you tried to pull up a clump. It was a miracle he'd even found the damned ball.

Never a man whose clothes quite fit, Fedderman's tall and lanky yet potbellied form even made his golf outfit look like it belonged on someone else. One sleeve of his blue knit pullover seemed longer than the other, and his muted plaid slacks made him look as if he were standing in a brisk wind even though the weather was calm. And hot. And humid.

As he approached the ball, Fedderman slapped at a mosquito and missed. His seemingly mismatched body parts made for an interesting golf swing as he took a practice swish, then moved closer and slashed the ball out of the rough. It rose neatly toward the green, carrying Fedderman's hope with it, then suddenly veered right as if it had encountered the jet stream and landed among some trees.

"You missed the sand trap, anyway!" Chet shouted. Fedderman was learning to dislike Chet.

Fedderman's shot again. His three fellow golfers were already on the green. He was isolated in what seemed a forest of palm trees near a running creek. There was his ball. Not a bad lie, on a stretch of grass that wasn't so high, because the sun never reached it beneath the closely grouped palms.

Something moved near the creek. Fedderman stared but saw nothing in the tall grass. He'd heard about alligators on the golf course but had never seen one, even on his frequent journeys into the rough. Still, he was sure he'd seen some kind of movement not human and it gave him the creeps.

He quickly approached his ball and set himself. He'd have to keep the shot low and get the ball between the trunks of two palm trees if he even had a chance to get near the barely visible green.

"Shoot the ball!" Chet yelled. "Shoot the ball, Larry!"
Shoot you, you dumb bastard!

Movement again, in the corner of his vision. There sure as hell was something over there in the shadows.

Fedderman took a quick practice swing, then hurried his shot.

He really nailed this one. Solid. It felt great.

The ball flew about ten feet, bounced off a palm trunk, and rocketed straight back and hit Fedderman in the head.

He threw down his club and clutched his skull, then staggered out into the searing sunlight. His cleated golf shoes snagged in the tall grass and he almost fell. Chet was yelling something, maybe laughing.

Damn Chet!

Damn golf!

Damn Florida!

He had to get out of here! Had to!

Fedderman's cell phone chirped.

4

Two months earlier

Shellie Marston paced in the vast glass and marble atrium of the CitiGroup Building at Third Avenue and Fifty-third Street. She walked again past a display window and tried to glance at her reflection without attracting attention. She saw a woman in her late twenties with medium-cut blond hair, a definitely filled-out but not *too* fat figure in a new maroon Avanti sweat suit and startlingly white New Balance jogging shoes. She wore a white scarf around her neck. *Too much?* Not considering that she was wearing no jewelry other than small gold hoop earrings, and her very practical-looking wristwatch with its black Velcro band. This was supposed to be a casual first meeting with . . . David Adams. It took her a second to recall his name. A meeting in a public place arranged by E-Bliss.org.

The atrium wasn't very crowded, but all the hard surfaces created an echoing effect that made it seem that way. Voices and shuffling soles created a constant background buzz. New Yorkers and tourists alike were strolling along the lines of shops or hurrying to and from the escalators.

As she looked away from the display window, Shellie saw that one of the small round tables set outside the shops was available. She'd bought an egg cream in a foam cup so she'd have something to do with her hands. Carrying it carefully so it wouldn't spill, she quickly laid claim to the tiny table and sat down. She placed the cup just so on the napkin she'd been provided.

His first impression would be of her seated. Was that okay?

If she sat gracefully enough. She made sure her thighs were together and placed one New Balance jogger slightly in front of the other, rested her left hand in her lap. That should present a reasonably graceful picture.

She raised her left hand briefly to glance at the watch on her wrist. He was five minutes late. She nervously took a sip of egg cream. Was he actually going to show up? Or was she going to sit here another—how long—fifteen minutes? The two old men playing chess at the nearest table had stolen looks at her; they knew she was waiting for someone.

Shellie tried not to feel embarrassed. It didn't matter if she was stood up, she told herself, not in New York. This city was full of improbable and unpredictable characters.

None of whom she knew more than casually, however. Shellie had been in the city a little more than a month. She was still operating on the inheritance she'd brought with her from Bluebonnet, Nebraska. All her mother had in the world, plus her mother's life insurance money. Shellie's dad had died ten years ago. A distant aunt had died only a few months ago, and Shellie had no siblings. She was on her own in the world, which was one reason why she'd decided to start a new life in New York.

Why not the biggest, most interesting city in the country? Shellie had her nerve, and her college degree in general education. Always a loner, there was no one she was particularly friendly with in Bluebonnet. There was nothing in the romance area, certainly, now that she'd broken off her affair with Mark Drucker. Hulking and ever-smiling Mark. Big high school football hero, college dropout, and TV addict. All Mark wanted to do was have sex and watch movies and shows on TV. Old *The Dukes of Hazzard* episodes. *My God!* Well, Shellie hoped that by now he'd found someone to share his passions, both in front of the TV and in the backseat of his meticulously restored '69 Camaro (his real true love). For her it was time for something more challenging and promising. Time to see if she could make it on her own.

And she could—she was sure of it. But she was so damned lonely. New York could do that to you. There you were, swimming in an ocean of humanity, and if you knew no one well, you were as isolated as if you were a castaway on a remote island.

Shellie had finally given in to something she'd been long considering. Using a matchmaking service to alleviate her loneliness hadn't seemed like the best idea she'd ever had, but she'd finally decided to give it a try. Sometimes in life you had to take a chance.

After spending weeks visiting the website of E-Bliss.org, she'd filled out the detailed questionnaire that allowed the agency to match her with the best possible bet as a future mate. Then she'd waited.

After slightly more than a week, the nervously antici-pated e-mail had appeared on her computer screen. The at-tached profile hadn't revealed much about her prospective soul mate, David Adams. It hadn't even included his photo. Well, that was okay. Shellie remembered how hesitant she'd been to send her photo to E-Bliss.org. After all, once your image was on the Internet, who knew where it might pop up? Someone might even superimpose her head on the body of another woman doing God knew what. Maybe even com-mitting unnatural acts. Shellie had heard of it happening.

She'd been permitted to choose the public place that was

to be the scene of their first meeting, so here she was at the agreed-upon time.

Now it was ten minutes past that time, and here was Shellie still waiting to share conversation and perhaps another egg cream with the first date she'd had since moving to New York. (She didn't count the scuzzy guy who'd stuck out his tongue at her and tried to pick her up outside Starbucks last week.)

On the other side of the atrium, pretending now and then to look into the show window of a luggage shop, David Adams watched her. Shellie Marston. From Nebraska, no less. He smiled. Maybe he'd been expecting too much. She wasn't perfect, but she'd do.

Adams was wearing neatly pressed khakis, a blue pull-over shirt with a collar, white jogging shoes. Even from this distance he could see that Shellie was also wearing white joggers. His smile widened. Already they had something in common. Maybe this would really work.

He was a handsome man with regular features not easily remembered from a glance. It took a while for his bland but masculine visage to register as attractive. His hair was dark brown, wavy, and worn a bit long to disguise the fact that his ears stuck out. He was slightly under six feet tall and moved with athletic ease. His body was compact and muscular, his waist narrow. His was the sort of physique that wore clothes well. He was all in all nonthreatening, and there was certainly nothing not to like about him. Easy manner, nice smile, clean, and well groomed. He was the sort who'd fit well in most women's romantic fantasies. And of course when he did finally bed them, they saw him as the ideal from the desires and dreams they'd carried since their first kiss.

He took another longer and bolder look at Shellie Marston and decided she was a go. He moved toward her with an easy grace, gaze fixed on her.

She'd spotted him now. These first few minutes were important. He watched her face.

It was, as usual, good strategy to be late. For an instant, relief that he'd shown up at all flooded her features. Then she had her mask on again.

He smiled at her and she managed to smile back.

Shellie made herself smile at the man she was now sure was approaching her table. He must be David Adams. She didn't know why she'd had to make herself smile. There was nothing wrong with this guy. Not that she could see, anyway. He didn't look like the type who'd need a matchmaking service. But then Shellie didn't see herself as that type, either.

She told herself again that there was nothing disreputable or dangerous about Internet hookups. Not anymore. This was a competitive and busy world, especially here in the largest and busiest of cities. People didn't have time to move tentatively in finding and developing relationships, as they often still did in Nebraska. She'd even known a girl in high school whose prospective suitors had to ask her parents' permission to date her.

Quaint, Shellie thought. And even if someone wanted to ask Shellie's father for her hand, she didn't have a father. She had only herself. And she could make up her own mind.

The closer David Adams got to her table, the more sure she was that she'd made the right decision in contacting E-Bliss.org.

"Shellie?" he asked when he was within a few feet of her. Even that one word—her name—was smooth and softly modulated. This was a gentle man, obviously. A bit hesitant and shy, like herself. A gentle man, but not at all effeminate.

"Shellie," she confirmed, then smiled and stood up. She felt the sole of one New Balance slide over the toe of the other. *Not noticeable.* "You must be David."

They shook hands. Gentle again.

Flesh upon flesh. Shellie hoped there might be some electricity there. Some arc of emotion that suggested a future truly meaningful. Physical attraction wasn't everything, except at first.

She wasn't disappointed.

5

The present

Cindy Sellers sat alone at a corner table in P.J. Clarke's on Third Avenue and Fifty-fifth Street. Around her were muted voices, the occasional clink of flatware on china, and laughter from the adjoining bar. The mingled scents of spices hung in the air.

The restaurant part of the venerable tavern was dim, with dark wood paneling, and there was something about the young woman seated in isolation before her bowl of stew and a Guinness that discouraged any of the rogues and business types at the bar or some of the other tables from approaching her. She was reasonably attractive, with inquisitive large brown eyes, short brown hair, and a trim figure, but there was an intensity about her that sometimes drove people away. She was very good at going after those people, overcoming their reluctance, and getting them to talk about matters they wouldn't have dreamed of telling anyone else.

It was still too early for the dinner crowd, and the place was quiet enough for her to think, which was why she'd come here. Before her on the table were her notes on what she'd chosen to call the Torso Murders, as well as a revised draft of what would be her story.

And a hell of a story it was. The time was near when she'd no longer feel obligated to keep it all off the record, as she'd promised Renz.

In fact, maybe the time *was* here.

Cindy took a sip of Guinness and allowed that the public had a right to know if a sadistic killer was in its midst and might kill again. It was, in fact, her professional obligation to inform the people, as long as it would sell papers and advance her journalism career. But Renz was police commissioner now, not just another workaday cop with rank, and he was riding a political high. Of course, he didn't know that he wasn't her only source, and that she was aware he'd called in retired homicide captain Frank Quinn, along with his detective team, that pushy bitch Pearl and the hapless but occasionally shrewd Fedderman, to work the case. There were people in the NYPD hierarchy who didn't like the prospect of semioutsiders covering themselves and Renz with glory so Renz could advance to an even higher office. These dissatisfied cops were people Cindy Sellers could and did use.

Certainly Renz wouldn't like it if the quasi-official presence of Quinn and his team was revealed too soon. On the other hand, he knew they'd be media subjects sooner or later—that was even the idea. They were, after all, part of Renz's team—working for him in particular as well as for the city. And Renz wouldn't be shocked by the fact that the NYPD had more than one leak.

Still, he *was* the commissioner. Cindy understood and respected power. She would give it its due, up to a point.

She took a long pull of Guinness and fished her cell phone from her purse on the chair beside her. Renz's direct number was on her speed dial.

No answer.

She tried his cell phone.

Apparently it was turned off.

Cindy dialed the general number of the Puzzle Palace, her term for One Police Plaza, and was politely put on ignore. She sighed and drummed her fingers. Waiting patiently for anything wasn't in Cindy's nature.

Hell with him, she thought, cutting the connection. She'd tried to give him a heads-up before releasing the story every other media outlet in the city probably knew about anyway but couldn't confirm. The clock was ticking and she'd done what she could.

Cindy had been here before and knew how it worked. When *City Beat* hit the newsstands and vending machines tomorrow morning, the hounds would be loosed. Renz as well as the killer would have to play the fox. Quinn and his detectives would occupy the area between hounds and foxes, perilous ground.

Keyed up as she was with anticipation, Cindy wasn't hungry. She took another long sip of Guinness and pushed aside her barely touched bowl of stew. Placing her half-rim reading glasses low on the bridge of her nose, she arranged the draft of her story—which was jotted down in her own custom shorthand that only she could read—before her on the table. Then she flicked down the menu on her cell phone and pressed the button that dialed her editor at *City Beat*.

"Are you sitting down?" she asked when he picked up.

Without waiting for an answer, she told him what she had and began reading aloud into the phone, but not so loud that anyone in the restaurant might overhear.

Just as she'd thought, he loved it.

By the time she flipped down the lid of her phone, Cindy's appetite had magically returned. She pulled the still-warm bowl of stew back close to her from across the table and ordered another Guinness.

He'd sawn the broomstick in half. Now he finished sharpening one end and began the sanding. He enjoyed this part.

He would use increasingly more finely grained sandpaper as he shaped the end into a gradually tapered fine point.

For almost an hour he sanded, idly watching television as he worked. An old spaghetti Western starring Clint Eastwood was playing. The TV was on mute, so he could only read Eastwood's taut dialogue in closed caption at the bottom of the screen. That was okay. He'd seen the movie half a dozen times and could practically fill in the dialogue himself. The rhythmic sound of the sandpaper on wood was soothing as he felt the tapering broomstick take shape in his hands.

Finally, when his hands and forearms began to ache from the effort, he set the broomstick and sandpaper aside. He ran a finger along the shaft of the broomstick, all the way to its point. The wood was smooth now and would require only about an hour's more sanding with the finely grained paper. Then he would go over it with tack cloth, and later he'd apply a good oil and rub it in well. Not too much oil. He wanted the sharpened broomstick smooth, but not too smooth. Feeling the resistance, that was part of it.

It wasn't supposed to excite him; that hadn't been part of the plan. But it did. There was no denying it. And it made him wonder, did they have to be dead?

His throat was tight. He swallowed.

Amazing, he thought, the things you discovered about yourself. It was his job that kept opening doors in his mind. He was so good at what he did, sometimes it scared him.

Eastwood chewed on his stubby cigar and squinted at him from the TV screen.

Eastwood, or at least the characters he usually played in his movies, wouldn't approve of him. But when the actor was younger, he might well have been handed altogether different kinds of scripts and would now be seen in an altogether different light. The man was an actor; his public image and probably his personal image had been shaped by the scripts he was given, written by someone he might never have met. In a way, we were all in the movies, whether we knew it or not.

He smiled at Eastwood, then went over to an antique roll-top desk and removed a drawer. Reaching into the cavity left by the missing drawer, he worked a wooden lever that opened a secret compartment in the side of the desk. From the compartment he withdrew a gray metal lockbox with the key in it. He turned the key, opened the lid, and reached in and got out a small Colt semiautomatic, holding the gun by its checked handle. It fired hollow-point twenty-two-caliber bullets and made little more noise than a loud slap. Not a powerful weapon, but the hollow points would penetrate a human being and break into pieces that would rip and tumble through bone and tissue and cause a great deal of localized damage. One careful shot to the heart was enough to bring someone down. If the wound itself wasn't sufficient to kill, the person would lie there in shock. And while the person lay stunned and disbelieving, almost certainly dying, two shots to the head would be enough to make sure. That's what the little Colt was—sure. He had a fondness for the gun.

He glanced at the silent TV screen. Eastwood was on a horse now, raising a lot of dust while galloping hell for leather over terrain that looked like Arizona but was probably in Italy.

What must that be like, flying across a purpling plain on a white and brown speckled horse? It must really impress the ladies. The ones in Rome and Milan, anyway.

He'd heard or read somewhere that Eastwood bought his cigars in a shop in Beverly Hills and cut them in half for his movie scenes. So much in life was an act.

Ignoring the TV, he removed a cleaning kit and some gun oil from the metal lockbox, along with a soft white cotton cloth.

He was about to clean and oil the gun when his cell phone, on top of the rolltop desk, played the first few bars of "Get Me to the Church on Time."

He glanced at the Caller ID before answering the phone. "I was hoping you'd call," he said, smiling.

A pause.

"Yes," he said, still smiling. "Of course. Of course. Yes. Yes. You know I do. Yes."

He put down the gun and wandered the room as he talked, as if motion would lend import to his words. Whoever was on the other end of the connection was receiving his full attention.

"Okay," he said, "I'll see you there. You can't know how much I'm looking forward to it." He idly picked up the broomstick and observed its sharpened point as he listened to the caller.

"See you there," he said again. "Love you."

6

Death had drawn them together again. They met at Quinn's first-floor apartment on West Seventy-fifth off Columbus in the room he'd converted into a den. Quinn sat behind his big cherrywood desk, his rough-hewn features sidelighted by the shaded lamp, making his oft-broken nose seem even more crooked. One of the Cuban cigars he had illegally supplied to him was propped at a sharp angle in a glass ashtray. The cigar wasn't burning. It was pointless to start things off with Pearl already bitching.

She was seated cross-legged in an armchair to the left of the desk, facing Quinn, wearing faded jeans, a blue Mets T-shirt, gray socks. The loafers she'd slipped off lay askew on the floor near the chair. Her raven-black hair was pulled back and wound in a knot. She wore her usual dark eyeliner, which made her almost black eyes appear even darker. Quinn thought she looked fabulous.

Fedderman, perched on the less comfortable wood and leather casual chair, looked his usual discombobulated self. Though his face had gotten thinner, it still had its expectant, hangdog look, as if he'd just committed some transgression and now needed forgiveness. He'd lost a bit more of his graying hair since Quinn had last seen him and was now almost bald on top. Quinn was sure he recognized the baggy brown suit Fedderman was wearing, and noticed that his right white shirt cuff was unbuttoned and hanging out of his coat sleeve. For some reason that often happened to Fedderman's cuffs when he used a pen or pencil for any length of time. Quinn almost smiled, seeing the frayed, loose cuff peeking out of the coat sleeve at him. Old times.

Fedderman looked over at Pearl. "I heard you had some trouble at the bank."

"Screw you," she said, dismissing Fedderman. She turned her attention to Quinn. "Lauri's no longer living with you?"

Lauri was Quinn's daughter, now almost twenty. "She and Wormy are living in California, trying to promote his music career." Lauri's lover, Wormy, so called because he was tall and painfully thin and kind of undulated when he walked, was front man for his band, The Defendants. Lauri's last letter said the group was close to a record contract. Her next-to-last letter had said that, too.

"I thought the boy had talent," Fedderman said.

"But what about his music?" Pearl asked.

"What about these murders?" Quinn said, reminding them why they were here. He picked up four green binders, then moved out from behind his desk and handed two to each of his detectives. "Renz supplied copies of the murder books. I made copies for you two."

"You must already have looked yours over," Fedderman said. "Any conclusions?"

Quinn sat back down behind his desk, automatically reached for his cigar, then drew his hand back when he noticed Pearl giving him a look. "I already told you some of the basics: two torsos, female Caucasian, each shot through the heart, no prints on file, and no way to identify them. Twenty-two-caliber hollow-point bullets. Both of them separated when they entered the victims, but the pieces stayed in the bodies and the lab managed to reconstruct them enough to be sure they were fired by the same gun. Both victims were sexually penetrated by what seems to have been a long, sharp stake of some kind that left a residue of oil."

"A sexual lubricant?" Pearl asked.

"Furniture oil," Quinn said.

"He polished them off," Fedderman said. He seemed obviously pleased by his humor.

"Shut up with that kind of stuff," Pearl said.

Fedderman noticed his shirt cuff was unbuttoned and fastened it. "Where were they found?" Mr. Serious now.

"The first in a Dumpster behind a restaurant on the Upper West Side. The second in a vacant building in lower Manhattan."

"Vacant why?" Pearl asked.

"Being renovated."

"Actively?"

"Yeah. A condo conversion." Quinn knew where she was going with this and was pleased.

"Found on a Monday?" Pearl asked.

"You guessed it."

"The workmen would be bound to find it, then. And the torso in the Dumpster would be found next trash pickup."

"Which was scheduled for the morning after it was placed there," Quinn said. "Restaurant employees said they would have seen it during working hours, so it must have been put in the Dumpster the night before."

Pearl uncrossed her legs and placed her stockinged feet on the floor, wriggling her toes. "The killer wanted the torsos found soon after they were dumped. Any idea why?"

"Not as yet," Quinn said.

"I take it there's been a missing persons check on the two victims," Fedderman said.

"Sure. No women their sizes, ages, or ethnicity have been reported missing lately in and around New York. Both were in their early thirties." Quinn leaned back slightly in his desk chair and began swiveling gently an inch or so each way.

He'd oiled the chair recently and it didn't make a sound. "Another thing. A journalist, Cindy Sellers of *City Beat,* knows everything I just told you and is sitting on the story as a favor to Renz."

"I remember her," Pearl said. "She's an asshole."

"No more so than the other media wolves," Quinn said, thinking Pearl would have made a good investigative reporter.

"Pearl's right," Fedderman said. "The Cindy Sellers I remember won't sit on the story for long. Not unless Renz has got something on her."

"If he does," Quinn said, "it isn't enough to keep the lid on very long. That's why he activated us. He wants to be out in front of the story."

"Wants to be mayor," Pearl said.

Still astute, Quinn thought.

Pearl suddenly wondered what she was doing here. Why had she chosen this option? She seemed unable to escape Quinn's presence and influence. Another appeal from Renz to Quinn, another critical case, another psychopath, the call to her from Quinn, and here she was again. This held the repetition of madness. It was as if she were on a masochistic treadmill that she couldn't get off because some part of her didn't want to leave. This case . . . she felt in her bones it was something special. She had to be in on it.

"Go over the files on both killings," Quinn said, "and we'll meet back here tomorrow and brainstorm."

"We gonna keep meeting here?" Pearl asked. She had lived here with Quinn and wasn't comfortable with the idea. Their bedroom had been right across the hall.

"Renz has promised to get us office space, as usual. He won't want us in a precinct house. The idea is we can be NYPD, but at the same time more independent than ordinary homicide detectives. We'll be reporting only to him."

"It'll be a roach-infested dump, as usual," Pearl said. "But anyplace is better 'an here." *Maybe not.* She remembered the last office space Renz had found for them, and the shrill scream of the drill from the dental clinic on the other side of the wall.

Quinn looked at his watch. It was almost midnight. Fedderman's flight out of Florida had been delayed, so the meeting had started late. "Nine o'clock tomorrow morning okay?"

Both detectives agreed to the hour, then stood up. Quinn got up to show them out.

As they passed the bedroom, Pearl couldn't help herself and glanced in at the bed. It was made, but not very neatly. A book lay on the table by the reading lamp on what she still thought of as Quinn's side, but she couldn't make out the title. Nothing seemed to have changed since she'd moved out two years ago. Quinn caught her looking and she glared at him.

She knew he was still in love with her, and it was a damned inconvenience. They'd tried to live together and found it impossible. Pearl didn't want to repeat the experience. It was obvious what the trouble was. Quinn was self-controlled, deliberate, and quietly obsessive. Pearl was impulsive, combative, and volatile. They clashed. Another difference was that Pearl knew when to give up on their relationship and Quinn didn't. He didn't know when to give up on anything.

At the street door, Fedderman said, "I've still got my rental. I'll drive you home, Pearl."

"Okay. Better than a subway."

"Better company, too," Fedderman said.

"If you don't count dress, manners, and intelligence."

Quinn was glad to hear them bickering. That was how it worked when they were a team, questioning and challenging each other, wearing away what wasn't solid or didn't fit, until only the truth remained.

Even if they might not like the truth.

Compared to most of the other New York papers, large and small, *City Beat* didn't have much of a circulation. But

Deputy Chief Wes Nobbler always picked up a copy, because he knew of the relationship between Commissioner Renz and Cindy Sellers. More than once Sellers had been Renz's conduit to the larger media.

Nobbler, a large, portly man with squinty blue eyes and a complexion that made him always appear to have been out in the sun too long, was thinking about *City Beat* now. His bedroom was still dark, but he couldn't sleep, and the red numerals on the clock by his bed glowed the time to him: 5:02 A.M. Too early to get up, and too late to bother going back to sleep. And his bladder was swollen, though not to the point of urgency. Why get up, switch on the light, relieve himself in the bathroom, and then go back to bed?

He couldn't think of a good reason.

Ten minutes passed. Now getting up or not wasn't the question. He had to take a leak.

With *City Beat* still on the periphery of his thoughts, he struggled to a sitting position on the squeaking bed, turned on the lamp, and plodded into the bathroom.

Might as well stay up now. He put on his wrinkled uniform pants from yesterday, knowing a freshly pressed uniform just back from the dry cleaners hung in the closet. He'd change into the clean uniform later, after he'd showered and shaved. He slipped bare feet into his shoes and left on the gray T-shirt he'd slept in. He went back into the bathroom, splashed cold water on his face, and used wet fingers to slick back red hair that hadn't a trace of gray in it.

Awake all the way now, he went into the kitchen and set up his Mr. Coffee to brew. Then he took a look out the window to make sure it wasn't raining and left the apartment to walk to the end of the block and get a *Times* and *City Beat* from their respective vending machines.

By the time he got back it was starting to get light out and traffic was just beginning to pick up. The apartment smelled of freshly brewed coffee, and he felt hungry and wished he'd found someplace open and bought some doughnuts. Not that he needed the calories.

He poured a cup of coffee, added a dash of cream from the refrigerator, and sat down at the kitchen table.

Nobbler glanced at the *Times* first. There was rioting in France, Congress was calling for an investigation into something Nobbler didn't understand, and beneath the paper's fold there was great consternation over the Yankees's seven-game losing streak.

The usual, Nobbler thought. All the money the Yankees had, you'd think they could buy some pitchers who didn't have arms ready to fall off. He put the *Times* aside, took a sip of coffee, and looked at *City Beat.*

Holy Christ!

Nobbler forgot all about his appetite, the Yankees, and his coffee as he read.

He'd known about the first female torso being found, and the second dead woman. He hadn't known that, like the first victim, only the torso of the second victim was at the morgue. And he hadn't yet seen the results of the ballistics tests. Commissioner Renz had certainly thrown a blanket of secrecy over the second woman, so it wouldn't be obvious right away that a serial killer was at work. And the thing with the pointed stake or whatever it was—Nobbler hadn't known about that, only that the first woman had been sexually penetrated. He had to admit he admired the way Renz had been able to maintain even partial secrecy over matters like this. Renz wasn't shy about working the levers of power.

Well, neither was Nobbler. And Renz had done something that really pissed him off. Frank Quinn was back on the scene, and on the Torso Murders case, along with his two detectives Kasner and Fedderman. Nobbler wasn't crazy about the three of them, and in his mind they were no longer NYPD. Especially Quinn, who shouldn't be able to get anywhere near the department. They gave him a ton of money and cut him loose, so what the hell else did he want? Nobbler didn't so much resent Quinn because he was bent, more because he was bent in the wrong direction. He turned his thoughts to Kasner and Fedderman, but only briefly. Couple of losers.

What power did Renz have, to call these three retreads in as his private detective squad to solve a case that would benefit him politically?

But Nobbler knew what power—that of position and popularity. No one in or out of city government wanted to cross Renz, and strictly speaking, it wasn't illegal for the NYPD to hire outside contractors or temporarily reactivate former cops. Especially if they were acting under the auspices of the commissioner.

Right now Renz was on a roll and wanted to stay that way. Ambitious bastard. Not that Nobbler could hold *that* against him.

Disgusted, he tossed the paper on top of the *Times* and sat back and sipped at his coffee, which was now almost too cool to drink. The information in the *City Beat* article was probably all over TV and radio news, and late-edition papers would pick it up. Nobbler knew how it would go, now that the media had a hand to play, and he knew how he'd deal with them if he were in charge.

But he wasn't in charge. He didn't like having what he considered his turf trespassed upon. And that was exactly what was happening. He was sure as hell going to do something about it.

For a long time he sat sipping cool coffee and thought about just what it was that he could or would do. There were possibilities, always possibilities. And future opportunities to be seized.

Whatever it took, he'd figure out something so that Renz and company would find themselves in a quagmire.

No, not a quagmire. Quicksand.

* * *

"It seems to have hit the fan," Fedderman said, as he claimed the chair he'd sat in last night in Quinn's den. The room was brighter today, with yellow sunlight spilling in between the opened drapes. There were a lot of dust motes swirling softly in the sunlight. Just looking at them made Pearl feel as if she had to sneeze. She figured Quinn didn't clean very often.

Pearl sat in the armchair again but didn't draw up and cross her legs this time. Her sensible black shoes were planted firmly on the floor, her hands resting lightly on her thighs. She was dressed in dark slacks, a white blouse, and a gray blazer with black buttons. She looked like a cop.

Like Fedderman, she was carrying this morning's edition of *City Beat.* "It'll be all over the TV news, too," she said. "Some of those talking heads read things other than their prompters." She twisted her newspaper into a roll and wielded it as if she wanted to hit someone.

She was right. Quinn had checked New York One TV before going out and walking to the Lotus Diner for an early breakfast. They were already broadcasting from the places where the two torsos had been found. Then, when he'd returned to his apartment, he'd looked in on CNN and Fox News. The story had already gone national. He wasn't surprised that news of the murders had hit so soon and with such impact. It was a sensational story, like one of those TV cop shows, only real. That was why political- and media-savvy Renz had been so desperate to hire them.

"Had time to go over the murder books?" Quinn asked, settling down behind his desk. The unlit Cuban cigar was still in the ashtray. He was smoking less and less these days, like other New Yorkers, being systematically backed into a physical and psychological corner by the mayor and his minions. Quinn reminded himself that the mayor had his health and well-being in mind. It kept him from disliking the mayor.

"Last night and this morning," Fedderman said.

Pearl simply nodded. Quinn thought she looked beautiful in the bright morning light that would expose other women's flaws.

She noticed the way he was looking at her and stared at him until he averted his gaze.

"Nothing jumped out at me that'd crack the case and make me a hero," Fedderman said. "I'm sure the police profiler will have plenty to say about the victims being dismembered. And that impaling business. Phallic symbolism. They're always quick to find that."

"There's a lot of it going around," Pearl said. "Maybe our guy is impotent."

Fedderman shrugged. "Just because some guy shoves something other 'an his dong up some broad doesn't mean he can't get it up."

"How would you know that, Feds?"

"I'm a detective, Pearl."

Quinn was looking at Pearl. "Something bothering you?"

"A niggling doubt." she said. "These two murders were obviously committed by the same psycho, but still there were only two of them. It's possible both women did something that set this guy off, maybe even together, and he doesn't have a grudge against other women, or some kind of fixation and compulsion to kill more. Maybe the two victims and the killer shared some kind of past that led to violence. I mean, do two victims make a serial killer?"

Fedderman said, "It's a good question."

"The media seem to think two's enough," Quinn said.

Pearl said, "It's still a good question."

Quinn leaned back in his chair and laced his fingers behind his head. "We all know how we'll find out the answer."

The truth of what he'd said sobered all of them.

Pearl sniffed the air. "You been smoking in here?"

"It's a good question," Quinn said.

7

Jill Clark sat in front of her computer staring at her screen saver of great Impressionist paintings gliding past. There went a Renoir, delicate and graceful in composition and color, so unlike the struggle and ugliness just outside her window.

She watched the painting disappear at the edge of the monitor screen.

She'd been sitting for a long time staring at the screen and had come to the conclusion that it was time to take stock.

The paintings were beautiful, but her own life seemed to be getting uglier and more of a struggle by the day. This was a hard city. Hard and merciless. If it were possible for a city to have a killer instinct, this one did.

Jill was twenty-nine years old with shoulder-length blond hair that often had a way of being enchantingly mussed. Her features were symmetrical, with perhaps too much chin. She had full lips, strong cheekbones, and an undeniably good figure, from jogging almost daily in her neighborhood or in the park. Her eyes were blue and she had a scattering of freckles on the bridge of her nose. Men seemed to find that an attractive combination.

She had a degree in accounting and a background in sales: office furniture, then insurance policies for antique and collectable cars.

Along with a nice smile, those were her assets.

Then there were her liabilities, mostly credit card debts. Revolving accounts to which she paid only interest while the balances ballooned. From time to time, Files and More, the temporary employment agency that found her part-time work, would land her a decent-paying job, but this was temporary employment. Jill would earn enough to make some headway with the charge accounts, but then there would be periods of inactivity and she'd fall further behind than ever. This seemed to be a cycle she couldn't break.

Jill had, in fact, come to think of herself as a professional temp. That was how she might fill in job applications and various other forms under "occupation." Temp. It at least kept prospective employers from thinking she might have just gotten out of prison. Now and then temporary jobs obtained through Files and More resulted in permanent employment—that's what the company had told her—but Jill soon learned it didn't happen very often. And she'd become convinced it wasn't going to happen for her.

Not only was the work temporary, but no matter where you were assigned the other employees treated you differently. You would never be one of *them*. They knew you'd simply fail to come in someday and that would be the last they'd see of you. They wouldn't exactly be rude to temporary workers, but no one wanted to form anything like a fast or permanent friendship. And romance seemed to be out of the question. Sex was always possible with the geeks she ran into who saw her as temporary in more ways than one, but romance, connecting with someone she might eventually love and depend on, that was as distant as the farthest star. Romance was, of course, what Jill wanted desperately. That and an infusion of cash.

A Monet smoothly crossed the screen. A garden scene:

water lilies; muted, beautiful colors; lush green at the edges but subdued, like the green of a faded dollar bill.

Romantic, but the painting had made her think of money.

If she didn't find steady employment soon, Jill would have real money problems. She had no family, hadn't since her brother in Missouri died last year, and she was only four months in New York.

It had seemed the longest four months of her life. There was no one she could turn to for a personal loan, or even a reassuring hug. What people said about New York was so true: It took a lot of money to exist here. And if you were by yourself in the city, the loneliness could crush you.

Jill was determined not to be crushed, not to return to Wichita, Kansas. That way lay defeat as well as more loneliness.

On one of her jobs, helping to label and box catalogs, a woman named Billie had told her about Internet dating, how she'd started to do it and it had turned out well for her. Sure, she'd met a lot of losers, but a few winners. Nothing permanent, but guys who wanted more than drinks, laughs, and a quick go-round and see you later.

At the time, Jill had been almost horrified by the idea. Having to resort to the Internet for romance seemed so wrong, and it was embarrassing. High tech meets the heart. She sure as hell didn't need that.

But now . . . well, it was different. Maybe because Jill hadn't had a meaningful date in months. The last guy had taken her to a Village dive and expected oral sex right there under the table. And he'd seemed so . . . normal at first. Maybe that was the trouble. Maybe she'd lost touch and he was normal and she was living outside the real world.

No, she refused to believe that.

There went a Manet, an ordered but vivid scene of revelers, a beautiful woman wearing a low-cut dress and a large locket standing behind a bar and looking out and smiling at whoever over time might observe the painting. A *Bar at the*

Folies-Bergère, no doubt a raunchy place in nineteenth-century Paris. Now it would seem tame. Its festive image had lost its lasciviousness and become art, and great art at that.

Jill had done some research, and it altered her opinion about Internet dating. Billie was probably right. It was a new world and things had changed. Jill would simply have to adapt. In this hectic life, in this mad city, there was nothing wrong, or particularly unusual, about using an Internet matchmaking service. Romance—possible romance, anyway—might be had at a price. Plenty of people were paying that price and finding romance. Why not Jill?

A Degas glided past, one of his poised and elegant ballerinas glowing in the limelight of the past.

Jill owed on her plastic cards, but she reminded herself that she wasn't maxed out. *Plastic and elastic.* Hope. The thing that sprang eternal.

One roll of the dice, and it could be a beautiful world.

She decided to take a chance.

There went a Van Gogh.

Quinn and his team members had exchanged ideas and information and decided they needed to start at the beginning and cover ground already trod. They'd visit the places where the torsos were found and question people in surrounding buildings, try to find someone who'd heard something unusual or happened to look out a window and see something that might be pertinent. Even if they'd given previous statements, the same questions after the passage of time could sometimes trigger memories.

They were about to get up and leave Quinn's office when they got a call from Renz saying he'd just finished taping a television interview that was about to air on a local channel.

Quinn aimed a remote at the small TV in the bookcase across from his desk and ran up the channels. Pearl got up from the armchair and closed the drapes to block the sunlight. Her motions were almost automatic, as if she still lived there and adjusted the drapes often.

By the time Quinn found the interview it was well under way. Michelle DeRavenelle, an impossibly cute local news anchor, was standing alongside Renz, holding a microphone. The interview was taking place in a sunny spot outside One Police Plaza. A slight summer breeze ruffled DeRavenelle's hair and made her look even cuter, while making Renz's sparse locks stand straight up so he looked as if he'd just gotten up from reading in bed.

". . . only the nude torsos?" DeRavenelle was finishing asking. She held the microphone out toward Renz as if offering him a bite.

There was a small, lonely potted tree just behind and to the left of Renz. He shifted slightly to his left and a branch seemed to be growing out of his head. "Serial killers operate out of compulsion," he said. "They feel they have no choice. While leaving the victims' torsos to be found seems—and in fact *is*—bizarre to us, it might not seem so to him."

DeRavenelle appeared to dismiss this answer. "Hopefully, the FBI or police profilers have analyzed this killer, Commissioner."

"Of course."

Quinn smiled. He didn't recall any profiler report in the files. What could anyone really surmise with any degree of certainty about a killer from a couple of unidentifiable torsos? That was the sort of thing that happened only in mystery novels and television drama.

"Do the police have any ideas as to who he is, what kind of madman he is? If indeed he is mad."

"Oh, he's mad by our standards," Renz said, "however anyone might decide to label him. Early on in a case, that's about the only thing we can be sure of when dealing with this kind of killer. Our profiler is examining evidence and working out a hypothetical composite suspect who I'm sure will eventually turn out to be much like the real suspect when we arrest him. Sadly, at this point there simply isn't much to work with, so it will take time."

"Can the same be said about Captain Frank Quinn and his detectives—that it will take time for them to assemble enough information to find the killer? Unfortunately, there might not be time to waste."

Renz wasn't thrown. "It's difficult to predict how this kind of investigation will go, but I'm sure that with Quinn in charge it will take the minimum amount of time to make an arrest. That's why I partnered with him and his team and tasked them to find the killer. I know they're the best, and in a case like this, one that impacts virtually all of our citizens who are women—or men who have lovers, wives, or daughters—the city deserves the best."

DeRavenelle cocked her head and smiled. This guy knew how to play the game. "But no suspects so far, Commissioner?"

"Not solid suspects. Because of the deviant sexual aspect to these terrible crimes—"

"You mean the sharpened stake?"

"Yes, the sharpened stake." It bore repeating.

"Does penetration of the victim occur before or after death, sir?" DeRavenelle grimaced, somehow prettily, and gazed out at her viewers. "Hopefully, after."

"Sadly, before," Renz lied.

Quinn saw Pearl and Fedderman exchange glances. They looked at him and he nodded. They approved of Renz's lie. This was something that only the killer and police would know was untrue, and it could infuriate the killer so that he might make a mistake. He might even contact the police or media to try to set the record straight.

"Good man," Fedderman said of Renz's deception.

"I wouldn't go that far," Pearl said.

"Do the police have any clues as to the whereabouts of the rest of these poor dismembered women?" DeRavenelle asked. "I mean, their body parts."

"I can only say at this point in time that we're cautiously optimistic."

"Anything more you'd like to add, Commissioner?" DeRavenelle was wearing her somber but inquisitive expression. Had one of the best in the business. She was short on time and knew this was a final rhetorical trolling for a juicy sound bite.

Renz knew it, too, and tried to oblige. "Only that I'm sure the Torso Murders will soon be part of this great city's past. We have the best people possible working around the clock to find the pieces and put them together."

Quinn winced.

"That would be a good start," Pearl said.

DeRavenelle didn't change expression as she looked somberly into the camera and returned coverage to the studio.

Deputy Chief Wes Nobbler sat behind his desk and watched the end of the Renz interview, then aimed the remote like a gun and switched off the TV just as the weatherman came on smiling.

Nobbler wasn't smiling. His pink jowls spilled over his tight collar and exaggerated the downward arc of his thin lips. "Plenty of people wouldn't mind seeing Renz's investigation fall flat on its face," he said. The bright morning sunlight searched his fleshy cheeks and couldn't find a single beard stubble.

Detective Sergeant Ed Greeve nodded, knowing when not to speak. He was one of those average-height men who seem taller because of their gauntness and slight forward lean. His long, chiseled features, and his serious brown eyes with lids that angled down at the corners, added to the illusion of height. He was wearing an unremarkable gray suit that seemed to match his mood. His nickname was "The Ghost" because of his skill at tailing people or remaining unnoticed at observation posts. Greeve was a man going through life hiding in plain sight, making a career out of it.

He was also a man Nobbler had used before, in ways that skirted the law but advanced the cause of justice, not to mention Nobbler's career. And Greeve was using his boss, Nobbler. What they knew about each other made them fellow travelers on the treacherous road up the ranks in the bureaucracy that was the NYPD.

"We need to monitor this situation," Nobbler said.

Again Greeve merely nodded. A wooden toothpick protruded from the left corner of his mouth. It waggled slightly as he maneuvered it with his tongue.

"Renz has found his rent-a-cops office space to work out of over on West Seventy-ninth Street. That should make it easier to keep tabs on them."

"We gonna need more people?" Greeve asked around the toothpick.

"Not yet, but when we do, it won't be a problem. A loose tail should be enough for now. If they split up, choose the one who looks most interesting and follow. It shouldn't take you long to figure out what they might know that we don't."

"They'll probably lock that office when they're out in the field, sir."

"Most likely," Nobbler said. "Most doors have locks."

That was all he said or had to say. He knew locks were seldom a problem for Greeve, who had been an officer in the old Safe and Loft division investigating burglaries. In fact, locks were something of a challenge to Greeve, who would probably pay a late-night visit to the office on Seventy-ninth. Late night was his time, and darkness his good friend. He could see like a cat in the dark, which was another reason for his nickname. Greeve was viewed by his fellow officers as being a little spooky.

"What about my caseload?" Greeve asked. He removed the toothpick and reinserted it, this time in the right corner of his mouth.

"I've reassigned it. You'll be on this more or less full-time. Report to me daily, or if anything notable needs to be shared."

"Understood," Greeve said.

"Needless to say, for now this is just between the two of us."

"Needless," Greeve agreed.

Nobbler felt a slight twinge. He couldn't be sure sometimes if Greeve was taking him seriously or secretly making fun of him. Well, that was simply Greeve's personality, or lack of same. One way or another, the man was useful and reliable.

Nobbler picked up a blue ballpoint pen and started playing with it using both hands, his elbows on the desk. He stared at the pen as if he'd never seen any kind of writing instrument before. He often did that with common objects. It gave the impression he was thinking of something other than what he was talking about, and was speaking in the abstract. "To be something like frank," he said, "I'm not sure a police commissioner should run his own team of detectives, brought in and controlled by him as temporary employees of the NYPD."

"I know others in the department who feel the same way, sir."

Nobbler held the pen vertically and studied it, as if gauging it for angle. "Damned shame, but there it is."

"Yes, sir. And splashed all over the media for everyone to see. There's not much you can say, though. As a politician and media darling, Renz is golden."

"There might be plenty we can do without saying anything," Nobbler said. "It's just a matter of deciding what, how, and when. There's not much question about why." He pressed the top of the pen and the point clicked out. Here was magic, his expression seemed to say. "I guess we'd both better get busy, Sergeant. The bad guys never take time off." He dragged over some papers from the corner of his desk so he could sign them.

The conversation was over. A conversation that would never be referred to, because it hadn't taken place. Like the tree that had fallen in the woods without anyone there to hear it. Anyone who mattered.

Greeve had experienced several such conversations with Deputy Chief Nobbler. The toothpick did a little dance and he almost smiled as he moved toward the door. "We're on the same page, sir."

Which didn't mean they were going by the book.

8

Two weeks earlier

What the hell?

Shellie Marston stood before her open closet door and stared at her meager wardrobe. The black dress with the gray polka dots was still in its plastic bag from the dry cleaners, but she was sure she'd hung it yesterday on the opposite side of the closet rod.

In fact, some of her other clothes seemed to be out of place. The white blouse with the lace collar—she wouldn't have jammed it between the two business blazers she seldom wore these days. And look, one of the lapels was bent.

This was damned odd. In fact, it made her flesh creep.

She recalled now the morning a few days ago when her cosmetics seemed to have been rearranged. Not drastically. Maybe a jar or bottle transposed or otherwise out of place. A can of hairspray she recalled as still useful had been dead when she picked it up, without the usual sputtering and irregular spray that could go on for several more uses.

She looked at herself in the vanity mirror. What? Was she getting paranoid? No one was getting in here. No one had the key, except for the super, a man in his sixties. She had to smile. Mr. Mercurio would hardly be wearing her clothes and using her cosmetics. He'd split all the seams if he tried to wriggle into the polka-dot dress. A vision of the dignified, mustached, and paunchy Mercurio struggling with her wardrobe almost made her laugh out loud. No, he was definitely not a suspect.

Of course, you never knew about people.

Yeah, she thought. Some people suspect things that never happened.

She had to admit it was possible that she'd hung her clothes in the closet exactly as they were. Same way with the cosmetics. The mind could play tricks. Memory was a joker.

The phone jangled, jarring her out of her thoughts. Not her cell phone. She ran to the table near the sofa, where the land line phone rested.

It was David.

The receiver pasted to her ear, she dropped onto the sofa and sat slumped in a cushioned corner. "The oddest thing just happened," she said. "When I opened my closet it struck me that some of the clothes weren't where I'd hung them."

"Never mind that," he said. "I've been thinking about you."

She smiled. "I should hope so."

Their journey from acquaintances to lovers had been smooth and natural, and Shellie couldn't imagine being happier. Their personalities meshed perfectly, which added to the sexual sparks. He left nothing to wish for, in any respect. David was a gentleman who knew his way around, both in and out of bed.

Especially *in* bed.

"I want you to move in with me," he said.

She was pleased but surprised. This was so fast. "I don't know. . . ."

"I didn't think you'd hesitate." He sounded disappointed.

"I mean, this is so sudden. I've been stuck in a routine: my apartment, my job—whenever I work."

"You won't have to worry about a job, darling. I'll support you. I can afford it easily. I'd say I won't even notice you're around, only I'll notice you all the time, even when I'm not home."

"I don't know, David. . . ." But she did know. She'd already made up her mind.

"Two apartments," he said. "All that money unnecessarily spent on rent."

She laughed. Didn't he know she was already convinced? "We've left the subject of love and we're talking about money now."

"I didn't mean—"

"I'm only kidding, David. Of course I'll move in with you. It makes perfect sense. Why should we rotate where we spend our nights?"

"I don't care where they're spent as long as we're together. I thought about giving up my apartment and moving in with you, taking over the rent payments."

"This place is a broom closet compared to your apartment."

"That's what I decided. You deserve better, darling."

"David, I've *got* better. You."

"You know I love you."

"I do know that. It's more important than my address."

"Tomorrow?"

"Nobody makes up their mind and then moves *tomorrow*, David. I need time to pack, decide what I want to keep, put things in boxes."

"Get busy. I'll come over and help you."

"Why so fast?"

"I don't want you to change your mind."

* * *

Within four days, Shellie was totally moved into David's apartment. He'd paid the remaining time on her lease, making the real estate agency that managed the building happy. A small moving company transferred the things Shellie wanted to keep. What was left was bought and moved out of her old apartment by an estate liquidation company. Most of it would probably turn up in flea markets, where Shellie had bought it. Life could certainly change in a hurry, sometimes for the better.

There was only one hitch.

David explained it to her over their first breakfast at home. They were almost like a married couple talking over . . . the things Shellie imagined married people discussed.

"I sublease the place," David said, after swallowing a bite of buttered toast. He took a sip of the coffee he'd assured her was just right. "Part of the deal is that I can't have a room-mate."

Shellie paused in raising a bite of egg on her fork. "You mean my living here has to be a secret?"

He laughed. "I wouldn't put it so melodramatically. I mean, you don't have to hide or skulk around. A big apartment building like this, hardly anybody knows or even notices their neighbors. Once you close the door to the hall behind you, they don't know which apartment you've just exited. In the elevator, they don't know which floor you've come from. What's more, they don't care. There's a rapid tenant turnover here."

"Am I supposed to look both ways in the hall before I go out the door?"

He smiled. "It wouldn't hurt. What I mean, though, darling, is just don't make it a point to get to know the neighbors. You don't have to run and hide if anybody sees you."

"You make it sound like a game."

"It is one," he said. "The way subleases and rental agreements work, lots of New Yorkers play it. If we lose, they'll throw you out. Which means they'll throw us both out, because I'll go with you." He shrugged. "Getting evicted wouldn't be the end of the world. It happens somewhere in the city every day."

"Not to us," she said, then chewed and swallowed her bite of egg. "Not here. I promise to be careful."

"Probably," he said, "no one would turn us in even if they did notice you were staying here. Most people mind their own business. They might even approve of your presence. Who couldn't approve of you?"

A game, she thought, and finished her breakfast.

More like a romantic movie. *The Phantom Tenant.*

Like a movie. And I'm the star.

David wouldn't know that was how she saw it, she thought, so why not give herself top billing?

It worked so well. David was right: no one in the building paid much attention to anyone else. If the tenants passed in the halls or found themselves with one another at the elevator, they usually merely nodded, sometimes smiled. On the elevator itself, they followed elevator etiquette and stood stone-faced staring at the ascending or descending number above the sliding door.

Entering or leaving the building was the same way; often there wasn't even an exchange of glances. A few times someone held open the heavy street door for Shellie. She'd thanked them perfunctorily and hurried along. She acted the way they did, the way most New Yorkers acted—preoccupied. They passed or had brief contact with thousands of people every day and within a few days forgot all but a few.

Shellie was happy. And the apartment was spacious by New York standards, and with a nice view from a high floor. The furnishings were traditional, with a pale tan leather sofa and matching armchair, a TV behind the doors of a wooden wall unit that also had shelves holding knickknacks and a lineup of books that seemed chosen more for color than content. The furniture, the complementing drapes and carpet, the framed art prints on the wall gave the apartment a com- posed, decorator look. It was a look she liked, and it took only a few weeks for Shellie to regard it as home.

She would have been even happier if David spent more time in town, but they made the most of it when he was home.

And the most of it was quite a lot.

9

The present

Renz had shot off his mouth about a profiler, so he figured he'd better have a profile. He was with Quinn and his team in the Seventy-ninth Street office he'd gotten for them at city expense. It was a ground-floor apartment, really, in a building that was being renovated. This unit hadn't been touched yet, but it wasn't in bad condition, with cream-colored walls and blinds still on the windows. There were light rectangles where wall hangings had been removed, and an outline on the hardwood floor where the carpet had been taken up. But the paint was clean. Renz had ordered three desks and four chairs, a four-drawer steel file cabinet, a printer and fax machine, and a used desk computer. He knew they all had laptops, except maybe Fedderman. As far as a coffee machine or other niceties, the detectives were on their own.

Pearl had bought a Braun brewer and dragged in an old table the workmen upstairs were going to throw away. An NYPD computer whiz had set up a broadband wireless system for their computers, with a router over near the coffee machine. The door had a good lock, the workmen upstairs usually didn't make too much noise, and there was an old air conditioner that no one would bother stealing in one of the windows.

Quinn was within walking distance of the place but would sometimes drive his old Lincoln, and Renz had gotten them an unmarked city Chevy.

They had a home. They had wheels. It was an efficient setup.

Quinn and Fedderman sat in the identical wood swivel chairs behind their identical gray steel desks, while Pearl perched on her desk's front edge. Renz had pulled her desk chair out and was seated on it. So there was a chair for the profiler when she arrived, as long as Pearl was content without one. Quinn made a mental note to scare up another extra chair. He'd have asked Pearl to do it, but she'd let him know she'd done enough, donating the coffeemaker.

There was a knock on the door. Then it opened and the profiler, Helen Iman, cautiously stuck her head in. "Morning, all," she said, smiling as she entered all the way. She was a very tall woman with a bony but not unattractive face and carelessly styled red hair, as if she cut it herself with dull scissors. Seeing her, Quinn thought, as he often did, that with her long, muscular frame, she'd make a hell of a basketball or volleyball player. But Helen wasn't into sports. She was into killers. A few years ago she'd quit the NYPD to go into private practice as a corporate psychologist in New Jersey, but she'd soon returned. For her it was no contest between the corporate and the criminal mind. They weren't *exactly* the same, and the criminal mind was so much more interesting.

Renz had requested her presence here so Quinn and his team could hear what she had to say.

Pearl offered her coffee, but she declined and sat in the uncomfortable extra chair. It was stained oak with a straight back and had a sturdy but crude look about it, as if it might have been made by one of those religious sects that thrived on discomfort. She was wearing a green business suit and white blouse with a man's green and black tie. She placed the large brown purse she was carrying on the floor so it leaned against a chair leg.

"Did you read the material I gave you?" Renz asked her.

Helen nodded. "It wasn't very enlightening."

Renz looked disappointed.

Helen calmly gave each of them a look, her eyes lingering on Pearl. "There really isn't much to surmise, since we know nothing about the victims."

"I need something to feed the media," Renz said. "Something for my people"—he nodded toward Quinn, Pearl, and Fedderman—"in case they get cornered by some smart-ass journalist."

Helen crossed her long legs. It was quite a show. "I understand, and I can give you the usual, even though I'm sure you already know most of it. Our killer's probably between twenty and forty and had a horrible childhood during which he developed a hatred for women. He might be married—"

"Married?" Renz interrupted.

"I said might. And he probably has a history of sadistic behavior."

"The thing with the sharpened stake," Quinn said.

Helen nodded. "Not to mention the dismemberment. Usually people don't unaccountably start doing such things all at once." She reached into the big purse and pulled out a buff file folder, took a few moments to check its contents. "The insertion of the stake occurred after death. That's interesting. Necrophilia with a substitute penis."

"You think?" Pearl asked, glancing at Fedderman.

"Looks that way," Helen said. "The dismemberments were neatly done, but apparently not by someone with a medical background. He might have practiced on animals. Possibly on family pets."

"Jesus!" Fedderman said. He swiped his shirtsleeve across his mouth. "Will I never get used to these assholes?"

Helen smiled at him. "It's good that you don't." She sat back as best she could in the rigid chair.

"That's all you can give us?" Renz asked.

"I'm afraid so, at this point. It would be good to have entire bodies, maybe a witness or two. Oh, there is one other thing. He wants you to know both women were killed by him—that's why he used the same gun."

"And the stake?"

"I don't know about the stake. Especially after death. Some of this doesn't yet add up. There's something especially creepy about this killer."

"They're all sickos," Pearl said.

"That's not the medical term I'd use, but it's fairly accurate," Helen said. "This guy, though—and we all know the killer's almost certainly a guy—promises to be particularly interesting. His mental processes might be unfathomable, even after he's caught and studied. For instance, he hides the torsos, but not so well that he doesn't want them found."

"Trophies," Fedderman said.

"No. More like his calling card. But trophies aren't uncommon. Maybe he's keeping the heads as his trophies."

Pearl took a noisy gulp of her coffee, burning her tongue.

"This guy" Helen crossed her legs tighter—"one thing's for sure about him, he's a very special case."

Tonight he'd just arrived home after a weekend of doing business in London. Whenever Shellie asked David about his business, she got the same vague answers, but she was less and less concerned. She was convinced now that David was a good man. Whatever he was involved in was sure to be benign and legal. He was simply one of those men who wanted a firewall between home life and business. Between love and the real and ugly world outside of love. Shellie understood that. She felt the same way herself.

Her wardrobe had grown and improved since she had

moved in with David. She had on the navy blue dress she knew he liked, bone high-heeled pumps, a double strand of pearls around her neck. Her hair was artfully mussed, the way he liked it. The top button of her dress was undone to reveal a glimpse of cleavage, the way he liked it. Later they would make love, the way he liked it. She was the way he liked her, and she was happy. She was sure David was happy, too. They each had an interest in the other's happiness. It had kind of surprised Shellie, the way she'd come to feel. Nothing in life pleased her more than pleasing David.

"Italian tonight?" he asked. Her favorite dishes were Italian. "I thought maybe Randisi's."

Randisi's was a five-star restaurant on the East Side. Some thought it was the best Italian restaurant in the city.

"Sounds wonderful."

He smiled. "Good. I made a reservation."

At the restaurant Shellie heard David tell the maitre d' there was an eight o'clock reservation for Clyde. Shellie smiled. David always used the name Mr. Clyde when he made reservations, or simply the first name Clyde when asked to leave a name on a waiting list. It wasn't a bad name, but it certainly didn't fit his handsome, assured, and debonair presence. She looked at him, so well tailored in a dark blue suit, white-on-white shirt, gray silk tie. Not your usual Clyde. She felt a swell of pride. Her David.

"Mr. and Mrs. Clyde" were almost immediately shown to a good table near a wide window with a view of the East River.

They had martinis, then ordered antipasto and cannelloni. David asked for a good red wine. "To celebrate," he said.

"What are we celebrating?" Shellie asked.

"My arrival home."

"You've only been gone a weekend."

"It's always a cause for celebration when I return to you."

"Am I not worth champagne?"

He grinned. "Shellie, Shellie. You must know you have me in your spell." He leaned over the table, looking serious. "Do you want champagne?"

She shook her head no, feeling ashamed. "No, darling. I was only testing you."

"Do I pass?"

"A-plus," she said. They were talking like two people in a sophisticated play, she thought. This amused her and made her feel slightly silly simultaneously. The swank surroundings must be affecting them. Role playing again. Well, so what? That was all everyone actually did, when you came right down to it. She didn't see what was wrong with that when she could see so much of what was right with it.

The food, as usual at Randisi's, was wonderful. As was the wine. David knew how to choose.

Outside the restaurant, they were both a bit tipsy. Shellie leaned against David for support.

He was about to hail a cab when a gleaming dark car pulled to the curb near them. It was a big car, a Chrysler. They were on a one-way street, and the driver's side was only a few feet away from the sidewalk. The window glided down.

Shellie assumed the driver would be with a service and he'd try to talk them into taking the car instead of climbing into a cab. She was surprised to see an attractive, hard-faced woman about forty with a gray buzz cut and no makeup. She wore a black pullover shirt with the collar turned up. Her arms were slim but muscular, and Shellie saw that the hand resting on the steering wheel was gloved. Driving gloves, she assumed. Maybe this was a professional driver and the big Chrysler was a car for hire.

"Need a ride, bro?" the woman asked, looking at David.

"I'll be damned," David said. "What are you doing here, Gloria?"

"I was on my way home and happened to see you. New York's not so big that coincidences don't sometimes occur."

"Obviously not," David said.

"Anyway, this is my neighborhood. Or at least I regularly drive through it."

Now the woman looked at Shellie. She had dark eyes, deeply set and intense. "You must be Shellie."

David squeezed Shellie's arm. "This is my sister, Gloria, Shellie. The only person in New York I've told about us."

"David and I always share the good things," Gloria said. Her dark eyes took on a glitter in the reflected red light of the restaurant's illuminated sign. "That's the way it's been since we were children. I know my brother well, and I haven't seen him fall so hard for a woman in years. It's a real pleasure to meet you."

"Same here," Shellie said. She moved forward, one foot off the curb, and shook the leather-gloved hand proffered through the open window. Gloria smiled at her, an unexpectedly beautiful smile that caused Shellie to smile back.

"Listen," Gloria said, her dark glance darting from one to the other, "why don't you two come up to my place and have a drink? Afterward, I'll drive you home. I really do want to get to know you, Shellie. Everything I hear is so positive. Like, finally, you're *the one.*"

Shellie felt a warm rush. That was always what she'd wanted to be to some man, what she was now—special, the one. She could hear David saying it to his sister. "She's the one, Gloria."

"Maybe some other time," is what he was saying to Gloria now.

Shellie tugged at his arm. "It's okay, David. We have time."

He was shaking his head. "I don't think it's a good idea."

"What are you, ashamed of me?" Gloria asked. She seemed amused by the idea.

"You know better than that, Gloria."

"Then don't be so damned secretive, David. The way you've been bragging about this woman to me, I should think you'd want us to get to know one another." Her dark eyes fixed on Shellie. "I mean it, Shellie. This brother of mine is gaga for you. We really should talk about *him* for a change."

"She has a point, David."

He moved closer and looked down at Shellie. There was a strained expression in his face she hadn't seen before. The wine, maybe. They'd certainly had enough of it. "You're sure?"

"It sounds wonderful. Your sister!" *Family.* "We really should get acquainted."

After a slight hesitation, he smiled. "Okay. As long as you two don't gang up on me."

He opened the big sedan's rear door and let Shellie enter first. Then he took a seat beside her. There was over a foot of space between them on the seat. It was as if David didn't want to demonstrate his affection for her in front of his sister by sitting too close.

As Gloria pushed the selector to "drive" and the car pulled away from the curb, Shellie noticed a pungent, brackish smell.

"Do you smoke?" she asked Gloria, without thinking. "Not that I mean to pry."

"It's that obvious?"

"I'm afraid so. Unless somebody else who smokes has been in the car recently."

Shellie saw Gloria's right cheek change contour in the shadows, maybe a smile.

"I thought you might be asking for a cigarette," Gloria said.

"No, I don't smoke. Not that it's any of my business whether or not you do. I wasn't meaning to be judgmental."

Gloria laughed, concentrating on her driving and looking straight ahead. She had the long neck and erect posture of a ballet dancer, as if an invisible string were attached to the top of her head and constantly tugging her upright in case she even thought about slumping. "That's okay. You caught me. Tobacco's my only vice. I've been trying to quit. David will tell you, I've tried off and on for years."

"Those damned things are going to kill you, Gloria," David said.

Gloria managed to shrug her narrow, hard shoulders as she spun the steering wheel to make a sharp right turn.

"That's okay," she said. "If they don't, something else surely will."

10

Life could be so good it almost hurt. It prompted Shellie to nestle close to David as Gloria jockeyed the big Chrysler north on Broadway. The car drove smoothly and seemed to glide over the potholes that dotted the street. The evening had cooled, but the warmth of the car's interior, and of the wine she'd earlier consumed, made Shellie deliciously drowsy.

The sound of a blaring horn jolted her alert. She opened her eyes and realized Gloria had been the one leaning on the horn.

A cab that had pulled past the Chrysler was swerving in front of it, seemingly inches off its front bumper.

"Jerkoff!" Gloria said softly but vehemently.

"New York cabbies, that's all," David said lazily. "You oughta be used to them."

"Being used to them doesn't mean I don't hope they should all come down with the plague." She raised her voice. "Lord, deliver to them locusts and fire and sickness, and let them drive fareless through eternity."

David chuckled and held Shellie closer in the softly up-holstered backseat. "Did I mention to you Sis has a bit of a temper?"

"I hope it isn't hereditary," Shellie said. She saw with relief that the cab had pulled a safe distance ahead.

"David fights a constant battle with his genes," Gloria said, from the front seat. "Not to mention the devil. Or maybe it's all the same thing."

The cab's brake lights flared and it slowed abruptly, causing Gloria to stand on the brakes and the big Chrysler to cant forward. "Now that this asshole's ahead of me, he doesn't wanna go fast," Gloria said. "The guy's a great argument for the legalization of hand grenades."

"Ease up," David said. "You don't want to attract attention now."

Shellie thought that was an odd thing for him to say, but she was too comfortable and drowsy to give it much thought. She decided her life was fully in Gloria's hands and there wasn't much she could do about it, so she closed her eyes, rested her head against David's warm shoulder. There were times when the wisest and easiest course was to be a fatalist.

Shellie came awake when the car stopped. She heard a low rumbling louder than the engine. She'd dozed off, but had no idea how long she'd been sleeping.

David's arm was around her. He realized she was awake and gave her a comforting squeeze.

They'd reached their destination. Through the wide front windshield Shellie saw a gray steel overhead door rising. Beyond it, headlights illuminated a dark area with some barrels and boxes stacked on one side. About fifty feet beyond them was a brick wall, obviously very old. The wall bulged inward. The bricks were no longer aligned and ledges of broken gray mortar protruded from between them like too much icing between layers of cake. There was an old wooden workbench with what looked like tools stacked on it in the shadows near the wall.

"Apartment's upstairs," Gloria explained, nudging the accelerator so the big Chrysler glided inside. "It's furnished better than the garage."

"Much better," David said. "And it doesn't smell like petroleum products." He bowed his head and kissed Shellie's just above the bridge of her nose.

The overhead door descended with a clatter and closed behind them. Gloria turned off the engine, and the garage was suddenly very quiet. The headlights were on time delay and stayed on. They deepened the shadows not directly in their twin beams.

In the dimness of the car's interior, Gloria glanced over her shoulder. "Be careful getting out and walking. There's a plastic drop cloth on the floor because the car leaks oil." The Chrysler's interior light came on, and before David or Shellie could move, Gloria climbed out of the car and threw a wall switch.

The light from two bare overhead bulbs didn't cheer up the garage at all. The carelessly stacked fifty-gallon barrels were rusty. The cardboard boxes were taped, unlabeled, and coated with dust. Leaning against them was a tall roll of something opaque, maybe more plastic sheeting. There were no windows.

David got out of the car before Shellie and held the door open for her, like a gentleman. She was still a little drowsy, unsteady, and needed his support.

"Before we go upstairs," he said, "I have a present for you."

"Present?" Shellie saw Gloria get an unfolded black umbrella from where it was leaning in the shadows by the boxes and lay it on the car's hood. The cooling engine began to tick.

"A surprise. Before we go upstairs for our drinks."

For a wild second Shellie thought he might mean the umbrella, but that didn't make sense.

The car's headlights winked off, making the garage even gloomier. Shellie glanced around and didn't see an elevator.

No stairs, either. There must be a door somewhere leading to an elevator or stairwell.

"Let's go upstairs and get comfortable and you can surprise her," Gloria said. She was smiling at Shellie, her dark eyes intense. Whatever light there was in the garage, they reflected.

"Better right here," David said, and again he kissed Shellie on the forehead. His lips felt cool.

"Stubborn," Gloria said, shaking her head. "I guess that's why you love him."

"One reason," Shellie said. She really did love David. More than anyone or anything at any time in her life.

Stepping back, David smiled down at her and reached into a pocket of his suit coat. Beyond him, Shellie noticed Gloria reaching for the umbrella as if to open it.

She didn't open it. Instead, she withdrew a long, pointed wooden shaft that had been concealed inside it.

"Close your eyes, darling," David said.

But Shellie didn't. Even through her wine-induced drowsiness and love and trust for David, the feeling of security she always had in his presence, she realized something was very wrong. A tingle of fear played up her spine.

Foolish. Why should I be frightened? He's here.

His hand emerged from his pocket not with a piece of jewelry or a gift box, but holding a small gun.

"David?"

He shot her through the heart.

She dropped to a sitting position, her legs straight out, and then toppled backward. He immediately took two steps, leaned down, and shot her again, twice, through the forehead.

Gloria tossed him the pointed shaft so it remained vertical in the air, as if she were a dancer tossing her partner a cane. Matching her stagecraft, he snatched it neatly with one hand. He felt the point with his index finger, testing for sharpness.

Gloria walked around closer to stand next to him over Shellie's dead body.

"Look at her face," she said. "She was surprised. You didn't disappoint her."

"I never disappoint the ladies," David said.

He bent low with the sharpened section of broomstick, and then slowly straightened up without it.

Gloria was breathing hard as she stared down at the foot or so of wood protruding from Shellie.

"Don't you ever wonder, David, how it would be if you didn't wait until they were—?"

"Grab the other end of this plastic sheet and let's move her so we can get busy."

"For everything there is a purpose under the heavens," Gloria said, still staring at the protruding section of broomstick. "Sometimes more than one purpose."

"Aside from your cynicism, this is no time to go biblical on me."

"It's exactly the time," she said, grinning. "And you didn't answer my question."

11

"Only an arm," medical examiner Dr. Julius Nift said, kneeling alongside the pale object before him on the wet bricks. "Yet look at the attention it's attracted. Some show. I wish somebody would give us a hand."

Pearl despised Nift and his callous sense of humor, but she said nothing, because, sick jokes aside, she agreed with him. A hand would mean fingerprints. She wasn't sure how much this arm that had been fished from the East River would be able to help them.

Nift continued to probe and examine the arm. He was a short, chesty man inflated by self-importance who dressed more like a banker than a doctor who spent a lot of time with corpses. He wore his black hair combed forward, resulting in sparse bangs that made him look Napoleonic. That was how Pearl thought of him, as a crude, cynical Napoleon. It was lucky the little bastard didn't have an army.

Quinn, standing a few feet away with Fedderman, gnawed his lower lip as he stared down at the handless severed arm. It had obviously been in the water a long time. He glanced around, squinting in the early afternoon sunlight. They were near Sutton Place, home of some of the most expensive real estate in New York. It wasn't likely the arm belonged to any of the neighbors. A missing arm in Sutton Place wasn't the sort of thing to go unreported.

The arm had been spotted by a Mrs. Grace Oliphant, while walking her Yorkshire terrier, Clipper. She'd noticed something pale snagged on some deadwood that had drifted up against the bank and thought at first it was a large, dead fish. She skirted a black iron fence and moved closer. Clipper began barking frantically, and she wasn't so sure she was looking at a dead fish. It was the forty-five-degree crook in the blanched object that made her peer more intensely and with fearful curiosity. There was something about the thing, something that reminded her of . . . an elbow.

Mrs. Oliphant straightened up immediately and backed away, nauseated, tugging at the leash to get Clipper away from the dreadful thing. The arm. It was no wonder the dog had been barking so frantically. He must have picked up the terrible scent, realized before she did what they were looking at. Yorkies were so smart.

She gave the leash a firm yank, momentarily choking off Clipper's shrill barking, then looked him in the eye and shushed him so he'd stay quiet while she used her cell phone to call the police.

The uniforms who'd arrived first knew immediately they were looking at a human arm that had been severed at the elbow. Its hand had been cut off at the wrist. One of the cops picked up a branch and edged the arm closer to the concrete wall where the water lapped, then gingerly inched it up and over and onto the bricks. He didn't like touching it, even with a branch, but he knew he had to move it before it broke free from where it was snagged and floated away, or maybe sank.

The water had blanched away most of the color, leaving the arm a dull white. The uniforms could see how the woman who'd called thought at first she'd been looking at a dead fish. There was some obvious damage from what lived in the river nibbling at the arm. Gleaming white bone showed beneath flaps of skin at both ends.

Both cops knew about the Torso Murders and recognized the possible significance of the arm. The police investigated weird things found in New York rivers almost every week, and those were only the ones that were reported. Still, human remains . . . and with the sicko on the loose killing and cutting up his victims . . . it was a situation that called for diligence.

One of the uniforms had listened to Grace Oliphant's story and taken notes, while his partner called their lieutenant. Up the bureaucratic chain the information went, but in a way tightly controlled. Within fifteen minutes, Renz had called Quinn.

"Right or left arm?" Quinn asked Nift.

"Does it matter?"

"It matters because I asked you," Quinn said in a flat voice that had unnerved hundreds if not thousands of suspects.

It didn't seem to unnerve Nift, armored as he was by ego. Still, he decided it was time to be businesslike. He pressed a forefinger to the side of his chin, striking a thoughtful pose, as he shifted slightly to peer at both ends of the arm. "I'd guess left, but I can't tell you for sure till we get this to the morgue and examine it more closely."

"How long's it been in the water?"

"I can only guess, but I'd say about a month."

Quinn figured it would belong to the first victim, if it *was* an arm from one of the mystery torsos. It almost had to be, he figured. Even in New York, it wasn't every day that the odd severed limb turned up. "Can you match it with either of the torsos we found?"

Nift glanced up at him with a confident, nasty smile. "With my skill, if it matches, I'll know. There'll be distinctive marks on the bone from the cleaver or hatchet. And comparable patterns in the way the flesh was cut away. Also, we should be able to match it by age to one of the torsos, if that's where it came from. And of course there's always DNA. Takes a while for a full report, but we might be able to hurry through a preliminary yes or no on a simple match."

A siren grew louder, then yodeled to silence, causing Clipper, held by Mrs. Oliphant, over by a small grouping of ornamental trees with orange berries, to fill the vacuum by emitting an earsplitting series of barks. A boxy vehicle with flashing lights had braked to a halt on the rise beyond steps leading to one of the pocket parks bordering the river at that point. Quinn could see a swing set and monkey bars and was glad some kid hadn't wandered down to the river and found the arm.

A white-uniformed paramedic jogged effortlessly down the concrete steps, then stepped over the low brick wall bordering the park and came toward them. While he was nimble, he was a chubby guy, holding a black rubberized zip case that looked like a portfolio an artist would carry samples in. Quinn figured there was no need for a stretcher here. The arm would fit in the case diagonally with room to spare.

The paramedic had dark hair combed severely sideways and a name patch that said JEFF.

He glanced around, noticed the black leather medical bag, and aimed an expectant smile at Nift. "Ready to remove?" He motioned with his head toward the pale arm on the bricks.

"I'm finished with it for now," Nift said.

Quinn nodded and stepped back, along with Pearl and Fedderman, and Jeff set to work.

"Careful with that," Nift told him as Jeff eased the arm into the case and worked the zipper. "It's part of a set."

Jeff didn't crack a smile.

12

Nobody was laughing in the office on Seventy-ninth Street. Quinn and Fedderman were seated at their desks, facing each other across the room. Pearl was perched on the edge of her desk with her legs crossed, sipping coffee. The office smelled strongly of overbrewed coffee, which was an improvement over the usual smell of sawdust and powdered plaster. The workmen doing the rehabbing on the floors above were sawing and hammering, destroying so they could create. The noise wasn't loud enough to be a bother, but it was almost constant.

Quinn had just hung up his desk phone. He sat staring at it for a long moment before speaking, as if it was a memory aid.

"The M.E. says the arm belonged to a woman in her early thirties, maybe five feet nine or ten. She was average weight. The swelling and loose flesh we saw was from exposure to the water. No distinguishing marks or jewelry." He leaned backward in his chair and crossed his arms. "Nift says the arm doesn't match either of the bodies."

"He sure?" Fedderman asked in a surprised voice.

"The little twit's always sure," Pearl said.

Quinn ignored her, as well as a burst of violent hammering. "Bones and flesh patterns don't match up, Feds. Also, we got a rush preliminary on DNA analysis. Enough info to know it doesn't match that of either of the two victims whose torsos we have. Even the blood type is different."

"We might still be able to find out who she was. The woman whose arm we found. What about a DNA database match?"

"The FBI's running it through its computers, but I don't think we can hold out much hope there."

Quinn knew the already vast database was still in its initial stages. The severed arm would have to belong to a woman who was a recently convicted felon and also had her DNA in the database. Those were long odds.

All three detectives sat silently and listened to the muffled hammering that punctuated the shrill cry of a power saw.

It was Pearl who finally said it. "We've got a third victim."

"Or else another killer who's dismembering bodies," Quinn said.

Fedderman noticed his shirt cuff was unbuttoned and fastened it. "Maybe the arm was cut off accidentally. By a boat propeller or something."

Quinn smiled wryly. "River patrol's got no reports of any such accident, and nobody's reported their arm missing."

"Third victim," Pearl said again.

Nobody disagreed with her.

"The killer chopped off her hand, too," Fedderman said.

"To be on the safe side and not risk fingerprints being lifted and compared someplace," Pearl said, "even if they're not on file. His cautious nature worked in this case."

Quinn sighed and stood up. "The rest of her might still be in the river. The rest of all of the victims might be there, or in some lake or tributary somewhere. I'll call Renz and see if we can get a search going, check bodies of water in or around New York."

"Grappling hooks," Pearl said. "That's how they drag a lake, with grappling hooks." Though she'd seen several such operations, the thought of this one, for some reason, chilled her. Hard steel seeking soft flesh in the dark.

"They use underwater cameras now, too," Quinn said.

"Divers," Fedderman said. "Eventually somebody's gotta swim down there in murky water and look for weighted-down arms, legs, and heads." He made a face and ran a hand over his almost nonexistent hair. "I'm glad I'm too old for that kinda stuff."

"They might drain some of the smaller lakes," Pearl told him.

He shook his head. "Yeah, but try draining the river. That's where we found the arm."

"He's got a point," Pearl said to Quinn.

"Global warming," Fedderman said. "Eventually it'll dry up all the rivers. That's when we'll find the missing body parts."

Pearl sipped her coffee.

"Global warming," Fedderman said again. "A cop's best friend."

"Severed arm?" Cindy Sellers asked into the phone. She was at her desk at *City Beat*. She kept her voice low so Howie Baker, at the next desk, wouldn't overhear. "Just an arm? How do we know it has anything to do with either of the two torso victims?"

"We know for sure it doesn't," Nift said nervously. He was calling with his cell phone a few blocks from the morgue. You never knew about phones. Just about any phone might not be secure these days. Not to mention cameras. They were getting to be all over the place in New York City. He wanted to get the call over with as soon as possible. "I can guarantee you that arm's not connected to either of the other victims' torsos."

"Obviously," Cindy said.

She was used to her informer's gruesome sense of humor and assumed that was what she was hearing. She thought Nift was a jerk, but he was reliable. And she'd been kind enough not to mention him in her exposé of unlikely pornographic video rental customers. She had mentioned to him that she had photographs of some of the customers arriving at and leaving the video rental stores. She hadn't mentioned that, though Nift was observed renting a DVD about drunken coeds on a horse farm, he wasn't in any of the photos. Let him assume.

"So what else do we know?" she asked.

Nift told her what they'd discerned from examination of the arm.

"A third victim," Cindy said when he was finished. "And the killer's probably weighting down the body parts and hiding them underwater. The arm must have somehow broken loose from whatever was holding it down and floated to the surface."

"You're jumping to conclusions," Nift said.

"Hey, it's my job." She was grinning. "Be sure to keep me posted."

"I will," Nift said and broke the connection.

Cindy knew he would.

Gloria turned off the narrow secondary road onto a mostly overgrown dirt road and drove until she came to a rickety wooden swing gate with a faded NO TRESPASSING sign nailed crookedly on it.

David climbed out of the big Chrysler and opened the gate, then waited until Gloria had driven through. He glanced around in the fading light, thinking they had about an hour until sundown, then closed the gate, fastened its rusty latch, and got back in the car.

They were on a farm in New Jersey, an hour's drive from the city. The farm was deserted and had been in the legal limbo of estate law for several years. There had once been a frame house with a detached garage, a barn, and another outbuilding for equipment and tools. The house and garage were deserted wrecks. Two walls of the outbuilding had collapsed, allowing the elements to lay rust over an old Ford tractor without an engine, and some shovels and other implements leaning against a remaining wall.

Gloria drove the car around behind the garage, popped the trunk lid, and sat for a few minutes watching tall, shadowed grass dance rhythmically in the breeze.

"Place is as deserted as the moon," she said.

"Time for the astronauts to get to work," David said beside her, then unclipped his seat belt and opened the door. (He would continue to think of himself as David until they were finished with their work here.)

He was always in a good enough mood if not downright cheerful, Gloria thought. Always optimistic, no matter the situation. No doubt that was part of his appeal to women.

They walked around to the open trunk.

The two of them carried four bulky black plastic trash bags down a grassy slope and about twenty feet into the woods. The bags contained the clothing and remains of Shellie Marston, except for her heart-shot torso, which they'd left next to a construction Dumpster on the Upper West Side.

They chose a spot in the darkening woods and laid down the bags. David returned to the car to get the shovels.

While he was gone, Gloria used the side of her foot to clear away last year's leaves. It took her four or five minutes. Satisfied, she scraped mud off her shoe, then tapped her back pocket to make sure her small leather-bound Bible was still there.

She heard a sound and looked over to see that, besides the

shovels, David was coming back with a rusty, long-handled pickax he'd found somewhere. That would make digging a lot easier, as it hadn't rained in three or four days and the ground was hard. Gloria smiled.

God was easing their task.

13

Pearl exhaled, inhaled, and said, "God, that was good!"

It was apparently what Milton Kahn wanted to hear. He turned back toward her on her perspiration-soaked mattress and nuzzled his head between her breasts. Kissed her precisely there, then kissed both nipples. Pearl wasn't sure she was in love with this guy, but it wasn't bad having him around.

Milt was, in a way, a gift from Pearl's mother and her friend Mrs. Kahn at the Golden Sunset assisted-living apartments in Teaneck, a sort of arranged affair if not marriage. Mrs. Kahn was Milt's aunt. Under duress, Pearl had agreed to meet the elderly women and Milt for lunch in Golden Sunset's bleak dining room, and Pearl was surprised to find that she actually liked the guy. He was short, like she was, and good looking in a dark way, with a tiny imperial beard on the tip of his chin that tickled in the right places and made him look more like a magician or renowned psychiatrist than a struggling dermatologist.

Pearl discovered that he was a good conversationalist with a sense of humor, a funny guy for a dermatologist. After their second date, he'd removed some bumps from

Pearl's neck. She'd somehow found that very intimate. To Pearl's mother's delight, the spark had struck and now there was flame if not a raging inferno. Flame was better than nothing. It was cold out there.

Pearl sat up and used both hands to smooth back her hair so she wouldn't look insane. She was aware of Milt watching her and smiling as she swiveled on the mattress. She felt his fingertips brush the curve of her right buttock.

"Got someplace to go?" he asked. He had a deep voice for a small man, husky. He wasn't husky himself, but lean and muscular. Tan, with a lot of dark hair on his chest. Some hair—maybe too much—on his back.

"The shower," Pearl said. "Gotta get outta here."

"You live here," Milt reminded her.

"But I don't work here."

He sighed. "Your job. Always your job."

"You sound like a lot of cops' wives."

"Sexist thing to say."

"And husbands," Pearl amended. She stood up and padded barefoot across the bedroom toward the bathroom.

"You know you're beautiful," Milt said huskily behind her.

"Oh, sure."

"And your job's okay with me except for the danger."

"Well, if I could be chief of police I would be."

"This Torso Murders case you're on, how do you know you won't become one of the killer's victims?"

She paused at the doorway and turned to face him. "That guy wants to stay as far away from me as possible, Milt."

He was propped up on his elbows, grinning as he gave her an up-and-down glance. "Hard to believe."

"That's not the only thing that's hard," she said and continued her sleepy, sex-sated trek into the bathroom.

By the time she'd showered and dressed, her hair still glistening wet, he had toast, orange juice, and coffee waiting for her on the kitchen table. The toast was slightly burned, the way she liked it, and along with the freshly brewed coffee made the kitchen smell great. Milt was barefoot and bare chested, but he had his pants on and was actually wearing one of Pearl's old aprons that she'd received as a gift from her mother. Pearl thought she'd thrown the thing away, but here it was in her kitchen on a man she'd just had sex with. Good sex. She'd never seen Quinn wearing an apron and couldn't imagine it.

"Cops' wives," Pearl said. "They're saints."

"And cops' husbands," Milt added, as he sat across from her at the table.

Domesticity, Pearl thought. It can't be beat. Until it beats you.

They were in Renz's office at One Police Plaza. It didn't look like a working cop's office because it wasn't. No clutter, no bulletin board with rosters and notices, no visible file cabinets. Harley Renz had risen way above all that and, like many before him, regarded the position of police commissioner as primarily political. Not surprising, as he'd gotten there more through politics than police work.

The office was carpeted in a deep maroon and had oak-paneled walls. Requisite trophy plaques, commendations, and photographs were arranged on the wall behind the desk. The desk itself was a vast slab of speckled dark granite. Whatever electronic equipment was in the room was concealed in a huge, many-doored oak hutch that almost perfectly matched the paneling. Two brown leather armchairs faced the desk. There was a small table with four chairs off to the side, for miniconferences, and what looked like an antique table with a cut-glass vase on it stuffed with colorful flowers.

Quinn guessed that fresh flowers were brought in every day. Harley Renz, bureaucratic climber, living the high life. Wanting to climb still higher. Quinn had heard that cockroaches did that, inexorably climbed upward in a building. He wondered what they did when they reached the roof.

Along with Quinn and his team, Helen the profiler was there. She was wearing a green blazer and gray slacks, with high heels that made her even taller than her six feet plus.

Pearl had on a lightweight navy blue business suit that made her features and hair appear darker. She looked vital and alive this morning, Quinn thought. Healthy and glowing in a way that was wholesome and beautiful. Health had a lot to do with sex appeal, Quinn was beginning to realize.

She caught him looking at her and he looked away. At the same time, he was sure she'd abruptly looked away from him.

Renz pulled a *City Beat* from somewhere below his desk and laid it on a granite corner. "Cindy Sellers is asking why the killer doesn't conceal the entire body. Why leave the untraceable torsos where they'll surely be found."

"We've been wondering the same thing," Quinn said.

Renz glanced over at Helen, who'd moved to stand in front of the office's window. It was her time to speak. It occurred to Quinn that she liked to stand in front of windows, maybe so she appeared in silhouette.

"That would be why I'm here," Helen said in her Lauren Bacall voice. She even looked a little like a young Bacall, only much taller and more athletic. "The killer's actions suggest that the torsos are part of his ruling compulsion and megalomania. He has to brag about what he's done. He must make sure that someone knows a murder's been committed, and that he's gotten away with it."

"By someone you mean the police?" Fedderman asked, from where he sat in an uncomfortable-looking chair near the table with the floral arrangement.

"Definitely. But the public, too. The torsos are his public souvenirs that he's sharing with them."

"Generous," Fedderman said.

Helen might have smiled. It was hard to know from her

silhouette. "They're also a way of taunting the police and terrorizing the city."

Quinn was long familiar with the games serial killers played, and he wasn't convinced. "Isn't it possible the killer makes sure his victims' remains are anonymous simply to hinder the investigation into their deaths?"

"Quinn's right. I can buy into that part," Pearl said, before Helen could answer. "And to taunt us." She shook her head. "The rest, the souvenir business, I'm not so sure. Some serial killers like to keep souvenirs of their victims—a lock of hair, that sort of thing—but they don't generally want to share them with the public or anyone else. They want to keep them where they can look at them from time to time, like all collectors."

"True," Helen said. "They like to relive their conquests. It gives them a feeling of power and importance."

Quinn shifted in the soft leather chair nearest Renz's flight deck–sized desk and crossed his arms. "None of this is for sure."

"Agreed," Helen said. "Like you, I don't have much to work with."

"We do know for sure he's one sick puppy," Fedderman said.

"The stakes, or whatever he uses to penetrate his victims," Pearl said.

"After they're dead," Renz reminded them. He looked inquisitively at Helen. "Why *after* they're dead?"

"As of now, I don't know," Helen said.

"A necrophiliac who can't get it up," Fedderman suggested.

Helen shrugged. "Good a guess as any."

Some profiler, Quinn thought. An honest one. "Truth is, this guy's got us operating pretty much in the dark."

"We can deduce from that that he's smart," Helen said sarcastically.

"Now you're cookin'," Renz said.

The poised silhouette that was Helen seemed unmoved by his return sarcasm.

Quinn wanted to stop them before a volley of sarcasm got going that might lead to a real argument.

The phone beat him to it. He hadn't even seen the phone; it was concealed in a sunken alcove on the far side of the desk. It had a soft, controlled ring that wasn't a ring at all. It sounded more like a repetitive, soothing note of a violin about to begin a gentle melody.

As Renz lifted a dark plastic receiver that matched the desk, he looked annoyed that they should be disturbed. Almost immediately, his expression became serious. "Yes. Yes," he said. He produced a notepad from the sunken alcove. "Christ!" he said, looking in turn at everyone in the office. He might have been identifying the caller, judging by the somber, dazed expression on his bloodhound features.

He switched the phone to his left hand so he could write on the notepad. He kept saying yes intermittently while scribbling with his pen. Finally, he thanked the caller and hung up.

He sat for a minute running his fingertips along the loose flesh of his sagging cheeks. It stretched the skin around his eyes downward and made him look even more like some upright breed of hound.

"We've got us another torso," he said. "Found alongside a Dumpster on the Upper West Side."

"Maybe a match for our arm," Fedderman said.

Renz shook his head no. "This one's too fresh. Killed within the last few days."

Pearl, who'd been leaning back so only her chair's back legs were on the floor, realized the import of Renz's words. She sat forward so the chair's front legs made a soft thump on the thick pile carpet.

"Victim number four," she said.

Renz was staring down at the folded *City Beat* on his desk. "I guess I oughta call Cindy Sellers." He looked at

Quinn as if for help. "The woman's become one big pain in the ass."

Quinn shrugged. "You're the one who made the deal with the devil."

"I do it all the time," Renz said. "Usually it works out okay."

He shoved his notepad forward so Quinn could copy the information on his own.

"I need you to find this bastard, Quinn."

Quinn didn't think that required a reply and kept on silently writing.

They left Renz in his office to go to the West Side address where the torso had been found. Left him in the suddenly smaller room with his plaques and commendations and ego-inflating framed photographs.

Right now, it wasn't a comfortable place for him.

14

The three of them were in Quinn's old Lincoln on the way to the West Side address where the latest torso had been found. Quinn was driving, Pearl beside him, Fedderman in back. They were headed uptown on Broadway. Traffic was heavy, and there was a haze that smelled like exhaust fumes over everything. The sun angled in low along the side streets and turned the haze golden.

As Quinn veered around a sightseeing bus to make better time, Pearl's cell phone buzzed and vibrated in her pocket.

She fished it out and saw by caller ID that the call's origin was Golden Sunset.

Her mother. Had to be. A familiar dread and anger closed in on her.

Quinn glanced over at her, wondering if she was going to answer her call.

Feeling that she had little choice, Pearl made the connection. "Officer Kasner." Let her mother know she was working. She glanced at Quinn, who was staring straight ahead. Was he smiling? Was that bastard smiling?

"It's your mother, Pearl," came the strident voice from the

phone. Pearl didn't want to hear it, yet she had to press the tiny phone close to her ear so Quinn and Fedderman couldn't overhear.

"Pearl? Is that you, dear?"

"Yes." *Keep it terse and simple. Brief.*

"I called your apartment, dear, and got your machine. Such a world since we started using machines to answer our phones. Maybe the phones could just talk to each other. Don't you ever check your messages?"

"Sometimes." *Brief.*

"Maybe your machine erases mine. What I wondered, dear, is if you and Milton Kahn left each other on good terms."

Huh?

"I mean, after last night," her mother said.

What? This was unacceptable. "Who told you? What do you mean?" *Unacceptable!*

"That's two questions, dear."

"Then answer them both."

"Don't snap, Pearl. That's very rude. Mrs. Kahn told me. And why not? It's no secret you and her nephew Milton are hotsy-totsy."

Pearl had a pretty good idea where Mrs. Kahn had gotten her information. She fell silent, noticing Quinn watching her from the corner of his eye. "Some things you don't talk about," Pearl said.

"Don't you know I agree with you, dear? But these were extraordinary circumstances. Mrs. Kahn tells me Milton is worried sick about you. About your personal safety. They— Mrs. Kahn and wonderful Milton—thought I should talk to you about it."

Wonderful Milton's going to learn to keep his mouth shut. "I appreciate his concern, but it's really none of his business. Or the business of whomever he might have told."

"The people who love you, darling Pearl, they're concerned. What else do we have in this world where everything, including your own mother, will someday turn to dust? Someday soon, I might add in all sincerity, feeling more and more distressed every day as I do here in this nursing home hell."

"Assisted living. It's not a nursing home. Assisted-living apartments with televisions, comfortable beds, kitchens, private baths, recliners, all the food you can eat—including the pot roast you likc so much. People who were on *The Lawrence Welk Show* come there to perform. There are game rooms, buses to Atlantic City. They're assisted-living apartments."

"Death's waiting rooms, dear."

Pearl was seething. "I think not." She so yearned to terminate this conversation. "Is that all you wanted? If so, I'm busy."

"You're being snappish again."

"I mean to be."

"What I want is for you to consider the future, Pearl. Milton and a home—and children, God willing. A place without killers and guns and knives and rap talk. There are other jobs, Pearl. Milton said to Mrs. Kahn that you could work as his receptionist. It would be safe there. He wants you off the streets, Pearl. We all do. The people who—"

"Yeah, yeah. This is my job."

"What I'm saying, Pearl, is there are other jobs."

Like dermatologist receptionist.

Quinn blasted the horn and cursed at a battered, dusty cab that had cut him off.

"Is that that nice Mr. Quinn I hear, Pearl?"

"The same."

"Such a good man. A protector and a provider. You should feel blessed, Pearl. You have your choice between two good men—one a mensch policeman retired with a generous pension, and the other a medical doctor, no less."

"An obsessive maniac and a weasel."

"What?" Quinn asked.

"I was talking into the phone."

"What, dear?"

"I have to end this conversation, really."

Quinn blasted the horn again, still focused on the cab that had cut him off. The driver extended his arm out the window and raised his middle finger.

Quinn leaned on the horn again. "If we had time I'd pull that bastard over."

"We've got time," Fedderman said from the backseat. "Lady we're going to see is dead."

"Look at that asshole, Feds!"

"Cabbies think they own the road like cops," Fedderman said.

"Screw a buncha cabbies."

"Pearl? Dear?"

"I need to go now. Sorry."

Pearl broke the connection and sat seething over weasel Milton yammering his business to his motormouthed aunt.

What was wrong with the world?

"Was that your mother?" Quinn asked, seeing clear pavement ahead and goosing the car to higher speed.

"How'd you guess?" Pearl asked.

"Shoulda told her I said hi."

"I should have, since she thinks you're God."

"Shoulda told her hi from me, too," Fedderman said from the backseat.

"She thinks you're a prick," Pearl said.

The passageway where the dusty green Dumpster squatted like a military tank without a gun was blocked off at both ends with yellow crime scene tape. CSU techs were swarming busily about the scene with their luminol, magnifiers, tweezers, and plastic evidence bags. Tagging and bagging. The photographer was finished and tinkering with her equipment. Nobody seemed to want to look directly at the pale, waxy flesh object beside the Dumpster.

Quinn glanced around and didn't see Nift. Maybe the Napoleonic little pest had come and gone.

Then a woman wearing jeans, a black T-shirt, and one of those vests with a thousand pockets approached. She was in her forties and had short brown hair in a practical cut, a trim body, and a sweet, lined face that was slightly red around the nose and eyes, as if she had rosacea. She was carrying a black medical bag.

"Detective Quinn?"

He admitted it.

She smiled. Nice teeth—probably used whitener. "I'm Dr. Chavesky from the medical examiner's office."

"I expected Nift."

"He had to go out of town on business." Again the smile. Blinding but natural. "Disappointed?"

"Not so far." He nodded toward the torso. "Finished with it?"

"Her? Yeah. I'm up on the case. As far as a preliminary gets us, she's the same as the others. Shot through the heart, obvious postmortem trauma to the vaginal area. The point of whatever was shoved into her snagged on her labia minor. The way she was taken apart—crude but effective dismemberment."

"Bullet still in her?" Pearl asked. She and Fedderman had been standing off to the side, listening.

Dr. Chavesky turned her attention to them, knowing they were with Quinn, a set. "Yes. No exit wound. It's a small caliber and it feels like it went through the sternum. We'll have to see if it didn't break up too much to run a comparative ballistics test."

"Kill her right away?" Fedderman asked.

"Probably not. But within a few minutes. Of course, it's also possible the killer shot her more than once. Obviously, the entire body isn't here."

Quinn looked over at the torso, the headless end. He quickly looked away. "How long's she been dead?"

"My estimate's ten to fifteen hours. I'd say she was in her early thirties when the clock stopped for her."

"Any other trauma to her body?"

She gave him a look. "Besides the vaginal penetration and dismemberment, no. Just the bullet. It appears to have entered from a point directly in front of her while she was standing." Chavesky glanced at her watch. "EMS should be here any minute to remove the body, unless you want them to leave it for a while. I gotta go."

"We won't be long looking it over," Quinn said.

Dr. Chavesky nodded. "I'll get a comprehensive post-mortem report to you as soon as possible."

She and Quinn exchanged cards. He glanced down at hers and saw that her full name was Dr. Linda Chavesky. He slipped the card into his shirt pocket, behind his folded reading glasses, and watched the doctor duck gracefully beneath the crime scene tape and climb into a gray city car. Though she was slender, she had to be strong, judging by the effortless way she handled the large black medical bag.

Quinn and his two detectives walked over to the nude torso.

Nift would have remarked on the victim's breasts, which were not large, but well formed even in death. A young woman, all right. So much life stolen from her. Quinn quickly examined where her arms had been severed, where her head had been severed. He was able to do so without suffering any reaction. That would come later, when he was alone and not on the job. She had black pubic hair, and it didn't take a doctor to know that violence had been done to the vaginal area.

"It would have been easy to put her behind the Dumpster," Pearl said. "Even inside it." The sweet, rotting smell coming from the Dumpster—she hoped that's where it came from—was making her nauseated.

"Our guy wanted her found as soon as possible," Fedderman said.

"Question's why," Pearl said.

"We'll think on it," Fedderman told her, giving her a look that let her know she'd stated the obvious.

"Sure. We're detectives."

"Act like it," Quinn said. He didn't want them getting into a spat, especially in front of the CSU people. They were pretending not to be listening, but he knew they were.

"No tattoos on any of the victims," Fedderman said. "Could just be coincidence."

"No nipple, nose, or belly button rings, either," Pearl said.

Quinn looked at her with something like approval.

"What the hell does that mean?" Fedderman asked.

"Maybe nothing."

"Means they probably didn't run with a kinky crowd," Quinn said. "Not part of the S&M scene, that kinda thing."

Fedderman pointed at the lifeless, violated torso. "You don't call that sadism?"

Quinn let out a long breath. "You've got a point."

"An interesting one to ponder," Pearl said.

"Whether they're S&M snuff victims?" Fedderman asked.

"No. Whether you've got a point."

She'd said it thoughtfully, obviously not trying to rag Fedderman.

Neither man questioned her about it. When Pearl let her mind go off on its own, which she often did, they knew not to disturb her.

Let her ponder. It would keep her mind off her phone call from her mother, or whatever had upset her. Keep her from snapping at people.

Later that day, Linda Chavesky phoned Quinn on his cell. She told him the victim's heart had been struck by a fragment of a twenty-two-caliber bullet that had nicked the sternum going in and broken into three pieces.

"It wouldn't have killed her right away," she said, "but it probably would have put her down, into shock."

"A second shot, then," Quinn said, "to a part of the body not found. Her head, probably."

"Most likely. Or the severing of a large artery in her neck or thigh by a knife. We don't know if she bled to death or the blood simply drained out of her when she was dismembered. That could happen if she was dismembered soon after death, and the blood hadn't had time to coagulate."

Quinn didn't say anything, thinking this was sounding more and more like a professional hit man—the shooting part. One to the heart, another shot or two to the head, to make sure.

"Another thing. She suffered vaginal penetration, then beyond, by a cylindrical, sharply pointed wooden object, consistent with a sawed-off and sharpened broomstick. This was after she was killed."

"How do you know it was wooden?" Quinn asked, figuring he was going to hear again about the furniture polish lubricant.

"I put in some extra time on this one. Found a splinter."

"Excellent. That's something for sure that we were only guessing at before."

"That a compliment?"

"You bet."

"Whatever penetrated her left a slightly oily residue."

"Furniture polish," Quinn said. "It was in the other victims. But it didn't necessarily mean wood for sure, until you found the splinter." He could imagine the killer lovingly sharpening and polishing the deadly piece of broomstick—if that's what it was. Helen Iman would suggest it was a phallic symbol. She might be right.

"I'd put the victim in her early thirties, average weight, and most likely curvaceous," Linda said. "A magnet for men." She kind of surprised Quinn. Usually M.E.s weren't so voluble or willing to speculate, especially over the phone to detectives they'd only recently met.

"Hold on a minute," she said.

Quinn waited, the phone pressed to his ear, hearing unintelligible voices in the background on the other end of the connection.

Linda's voice came back on. "My friend from ballistics just gave me the report on the bullet. It was fired by the same gun that killed the other victims. So there's something else you know for sure. You wanna meet someplace for coffee?"

"Pardon?"

"You don't need a pardon; you're a cop. I'm asking you out on a date. You're not exactly a real NYPD cop, and even if you were, you'd be my superior officer, so it wouldn't be sexual harassment. A yes or no'll do."

Quinn got over his surprise and thought, what the hell. Laughed. "It's a yes, Linda. We'll meet somewhere for drinks."

"I did say coffee."

Quinn sensed that he'd tweaked a nerve. "Sure. Coffee it is."

"I used to drink alcohol for nonmedicinal purposes. I'll be up front about that."

"You've got lots of company if you used to have a drinking problem," Quinn said, thinking immediately that he shouldn't have told her that. She hadn't exactly said she'd had a problem.

"Nobody 'used to have' a drinking problem, Captain Quinn. I've been dry for over two years and intend to stay that way."

"It's just Quinn, Linda. Tonight at the Lotus Diner on Amsterdam suit you?"

"Sure does. I know where it is. About seven?"

"Let's make it six. We might have coffee, then decide to go out for dinner."

"We've got a date, Quinn."

Quinn was smiling. Then he remembered this was an official conversation. "Anything else about the victim, Doctor?"

"She didn't drown."

A date, Quinn thought, staring at the phone's tiny blank screen. What unsettled him somewhat wasn't that Linda Chavesky had come on to him. In his early fifties, he was still at least presentable enough to be in the game. What struck him was that not once during his conversation with Linda had he thought about Pearl.

He knew he was as obsessive and stubborn, as Pearl often told him he was, but even the most determined person finally got tired of knocking on a door and not getting an answer, of waiting patiently and then waiting some more.

Maybe Pearl had finally convinced him that any possibility of them ever being in a loving relationship again was gone forever. Possibly she was right and that was how it should be, accepted by both of them and not just her.

Or maybe he was simply giving up hope.

And grasping for more hope.

15

Jill had settled on E-Bliss.org.

She'd checked out several of the matchmaking services on the Internet, limiting them to those based in or serving New York City. There was no shortage of them, especially if you had some sort of exotic sexual preference. A few of them seemed respectable if not downright staid. It was among those that she'd found E-Bliss.org. She'd carefully filled out its online questionnaire for its personality profile. She'd had a flattering photo, a head shot from a wedding she'd attended a few years ago back home, already on her hard drive. She'd attached the jpeg along with the filled-out, surprisingly detailed questionnaire, then put it on "Mail Waiting to Be Sent" and given herself two days to reconsider.

Two days later, to the hour, she'd drawn a deep breath and clicked her computer's mouse on SEND.

Almost immediately she'd received an e-mail telling her what a wise choice she'd made, how wonderful she appeared in her photograph, how perfect was her personality profile. She could be assured that there were many suitable males who would request a meeting with her. She could establish a password and browse through profiles of potential partners or, as most clients did, wait for the experts at E-Bliss.org to use their comprehensive database and special software to match her with the best possible choice.

Jill didn't hesitate before moving her computer's cursor to the button requesting expert matchmaking. That was what she was paying for on her Visa card. God knew she hadn't done well on her own when it came to attracting and choosing among men. Let the experts do it for her. If they could design her closet and scrapbook, they could design her life. She clicked the mouse and immediately felt relieved. She'd made her choice and followed through.

Time to wait, and at that she had become an expert.

They sat in a window booth in the Lotus Diner, by chance Quinn's favorite booth, where he often had breakfast and read the papers over coffee. Daylight was battling dusk, and the sidewalks were still crowded. The steady stream of pedestrians hurrying past were mostly unaware of Quinn and Linda Chavesky, though they were at times less than a foot away on the other side of thick plate glass.

Quinn and Linda were ill at ease with each other at first, but by their second cup of coffee were somewhat more open. Quinn liked Linda, and he sensed that she liked him. Dressed in slacks and a loose-fitting yellow blouse, with her hair calculatingly mussed and a gold chain necklace, she seemed much more attractive than she had at the earlier crime scene. The light they were sitting in didn't do her any favors, and she didn't need any. Judging by the crows-feet just beginning to show at the corners of her intelligent blue eyes, Quinn guessed her to be in her early forties. That was the principal thing about her, he thought, her obvious intelligence. And a subtle sadness born of hard experience. Quinn recognized that expression; he'd seen it often in the mirror. She had some kind of makeup on this evening that mostly disguised the redness of her cheeks and the bridge of her nose.

"Rosacea," she said, smiling at him. She'd noticed him staring.

"Pardon?"

"It's a hereditary affliction that causes a kind of redness in a ring pattern on the face. At times it makes me look something like a raccoon."

"I wasn't thinking raccoon," Quinn assured her, taking a sip of coffee.

"Also makes me look like a drunk, since alcoholics sometimes have the same look from ruptured capillaries."

"Obviously, you're not a drunk."

"Well, I am, but a dry drunk. I intend to stay that way."

"I had my own go-round with the bottle a few years ago," Quinn said. "When I had the problem in the department and my wife left me."

"When things finally worked out at least somewhat for you, did you have trouble quitting?"

"Not really. I don't think it ever became a problem in itself. And I still have a drink now and then."

"There's the difference between you and friends of Bill, like me."

They both knew "friends of Bill" was code for Alcoholics Anonymous.

Linda rotated her coffee cup on the wet saucer ring with both hands and fixed her blue eyes on Quinn. "You have a daughter, right?" The way she looked at him and spoke, her words and eyes boring into him, made it seem as if they were alone in the diner.

"Uh-huh. Lauri. A great kid. Woman. She's living out in L.A. with her true love, a guy named Wormy who fronts a band."

"I married young and divorced, never had kids. Too late now, and the alcohol messed me up when I could have gotten pregnant. Thank God I didn't. An alcohol addiction doesn't leave room for much else, including love or sex. My hell years."

"Over now," Quinn said. "For you and for me. Where's your ex?"

"Back in St. Louis, selling mortgage insurance, last I heard. We don't keep in touch. Not much sense in it." Linda stared down into her cup, then up again at Quinn. "I damned near lost my medical license in St. Louis. Then I quit practicing and fought the booze for a few years, and came to New York for a new start. That was five years ago."

"That's when you started in the NYPD," Quinn said. "In Latent Prints. Wasting your talents and qualifications. Couple of years and you became an assistant M.E. And a good one. I researched you." *Best to start off with honesty.*

"Sure you did. You're a cop. So am I, in a way. I ran a check on you, too. It's too easy on the computer. I really didn't have to do much bouncing around on NYPD databases to learn about you. You're something of a legend in the department, Quinn. That's why I was so nervous at first when I sat down here."

"You didn't seem nervous."

"I still am, a little bit."

He smiled at her. "We'll have dinner." He'd almost said, "*with wine*," but caught himself. "A good meal will relax both of us. I'm still a little nervous, too. I remember seeing you at a few other crime scenes. You attract the eye."

She blushed at the compliment. The rosacea made itself evident, as if she'd been wearing a mask and it had left faint marks. Quinn found it somehow attractive, this disorder.

"Your ex-wife, May, is in California, too," she said. "Anywhere near your daughter?"

"Close enough. I'm sure they see each other, but not often. May doesn't like Wormy. Who does?" He felt a little stab of guilt. "Well, tell you the truth, I've become sorta fond of him."

"What about you and May?"

"We get along with each other. She's remarried to an attorney out there. Elliott. Not a bad guy. She and I talk, but only about Lauri. Our marriage ended because May couldn't be a cop's wife."

"Familiar story."

"Yeah. I don't hold it against her. I wouldn't hold it against anyone. Don't worry about May."

"Should I worry about Pearl?"

"That's over," Quinn said, thinking, *We're only meeting for coffee, then some dinner.* But he knew there was much more going on here than that. They both knew it.

"Pearl know it's over?" Linda asked.

"It's her idea. I accept it."

"You sound as if you're trying to talk yourself into accepting it."

"Maybe a little," he admitted. "But it's over."

"You sure?"

"I think so."

Linda sighed and sat back in the booth. She glanced at the people streaming past out on the sidewalk, so near yet separated by a wall of glass. "So many people in this world. And cops seem able to make it long term only with other cops, or people in the same business."

"I'm not so sure I believe that," Quinn said.

Linda looked back at him with all her somber intelligence. "Sure you do. That's why you're here. That's why we're both here."

"We don't know each other all that well," Quinn said, "but already I hate it when you're right."

Deputy Chief Wes Nobbler sat behind his desk and waited patiently for Greeve to enter his office. He knew "The Ghost" wouldn't have wanted to see him so early in the morning unless he had something interesting to report.

There was a perfunctory knock on the door, and Greeve

entered. As he did so, Nobbler absently lowered the file folder he'd just finished reading, placing it out of sight in a partly opened desk drawer.

Greeve looked this morning as he always did, slender and faintly mournful. He was wearing a dark suit, white shirt, and a neatly knotted black and red tie, mostly black. His dark hair was combed straight back, making it obvious that it was receding and thinning. His long face was pale and closely shaven; no dark whiskers to offset his pallor.

"This about the Torso Murders?" Nobbler asked, wanting to get straight to the point.

Greeve gave a somber nod. "I followed Quinn and his team from Renz's office yesterday," he said. He didn't sit down but stood with his hands in his pants pockets, his feet close together. His long body was at a slight forward lean, his narrow shoulders hunched. The man knew how to loom. "Quinn and company hauled ass out of there. There's no way to know what they were discussing, but I know why the meeting broke up."

"The latest Torso victim," Nobbler said. He'd learned about the most recent victim late yesterday afternoon, and it was all over the papers and TV news this morning.

"Yeah. They went to the crime scene, and I figure they'll be back there today canvassing the neighborhood. Probably just Pearl and Fedderman, though."

"You'd be better off staying with Quinn, then."

"That's the way I figure it," Greeve said. "The word I get is that ballistics tests already made the gun as the same one that killed the other victims. Little twenty-two-caliber pest pistol. One to the heart that probably didn't kill the victim right away. Same kind of sexual mutilation." Greeve shifted his weight slightly from one foot to the other, then settled in again so it was evenly distributed, almost like a macabre dance step. "None of this is confirmed yet."

Nobbler nodded. There was no need to tell Greeve he was way ahead of him on the postmortem information.

"Actually," Greeve said, "I stayed on Quinn last night after he parted company with Pearl and Fedderman. He met the M.E. who examined the victim at the scene of the crime, Dr. Linda Chavesky."

Nobbler sat forward over his desk, interested. "You mean they met someplace other than the crime scene?"

"They had coffee at a diner over on Amsterdam. Then they took a long walk and went to dinner at an Italian restaurant on Broadway. Had antipasto and rigatoni carbonera. Then he put her in a cab. No good-night kiss." Greeve smiled. "Coulda been the garlic."

This fascinated Nobbler. "You saying it was more than a professional meeting?"

"I'm sure it was. Looked like they were more interested in each other than whatever else they were talking about. I was hoping he'd jump her bones. I'm kinda disappointed. But then, I guess Quinn is, too."

Nobbler drummed his fingertips on the desktop and thought for a few minutes, trying to process this and figure out how he could use it.

Greeve seemed comfortable with the silence.

"Dr. Chavesky . . ." Nobbler said at last. "I think I know which one she is over there."

"Nice-looking woman," Greeve said.

"We need to find out more about her."

"Definitely. I've heard rumors she's got a past. Has to do with the bottle. Not here in New York, though."

"That we know of," Nobbler said.

Greeve smiled. "So far."

Nobbler shook his head, causing his fleshy jowls to quiver. "Quinn oughta know better."

"You'd think," Greeve said. "For now, I'll spend some time trying to find out more about the postmortem. See if there's anything pertinent there that's being kept secret, since these two have gotten so close."

"No. Just stay on Quinn."

Greeve nodded. "Your call."

"I can catch up on the postmortem," Nobbler said. "I've got a confidential contact in the medical examiner's office. Guy named Nift."

Greeve smiled mournfully. "Confidential contact. That the same thing as a snitch?"

"It's a difference without a distinction," Nobbler said.

Greeve nodded. "You see a lot of that these days."

16

He sat on a stool in Has Beans coffee bar and watched her approach on the other side of the glass door.

She was attractive enough that almost every male reacted in some way when she came through the door. Very well built under that blue sweat suit, he thought. Medium-length blond hair cut in some kind of layered way so it would always look slightly mussed, just the right amount of makeup. Her jaw was strong—what used to be called mean—but her full lips took away its severity. There was a slight angularity to her blue eyes that made them interesting. She looked a little like that sexy movie star Charlotte Rampling, only younger. Just the right age.

He slid off his stool at the bar, moved toward her with a smile, and gestured with his arm toward one of the vacant tables near the back of the place, where it was less crowded. Not coming on too strong, but already taking charge. Friendly and firm. They liked that, or they wouldn't have sent in the questionnaire in the first place.

She smiled back, nodded, and their paths converged at the table. He saw that she had a small galaxy of light brown freckles scattered across the bridge of her nose. Charming. He made a mental note to memorize their pattern.

Jill liked it that he sort of took charge of the meeting but waited until she'd sat down before he sat. And he had a wonderful smile that dissipated much of her nervousness. He certainly was handsome enough, and he was tastefully dressed in tan pants and a darker brown sport jacket. His cream-colored shirt beneath the jacket was open at the collar, revealing a few dark chest hairs. The hair on his head was parted and neatly combed and there was no beard stubble on his face, so he wasn't going for the macho need-a-shave look.

Jill decided there was nothing here not to like. So far so good.

When he'd sat down opposite her, he said, "Tony Lake," and extended his hand.

She laid her hand in his and felt a gentle pressure. Just right. "Jill Clark."

"As advertised," he said, with the smile again.

"You too," she said, not knowing how else to respond. She raised her chin and a look of pleasure moved over her features. "It smells terrific in here," she said. "I love the aroma of roasting coffee."

"Me too. And there's a touch of cinnamon in the air. Makes it smell all the better."

"I agree." *My, don't we already have a lot in common?*

He nodded toward the oversized gray mug he'd brought with him to the table. "I'm having a Honduras," he said. "It's a caramel latte. They've named their coffee drinks after Central and South American countries."

"I know," she said. "I've been here a few times before." Then she quickly added, "By myself, though."

"Could be the countries are where the beans come from," he said.

That had never occurred to her. "You think?"

"Truthfully, I have no idea." He seemed amused by the detour their conversation had taken. First-date talk. "So which piece of geography do you want to order?"

"I like their El Salvador."

He went to the bar and returned a few minutes later with a large mug topped with creamy froth.

"I'll have to try one of these sometime," he said, placing the mug before her on the table and sitting back down. He took a sip of his Honduras and studied her over the mug's thick rim. "So tell me about yourself, Jill."

"I guess you read my online profile."

"Sure. Like you read mine. They go only so deep. People tend not to confide in computers. Being online isn't like sitting across from someone and talking face-to-face."

"You're right. We should do some confiding." She sampled her El Salvador, found it too hot, and set the mug back on its coaster. Foam might be sticking to her upper lip. She dabbed it gently with the back of her knuckle and felt no dampness. "I hope you won't find me too dull."

"Not hardly. You already cleared that hurdle by just walking in the place. A lot of Central America came to a boil."

She laughed. "Well, let's see. I haven't been in town all that long. Like a lot of other people, I came to New York for a fresh start. There are more possibilities here."

"Opportunities."

"I haven't run into too many of them yet."

"Maybe this is one."

She put on her best smile. "Maybe it is. I've been working for Files and More. That's a temp place. And for the past week I've been a temp at Tucker, Simpson, and King, a law firm on the East Side that specializes in traffic violations and domestic disturbances."

"AWD. Arguing while driving."

She laughed. "Fixing traffic tickets, actually. As for the

domestic cases, from what I've seen they go further than arguing."

"Yeah, I suppose they do." He appeared genuinely concerned. "It's a problem."

She tried the El Salvador again. Better. "All I'm doing there is filing, which gets old fast. And you know how temps get treated—especially at the smaller companies, like this one. When they know you'll be leaving at the end of the week, no one bothers to get to know you."

"Jill, I can't imagine someone not wanting to know you better. Especially people of the male persuasion."

"Uh-huh. They want to know me in the biblical sense, and skip the Old Testament."

He threw back his head and laughed. She approved of his sense of humor, and he seemed to approve of hers. She'd been afraid he was going to be a dry stick. Who could tell from an online profile that might be 90 percent lies? She glanced around at the place she'd chosen to meet him. Strangers around them who were supposed to provide some sort of comfort and assurance.

Am I really doing this? What do I actually know about this man?

"So what do you do?" she asked.

"For a living? I sell advertising space in international publications. There's some traveling involved, but I don't mind. Kind of enjoy it, in fact."

"Sounds interesting."

"About like Files and More."

"Oh, I think not."

"You a religious person?" he asked.

Where'd that come from?

She answered carefully. "Not particularly. There should be plenty of time to get around to that."

"So you want to have fun first."

Ah, there's *where he was going.*

"I didn't exactly mean it that way," she said. She didn't want to give him the wrong impression. A toss between the sheets she could have in this town any time; she was, after all, a woman who could bring Central America to a boil. She wanted to be clear she was looking for something more here. And wanted him to be looking for more than casual sex.

"I hope you didn't take what I said the wrong way," he told her. "I mean, you know, about having fun . . ." He looked terribly concerned that he might have offended her.

She smiled and patted the back of his hand. "Not to worry, Tony. I'm neither a bimbo nor a nun, nor a combination of the two."

"Let's hope they're mutually exclusive," he said.

"Let's hope. Hope is a good thing."

And she did hope.

Jill and Tony talked for more than two hours except for a few minutes when Tony left the table to talk on his cell phone.

Jill decided that their coffee bar date had gone marvelously. He'd been about to kiss her on the forehead when they'd parted outside of Has Beans, but then he'd changed his mind, despite her unspoken wishes. Obviously, he didn't want to push too soon and too hard.

Maybe later.

Still high on caffeine or Tony Lake, Jill now began to walk.

It was interesting how her nervousness had left her only moments after sitting down with Tony. And their conversation had flowed so smoothly. Most of it, she realized, had been about her. She told herself not to be so selfish next time they met. But he had a way of making her feel important and the natural subject of the conversation. He wanted to know all about *her*. He was genuinely interested in her. More than interested—fascinated.

Yes, *fascinated* was the word.

She smiled at her happiness that lay right there in front of her like a gold coin waiting to be picked up.

Face it, doomster, the meeting was a roaring success.

Now and then in this crappy, difficult world, something went wonderfully right.

As she strolled away from Has Beans toward her subway stop, Jill actually found herself whistling.

17

The traffic light at the intersection was a DON'T WALK, so Jill stopped and stood with a few other people waiting for it to change. Since she had on her sweats and Nikes, she began idly jogging in place on the sidewalk, her body revolving in a slow circle. She could feel a slight bouncing of her breasts, but she didn't mind. Let people look. Let them guess how happy she was. Someone passing in a car honked the horn and shouted something.

At me?

For me?

Almost certainly.

As she turned to face back the way she'd come, her mood suddenly changed for the worse. She saw a woman, a street person in filthy clothes and with unkempt dirty blond hair, standing about fifty feet away and openly staring at her.

What bothered Jill was that the woman seemed oddly familiar.

Then she realized why. Jill was sure she'd seen her across the street from Has Beans when she and Tony had emerged from the coffee bar. Jill remembered the pang of pity she'd felt for the woman, who'd been standing alone and motionless as if lost, clutching a wrinkled brown paper sack beneath her right arm.

The woman was staring at her now in a way that evoked more fear than pity. As if there was some kind of connection between them.

Jill didn't want a connection. With a little bad luck, *she* could be this woman. Maybe only her dwindling checking account was the difference between them now. Homelessness happened. This city was cruel and could crush.

The woman took a faltering step toward her.

Jill looked away, continuing to jog in place, turning her back to her.

The woman had to be close now. Getting closer.

Jill continued facing away from the sad specter of a horrifying future and stared hard at the traffic signal across the intersection.

Change, damn you. Change!

The light did change.

Jill lengthened out her foot motion and jogged across the intersection. After veering around an old woman pushing a shopping cart full of groceries, she accelerated into a brisk run. Her rhythmic arm motion and the strain on her thighs felt great, liberating.

The homeless woman didn't figure to be a runner. Jill didn't have to glance back to know she was leaving the ragged figure behind. Her bleak alternative future receding into her past.

Running faster made Jill somehow breathe easier.

On the way home from work the next evening, Jill saw the woman again. It was when Jill stopped to look at a shoe sale display in a small shop. There, superimposed in the show window over the red high-heeled pumps she was considering, was the woman's reflection. She had to be close, not more than ten feet behind Jill.

There was something about the woman's reflected image that horrified Jill to the point that Jill was faintly nauseated.

To be in this woman's thoughts, her intentions . . .

It wasn't simply that Jill knew for sure now that the woman had truly been following her, had for some reason fixated on her. It was more a creepy certainty that she'd seen the woman before, other than just that evening outside Has Beans.

How long has she been following me? Watching me?

Had they met? Did they somehow know each other?

Had she simply pegged Jill as a soft touch, wanted a handout and was too shy to ask? It was a possible explanation. Maybe the poor thing was driven more by hunger than malice.

Either way, Jill had to find out.

Better to face your fears.

Jill decided to turn around and simply ask the woman, get to the bottom of this nonsense. She'd look the woman in the eye. Force a smile. Force a question.

Do we know each other?

She knew from experience that when you confronted your terror, it could quickly dissipate.

And this woman, determined, homeless, terrified her.

This will all end in a moment.

She tensed her muscles and whirled to face what waited behind her.

The woman was gone.

18

Mexico City, two months earlier

Maria Sanchez lay next to her husband, Jorge, in a circular bed in the honeymoon suite of the plush Hotel Casa Grande on the busy Paseo de la Reforma. They were on the twelfth floor, far above the noise and bustle in the streets below.

The only sound in the room was Jorge's even breathing, but Maria knew he wasn't asleep. He'd seldom slept at all the last few weeks because of the pressure. Political winds had shifted, and Jorge Sanchez, once an almost invincible drug lord and master of cocaine, was now vulnerable. New drug money, in larger amounts, had found its way to Jorge's friends in the government and made him dispensable. Over the past few months, routes into the United States had closed or become too dangerous. Just last week a sleek cruiser running drugs into southern Florida had been intercepted at sea, actually boarded after two of its crew had been gunned down from another, faster boat. After the cargo was transferred, the surviving members of the crew were allowed to live.

They, along with the boat, might prove useful to Jorge's successor.

The alarm by the bed began to buzz, and Jorge sat up immediately and turned it off. He was a lean, muscular man, dark and with a black, carefully trimmed beard and mustache. The fierce downward trim of the mustache was overmatched by the liquid softness of his brown eyes.

In the silence after the alarm, he lay back down and drew Maria to him. Both were nude, and sexually satiated after last night, but for a moment Maria thought he might want to make love again.

Unlike her husband, Maria had a light complexion, though her long, straight hair was auburn, like his. Her features were symmetrical and well sculpted, and her body was trim and athletic. Maria was the daughter of staid Midwesterners and had met Jorge three years ago when she was an art student at UCLA and he was studying business. Supposedly. What Jorge was really doing in the United States was establishing a drug distribution network.

With Jorge's help, Maria's basic grasp of Spanish soon improved, and their friendship quickly developed into a love that transcended any cultural differences. In fact, it gained the momentum of a freight train, and there was no leaving the rails without a fatal smashup.

When Maria learned from one of his friends that Jorge was a major drug dealer, she was thrilled rather than repelled. She confided this to him, and their love affair became even more heated. The friend who'd told her about Jorge disappeared. Maria never asked why or where to.

She regretted nothing of the life that had led to them being here in this room at the Hotel Casa Grande. Her family considered it sinful, and they didn't know the half of it. With Jorge, boundaries fell one after another, and behavior changed, along with what was unacceptable. Life was something to be seized. If it was selfish to live it to the fullest, so be it. People might not approve. Screw them, Maria thought.

Jorge didn't want to make love again. He leaned back away from her and rested his head on his pillow. The air conditioner kicked in with a soft rushing sound, almost like water flowing, sending a cooling breeze like a benediction down from the vent near the bed. It might not have been so pleasant lying here under different circumstances.

"A sad day for us," Jorge said. "After this morning, we won't be able to see each other for quite a while."

Maria scooted nearer to him on the bed and kissed him on the lips. "I understand," she said.

And he knew she did. And she accepted. He smiled. "You are unlike any other woman."

"So is every other woman, but no other woman is yours."

His smile widened. "That is because you would cut off my testicles."

"You are so right. And I love you so much."

"And I you."

They kissed again and she moved away from him and climbed out of bed. She didn't see any point in drawing out what for both of them was going to be a painful but necessary parting.

Raising her arms high, she stretched the length of her sleek body. "I'll shower first."

"Perhaps I'll join you. Save the hotel some water."

She paused and grinned at him. "Yes, you've always been interested in hotel water conservation."

"If it involves you, I find it a fascinating subject."

An hour later, Maria left the room first. She rode the elevator down to the lobby, walked to an archway beyond the reservation desk, and found a table in the coffee shop.

She ordered an espresso and sat calmly sipping it, waiting for Jorge to finish dressing and come downstairs.

As she sipped her espresso and gazed out the coffee shop's wide window that provided a view of the street, she noticed two identical black Volkswagen Jettas parked at the curb near the hotel's entrance. Though they were in the way of taxis, and a shuttle bus, if one were to arrive, the uniformed doorman was obviously ignoring them.

He also ignored the three men in dark suits who hurried past him, walking side by side. From her table, Maria could see beyond the entrance arch as the three men entered the lobby and strode across the terrazzo floor toward the elevators.

Only there were four of them now, all walking in step. One suddenly veered off and stood leaning against a wall with his arms crossed, staying well out of the way of guests and bellhops scurrying past. Through the window, Maria saw a third black Jetta. A van peeled away from the traffic and parked directly across the street. Several men emerged from it and began to cross.

Maria's heart was hammering as she drew her cell phone from her purse and called upstairs.

After breaking the brief connection, she kept her eyes trained on the lobby, and a few minutes later there was Jorge. He must have passed the men in the elevators, descending in a different car as they were going up. He was hurriedly making his way through the lobby, his shirt untucked, his hair uncombed. He didn't glance toward her as he passed the coffee shop entrance and walked faster toward the street exit.

Quickly he passed from her sight.

Almost immediately she heard gunshots and screaming. She watched through the window as the figure with the half-tucked shirt came into view and began to run. His pace faltered, and red splotches appeared on the broad back of his white shirt.

Then he stopped, raised both hands, and collapsed dying on the sidewalk.

People in the hotel and out in the street were rising from where they'd sought shelter and moving around now. Some of them were running. People were hurrying from across the street, weaving between the stopped cars. All were moving faster and faster toward the scene of the shooting.

Maria rose from her table, hurried to the lobby, and joined the throng of people rushing to see what had happened. Car horns were honking. There was much shouting. The wailing of sirens drifted over the city.

Like banshees, she thought. *They sound like banshees mourning for Jorge.*

But she knew the sirens meant only more police closing in to help establish and maintain order.

Out on the sidewalk, she avoided elbows and shoulders, pushed her way against the flow of the crowd, and slipped away.

19

One of those days.

Quinn sat at his desk, leaning far back in his swivel chair, and watched the rain fall outside the window of the office on West Seventy-ninth Street. It must have been cool where the rain fell from, because steam was rising when the angled drops struck the warmed street and concrete sidewalk.

Pearl was, for a change, in her chair, rather than perched on the edge of her desk. Fedderman was slouched in his desk chair nursing a mug of coffee. They were looking at the rain, too, aware of the constant trickling noise from a ledge above the window, and the occasional rattle of the loose pane when the summer wind kicked up. The city had slowed perceptibly, unaccustomed to such a gray morning in midsummer. This was somehow more depressing than the relentless heat they'd been enduring. The mood from outside had penetrated inside to the office.

Fedderman lifted his coffee mug and observed it carefully, as if he suspected a leak.

"We're not," he said, "getting a helluva lot done this morning."

"I am," Pearl said.

Quinn adjusted his chair slightly so he could look at her. She seemed small in the black vinyl swivel chair that was identical to his. Small and unproductive. Was she serious?

"I've been thinking," she said.

"Oh, Christ!" Fedderman said. "Let's hope it hasn't borne fruit."

Pearl looked at him as if he were an insect. "But it has. It's a big juicy theory."

"Like with relativity?"

"Let's hear her out, Feds," Quinn said. He leaned farther back in his chair, as if to gain distance from Pearl and her theory.

"You're going to fall on your ass," Pearl told him.

"Is that your theory?"

"No, it's about our killer."

"I assumed," Quinn said, with a smile.

They all listened to the patter of rain for a moment. Then Pearl sat up higher and leaned forward with her elbows on her desk. "It's possible that the victims' unidentifiable torsos are left where they're sure to be found not as the killer's calling card, or simply because they're deemed untraceable, or even to taunt authorities, but so the police will *assume* the women were victims of a serial killer."

Quinn and Fedderman stared at her.

"I hate to point out the obvious," Fedderman said, "but whoever killed those women is by definition a serial killer."

"But maybe one who kills with a logical purpose," Pearl said, "who might have a real and practical motive."

"They all think they have a real and practical motive," Fedderman said. "It always turns out to be psycho squirrel shit."

"Maybe not this time, though. Our guy might be pretending to be a psychosexual killer so that's what we'll be hunting."

"The old serial killer diversion," Fedderman said. "While we're searching for a killer, our perp might actually have a bunch of unpaid traffic tickets."

Quinn thought, *You seldom hear people say* perp *anymore. Where did it go?*

"If it's an act," Fedderman said, "it's sure as hell a convincing one."

"So why's our perp leaving the torsos and concealing the rest of the bodies?" Quinn asked, thinking it felt odd to say *perp*.

"I'm not sure. All I'm saying is, it might really *be* a kind of diversion, so we're looking for a nutcase killer and not for whatever else he is," Pearl said.

"The weather's getting to you," Fedderman said.

"Screw you and the weather," Pearl said.

Quinn was silent. He knew this was the kind of thinking that made Pearl such a talented detective. He also knew she wouldn't easily turn loose of the idea.

"Are you convinced of this?" he asked her.

"Of course not. I told you it was a theory."

"Did you say crackpot theory?" Fedderman asked.

Pearl ignored him and pointedly addressed only Quinn: "Here's where we are, spinning our wheels: We check the mental hospitals and psycho wards in New York and surrounding states, and there's no one missing who likes to carve up people or animals. No one with those characteristics has been released from prison lately. We check with other cities and there are no similar cases. We use Helen's profile as our guide and it gets us nowhere. That's because her profile's wrong. He's not a nutcase in the conventional sense, and thinking he is throws us off the scent. That's the object of his game."

"He has the earmarks of a genuine psychosexual serial killer," Quinn said. "He kills each time in the same manner, ritualistically dismembers his victims and leaves grisly calling cards we're sure to find, uses the same gun we're sure to match with the bullets, does the sexual mutilation and penetration with the sharpened wooden broomstick—"

"The goddamned furniture oil," Fedderman interrupted.

"It all might be part of his plan," Pearl said calmly. "Don't you see? He's creating a profile for our profiler."

"Jesus," Fedderman said.

"It might be part of a plan," Quinn said, "but so far there isn't any evidence that it is. So we have to proceed on that basis."

"Consider the way everything is too damned pat," Pearl said. "That's its own kind of evidence."

"If it is," Quinn said, "what are we gonna do with it?"

"There's a good question," Fedderman said.

Pearl sighed, knowing they were both right. "Yeah," she said. "What can we do?"

"Keep it in mind, is what," Quinn said. "That's the kind of evidence it is, the kind you keep in mind."

"Sure," Pearl said. "I'll do that."

Quinn knew she would.

Fedderman stood up and wandered over to the coffee brewer. He glanced back at Pearl. It was obvious that he felt he might have been too hard on her.

"It's the weather," he said. "You want some coffee, Pearl?"

"Up your ass with your coffee," she said.

He poured her a cup anyway, then reconsidered, staring at the way it was steaming. It was scalding. She shouldn't have it right now.

He poured it back in the pot and returned to his desk.

"Let's go back to where we found the last one, by the Dumpster, and reinterview anyone who might have seen or heard something," Quinn said.

"In the rain?" Fedderman asked.

Quinn was already putting on his light overcoat.

"In the rain."

"Most of them will probably be at work," Fedderman said.

"So will we," Quinn said.

It wasn't just that Quinn kept Pearl's theory in mind the rest of that day; he couldn't get it out of his mind. Sometimes sitting around drinking coffee, or talking while it was raining outside a precinct house or stakeout car, there'd be a breakthrough in a case.

Maybe today in the office had been one of those times.

20

By early evening the rain had stopped and a cooling breeze wafted in from the east. The city looked and smelled fresh, disconnected from any sordid past or questionable future.

Quinn and Linda Chavesky met again for coffee and then went for a walk. They were on Broadway, near Columbus Circle. Traffic was heavy, mostly with cabs taking people shopping or to early dinners before the theater. Quinn was on Linda's right, between her and the street. They were strolling casually, taking their time, stringing out the experience of being together. When the lights temporarily stopped traffic on their side of the street, they could hear their footfalls on the damp sidewalk.

"Wanna talk shop?" Quinn asked.

Linda shrugged, bumping her hip against him, maybe accidentally. "You're always a cop, I'm always an M.E."

Quinn told her about Pearl's theory.

"Doesn't sound likely," Linda said after listening closely.

"Pearl's an original thinker."

"So I've heard."

Quinn hoped he'd detected a note of jealousy.

They both veered left automatically to let a couple of chattering kids in gangsta pants bounce past.

"Not being critical," Linda said, "just asking, how the hell do they keep those pants up?"

"I dunno. I guess they enjoy the suspense."

She laughed.

They'd walked another fifty feet before she said, "You run Pearl's theory past Renz?"

"No. I think we should wait till we have something more."

"There might not be any more."

"Might not."

Another five measured steps. Ten. Quinn could sense that Linda hadn't let go of what he'd told her. She was toying with it in her mind, like a cat with a ball of yarn. Here was something about her that intrigued him, and for some reason immensely pleased him.

And something else, he realized; they were comfortable in their silence.

"Maybe you should try it on the profiler, Helen Iman," Linda said.

"According to Pearl, Helen's the one being conned."

"Well, she might at least want to be aware of the possibility."

"Also," Quinn said, "it might be a mistake to plant the idea in Helen's head. Might throw her off her game."

"Uh-huh." They walked a bit farther. "That's one for you to decide."

"I know," Quinn said. "You just examine what's left of the victims."

"Not anymore," Linda said.

They stopped walking and Quinn looked at her.

"Dr. Nift has taken over all duties connected with the Torso Murders."

"He give a reason?"

"To maintain continuity, he said."

"He's a continual asshole," Quinn said.

"He's my boss."

"Which is why I can say it and you can't," Quinn said.

Linda didn't disagree.

Jill and Tony met at Has Beans again. He'd suggested a genuine night out, dinner at an expensive restaurant, maybe a show. Who could tell what might come after? She wasn't ready for that. She'd let him know and he'd smoothly backed off.

They were in the same booth where they'd first met. He was sipping a Honduras again. She'd taken a chance and ordered a Nicaragua.

When she sipped the foamy coffee drink, she decided she liked it.

"Yum," she said, "but do they even grow coffee in Nicaragua?"

"I don't know," Tony said. "They grow revolutions." He sipped and smiled. "On the phone you mentioned there was something you wanted to tell me. Something personal?"

"It's something that's got me kind of rattled," she said. "A little scared."

"About me?"

She rested her hand on his. "God, no!" She didn't know quite where to begin, not wanting to sound paranoid. "There's this woman who seems to be . . . well, following me."

He sat forward, interested. She was gratified by his obvious concern for her. "You know who she is?" he asked.

"I've never seen her before. I don't think. She does look familiar, but maybe she has one of those faces. She's a street woman, Tony. A homeless person. Dirty clothes, stringy blond hair. And she looks as if she could use a bath and a good meal."

"So maybe she's just panhandling."

"No, she's never asked for anything. It's just that now and then I turn around or glance to the side, and there she is."

"Coincidence?"

"I wish. She's usually staring at me. Once she even started toward me."

"What do you mean, started toward you? In a way that was threatening?"

"I . . . well, I'm not sure."

"So what did you do?"

"I ran. I mean, that sounds worse than it is. I had on my sweat suit and jogging shoes anyway, and I was sort of running in place, so I just . . . jogged away from her."

"Good." With his free hand, he scrunched up his lower lip between thumb and forefinger, looking worried.

"What are you thinking, Tony?"

"I don't know what to think. If you see her again, just avoid her. Do whatever's necessary to stay away. She might be dangerous."

"Whether she is or not, I admit she makes me afraid."

"Maybe you know something about her you don't think you know," Tony said. "If you know what I mean."

Jill didn't. "There's something else." She hesitated. "I don't want you to think I'm some kind of nut."

Tony gave her hand a squeeze. "I don't and I won't."

"I get the feeling sometimes that someone's been in my apartment while I was gone. No, more than a feeling, actually. I'm sure things aren't exactly as I've left them. There've been small changes, barely noticeable, but they're there. Maybe a lamp shade's crooked, or a sofa cushion's propped up at a corner when it wasn't before, or my clothes aren't hung in the same order in my closet. Things like that." She looked at him. He *must* think she was crazy. "I'm sure about these things, Tony. They're real and not my imagination."

"Not necessarily your imagination," he said. "But maybe

your memory. Maybe you're just spooked and seeing things you hadn't noticed before."

She tried a smile. "Sort of the opposite of déjà vu?"

"I guess you could put it that way. If you had a sense of humor. You might simply not recall things exactly as they were. We all do that from time to time."

"You could be right." But she wasn't so sure. These differences in her apartment, however minute, did seem real.

He sat back and seemed suddenly alarmed. "Jill, you don't think these two things are connected, do you? I mean the homeless woman and the idea that somebody might have been in your apartment?"

The possibility *had* been on the edge of her consciousness. But she said, "I don't know. I don't see how they could be, but who knows?"

Tony abruptly leaned toward her, giving her hand another squeeze. "You have my cell phone number, Jill. Do me a favor. If you see this woman again, give me a call. Wherever I am, I'll get right there and confront her."

"All right. But I could call the police."

"If you want."

She didn't and he knew it. She wanted him and not the police to come to her rescue. Besides, what could she tell the police, arrest the woman for staring at her?

"The trouble is," Jill said, "you're out of town so often. Your job."

"If I'm in town, I'll come running."

She placed her hand on top of the one holding hers and aimed a smile across the table. "I know you will, Tony. But all of it, I mean, it's all probably nothing. Maybe it is my imagination. I mean, the woman's real, all right, but she probably does simply want a handout. She might see me as a soft touch."

He grinned at her. "Now, that's possible."

They leaned toward each other across the table and kissed lightly.

"But call me anyway," he said.

Jill assured him that she would, but she'd decided not to. These problems she should handle on her own. She didn't want Tony to think she was some kind of head case.

One he wouldn't want to see again.

21

He wasn't there. He was.

Deputy Chief Nobbler glanced up from what he was reading on his desk, and there stood Greeve. Also standing was the hair on the back of Nobbler's neck.

Nobbler had just a moment ago told his assistant in the outer office to send Greeve in, but Greeve had somehow opened the heavy door, entered, and closed the door without making a sound. Living up to his "Ghost" nickname. Nobbler wondered if the silent entry had been deliberate. He was sure that from time to time Greeve played with his mind.

"Morning," Greeve said. He made it sound like *mourning*. Or maybe Nobbler just thought that because of Greeve's mortician looks and attitude.

Mourning yourself. "I've been thinking about that Quinn and Dr. Chavesky thing," Nobbler said.

"It bears thinking about." Greeve methodically unbuttoned the coat of his dark suit. His idea of getting casual.

"Word I get is that he's porking her on a regular basis," Nobbler said.

"Quinn'd be an idiot if he wasn't."

"We got us a bona fide romance going here," Nobbler

said, with a smile that made his fat cheeks crinkle. "A reformed alky and a pensioned-off cop. Think it has a chance?"

"Love's strange," Greeve said. "If it is love."

Nobbler narrowed his eyes at Greeve. "You think it might be something else? Somebody using somebody?"

"That's love," Greeve said.

"Maybe it is at that. There's jealousy, too. And hell's fury. They can be part of love. Even part of love's embers."

It wasn't like Nobbler to be poetic. It took Greeve a few beats to figure out where the deputy chief was going. "Pearl?"

"Uh-huh. Even though she and Quinn are no longer a couple, she's working with Quinn, seeing him every day. She can't be happy knowing he's humping the good Dr. Chavesky."

"I'll bet she is good."

"You're digressing."

"Pearl knows about Quinn and Chavesky?"

"If she doesn't already, she will soon," Nobbler said. "She won't like it."

Greeve looked doubtful. "I don't know, sir. Pearl's different. Way I got it, she's the one who broke it off with Quinn. He's been trying to get back in and she wants none of it."

"She'll feel different when she realizes Quinn's suddenly no longer available to her. Women. What they can't have is what they want, and why they want it."

It took Greeve a few seconds to work that one out in his mind. "I've seen Pearl Kasner work. She's not women. She's different."

"Yeah. From what I hear, she's a goddamned alley cat. She'll fight for any morsel just because it's hers. Even if it's Quinn. Then she'll spit that morsel out."

Greeve wasn't so sure. If only from a distance, he knew Pearl. She was a hardhead but smart in a weird way. He chose silence as the wisest course.

"Quinn's also a problem," Nobbler said.

"That's for damned sure."

"But starting today, I want you to get off Quinn and start shadowing Pearl."

"Quinn's the one in charge," Greeve reminded Nobbler. "And we just agreed he's a problem."

"He's *the* problem," Nobbler said, "and Pearl's his vulnerability."

Greeve stuck out his lower lip and slowly nodded. Nobbler could, at times, be smart in a weird way, too. "Woman scorned, hell hath no fury, that kinda stuff?"

"Exactly," Nobbler said.

"Pearl will feel the way you say. Get distracted and screw up some way. Maybe even sabotage Quinn."

"She will if she's female," Nobbler said. "And she's definitely that."

He began carefully arranging the papers on his desk, letting Greeve know their meeting was at an end.

"I suppose it makes sense," Greeve said.

"I'm glad you think so," Nobbler said, looking up.

But Greeve was gone.

Jill Clark fought her way between a man with a duffel bag and a woman with a purse the size of a house and made her way onto the crowded subway. Getting mobbed and sometimes groped or pinched on the subway wasn't Jill's idea of recreation, and she wished she didn't have to go through the ordeal. But riding the subway was the cheapest way to move around New York other than walking, and the offices of Tucker, Simpson, and King, where she'd filled in for a second vacationing employee, were too far away for her to walk.

When she transferred after two stops to an uptown line, the train wasn't so crowded. In fact, she was one of about twenty passengers. They were the usual mix, business commuters, solemn readers of books and newspapers, dozing

night-shift workers on their way home, a few of the homeless, a few truly dangerous-looking men whose dress and
manner suggested aggressive mental derangement.

Jill had entered the end door. Immediately to her left
there were facing smaller seats with chipped decals on them
saying they were priority seating for persons with disabili-
ties. That didn't mean Jill couldn't sit in one and get up if
somebody with a disability got on the train. Besides, there
were plenty of empty seats. Both of the disability-designated
seats accommodated two passengers and were unoccupied.
Jill settled into one.

The train accelerated into darkness with a roar and a
squeal of steel on steel. Jill sat back and watched her waver-
ing reflection facing her in the dirt-streaked window. A corner of the window was smeared with a gooey substance that
might be anything.

She remembered reading about a study concerning germs
on subway cars—they were everywhere on everything. She
rubbed her fingertips on her slacks.

The roar of the train grew suddenly louder, and cooler air
swirled around Jill's ankles. The sliding door at the end of
the car, leading to and from the next car, had opened. Someone was moving from one car to another. Teenagers did that
a lot. So did panhandlers, as well as gang members looking
for trouble. Jill told herself this was probably just someone
looking for someone else and kept her gaze focused on the
floor.

She saw movement in the periphery of her vision; then
the door swung shut. There was sudden silence, and the air
around Jill's ankles became still. She waited for whoever had
entered the car to move past her, possibly toward the door at
the opposite end.

Instead she saw a pair of worn-out, scuffed black shoes
protruding from wrinkled brown slacks, and a body dropped
with a sigh next to hers on the small seat so that their thighs
were warmly touching.

Jill saw dirty hands, chipped fingernails, and recoiled at the stench of stale perspiration and perhaps urine.

She turned her head and was looking into the desperate bloodshot eyes of the woman who'd been following her.

Jill's throat constricted with fear.

A viselike grip closed on her right bicep, squeezing so hard that it hurt.

"We've gotta talk," the woman said in a raspy voice. "Whether you want to or not."

"I don't want to!" Jill managed to force the words through her tightened throat as she tried to yank her arm away. She couldn't break the iron grip. "We have nothing to say!"

"What you need to do is listen. I'm warning you."

"Warning me?" Jill tried harder to escape the fingers digging into her arm. The woman's grip got even tighter.

"Something bad could happen to you," the woman said. Her breath was foul enough to turn Jill's stomach.

"Damn it! Let me go!" Jill began working her arm back and forth, desperate to get away. "Stop following me! Leave me alone!"

"You'd better watch out."

Jill stood up this time, pulling her arm away and twisting it violently, causing it to flare with pain.

Suddenly she was free.

She took two wobbling steps and bumped into one of the vertical bars for standing riders to grip when the car was crowded. Her forehead hit the hard steel, momentarily disorienting her. She almost fell.

Then she got her balance and started to stagger toward the front of the car. A man was staring at her. He quickly looked away.

No one looked at her other than briefly and with mild and guarded curiosity as she lurched and stumbled the length of the car. The other passengers seemed not to have noticed anything was wrong. They were studiously reading or gazing up at the advertisements running along the sides of the car above the windows. Or they stared at the dirty and littered floor. They didn't want to get involved with violence, insanity, the unpredictable. The predictable they faced every day was difficult enough.

Jill gripped another vertical bar and looked back to see if the woman was pursuing her.

The other end of the car was unoccupied. The woman was gone.

Jill fell into an empty seat and hugged herself. She began rocking in the seat, exaggerating the motion of the train. This was insane. Maybe she *was* insane.

Is my mind slipping?

Was the woman real?

Jesus! Oh, Jesus! This city . . . This city . . .

She glanced around, embarrassed and still afraid.

Still, no one looked at her. The train thundered through the darkness.

22

Jill had calmed down by the time she got to work. There was no one at Tucker, Simpson, and King she wanted to tell about the subway incident. She didn't know anyone there well enough. And they might think she was crazy. They *would* think she was crazy. The incident now seemed almost as if it hadn't happened. It was so incongruous to her surroundings aboveground, at work, in the normal world.

But of course it had happened.

Something had happened.

She'd been at work about half an hour and was filing papers concerning a traffic violation appeal when a voice said, "It's for you."

Jill turned around. The receptionist, an older woman named Judy, was staring at her. "Line three."

"Excuse me?"

"You said your name was Jill Clark, right?"

"Right," Jill said.

"You have a phone call. Line three."

Jill straightened up. She looked around and then went to a phone on the other side of the office, where she'd have some privacy.

She pressed the glowing line button and said hello.

"Is this Jill Clark?" A woman's voice. Familiar.

"Yes. Who is this?"

"The woman from the subway."

Jill's heart jumped. She told herself the caller was lying. The voice on the phone wasn't so hoarse, and it was controlled, almost cultured. Not like the subway woman's. But it carried the same note of desperation.

"Don't hang up, Jill. Please!"

"Why shouldn't I? My arm still hurts!"

"I'm sorry about that. You have to understand my state of mind."

I think I do. Insane.

Behind the receptionist's desk, Judy glanced at Jill, then looked away.

Jill lowered her voice, not wanting to attract attention. "Leave me the hell alone! Stop following me! Stay away from me! Stay out of my apartment!"

"Don't hang up!" the woman pleaded again.

"I haven't, have I?"

"I've never been in your apartment," the woman said. "My name is Madeline Scott, and we have to talk."

"I can't imagine why."

"That's the point, damn it!"

"My arm still hurts," Jill repeated.

Jill hung up, careful not to bang the receiver.

American Airlines flight 222 out of Mexico City via Atlanta arrived ten minutes early, and the plane touched down gently on LaGuardia Airport's south runway. When the reverse thrust of the plane's powerful engines had brought it almost to a halt, it taxied toward its assigned gate.

The plane veered gently and arrived at the mobile enclosed ramp to the concourse. The engines stopped whirring, a faint bell chimed pleasantly, and the clacking of unfastening safety belts rippled through the fuselage.

Maria Sanchez, who'd been sitting in a coach window seat just beyond the wings, wrestled her carry-ons from overhead storage and filed off the plane with the other passengers.

She exchanged a polite and perfunctory "G'bye" with the smiling flight attendant at the plane's door. Maria's formerly long dark hair was dyed blond, and she was traveling under forged identification. She'd made it a point not to be at all memorable to the other passengers or the flight crew.

When she emerged from the enclosed walkway into the terminal, she lowered both of her large red carry-ons to the floor and raised their telescoping handles. She followed the stream of passengers along the concourse toward the baggage area, then increased her speed, lengthening her stride and pulling the two rolling suitcases behind her.

She went outside the terminal and waited her turn in line for a taxi. A cabbie finished stuffing a young couple's tons of luggage into his taxi's trunk, then got in and drove away with a brief squeal of tires. The cab lying in wait behind his leaped forward to take its place and came to a rocking stop. Maria's turn.

She watched her driver place her two suitcases in the trunk, then got in the cab and waited for him to join her. When he was settled into his seat and had turned an ear toward her, she gave him an address in Manhattan.

The cab made a squeal like its predecessor's and shot forward, speeding toward the island like a wolf returning to its lair.

Jill stood in the hall outside her apartment door and used two keys to unlock two dead bolts. She was exhausted from her day of filing and following instructions at Tucker, Simpson, and King. That and her morning's misadventure had left her weary and uneasy. It would be good to kick off her shoes, get a bottle of water from the refrigerator, and slump onto the sofa. In fact, it would be heaven.

She opened the door and was immediately aware of an unpleasant odor, then a presence close behind her, crowding her. She was abruptly pushed into the apartment and followed. The door clicked shut.

Jill took two skidding steps on the hardwood floor, almost falling, then whirled and saw the homeless woman from the subway, the one who'd called her at work and identified herself as Madeline Scott. Fury and indignation rose in Jill. She didn't know any Madeline Scott and didn't want to know this one.

Then her anger became fear. She was alone with this woman who might be crazy, who might do anything.

Mad Madeline.

The woman's hair was unkempt and her eyes were wild. Her clothes were wrinkled and frayed. She'd obviously been living on the streets and might be crazy or on drugs. Unnaturally strong. If it came down to it, Jill didn't think she could subdue her. Didn't want to touch her.

Her fear must have shown on her face.

"I'm not going to hurt you," Madeline Scott said. Her wild blue eyes paralyzed Jill. "But I'm determined you're going to hear me out."

Jill was ashamed of the terror in her own choked voice as she backed on stiff legs into the living room and said, "I'm listening."

Madeline smiled and said, "That's all I ever wanted."

23

Madeline Scott didn't sit down. Jill didn't make the offer.

The two women had drifted farther into the living room and stood facing each other, keeping their distance. The odor coming off Madeline seemed to have dissipated, or maybe Jill was simply getting used to it. Some of the wildness had left Madeline's eyes, leaving Jill at least reassured that the woman wasn't going to abruptly attack her.

"I only want to talk while you listen," Madeline said with surprising calm.

Jill swallowed. "All right. So talk."

Get whatever you have to say over with, and then get out. Get out.

"Not so long ago I was in your position," Madeline began. "I was from out of town, with no real family, and not very long in New York. Things hadn't gone as well as I thought they would when I moved here from Illinois."

Jill began to feel somewhat relieved. Madeline had obviously rehearsed this, or at least given it a lot of thought. This was going to be a sob story, ending, she was sure, in an appeal for money. Okay, maybe she could buy her way out of this. Out of this dread she hated to admit to herself.

"I was working dead-end, impersonal jobs," Madeline continued, "where they'd hardly miss me if I didn't show up. I had no real friends to speak of. Dates? Yeah, a few. But you know how that goes. The men I let pick me up wanted the usual and then out. All the acquaintanceship you might want is out there, but not friends, not people who'll remember you even the next day. So I did what a lot of lonely people in New York do after they've wasted time dating enough losers. I contacted a reputable matchmaking service."

Jill's mind had been distracted, still trying to figure a way out of this awkward situation, a way to cut it short. What would it cost her? Suddenly she began paying close attention.

"It was the same online matchmaking service you used," Madeline said. "E-Bliss.org."

Jill moved to a chair and sat down. Madeline went to the sofa and sat on the very edge of one of the end cushions.

"Everything I just told you about," Madeline said, "E-Bliss learned about on my personality profile form. That and more."

"There's nothing wrong with E-Bliss," Jill said, wondering as she spoke why she was defending the online dating service.

But she knew why: she wanted desperately for the matchmaking service to be legitimate. So much of her intimate and vulnerable self was invested in it now.

Madeline smiled sadly, as if knowing what Jill was thinking. "I believe they're mostly a legitimate matchmaking service," she said, "but they operate another service within that one. It requires women without close family, new to the city, and still mostly without close friends or connections. I fit the profile, and so do you."

Jill took a deep breath and tried to organize her thoughts. "What does this service within a service do?"

"It searches through all the profiles, probably with some kind of computer software, and settles on the right applicant.

Then the company sends someone to gain your trust and learn all about you. Everything from your Social Security and charge account numbers to your favorite candy. Meanwhile, someone else is learning about you, watching you, spending time in your apartment when you're not there, wearing your clothes, even being glimpsed around the building as you. Practicing to be you. And then . . . she becomes you."

Whoa!

"You said, 'becomes me'? What's that supposed to mean?"

"Exactly what it says."

Madeline stared at her silently.

"Why me in particular?" Jill asked, astounded. And afraid again, but not exactly in the same way. There was something creepy about this that was working its way into her marrow. Something some part of her mind knew that the rest of it hadn't yet caught up with. "I mean, there are plenty of women like you described living in New York. This is the most anonymous city in the world."

"Why you?" Madeline said thoughtfully, obviously considering. "I don't know for sure. But I followed the man you know as Tony Lake from the offices of E-Bliss to you. Only I knew him as Dwayne King. I've given this a lot of thought. In fact, it's all I've thought about for weeks. My guess is you resemble someone who wants to disappear, and who's paid E-Bliss so she can take your place."

"What about the real me?" Jill asked, dreading the answer even though she wasn't sure she believed any of this.

"The real you ceases to exist. You're shot and killed, as they tried to do to me. I managed to break free and run. They kept shooting at me, but I escaped by climbing into an approaching car and urging the driver to get us away. I read in the paper a week later that a man I'm sure was the driver was found dead in Riverside Park from a drug overdose. I don't think it was suicide or an accident."

Jill's mind was still wrestling with what she was hearing. "But why would they do this, substitute people for each other?"

"Money," Madeline said simply.

"Of course. Money. Like everything else. But what do their clients want? What's the reason for the substitutions?"

"I don't know," Madeline said. "But I know that what E-Bliss is doing must work. They choose their victims carefully from thousands of Internet applicants for relationships. These women must meet the qualifications and resemble whoever's going to become them. If you're a victim client and you've happened to make a friend who might care or suspect there's something wrong, the new you simply moves away suddenly, as people often do in Manhattan, leaving a note or the last month's rent so there's no doubt the departure was voluntary. I've seen the other Madeline coming out of my apartment on West Seventy-second Street. She isn't my exact double, but with the same hairdo, makeup, and my wardrobe and apartment, not to mention identification, charge cards, and passport, maybe even some minor cosmetic surgery, she *became* me."

"My God!" Jill's mind was working furiously, warning her again that this woman was crazy, that what she was saying was impossible.

Only it *was* possible, and Jill knew it. Loneliness made it possible. Jill remembered loneliness.

Madeline, knowing what Jill must be thinking, again showed her sad smile. "People who don't know us well or long don't look at us all that closely, Jill, and the new me even has my gestures and speech patterns down pat."

"This other you," Jill said, "why didn't you confront her?"

The gleam of terror in Madeline's eyes was answer enough for Jill.

"Why don't you go to the police?"

Madeline shook her head. "I tried. They brushed me off as just another deranged street person. And there's no way for me to prove I really *am* me. Sometimes I doubt it myself. This is larger than either of us knows, Jill. The police might be in on it."

Jill was jolted by the thought. And again she thought Madeline might simply be paranoid, one of the poor and forever lost who roamed the Manhattan streets talking to everyone and no one, suspecting everything and everyone.

And yet . . .

"How could the police even know we talked?" Jill asked.

"They'll know. Or at least there's no guarantee they won't. And you can't take the chance, Jill. I'm sorry I did this to you, but I need your help. I was like you, living my life, and suddenly I'm mixed up with . . . I don't know. Organized crime would be my guess. Or maybe anyone who can pay whatever E-Bliss.org charges for its special service. They might have infiltrated the police and they'll learn what's going on and see that any investigation stops. And that I'll be killed. And now that I've talked to you, that you'll be killed. How can we know whom to trust? If we confide in the wrong people, we'll wind up like the rest of those women. What's left of our mutilated bodies that can't be identified will be put into a pauper's grave or cremated by the city."

"Left of our bodies? You mean the Torso Murders—"

"Being on the run, I didn't watch or read the news regularly, but when I happened to learn about the Torso Murders, I knew there was probably a connection. That was what was going to be left of me after I ceased to exist as a person. And that's the plan for you, Jill. I'm sure you've never been fingerprinted or submitted a DNA sample, and if you disappeared there'd be no one to miss you or even report your absence."

Jill had to admit that Madeline was right about the fingerprints and DNA. And the family she didn't have. There was no one who cared enough to make a spirited inquiry.

"You're halfway to nothing already." Madeline took a deep breath. "Do you believe any of this?"

Jill sat silently for almost a minute staring at the woman who might be mad. Who certainly appeared mad.

Only she wasn't mad. And Jill knew it.

"I believe enough of it," she finally said, remembering filling out her endlessly detailed and personal E-Bliss.org profile.

Do you take cream in your coffee?

What brands of cosmetics do you use?

Do you ever wear a hat or cap?

Would you drink from someone else's water bottle without first wiping it?

Do you jaywalk?

Do you use an electric toothbrush?

Madeline stood up from the sofa. The look on her face suggested she might rush over to Jill and hug her.

But she didn't.

"I'll go now," she said. "I know your mind must be whirling. You need time to think about all this. Let's meet tomorrow, around noon, just inside the main library on Fifth and Forty-second. They don't throw anyone out of a public library, and I can neaten myself up enough so they won't think I'm a panhandler. We both need to think this over and then have a talk, try to come up with some kind of plan."

"A plan . . . ?"

"Some kind of plan," Madeline repeated. Her eyes brimmed with tears, pleading. "Will you be there, Jill?"

Jill couldn't look away from those eyes. They didn't seem insane now. Desperate, but not insane.

"I promise I'll think about it," she said.

Madeline nodded.

"If you think about it, you'll be there."

24

So here Quinn was in a blazing forest, terrified animals streaking past him, ignoring him. Deer, bears, rabbits, a lion. *What next? A unicorn?*

Quinn had fallen asleep in the brown leather chair in his den while reading about the Torso Murders in the *Post*. It amazed him how so much could be written on something everyone knew so little about. The Cuban cigar he'd been smoking lay smoldering in an ashtray on the carpet beside his chair. That was the sort of thing Pearl often warned him about. He was going to start a fire, kill them both, kill everyone in the building. Pearl, who'd melted the shower curtain with her curling iron.

He smelled cigar smoke and almost woke up. But not quite. His dreams weren't ready to release him. The smoke grew denser.

He was wearing only a plastic raincoat with a hood and, like the animals surrounding him, he was terrified of the advancing wall of flame. Even without the heat of the forest fire, he was sweltering in the plastic NYPD coat. The California heat was merciless.

California?

Where was Lauri? Was she safe from the fire? Was Wormy?

Pearl?

A phone was ringing. Or was it the urgent jangle of a fire engine? *Gotta pull the damned car over to the side of the road.*

Hold on! He wasn't driving. He knew that because he couldn't find a steering wheel.

He realized he'd fallen asleep. He struggled up out of the chair, wearily stumbled toward the phone. Snatched up the receiver and almost said, "Pearl?"

But he didn't say it. The word hadn't quite escaped.

Why did I think of Pearl? I was worried about Lauri. Even Wormy.

He smelled something burning and terror took a swipe at him. Then he noticed the smoldering cigar in the ashtray on the floor.

"Quinn?" a woman's voice said on the phone. Not Pearl's voice. "Quinn? It's Linda."

He suddenly wanted to see Linda. To hold her and feel her holding him.

"Linda," he said stupidly, still tangled in the cobwebs of sleep. He dropped the receiver but caught it just before it could bang against the desk. "I dozed off in my chair," he explained.

"You're working too hard."

"Not hard enough, though."

She was silent for a moment.

"I need to see you," he said.

"That's why I called. I need to see *you*."

Jesus! Quinn thought. *Where is this going? So fast. Like being caught in a strong current propelling me toward a sea I know is dangerous.*

"Quinn?"

Sharks. Not fire—water. Wake all the way up, numb wit!

"Quinn?" Linda said again, concerned.

"The Lotus Diner in half an hour?"

"I'll be there."

He hung up the phone and stood staring mutely at it for several seconds. Then he went into the bathroom and splashed cold water on his face. On his shirt, too. He decided he needed a fresh shirt. Realized he still had a bitter taste in his mouth from the cigar. Brushed his teeth. Went into the bedroom and changed his shirt. Back to the bathroom to comb his hair.

Before leaving the apartment, he picked up the cigar and ashtray and carried them into the kitchen. He ran water on the cigar and threw it away, then wiped the glass ashtray clean and set it on the sink counter.

He found an aerosol can of air freshener and sprayed it around the apartment, especially in the den, where he'd been smoking.

As he left the apartment, he wasn't thinking about his dreams, about the Torso Murders, about dead women.

Only about Linda, alive.

At first Jill was awkward around Tony when they met for dinner. He seemed not to notice, and by the time they were seated at Scampi, a four-star restaurant near Sixth Avenue and Fifty-second Street, she was much more at ease. Tony was so attentive, so reassuring, so . . . nonthreatening that Jill's conversation with Madeline receded in her mind and seemed more and more unreal.

Surely it *was* unreal, the delusional ranting of a mentally ill street woman. *This* was reality, sitting here with Tony in the soft light from the candle in the center of the white-clothed table, their half-eaten meals before them, the waiter bringing more wine.

Tony couldn't—he simply *couldn't*—be the kind of monster Madeline had painted. Surely if the story were true Jill would be able to see it in Tony. Not that he'd have horns and his eyes would glow red, but there'd be *something*. A person simply couldn't be as Madeline had described and at the same time be like Tony.

Besides, Jill knew this man. They'd had several dates now and were moving toward sleeping together. While making it obvious that was what he expected, Tony hadn't rushed her in any way while they continued to explore each other, making sure of what they wanted. Making sure of Jill, really. Tony seemed to know he wanted her, and for more than simple sex.

That was what had emerged from their time together, an intimacy that would be cemented by commitment when they were ready. A mutual trust. Their very private conversations had provided insights into each other's souls.

"You seemed a little unsettled when you got here," Tony said, as the waiter finished pouring the wine. His grin was beautiful and boyish. Toothpaste-commercial white, yet genuine as Tony himself. "Still worried about someone trespassing in your apartment?"

"Not anymore." Jill smiled, wondering if she should tell him about Madeline. Mad Madeline.

Actually mad?

Better to say nothing. Tony, handsome and perfectly normal Tony, might think *she*, Jill, was the one with the overactive imagination. The paranoid tendencies.

Maybe I am the mad one.

But she knew she hadn't imagined Madeline.

And somewhere deep in her mind she knew she couldn't entirely dismiss Madeline's mad tale.

Somewhere.

Far away.

The wine was relaxing her, making her feel warm inside. So warm and safe.

With Tony.

* * *

Over coffee at the Lotus Diner, Quinn and Linda made easy small talk. The evening was warm, but it was cool in the diner and unusually quiet.

It hadn't taken long before Quinn felt totally comfortable talking with Linda, and she seemed comfortable talking with him. Strangely, the coffee cups between them helped. They were similar to other containers of liquid from the hell they'd both visited, reminders of who they'd been, and who they were. The present, where the liquid containers had handles, was infinitely better than the past, and getting better.

Quinn hadn't taken a sip of his coffee in a long time. He sat toying with the warm cup, enjoying the scent of the coffee and the heat on his fingertips. "It was a good idea, meeting here tonight."

"I think so," Linda said. She was wearing a dark blouse, pale Levi's that she had the figure for, no jewelry except for four or five thin silver loop bracelets that jangled together ever so faintly whenever she lifted her right arm to sip coffee.

There were only a few other people in the diner, and no one was paying them the slightest attention. Outside the streaked window next to their booth, traffic on Amsterdam had slacked off and there weren't so many pedestrians—the city as relaxed as it ever got. Across the street, a woman waving a folded newspaper lured a cab to the curb. She opened its rear door and climbed in. The white of the newspaper showed behind the cab's reflecting windows as it drove away.

"My place is within easy walking distance of here," Quinn said.

Linda smiled. "Seeing that woman hail a cab make you think of that?"

Quinn looked into her eyes, not smiling. "You made me think of that."

Linda felt a stirring she hadn't experienced in years. She

knew they could both feel their relationship shifting toward the tipping point and wondered if Quinn was as nervous about it as she was. Nervous and a little bit afraid. He couldn't be as afraid. He'd been the one who'd nudged things in a new and faster direction. Linda's heart wouldn't slow down.

Her smile faded and she raised a hand to run her fingertips lightly along the contours of his face, like a blind woman assessing someone's true self.

"I'll get the check," she said.

"Wouldn't think of it," Quinn told her.

"No, you wouldn't."

She thought that from this point on it wouldn't matter much which of them paid.

25

"Pearl's pissed off," Ed Greeve said to his boss. "Has been ever since we made sure she knew about Linda Chavesky."

"That's a good way for her to be," Nobbler said from behind his desk. He scratched his fleshy neck. "Walking around pissed off and with her mind not on her work."

Harsh morning light streamed in through the office window, making the brightly illuminated half of Nobbler's face look red and raw, as if he'd shaved way too close and planed the skin.

"Think we might be able to flip her?" Greeve asked. "Get her to let us know what Quinn's up to?"

Nobbler thought for a few seconds and shook his head. "Not that one."

"A woman scorned," Greeve reminded Nobbler.

Nobbler smiled. "Remember, she's the one who dumped Quinn."

"I will say she's trying to get over him. Got herself a replacement. Guy named Milton Kahn, who's been humping her heavy."

"Well, well . . ." Nobbler drummed the plump fingertips

of his right hand on the desk and looked off into the brilliant light, maybe calling up the image of Pearl and whoever this Milton Kahn was.

"Pearl's probably a sexual dynamo," Greeve said.

"The type," Nobbler agreed. "Lucky Milton Kahn."

He sat back in his chair, made a tent with his fingers, and tapped their soft tips lightly together.

"Pearl's got this mother in a retirement home," Greeve said. "Way I got it, she and another old broad there set up Pearl with this Kahn guy, and the chemistry was there. Matchmaker moms. Always a pain in the ass."

"You never had a wife."

"Other peoples'," Greeve said.

"Hardly counts."

"Counts where it counts, depending on who's counting."

Nobbler didn't want to get into that kind of conversation with Greeve. The guy was a mystery anyway, even without going all Zenlike. "This Kahn character, is he a player?"

Greeve knew what Nobbler meant. Might Milton Kahn develop into a problem? "Naw, what he is is a dermatologist."

"It gets better and better," Nobbler said.

"I'll tell you something else I think," Greeve said. "My feeling is they might be humping like crazy, but they're not in love."

"How the hell would you know that?"

"I can just tell. It's not the real thing."

Nobbler gave him an incredulous look. "Christ on a stick! What are you, a romance columnist?"

"I'm somebody who knows people."

"He's humping her," Nobbler said. "That's good enough for me." He tapped his fingertips together faster and faster, as if to demonstrate.

Greeve might have shaken his head in disapproval as he left the office, or it might have been Nobbler's imagination.

* * *

Jill had never been in the main library. After climbing stone steps to the entrance, she found herself in a vast atrium of richly veined cream-colored marble with tall columns. The floor was also marble. A wide stairway led to upper floors. There was a mezzanine with a railing high above. A girl about ten was leaning over the railing looking down at her. She smiled at Jill, then ducked back out of sight. People walked past, their footsteps and voices echoing in the vastness.

Jill found a spot out of the flow of foot traffic and looked around.

There was no sign of Madeline. Or the woman who called herself Madeline. As far as Jill knew, the woman might be someone other than she said she was, someone so mentally deranged she might be imagining a different identity as well as the bizarre story she'd told.

Or was it so bizarre? When Madeline told it to Jill it seemed to possess a stubborn if frightening truth that kept finding its way to the surface. Jill had believed her enough to be afraid, to need to know more. Which was why Jill was here.

But where was Madeline?

Madeline never did show up. Jill waited fifteen minutes more inside the library, then went outside and stood in the shade near the entrance and waited another ten. People came and went. None of them was Madeline.

Jill rode the subway back toward her apartment half expecting, maybe fearing, that the door at the end of the car would open with a blast of air and noise and in would burst crazy Madeline to slump down next to her again and fill her ears with madness.

But the subway ride was uneventful except for a desperate man who set half a dozen small stuffed animals to bound about on the car's floor and tried to sell them for five dollars each.

During the next few days, as Jill entered or left her apartment, walked the streets, and rode the subway, she found herself watching for Madeline. Now and then she'd spot a bundle of rags that turned out to be human and her heart would jump, or she'd spot a haggard, lonely homeless woman who only vaguely resembled Madeline when she got up close. No Madeline. She seemed to have left Jill's life as abruptly and mysteriously as she'd entered it.

Jill couldn't leave the matter alone. She caught up on the news reports about the Torso Murders, spending much of her time reading daily papers and then more time online searching local newspapers' archives.

Without Madeline there to make the murders seem connected to E-Bliss.org, Jill began to doubt that either of them was in any real danger. Madeline must simply be one of the many mentally precarious and delusional souls wandering the New York streets. Perhaps Jill could find help for Madeline. If she could find her.

If she truly *wanted* to find Madeline.

What she wanted to do, really, was forget Madeline, though she didn't like admitting it to herself.

Each night before Jill slept, and in the dawn just after waking, she found herself thinking about Madeline. There was no way she could keep her mind from working on Madeline's story. If Madeline was telling the truth and was found and murdered, her killers wouldn't necessarily leave her torso to be discovered and examined by the police. The fact that she'd escaped for a while might have put her in a different category, someone E-Bliss.org wouldn't want in any way connected to the other murders.

But what bothered Jill most about Madeline's story, what snagged her thoughts whenever she let her guard down, was that Madeline, who'd been vibrating with the urgency that they meet and discuss some kind of plan, was nowhere to be found. Not in Jill's banal, workaday world, anyway.

But Madeline was real. Jill kept reminding herself of that. Had to be real.

Five days after they were to meet in the library, Jill tuned her TV to NY1 local news and learned that the decomposing body of a woman had been found in the shadows of a subway stop on Fifty-first Street. No one had noticed the body at first because it was just inside the dark tunnel at the very end of the platform, down in the deeper darkness alongside the tracks. Train after train must have traveled alongside the dead woman, barely missing her.

There was no identification on the body.

In the *Post* the next morning was a police artist's depiction of what the woman might have looked like when alive. Jill saw it while riding the subway when the man seated across from her opened his newspaper wide to read the inside pages.

Jill sat rocking gently in her seat with the subway's constant swaying motion staring at the sketch. The woman's eyes seemed to stare back at her.

The woman looked like Madeline.

Charlotte Lowenstein kissed Dixie on the lips as they were about to leave The Bad Sister and walk the few blocks to Charlotte's apartment in the Village. Charlotte was slightly drunk and knew it but didn't care. Dixie would take care of her, make sure she didn't stumble and fall or walk out in front of a car. Not that there was much traffic this time of night in this part of the Village.

Dixie helped her to stand up from her chair at the tiny table where they'd been sitting. The tabletop was a clutter of empty glasses, wadded paper napkins, miniature plastic swords, and bent swizzle sticks. They'd been sitting and talking, lost in each other, for at least two hours.

The bartender smiled and told them good night as they made their way along the bar, where about a dozen women sat, then past an old-fashioned glowing jukebox near the street door.

Outside, walking wasn't as much of a problem as Charlotte had assumed. Dixie lent her an arm for support, but it wasn't necessary. Charlotte could walk a straight line. She pretended anyway that she required Dixie's assistance. It was so nice, for a change, to have someone taking care of her.

So much better than the loneliness, the emptiness that was becoming vaster and vaster and threatened to leave a hole in her soul.

The dating service had worked the first time. First time for Charlotte, anyway. Its website had boasted about same-sex matchups, and it had been true to its word. Dixie, tall, dark haired, with strong features and a slim, powerful body, was exactly what Charlotte needed. Maybe opposites did attract, up to a point.

Unlike the sleek and sensual Dixie, Charlotte was short and blond, and about fifteen pounds overweight, most of it in her hips. She had a heart-shaped, sweet face, as opposed to Dixie's chiseled features and sharp vulpine profile. Dixie was undeniably sexy, but in a way that when she got a few years older might prompt people to refer to her as "handsome." Well, she was handsome to Charlotte right now, tonight.

And tonight was going to get better. Each night during the month since they'd first met by appointment at Starbucks seemed better to Charlotte than the last. It was tough enough in a new city without being one of the sisters. True, you could hook up easily enough in New York, but there were risks involved. Sometimes serious risks. There were people, male and female, out there who would hurt you in the worst ways.

Charlotte found Dixie to be delightfully perfect. Dixie knew just how far not to go.

The two women leaned toward each other for mutual support, though Charlotte was sure Dixie had downed only one drink, maybe two. Charlotte's memory was fuzzy. She heard Dixie draw a deep breath.

"Beautiful night."

"Every night's beautiful with you," Charlotte said.

Dixie smiled. Two men, maybe a couple, passed on the other side of the street and glanced over at them. Charlotte knew that one way or another it was probably Dixie who drew their attention. Dixie, with her slicked-back black hair, her dark leather jacket and black tights, her high-heeled black leather boots that made her long legs look even longer. And the red scarf tied loosely at her neck, a splash of brilliance like blood. Man or woman, who wouldn't stare? Who wouldn't want?

Charlotte rested her head on the point of Dixie's shoulder as they strolled. "We gonna put on a CD tonight?"

Dixie smiled. "If you'd like."

"I like it with music."

"You like it with or without," Dixie said. She pinched Charlotte playfully on the cheek. Not that it didn't hurt a little. Charlotte didn't mind.

Headlights behind them bathed the street in yellow light, but they didn't alter stride or stance. This was friendly territory late at night.

But Charlotte's heartbeat did pick up when the lights got brighter and the car was obviously slowing behind them. She could hear its engine ticking. She didn't look back, though. Neither did Dixie.

The front of the car came into view beside them. A large black car, shiny and with lots of gleaming chrome. Charlotte couldn't help but glance over at it. She thought it was a Chrysler.

It pulled right alongside them and a little ahead and

stopped at the curb. The driver buzzed down the passenger-side tinted window and leaned across the seat to look out at them.

"Dixie?"

A man's voice.

Dixie stopped walking and gave Charlotte a brief squeeze, letting her know there was nothing to fear.

"What are you doing here?" Dixie asked the driver, sounding surprised but not particularly afraid. The sure tone of her voice made Charlotte feel better. There wasn't much Dixie couldn't handle.

The driver was smiling. A nice-looking guy. "I just dropped a friend off at his apartment and was on my way home. Didn't expect to bump into anyone I knew, much less you." Still smiling, he looked at Charlotte, then back at Dixie.

"This is my friend Charlotte," Dixie said. Her arm stayed reassuringly firm around Charlotte and contracted again in a gentle squeeze. "Charlotte, this is my brother, Don."

"On your way someplace?" Don asked.

"Just left someplace," Dixie said.

"We haven't seen each other for quite a while."

"That's for sure," Dixie said.

"I've got an idea," Don said. "Why don't we go to my place for drinks? The three of us. I can drive us there, then afterward take you wherever you want to be dropped off."

Dixie felt Charlotte draw back. But then, she knew what Charlotte wanted. She kept her arm tight around Charlotte at the shoulder and looked down at her, smiling encouragingly. "Charlotte?"

"I don't think so, Dixie. Not tonight. I'm feeling pretty dragged down."

"You sure?"

"Certain." She gave Don a tentative smile, asking for help.

The two guys who'd passed on the other side of the street appeared again, walking the other way.

Don seemed to think about it. "Don't force her," he said to Dixie. He grinned up at Charlotte. "There's always another time."

"Okay," Dixie said. "We'll give you a call."

Don was still looking at Charlotte, still smiling warmly at her. He winked. "It's a date."

He drew back into the shadowed confines of the car and the window glided up. Charlotte and Dixie watched as the big Chrysler pulled away from the curb and turned the corner at the next intersection.

"Your brother," Charlotte said, as if still digesting this new piece of information about Dixie.

Dixie took her arm and they began walking again. "My brother. We don't see each other often, but we get along. I think you'll like him."

Charlotte kept pace and leaned into Dixie again so that they were almost thigh to thigh. "He seems nice."

"Everyone says that," Dixie said.

26

It was moments like this when Pearl emitted a kind of energy that anyone near her could feel. Quinn felt it now. Something was up with Pearl.

They were riding along in Quinn's big Lincoln on a fine New York morning. The slanted sunlight cast stark, sharply angled shadows of tall buildings so that light and dimness danced over the vast expanse of metal that was the car's gleaming black hood. Pearl had shown up at the Seventy-ninth Street office early in the unmarked car, and now they were driving to pick up Fedderman so the three of them could meet with Renz in his office at One Police Plaza. Quinn felt his hands tighten on the steering wheel as Pearl spoke.

"I understand you're seeing that M.E. who smells like formaldehyde."

Quinn braked to avoid rear-ending a dusty white delivery van and let the Lincoln edge forward in the blocked traffic. "I never noticed a formaldehyde scent." He felt his jaw setting. Who was Pearl, anyhow, to worry about whom he was seeing or sleeping with? Pearl and that asshole Milton Kahn.

Quinn cautioned himself about his anger. After all, he'd never even met Kahn, only heard about him.

"I didn't say scent," Pearl told him. "I said smell. More like *stench*."

Quinn shrugged, which seemed to infuriate Pearl. He could sense her seething beside him. They drove along. The motor hummed. Pearl seemed to hum, though she wasn't uttering a sound.

She was trying to start something, Quinn knew. *Always trying to start something. Born with a burr up her ass.*

Finally she said, "Goddamned car stinks, too. Like you've been smoking cigars in it."

Screw this! Quinn had wanted a peaceful morning, but if she was determined to make trouble, he was going after her. She'd brought it on herself. "That might be you burning, Pearl."

"Why should it be?"

"You seem upset about me seeing Linda. Not that you oughta be. You're the one who's always harping about the end of our relationship."

"What's to harp about?" she asked. "It's over. There is no relationship."

"Then why are you—"

"Who said I was?"

"So pissed off about—"

"I'm not in the slightest angry over anything concerning you, Quinn. Who you're seeing. Who you're screwing."

"You brought up the subject."

"The Linda subject?"

"Doctor Chavesky," Quinn corrected, still in an unforgiving mood.

Pearl played it cool. She knew him, knew what he was doing, and how he usually refused to engage her in argument unless he was particularly angry about something. She must have pushed the right buttons. This *Doctor* Chavesky must've really gotten to him, for him to react by coming after Pearl so hard and tough. What was she supposed to do, shrink away in fear? Is that what the overgrown Irish thug expected?

"Move the goddamned car," Pearl said. "Try to keep up with traffic."

Quinn glanced up. It was true, traffic had begun to move forward. The dusty back of the van he'd almost hit was half a block away and picking up speed. He goosed the big Lincoln so it would keep up. He ignored Pearl.

She wouldn't let it go.

"So now you've got something new to obsess about," she said.

"You're the one with the new obsession."

"Which would be?"

Screwing Milton Kahn. "Disliking Dr. Chavesky."

She laughed loudly and without a shred of humor. "You talk like I should actually give a shit about you two getting it on."

"You talk like you care."

"Why should I care?"

"You shouldn't. I won't obsess about you anymore, Pearl. That's what you always accused me of doing. That's over. No need for you to get upset about it any longer."

"Is this me being upset?" she asked, pointing her forefinger at her deadpan expression. "Is it?"

"I've gotta keep an eye on the traffic," Quinn said, not looking at her. God help him, he was beginning to enjoy this. A little.

Pearl seemed to sense it. "You do that," she said. "You keep an eye on the traffic while you obsess about your doctor friend. You're not careful, you're liable to drive right up somebody's ass. Maybe like you—"

"Pearl!"

They were both silent while he tailed the van along Forty-ninth Street in stop-and-go traffic. About five minutes passed.

Quinn thought maybe Pearl had run down. He settled back in the leather upholstery and paid more attention to his driving.

"Know what I think?" Pearl asked.

"Usually not."

"I think you're so good at getting inside the minds of serial killers because you're obsessive just like they are. You're psychotic. You and the killer are opposite sides of the same coin."

"That's important, being on the opposite side." But Quinn knew exactly what she meant and it bothered him. He'd always been stubborn, tunnel visioned, obsessive. . . . Or was it persistent, unrelenting, determined . . . ? And what the hell was the difference? These were fine distinctions that had now and then gotten Quinn in trouble. Pearl's hard head had gotten her into more than a few messes, too, so she had a lot of nerve talking to him that way, comparing him to serial killers.

He took a few deep breaths and swallowed his irritation.

So he was obsessive. So what? He put it to work and did some good in the world with it. If his obsessive nature helped to nail these assholes who killed women in the worst ways, so be it. That was their problem and he was coming after them hard. And didn't every coin have its opposite side?

"Whatever's going on in our personal lives, we have to work together," he said calmly. "Can you manage that, dear?"

"Don't give me that sarcastic 'dear' bullshit. I'm not one of your gullible suspects or witnesses who fall for it and spill their guts."

"Can you manage it?" he asked again.

"I'm still in the car, aren't I?"

He glanced over and was surprised to see that she was smiling.

She was actually smiling.

Pearl enjoyed combat. But Quinn knew that. He didn't say anything, and within a few blocks he found himself smiling along with her.

At Second Avenue he stopped for a red light, first in line, then suddenly ran the light and went the wrong way up Second while there wasn't any traffic coming. A uniformed cop was standing by his squad car halfway up the block. As they passed, Quinn slowed the Lincoln and held his shield up tight against the windshield so the cop would see it. The cop recognized the shield, maybe recognized Quinn, and nodded.

As they turned the corner at the next block so they could zigzag uptown and get going in the right direction again, Pearl twisted around in her seat and saw the roof bar lights on the squad car winking and the cop standing alongside a gray Ford sedan lecturing the driver about traveling the wrong way on Second Avenue. She knew the Ford was a press car, one of those that had been staked out near the detectives' office so media wolves could sneak photos or video footage, and sometimes follow them when they left.

Quinn cut over another block and got back on course, checking his rearview mirror to make sure the press car was nowhere in sight.

"That was nifty," Pearl said.

Quinn nodded and drove on.

Jill knew she was being obsessive about Madeline. That was the only way to explain it. After all, the police artist sketch that was in all the papers and seemed to pop up every fifteen minutes on TV didn't really look *that* much like Madeline.

But Jill had worked her last day for Tucker, Simpson, and King, though they said there was a slight possibility she'd be called back in a week. It all depended on when Mr. Tucker's hernia operation was going to be scheduled. Things at the office would be hectic while he was off, and they'd need someone extra who could answer the phone and knew the filing system.

I know the filing system but no one there knows me.

On top of the situation at the law firm, Tony was out of town on business and would be for another four days.

For the first time in a while, Jill had time on her hands. That was why she couldn't stop thinking about Madeline Scott. About what might have happened to poor mad Madeline. About whether she was still alive.

Jill had eaten the other half of her Chinese take-out meal for dinner last night, and this morning she'd walked a few blocks to a deli and gotten orange juice and a toasted bagel for breakfast. Now what was she supposed to do, watch *Oprah*? Hell, *Oprah* wasn't even on.

The apartment was so quiet.

Jill paced a while, then turned on the TV and channel surfed until she was tired of talking heads and SUV commercials and bad drama and unfunny comedies. What she didn't want to watch was the news. It would make her think about Madeline.

Jill used the remote to switch off the television. She stretched out on the sofa on her back with her forearm over her eyes. She knew she wasn't going to sleep. She wasn't tired. Her mind wouldn't be still.

She removed her arm from across her eyes and sat up, remembering something. Thinking back. Making sure.

There was no reason why she couldn't do something about Madeline, satisfy her curiosity about the woman. She was certain Madeline had mentioned that her former apartment was on West Seventy-second Street, the apartment where the new Madeline Scott (if by some chance there really was one) would be living.

If the apartment actually existed.

If what she'd heard hadn't been another of mad Madeline's flights of imagination.

Jill got up from the sofa and went to where the phone sat, on a table near the door. A stack of borough directories lay on the table legs' cross braces. She stooped and got the Manhattan directory from the top of the stack and carried it back to the sofa.

She leafed through the pages to the Scott listings. There were quite a few Scotts, but she found it almost immediately: "M. Scott," with a West Seventy-second Street address.

Jill sat motionless for a few minutes with the open directory on her knees. Seeing the listing had given her a start, even though it was the object of her search. Its existence in the phone book made the rest of Madeline's story seem much more possible.

Jill shook off that feeling. The listing might be for a different M. Scott, a Mary, Martha, or Margaret Scott. Or maybe a Mathew or Martin Scott. It wasn't only women who tried to give the impression a man lived in their apartment, by using first initials for their phone number listings and mailboxes.

One way to find out.

Jill gathered her willpower and carried the directory to the phone. She pecked out M. Scott's number.

And was told the number was no longer in service. It was now unlisted.

Jill hung up the phone and returned to the sofa. She sat down heavily, still clutching the directory.

Great! Now what?

But she knew what.

Her boredom, her curiosity, her fear were driving her.

She tore out the directory page with M. Scott's listing on it and stuffed it in a back pocket of her jeans, in case she'd forget the address.

She'd seen the weather report three times this morning on TV and knew it was supposed to rain. No matter. She wouldn't take an umbrella.

She felt lucky.

27

The West Seventy-second Street address listed for M. Scott wasn't far from Columbus Circle. It was an old building, at least twenty stories tall, with an ornate brick and stone front that was chipped and stained. Maintenance or repair was being done on the building. Blue iron scaffolding nestled tightly against it, across and above the entrance, though at present no one was working. A red plastic cone lettered CAUTION stood to the side of the three shallow stone steps leading to its entrance. Jill thought that was apropos.

It wasn't the kind of building that featured a doorman. In fact, one of the wide entrance doors was propped open by a crude wooden wedge. Jill stepped inside, where it was a few degrees cooler and dim after the hot brightness of outside.

To her left was a bank of tarnished brass mailboxes. In a card inserted in the narrow slot above the locked box of apartment 16C was the name M. Scott. It was in slightly smeared black ink and appeared to have been there a while. Jill peered through the narrow grille in the box's door and saw only darkness. There was no mail inside. None that showed, anyway.

Jill moved farther into the lobby. It was large, with mismatched upholstered furniture arranged in two groups around low tables. One of the tables had a left-behind newspaper scattered over it. The other had an arrangement of plastic flowers in a glass vase on its center. Two elevator doors stood at the opposite end of the lobby, across an expanse of gray and white tiled floor. There were ancient stains on the floor that looked like they'd been made by people stepping on cigarettes to put them out. The elevator doors were wood, with fancy brass inserts that were as tarnished as the mailboxes. The lobby obviously hadn't been redecorated in years, but it looked reasonably clean. A wide wooden stairway to the left of the elevators had rubber treads on the steps and stopped at a landing that turned out of sight.

The lobby was empty, as far as Jill could see. Unless someone was seated in one of the two high-backed upholstered chairs facing away from her. Sounds from outside were faint. The busy sidewalk and street seemed far enough away to be another world, though they were just beyond the propped-open door.

As she glanced back at the door and mailboxes, Jill noticed an intercom system on the wall opposite the brass boxes. She hadn't seen it before because it was coated with the same beige enamel as the walls.

She went to it and found 16C, then pressed on an enamel-glutted button, which, to her surprise, actually depressed under the pressure of her finger, and waited.

No buzz. No voice. No answer.

Jill gave the paint-coated button another push, thinking the ancient intercom probably hadn't worked since the fifties.

She gave it up, stood staring at the elevators for a moment, and then strode toward them. She'd come here to learn something, and so far she'd been shut out. She was frustrated.

At least the elevator buttons hadn't been painted over. She pressed the "up" button.

Nothing lit up. There was no response until the narrow brass arrow on the floor indicator above one of the elevator

doors trembled, then started to descend from the number
nine.

Jill waited patiently. Finally there was a grinding, clunk-
ing sound, and the elevator door slid open.

No one stepped out.

Inside, the elevator was surprisingly small and paneled in
dark wood with a heavy grain. Jill saw that the building had
twenty-five floors. She pressed the button for sixteen and
stood waiting for what seemed a full minute before the door
slid closed. When she was completely surrounded by the op-
pressive paneling, the elevator lurched and began its ascent.

The walls of the hall on the sixteenth floor were paneled
halfway up with the same wood as used in the elevator. The
upper half of the walls was a much lighter beige than that in the
lobby, and it was pinkish.

Jill left the elevator and turned right, then walked down a
dimly lit hall toward a small, dirty window and a sign indicating a fire stairs door. Apartment 16C was about halfway
there.

Its ancient, six-paneled varnished door looked like all the
other doors except for the apartment number. Just beneath
the brass numerals was a round peephole.

Jill found that her hand was quaking as she raised it,
made a fist, and knocked.

She kept her eyes trained on the peephole, watching for
movement or a change of light on the other side.

No answer. No movement. No sound from the other side
of the heavy old door.

Jill swallowed, then knocked again, much harder.

The door across the hall opened, startling her.

She turned around and saw a small, Hispanic woman in
her forties looking out at her. She had a shabby white robe
wrapped around her and tied with a matching sash. Her
graying dark hair was mussed. Jill noticed that her feet were
bare and her unpainted toenails needed trimming. The
woman said nothing, simply stared inquisitively at Jill.

"I'm looking for Madeline," Jill said.

"You were knocking so loud, I thought it was my door," the woman said, without a trace of accent.

"I'm sorry. Do you know Madeline?"

"Seen her a few times, is all. I'm not home a lot, and when I am . . ."

"What?"

"Nothing. People in this building pretty much mind their own business. You woke me up. Made me drag my ass in here and see who was at the door. Who was nobody. I don't mind telling you that pisses me off. I work nights and try to sleep during the day."

"I'm sorry."

"You should—"

"I said I was sorry. Twice."

The woman stared hard at her. "Apology accepted," she said abruptly and moved back inside and closed her door.

Jill was angry at first, and then she had to smile. At least the woman's rudeness had broken the spell of anxiety that had come over her. Or was she the rude one? She'd awakened the woman.

She shook her head and walked back toward the elevator. This little bit of detective work hadn't yielded a bit of information, but she felt better. At least she'd done *something* instead of sitting around her apartment letting the questions eat her alive from the inside.

She rode the elevator down to the lobby and waited while the old door took its time sliding open.

And was startled to see silhouetted against the light a woman entering the lobby.

Madeline!

Or someone who looked remarkably like her. She was the same size and shape as Madeline, had the same walk, the same tilt of the head.

Jill was rooted to the elevator floor. Couldn't budge.

The woman was walking toward the elevator. Toward her.

Jill's mind worked frantically. She'd been standing staring at the woman. She couldn't leave the elevator now. She'd stay where she was, as if she'd entered the elevator just before the woman came into the lobby.

Then the woman was ten feet away from her, no longer in silhouette.

She barely glanced at Jill and entered the elevator to stand beside her.

She wasn't Madeline, yet she was. They were so similar that anyone might mistake one for the other at a glance or from a distance. And after seeing this woman a few times as Madeline, there wouldn't be the slightest doubt as to her identity. At that point, even standing next to the real Madeline, this one would be chosen as the original.

This woman was perhaps slightly taller, and of course she was well groomed, with her blond hair cut the same as Madeline's, only clean and combed. Her eyes, her nose, the thrust of her chin, everything about her was like Madeline's. What wasn't like Madeline's—the slope of her forehead, the curve and fullness of her upper lip, the slight cleft in her chin (or did the real Madeline have such a cleft?)—all seemed to achieve a balance so the end result was that she *looked* like Madeline.

The woman pressed the button for the sixteenth floor, and Jill was afraid the woman might hear the wild hammering of her heart.

The elevator door slid shut.

Jill thanked God the buttons weren't illuminated. The woman wouldn't know that none of them had been pressed before she'd entered the elevator.

As the elevator rose, Jill knew what she had to do. She'd come this far, and afraid though she might be, she'd not stop now. Despite her fear, and the chance she was about to take, she'd go further.

But not farther up than the sixteenth floor.

Trying to seem casual, she exited the elevator first and

turned left, away from 16C. She walked slowly, and near the opposite end of the long hall she stood before a door and pretended to be fishing in her purse for her key.

From the corner of her eye she watched the woman who looked like Madeline walk the opposite way down the hall, stop, and enter an apartment. She hadn't glanced back at Jill, hadn't seemed at all curious about her.

Jill hurriedly walked back down the hall, extending her arm and pressing the "down" button as she passed the elevators, in case she had to get away in a hurry. She had to make sure. To be positive.

With a glance at the numbered door to the apartment the woman had entered, she was sure.

The woman had gone into 16C.

Jill strode swiftly back along the hall, breaking into a jog so she'd be in time to enter the elevator that was waiting, door open, already at floor sixteen level.

It seemed to take forever for the creaking old elevator to descend all the way to the lobby.

Finally, back out in the sun and bright air of Seventy-second Street, Jill made herself walk at a normal pace away from the apartment building toward Columbus Circle. Her breath came fast and uneven, in tiny gusts that she couldn't control. Her mind danced from one possibility to another, not liking any of them.

Now that she had this information, what was she going to do with it?

She remembered what mad Madeline had told her that day in her apartment: *"They'll learn about what's going on and see that any investigation stops. And that I'll be killed. And now that I've talked to you, that you'll be killed."*

"You're halfway to nothing already."

28

Palmer Stone's desk phone played the first seven notes of "I've Got You Under My Skin." That meant his direct line.

That meant something important. Only certain people possessed that number: his most trusted employees, and a few privileged clients. The clients were supposed to use it only in the direst circumstances. At a certain point, they were to destroy the paper it was written on and then forget it.

Stone was in his midfifties but trim and still handsome. His tailored gray suit was Armani, his tie Hermès, his shoes John Lobb. His full head of dark hair was expensively cut and salt and pepper at the temples. He had features that were craggy yet amiable rather than noble, with a smile that dazzled. If he was an actor, he could play the president of the United States. If he didn't drool or speak like an idiot, he could *become* the president of the United States.

Palmer Stone didn't drool, and he spoke with calm reason in a moderated tone. He was as suave as he looked. But he had no interest in the presidency. It didn't pay enough.

He picked up his desk phone on the third ring. "Palmer Stone here."

"This is Maria Sanchez, Stone."

An angry female voice, one he'd heard only a few times before. He didn't think he'd ever hear her or speak to Maria Sanchez again. Like his other special clients, she no longer existed except on paper and as electronic pixels.

He didn't get a chance to ask her why she was calling, what was wrong.

"I thought you told me that Madeline bitch was dead," she said.

"Maria! It's good to hear from you."

"I thought—"

"Please don't worry, really. Ms. Scott is no longer a problem. I can assure you of that."

"Funny, I don't feel assured."

"There is only one genuine Madeline Scott, and you are she."

"Sometimes I don't goddamned feel like it, and that's creeping me out. I got on the elevator this morning in my building and some bitch was waiting to go up. I had the feeling she'd been standing there a long time, and she had this weird look on her face. Then she got off on my floor, put on a transparent act of going to another apartment at the opposite end of the hall, and watched me enter mine."

"You're saying she looked like Madeline?"

"No, no! Listen to me, Stone. She was definitely giving me a close look, like it meant something to her, and I'm sure we never met before."

"Well, you're a beautiful woman, Maria. Even more beautiful now."

"She wasn't looking at me that way. She was . . ."

"What?"

"Scared of me. I'm sure of it. I've been around fear. I could smell it on her."

"Why would she be frightened of someone like you?"

"I can think of only one reason."

"What you describe might have been mostly your imagination, about this woman being so interested in you. It's natural. We've seen it in other clients. You couldn't look more like . . . who you *are* now. It's not uncommon to have doubts at this stage of the game. Things started out a little unevenly, but we soon got them under control. Believe me, you have nothing to worry about."

"Maybe you just think they're under control."

"Maria—Madeline, listen to me. When I tell you the other Madeline is gone for good, believe me. I can't give you the details and you don't want to know them, but you have my sincere promise."

There was only silence from the phone at his ear.

"Do you feel better, Madeline? Is my promise good enough?"

"I don't know," she said and broke the connection.

Stone hung up and sat drumming his manicured finger-nails on the arm of his chair. Maria Sanchez had turned out to be a skittish one, which was a surprise. E-Bliss.org had been assured she was the sort who seldom got rattled. Now here she was acting out of character.

Of course, what he'd told her was the truth. It was natural for special clients to be nervous and suspicious immediately after the identity exchange. They soon got over their fears once they settled in as who they had become.

The odds that the woman on the elevator actually sus-pected anything were long. The odds that someone in Maria Sanchez's position might think so were short.

There was nothing to worry about if only he could get his client to realize it and feel safe.

While he was at it, Palmer Stone made it a point to stop thinking of her as Maria Sanchez.

"Madeline Scott," he actually muttered under his breath, as he pushed Maria Sanchez from his consciousness.

Madeline Scott, the first and original, had had E-Bliss.org almost exactly right in her conversation with Jill. The legitimate matchmaking service was a protective shell for an operation that provided something similar to a witness protection program for those who could afford it. Its clients were mostly the wives or lovers of organized crime figures whose own lives and/or considerable fortunes were in danger because of competing mob elements or the law. Occasionally a client was concerned only with disappearing for his or her own sake. These clients, who would eventually take other clients' identities, were referred to in conversation and in E-Bliss.org files as *special clients*, to distinguish them from the bulk of legitimate clients, who often did find love, lasting or otherwise.

The special client would make obvious a move out of the country or into deep cover and instead take the place of another E-Bliss.org client who'd been culled with a computer program and carefully researched. Fees included teaching and coaching the special client to move smoothly into the new identity. The old identity would remain at large, while the basis for the new identity was murdered. The special client, who for safety's sake had severed all ties with E-Bliss.org, would wait patiently in hiding to assume the life of the victim client. News of the torso (useless in identification) being found was the signal that the switch in identities was complete; it was time to move into the client's apartment. Usually, as a precaution, the new identity would soon move out of the building, leaving a note and making sure the rent was covered. Officially, no one was missing.

This was a business model Palmer Stone had worked on for a long time before putting it into practice. It was a business model that worked.

That's why the phone call from Maria—Madeline—was particularly irritating.

It had been a mistake jumping the gun and letting a special client take over an identity before it was actually available. E-Bliss.org had made the exception in Maria Sanchez's case because she was an especially important, and demanding, client. And there had been a great deal of money involved. Who could have guessed the client to be deleted would somehow escape?

Well, nothing to be done about it now.

Stone didn't exactly forget about the new Madeline's nervousness, but he put it aside in a separate compartment of his mind. He'd always regarded compartmentalization as one of the most valuable business skills. He had other things to think about right now. Like printouts of the latest client profiles on the corner of his desk, awaiting his attention.

He stopped drumming his fingers. He'd probably never hear from the new Madeline again.

That, after all, was the whole idea.

He smiled and set to work, determined not to worry about what he couldn't change. He regarded that as another valuable component of his business skill set.

Victor and Gloria entered Victor's Sutton Place apartment at three A.M. They both looked tired and their clothes were rumpled.

As soon as they closed the door, Victor walked to the other side of the tastefully furnished living room and got a bottle of twenty-year-aged scotch from an antique mahogany credenza. He poured about two fingers of the scotch in crystal on-the-rocks glasses, straight up. Gloria had followed him halfway to the credenza. He handed her one of the glasses, and they both raised them in brief and silent toast, then sipped.

Gloria yawned.

Victor felt like yawning but didn't. "Want to sleep over?"

She shook her head no. "Things to do tomorrow morning." She looked down at her gray blouse and black skirt. Then she gave Victor a head-to-toe glance. "Not a drop of anything on us."

"Because we're professionals."

"Thank the good Lord for plastic," she said, smiling.

Earlier that evening they'd disposed of a male E-Bliss.org client. One of the same-sex clients who comprised a minority but growing part of the company's business.

Because the client was gay, they hadn't followed their usual procedure of luring the man into Gloria's car. Nevertheless, Gloria had been in a position to effect the man's death, and then drive him to the East Side garage where she and Victor did the dissection.

Victor's smile turned nasty, and curious. "I was surprised when we opened the car's trunk and I saw a broomstick."

Gloria shrugged. "We need to stay consistent."

"I just couldn't see you doing it," Victor said. "And to a man. And of course, you didn't wait for me."

"Since I handled the other preliminaries, I thought I'd handle that one."

Victor waited for her to say something more, but she didn't.

Instead she tilted back her head and swallowed the rest of her scotch, then began to move idly about, looking at the furniture, the art mounted on the walls.

This wasn't the apartment her brother actually lived in. That apartment, the one the clients saw, was owned by E-Bliss.org. and wasn't nearly so sumptuous—which was why Victor had taken to spending most of his time here, moving in most of his clothes and even his modest library.

Gloria paused near a bookshelf. Something new had been added to Victor's collection of nineteenth-century novels and contemporary mystery fiction and biographies. Two glossy hardcovers. She pulled one out and looked at the cover. " '*Vlad the Impaler*'?" The other book also appeared to be about the famous fifteenth-century Transylvanian despot who was the inspiration for the book and movie *Dracula*. Despite myth and movie, there was no proof that he'd actually drunk blood, though, at least not straight from the vein. His twisted pleasure was impaling enemies and sometimes friends on tall stakes. Sometimes by the hundreds or thousands. When one of his minions complained about the stench, the man was himself impaled on a taller than usual stake so he'd be up high where the air was better. Vlad had a sense of humor.

"Most of your biographies are of statesmen, military or literary giants," Gloria said.

Victor sipped his scotch. He was always a slower drinker than Gloria. "Vlad's not exactly my hero," Victor said, "but he was an interesting man. The more you learn about him, the more impressed you become."

"If you say so." Gloria returned the book to the shelf.

"Since we've decided to do this, we might as well learn technique. And we should do it together."

Gloria stared at him, then walked over and placed her glass on the slate inlay of the credenza. "We've had a long night. I'm going home, say my prayers, and go to bed."

"I got a call from Palmer Stone," Victor said. "He told me Maria Sanchez called him."

"Called Palmer?" Gloria looked irritated. "What the hell for?"

Victor recounted the phone conversation as Palmer Stone had told it to him.

"She should have known better," Gloria said.

"I wouldn't get too worked up yet. She's probably just nervous. That's what Palmer told her, and my guess is he's right."

"It didn't sound as if she thought so. Off-the-wall bitch!"

"She'll calm down. We'll probably never hear from her again. She got what she paid for, so she has no complaint."

"She sure won't have any trouble with Madeline Scott."

"Since she *is* Madeline Scott," Victor said. He finished his scotch, walked across the room, and placed his empty glass on the credenza next to Gloria's. He gave her a nervous grin. "This really is something, what we've gotten ourselves involved in, sis."

"Something extremely profitable." She waved a languid hand. "Here you are on Sutton Place. La-di-da."

"You're not living so bad yourself."

"Let's do what we must to keep it that way."

"Another scotch?"

Gloria yawned. "No thanks. I'm tired enough already." She moved again toward the door, this time with more resolution.

"The broomstick, Gloria."

She paused with her hand on the knob, posing, he thought. "What about it?"

"When you inserted it, was he alive?"

"Go to bed, Victor. Read yourself to sleep."

She slid out the door into the plushly carpeted hall that absorbed the sound of her leaving.

Victor poured another two fingers of scotch into his glass, wondering if he knew Gloria as well as he thought he did.

Or knew himself.

29

"A man," Quinn said, staring down at the bare torso wedged in with a cluster of black plastic trash bags and cardboard boxes of refuse.

"Obviously," Pearl said.

It was a warm night, and the cloying stench of corruption hung in the still air. It might simply have been from the garbage, but there was more than garbage before them.

They watched the CSU techs working around the torso inside a taped-off area alongside a pizza joint on the Lower West Side. The partial corpse had been discovered earlier that evening when one of the cooks carried out some garbage from the kitchen. A nearby neon sign advertising the best pizza in New York cast a greenish glare over the scene, making the torso seem more like a stage prop than what was left of a real human being.

"Our guy swings both ways," Fedderman said, pointing with a long finger protruding from his oversized sleeve. "Notice the broomstick?"

"Hard not to notice," Quinn said. "There's also a lot of blood on the stick. Not like the others."

Pearl understood at once what he meant. "Sweet Jesus! He was alive when it went in."

"Looks that way."

Fedderman moved in to take a closer look. "Not much doubt about it. And it wasn't gentle." He straightened up and moved away, wiping his sleeve across his mouth. "I hope to hell we don't have a copycat."

"Hard to imagine," Pearl said.

"This whole goddamned thing is hard to imagine."

"Whole world," Pearl said.

Quinn looked at her. Philosophizing at crime scenes wasn't like Pearl. The Milton Kahn effect, maybe.

"It makes my hypothesis more likely," she said. "About a compulsive, psychosexual serial killer not being what we've been chasing. That could all be a diversion."

"Profiler says no," Fedderman said.

"He's got her fooled," Pearl said.

"More likely a copycat," Fedderman said.

Quinn shot a glance at the ghastly green torso. At the two neatly placed small-caliber bullet holes in the chest, among hairs that were just beginning to gray. The victim might have been around fifty, but it would take the medical examiner to know for sure. Almost certainly the bullets were still in him. "We'll know about the copycat theory as soon as we get postmortem and the ballistics test results on the bullets."

Motion caught his eye and he looked toward the front of the building, where more cars were arriving. Not all of them were NYPD. The media had caught the scent and were on the scene. Quinn knew more were on the way.

"Wolves," Pearl said.

"Useful ones sometimes, though," Quinn said.

"That'll be a tough sell with me."

"I'm going back to the office," Quinn said. His Lincoln was parked out front, half a block down so it might not attract media attention. There were more black Lincoln Town Cars in New York than any vehicle other than cabs, but the media knew his car's license number, so he had to be careful. "You and Feds talk to the people in the restaurant, especially the guy who found the body, then drive the unmarked back to the office. Meanwhile, I'll be in touch with Renz and find out as soon as possible what comes out of the morgue and lab."

As Quinn was walking toward the street, he saw Nift approaching confidently from the opposite direction. He was wearing a well-cut black suit and lugging his black medical case, bouncing jauntily, as he always did, with each step.

He smiled when he saw Quinn. "Leaving so soon?"

"Miles to go before I sleep," Quinn said.

"Poetry, no less. And I thought you were the victim, you being so green and all."

"He's back there waiting for you," Quinn said, jerking his thumb in the direction of the torso.

Nift raised his eyebrows in surprise. "He?"

"I know it's a disappointment for you, but this time the victim's a man."

"The Torso Killer offed a man? What's that mean?"

"Means he's dead," Quinn said and walked on.

As soon as he turned the building's corner and started for his car, he heard shoe leather scuffing on concrete, a voice: "Captain Quinn, can we have a statement?"

"Sorry," Quinn said, "but no comment."

"But you *will* say we can assume this is another Torso Murder?" another voice, a woman's, asked.

"Assume away."

More shoe leather noise, even though Quinn was walking faster. He sensed numbers behind him, but he didn't want to turn around and count. It sounded as if they were about to close in on him. He could imagine the headline: MOBBED BY THE MEDIA. The Lincoln was still a hundred feet away.

"Anything different about this one?" the same woman asked.

Quinn put on some speed. "You might ask the M.E., Dr. Nift. He's back there now with him."

Several voices in unison: "*Him?*"

At first Quinn thought they were talking about Nift. Then he realized otherwise.

Shit! Quinn regretted his slip immediately. Not that it mattered; they'd learn it soon enough. Still, he didn't like goofing up that way. A victim of another sex was just the sort of information the police should have kept *away* from the press. Something cops could know and all those nutcases making false confessions wouldn't imagine.

Too late now.

"Is this victim a man?" several voices asked, almost in unison.

"Captain Quinn?" The woman's voice. Grating and insistent. "Is this victim—"

"I think that's what Dr. Nift said," Quinn told them, as he finally reached the car and pressed the fob to unlock the doors. "Dr. Nift knows more than anybody about this one." He got the door open and managed to ease his way inside the car as the media wolves crowded around him. "He's the little guy poking around the body who looks like Napoleon dressed like a banker."

Quinn removed some fingers wrapped around the edge of the door and got it closed, then hit the universal lock button, started the car, and got out of there.

In the rearview mirror he saw at least half a dozen shadowy figures hurrying back toward where the ghastly green torso lay, toward Nift and his black bag of tricks.

Quinn, sitting at his desk in the office, looked up when the door opened and Pearl and Fedderman came in. They looked tired. They should—it was almost midnight. It must have been a late night for some of the pizza people, too.

Pearl went over and slumped in her desk chair. Fedderman trudged to a brass hook on the wall and hung up his wrinkled suit coat, then rolled his chair out toward the middle of the room and sat down wearily.

"Anything?" Quinn asked, knowing the answer.

"Nothing," Pearl said. "Nobody saw, heard, or smelled a thing other than pizza. The guy who discovered the torso, kid named Enrico, was still shook up, but his story's simple enough. The head cook sent him out with the garbage to add to the pile of sealed plastic bags, and there was the victim. Kid thought it was a fake at first, some kind of prop. Then it dawned on him what he was looking at and he went back into the kitchen shaking and told the head cook. The head cook came out and verified his story, then went back into the kitchen and called the police."

"We talked to people in the neighboring buildings, too," Fedderman said. "Same no story there."

"Our guy's nothing if not careful," Quinn said.

"According to the pizza employees," Pearl said, "no one had gone out the restaurant's back door since about eleven this morning. The torso could have been there quite a while. It was half buried in all the trash, so the eleven o'clock employee might not have noticed it. Busy as the street is, our guess is that it was put there the night before, when hardly anybody was around. It's a block of businesses, so it's a good place to ditch a body after dark."

"Like the other places where we've found the torsos," Quinn said.

"Our guy," Pearl said.

Fedderman ignored her. It was clear they'd reached the point where they were getting on each other's nerves. Quinn understood.

"What's next, boss?" Fedderman asked. "More coffee, or bed?"

"Information, then bed," Quinn said. "Ballistics did a rush job, and the bullets in and near the heart were twenty-twos, fired by the same gun that killed the other victims."

"There goes the copycat theory," Pearl said.

Fedderman made an obviously Herculean effort not to reply to her taunt.

"We'll know more about the postmortem tomorrow," Quinn said. "Something different about the broomstick stake, though. The others were cedar; this one's made of poplar. And the cuts that sharpened it are more visible and were made by shorter, shallower strokes, and from a sharper blade. And it wasn't sanded as fine. Also, no traces of furniture oil."

"Ouch!" Fedderman said.

"Believe it," Quinn told him. "Nift did confirm the broomstick was inserted via the rectum when the victim was alive."

"After he was shot, though?" Fedderman asked.

"Nift couldn't be sure. The bullets might not have killed him right away. Nift said he might have lived another few minutes."

"Hard minutes," Fedderman said.

"All that blood," Pearl said. "Any prints on the broomstick?"

"Of course not," Quinn said. "And what you were looking at wasn't all blood."

"I guess not," Pearl said, remembering the foul odor in the vicinity of the torso.

Everyone sat silently for a long while. Quinn wondered what the other two were thinking. He wasn't even sure what *he* thought about this departure, undoubtedly made by the same killer they'd been stalking. There were variations, sure, most notably the gender of the victim, but they were still looking at the same gun, same grisly M.O., same killer. Had to be.

Pearl yawned. Didn't excuse herself. "Bed?"

"Bed," Quinn said, standing and switching off his desk lamp.

"I bet I won't dream," Pearl said.

"I bet I will," Fedderman said.

30

Jill hadn't been able to sleep since her visit to Madeline's apartment. She played it over and over in her mind, trying to remember the slightest details, trying to be sure the new Madeline hadn't paid her any undue attention. She couldn't be positive.

She paced her apartment, moving like a disassociated spirit from room to room. She was exhausted but couldn't make herself sit down. In the kitchen, she paused at the sink and ran water into a glass, gulped it down. She knew she should eat something, but her appetite had been replaced by anxiety.

It was possible—no, now it was likely—that mad Madeline's story was true. But even if it wasn't, there sure as hell was *something* creepy going on. And if Madeline's story was true, that meant Tony was . . .

Jill didn't dare let herself think about that. It seemed impossible.

She remembered mad Madeline's distrust of the police. But not all of them. The problem was, which ones could be trusted?

Paranoia.

Jill refused to let her mind tilt in that direction.

She realized she didn't have anyone to turn to. That was how she'd gotten into this mess in the first place. There was only Tony. Ordinarily he'd be the first person she'd go to for help, but if the real Madeline Scott was right, he'd be the last person she should go to.

Jill tried again to bend her mind around the seemingly inescapable conclusion, but again it was impossible for her to imagine Tony intending she should come to any harm. Incomprehensible. Gentle, loving Tony.

She ran another glass of water and carried it into the living room. She slumped in the corner of the sofa, feeling small and vulnerable, and absently used the remote to switch on the TV.

The set was tuned to a local channel, and a talking head wearing a serious expression said that another Torso Murder victim had been found. "The torso of a man . . ."

A man?

Jill turned up the volume and leaned forward, her elbows on her knees.

The news report had gone to tape. A tall, rawboned man in a white shirt and red tie, with strong features and a bad haircut, was striding just ahead of a gaggle of journalists dogging him with recorders and TV cameras. He ignored them and walked faster, nudged one of them aside, and opened the door of a large black car. It was a graceful but powerful movement. People instinctively got out of this man's way.

"Captain Quinn?" one of the media people, a woman, kept repeating. "Captain Quinn?"

The big man said something unintelligible as he lowered himself into the car. He had to remove the hand of a man from the door so he could get it closed. There was a shot of the knot of journalists standing and staring as the big black car squatted with power and drove away fast.

The camera moved in for a close-up of the woman who'd been calling the man's name. She was hastily rearranging her breeze-mussed hair with her free hand while holding a microphone with the other. Behind her, other media people were moving back in the direction they'd come from when they'd followed the big man. A few of them were running.

"As you can see," the woman said, "the police aren't yet giving out any information on this new and startling development." A lock of blond hair flopped over her left eye, and without closing the eye she shoved the hair back in place. "Lead investigator Captain Frank Quinn did let slip that this time the torso is that of a man. Speculation at this point in time is that this murder was the work of a copycat killer, as so often happens in these sorts of cases. This is something that impacts the entire city, and you can count on Team News to get the facts as soon as they're available and pass them on to you. Bill?"

The news anchor named Bill reappeared on the screen. "Thanks, Mary." He gazed solemnly at the camera. "As you just saw, Team News is on the scene and on the story, and we'll pass it on to you at the speed of electrons." He shook his head at the horror of the developing story. "Hopefully, this nightmare will soon be over."

He glanced down at his desk, then back up at the camera. "Do you ever wonder what your dog does when you're not home?"

Jill stopped listening. *Quinn. Captain Frank Quinn.* She recalled the big man's name from the papers and earlier TV news. The lead investigator.

There was something about him, something solid and strong. A calm island in an angry sea. He'd be a policeman she could trust. At least he was the best possibility she could think of, and she had to talk to *someone.*

She got the Manhattan phone directory, balanced it on her knees, and looked up the number of the precinct house closest to her apartment. She picked up the phone.

After punching in two numbers, she slowly put it back down.

It occurred to her what they'd want of her, what she'd almost certainly have to do if she contacted the police and told them everything.

They'd want her to look at a decomposed body. To identify Madeline Scott at the morgue.

Jill didn't know if she could do it. Didn't people sometimes get ill when they did that? Throw up? Sometimes pass out? Simply the thought was making Jill nauseated. She'd always considered herself to be a person with the willpower to do what was necessary, a person of commitment and courage. Now she wasn't so sure. She wasn't sure about anything. Her world seemed to have gone insane, and it was the only world she had.

She replaced the phone book and trudged to the sofa. Sat down and pressed her face hard between her palms. Her features were distorted as if squeezed in a vise. She didn't feel like crying; she felt like screaming. And screaming and screaming . . .

She held the screams inside, but it wasn't easy.

Eventually she might call Captain Frank Quinn, but not yet.

Charlotte was daydreaming while walking along Christopher Street and didn't recognize the car right away. There were so many big dark luxury cars running around New York. Then she used her hand to shield her eyes from the sun and saw the shiny Chrysler emblem. She realized it was Dixie's brother's car. What was his name? Ron? No, Don.

The car slowed and then pulled to the curb about twenty feet ahead of where Charlotte was walking. Uh-oh. This might become an awkward situation. She'd caught the way Don had looked at her the other night, when he'd tried to get her and Dixie to go to his place for drinks, and knew he might not know about Dixie's sexual orientation. He might think she and Dixie were simply friends.

Charlotte pretended she hadn't recognized the car and

kept walking at the same pace, hoping maybe she'd been wrong about it being Don's car. But when she was almost alongside it the tinted window on the passenger side glided down, and at a slant through the rear window Charlotte saw the figure behind the steering wheel lean over toward the passenger side to say something out the window.

"Charlotte."

Not Don's voice. Dixie's.

Relieved, Charlotte approached the car and bent down.

There was Dixie, leaning across the front seat toward her and smiling. She looked terrific, dressed in black, as usual, with her red scarf, her glossy black hair pulled back to emphasize the prominent bone structure of her face and the force of her dark eyes. It was her eyes that had first attracted Charlotte to her.

Charlotte grinned widely as she moved closer to the car, one foot down off the curb. "Dixie!" She bent even lower to look inside the rest of the car. Dixie was alone. "Isn't this your brother's car?"

"I borrowed it to drive down here to the Village."

"How come?"

"To see the woman I love."

"That would be me?"

"That would be you, sweetheart. Hop in."

"Why? Where we going?"

"Get in and I'll tell you."

No reason not to. Charlotte moved back so she wouldn't block the big door from opening, then lowered herself into the car.

The interior was cool. An air freshener attached by a suction cup to the windshield emitted a faint lilac scent that seemed to overlay some other, more acrid odor. The upholstery was soft leather and felt almost like velvet beneath Charlotte's exploring touch. *Nice.* As soon as she pulled the door closed, the car was filled with silence. She felt isolated but comfortable and cozy, being in here with Dixie.

"This some kind of surprise?" she asked.

"In a way it is. We're going to my brother Don's."

"Oh." Charlotte realized she'd sounded disappointed and regretted it. She didn't want to hurt anyone's feelings. "I mean, how nice! But how come?"

"He's home today and we were talking on the phone, and he said he wanted to meet you. Said you looked like a nice person."

"Is that why he wants to meet me? Because I look nice?"

Dixie gave her a sideways glance and pulled the car smoothly away from the curb. "He's interested. He figures you're my significant other."

Charlotte laughed. "I was afraid he might be interested in another way."

"Not Don. We know all about each other. He understands." Dixie braked the big car hard to avoid a cab making a wide turn. She glanced again at Charlotte. "Buckle up, hon."

Charlotte did as she was told. "Am I?" she asked.

"Are you what?"

"Significant to you."

Dixie smiled and ran the fingertips of her right hand along the inside of Charlotte's left thigh. Charlotte's body stiffened and she caught her breath.

"You have no idea," *Gloria* said.

31

Jill deliberated for hours. Finally she returned to the phone and called the precinct house nearest her address. They didn't know what she was talking about at first. Then they tried to convince her that if she had valuable information it wasn't necessary to talk to a particular officer. She told them patiently that she'd talk *only* to Quinn. It occurred to her that they might be tracing the call, but that was okay. She'd decided on her course and didn't care.

At last someone gave her the number to call to talk to Quinn. A detective named Fedderman told her that he'd be glad to help her, that Quinn wasn't available. Again she insisted on Quinn and only Quinn. Finally, maybe because Fedderman heard the desperation in her voice, he relented. He told her to hold and he'd put her through.

There was no unmemorable background music, only a series of clicks and buzzes as her call was patched through to yet another number.

A voice said, "Quinn," and the connection was made.

*   *   *

Charlotte was surprised when Dixie slowed the big Chrysler to a stop. They waited while a sectioned overhead steel door rumbled and clanked as it rolled up in front of them. She looked over at Dixie, who smiled reassuringly, as the door reached full open position and the long black car eased into what the dimness soon revealed to be a garage. Charlotte heard the steel door rattle closed behind them.

"Don's garage," Dixie explained.

Charlotte nodded. She hadn't been paying much attention, but it didn't seem to her that the garage was large enough to be part of a much larger building that would contain apartments. Of course, Don might live in one of those prewar brick or brownstone homes converted into apartments. Or it might be a rented garage; there must be plenty of them in Manhattan, considering the scarcity of parking spaces.

She felt better when a wooden walk-through door on the back wall of the garage opened and Don entered. He was wearing faded jeans and a gray T-shirt that might at one time have said METS. He was also carrying a white cardboard box.

As Dixie climbed out of the car on the driver's side, Charlotte opened her door. She heard Dixie say, "Hi," to Don, then, "See what I've brought." As if Charlotte was a pleasant surprise. But Don didn't seem surprised.

Charlotte got all the way out of the car and closed the door behind her. She thought she heard the electronic whisper of the doors locking. The garage smelled of gasoline and oil and something she couldn't identify. Heat rolled out on her ankles from beneath the car.

Don looked over at Charlotte and winked. "Hi, Charlotte." He placed the cardboard box on the floor, wiped his palms on the thighs of his jeans, and walked over to her. He was smiling. Charlotte thought he was going to offer his hand to shake. Instead he punched her hard in the stomach.

All the air *whooshed* out of Charlotte's lungs and she slumped forward. Didn't fall, though, because Dixie had walked around the back of the car and was there to catch her with her arms around her midsection just beneath her breasts.

Close to her ear, Charlotte heard her ask Don, "Bring everything?"

"Everything you wanted. This was your idea."

Charlotte's body wanted to draw into a tight curl. Her feet rose off the floor. But Dixie was strong and held her firmly enough so she didn't fall. She was hanging there in the air with her legs pulled up almost in a fetal position.

The vacuum in Charlotte seemed to be drawing every part of her toward it. Her head was bowed. She couldn't raise it as she tried futilely to suck in air. She saw that the garage floor was covered with something. A plastic drop cloth. She also saw that Don was wearing loose green booties of some sort, the kind doctors wore in operating rooms or other sterile environments. He reached into the cardboard box and pulled out a green surgical smock. It took him less than a minute to slip it on over his clothes, complete with cap. His movements were all very smooth and practiced, as if he'd done this many times before. He snapped on latex gloves with the same expertise.

Charlotte's heart was about to burst. She worked harder to suck in precious oxygen, and this time managed a quick, sharp intake of breath. A rasping sob.

"She'll be able to scream soon," Dixie said.

"Can't have that," Don said.

He bent down, got a thick roll of gray duct tape from the box, and walked over to stand in front of Charlotte. He reeled out about two feet of tape and ripped it off the role. Charlotte felt Dixie tighten her grip and shift one arm so her hand was cupping Charlotte's chin. She raised Charlotte's head and Don quickly slapped the tape over Charlotte's gaping mouth and wrapped it around her cheeks and neck, even her hair. He pulled out more tape and wound it tightly so she couldn't breathe in or out through her mouth, couldn't utter a sound. Then he stepped back and surveyed his work without really looking at Charlotte as a person. That more than anything scared her.

What will they do to me if I'm not human anymore?

"She won't suffocate, will she?" Don asked.

"She's breathing through her nose," Dixie said.

Charlotte was, but it took every bit of will and effort she could manage. The ache in her stomach had spread throughout her body. But she *was* breathing again. She could hear the air hissing through her nose. Getting louder. The frantic hissing reminded her that all they had to do was pinch her nostrils for a minute or so and she'd be dead. That was all that stood between her and nothing. Now she was truly terrified.

She calmed her fears somewhat by telling herself there was at least some hope. Don had been afraid she might suffocate with the tape over her mouth, so they didn't intend to kill her.

Did they?

She tried to convince herself that the answer was no. Then what *was* going on? A kidnapping? Hardly. There wasn't anyone who'd pay even a small amount of money to have Charlotte returned. There was no place for her to be returned to, since she'd cut off all family ties a month ago when she moved to New York after the inevitable blowup. It wasn't acceptable to be a lesbian in a small town in Indiana. Her parents had said that they didn't want to see her again, that she was no longer their daughter. Charlotte had accepted their judgment and pronouncement, and after meeting Dixie she knew she could live with the situation.

Now this. Some kind of sexual thing? Dixie was plenty kinky. Maybe this was all to frighten Charlotte, give her the ultimate masochistic kick. But they'd never gone this far before. Not half this far. Charlotte managed to crane her neck and look up at Dixie. Dixie smiled at her. Charlotte knew that smile. This time it frightened her. *Really* frightened her.

Was that the idea? She prayed it was the idea. A kinky game. Nothing more. In an hour or two at most it would be over.

She saw that Don had something else in his hand. A thin strip of white plastic. It was one of those ties that once placed around something had to be cut to be removed. Sometimes the police used them instead of handcuffs.

The police. Charlotte wouldn't mind seeing *them* right now.

Dixie momentarily released Charlotte, then grasped her wrists and yanked her arms behind her back. Charlotte felt the plastic tie go on and tighten, cutting painfully into her flesh. She screamed silently into the duct tape.

Now she struggled to stand on her own. Dixie helped her, grabbing her beneath each arm and supporting her. The way Charlotte's wrists were strapped behind her, she still had to slump forward, but she was standing.

While Dixie held her, Don went to the box and returned with some kind of cutter with a razor blade in it. Charlotte kicked out her legs desperately and banged her heels against the hard floor. She remembered the clear plastic sheet spread over the floor, the kind painters used so they wouldn't make a mess. Don was going to cut her throat. A single, quick slash and her life would gush from her. She knew it!

But he didn't use the blade that way at all.

Instead he used it to cut along the seams of her blouse. He yanked the blouse away as if performing a magic trick and tossed it over by the box. He cut her bra straps and removed her bra. Tossed it over to land on her blouse. She kicked out futilely. One of her sandals flew off and landed near the pile of clothes, as if she'd tried to place it there. Don was staring at her intently now, but while his eyes were alive his features were set, almost wooden. He cupped one of her bare breasts in his hand for a moment, then unbuckled her belt, worked the button and zipper on her jeans, and tugged at the waist. When he'd inched the jeans down a bit, he lifted her feet and clutched the denim around her ankles and pulled the jeans off, along with her remaining sandal. Charlotte wriggled and tried to kick him. He sidestepped her bare foot and had her panties off before she knew what had happened.

Don went back to the box and drew from it a folded clear plastic drop cloth, like the one on the floor, only smaller. He unfolded it and draped it over the hood of the car.

He came back and stood in front of Charlotte, just out of kicking range, and looked at Dixie.

"Do we really want to do this?" he asked.

"Both of us do," Charlotte heard Dixie say in a throaty voice. She could feel Dixie's warm breath in her ear.

Don went again to the box and this time drew out what looked like a broomstick, only it was shorter, and pointed.

At first Charlotte didn't realize what that meant. When she did, she was aware of a warm wetness flowing down her legs as terror took over every corner of her mind.

This isn't happening. This is a dream. Please, God! It has to be a dream!

Maybe God had heard her, because she became oddly detached from what was happening. It was as if there were no place, no time, only fear so deeply rooted she couldn't bear to accept its reality.

It was a mercy that she was in a trance as Don took her from Dixie and walked her as if she were a zombie to where the plastic sheet was draped over the hood. He shoved her onto the hood, lifting her slightly so her feet were off the floor.

She felt her legs being forced apart. She tried to put them together, but Don's body was between them now, easing them ever farther apart. Charlotte saw Dixie on the other side of the hood watching her. Both of Dixie's hands were on the hood and she didn't have the sharpened broomstick.

Don must have it.

Don must have it!

The trance was broken.

Through unbelievable pain, the terror and panic rushed in.

Charlotte began to scream, over and over. Each scream filtered through the tape as a muted, soft hum. Almost like coos of intense pleasure. Dixie leaned closer over the warm hood, still watching with glittering black eyes, her face like stone.

Charlotte loved Dixie. She really did.

Then there was only the pain.

32

It took Jill Clark almost half an hour to tell Quinn everything. When she was finished, she wasn't sure how she felt about what she'd done.

She still felt she'd had to do it, to talk to Quinn before her next date with Tony. But now she began to think again about what Madeline had told her and wondered if she really trusted Quinn. If she trusted anyone.

She hadn't been disappointed in Quinn. His strength and calm were obvious and reassured her, drew her out. He seemed to understand and to forgive her for any naïveté or foolishness that had led her to this predicament. But was that the idea? Was it a trick? Was everything a trick?

The sense of being drained, of absolution, after telling her tale was fast disappearing. She'd opened herself to new problems. She was still suspicious of everyone.

You're being paranoid. Like Madeline.

Dead Madeline, who'd had real *enemies.*

But she didn't know for sure that Madeline *was* dead. Jill had only been sure enough to come here, to talk to Quinn.

Tony. Why didn't I talk to him? Why didn't I trust Tony?

It was as if her heart had known secretly what hadn't yet

found its place in her mind. Her heart hadn't trusted Tony. Was her heart right?

It hadn't been right yet.

She was still afraid.

Appraisal time.

Quinn had been reviewing his notes when Jill arrived. He'd left his reading glasses on so he'd seem less intimidating. Anything to make her conversational and keep her talking. And she'd told him plenty, the words tumbling out sometimes so close together they got tangled up.

He leaned back in his desk chair and peered over the rims of his glasses at this young woman who'd just unburdened herself to him. She seemed entirely rational but obviously distraught. She was wearing lightweight blue slacks, a white blouse with a coffee stain on it, very little makeup. Her blond hair was carelessly combed and slightly flattened on one side, as if she'd been lying down. Her eyes were red, but he couldn't be sure if she'd been crying. She was perched on the very edge of the visitor's chair in front of his desk, facing him. Quinn, after all his years as a detective and all those lies he'd been told, could almost unerringly know if someone was telling the truth. Jill Clark seemed too frightened to be lying.

"I know it's hard to believe," she said, mistaking his silence. "I didn't believe it myself at first."

"And you think the woman you saw in the elevator on Seventy-second Street has taken over the identity of the one you referred to as mad Madeline. Has moved into her apartment."

His words were statements, not questions.

"Only Madeline wasn't mad," Jill said. "I'm sure of that now."

Quinn peeled off his glasses, folded them, and slid them into his shirt pocket.

"It's hard to believe," Jill said again.

"It's hard to believe we're finding human torsos lying around the city, but we are."

"Then you *do* believe me!"

He wasn't ready to give her that yet. "I think you and I should take a ride in my car," he said.

"To Madeline's apartment?"

He smiled. "It's a little premature for that, I'm afraid."

She shuddered and her lower lip trembled. "I know where we're going. I expected it."

"You've given this some thought."

"Of course I have."

And you'll give it more thought after today. Probably for the rest of your life.

Quinn scooted back his chair and stood up, then walked around the desk and placed his hand on Jill Clark's shoulder. He could feel the fear and tension like electric current in her slender body. "You're safe now, dear. You did the right thing coming here."

She surprised him and placed her hand on his and squeezed. "I don't think anyone's really safe," she said. "Not anymore."

"Relatively safe," Quinn amended. "And that's about all we get in this cockeyed world."

She managed a smile, but it wasn't much.

"Ready to take that ride?" he asked.

She nodded and stood up from her chair as if she were an arthritic old woman. The mind was forcing the body where the body didn't want to go. Quinn couldn't blame her for being reluctant.

"We'll make it as easy as possible for you," he said. "Nothing's as bad as the fear of it."

Almost nothing.

He scribbled a note to Pearl and Fedderman explaining where he was going. Then he placed a hand gently on Jill Clark's shoulder and steered her toward the door. He saw that the label on her blouse was sticking up out the back of her collar and deftly tucked it in. She glanced over at him and they exchanged smiles. He had to keep her moving, keep her from thinking too much.

They were on their way to the morgue.

Victor paced in his apartment, roaming through all the rooms, head bowed, his mind processing new experience, the new Victor.

It wasn't supposed to be this way. It was business. He'd started out so detached. The dismembering was useful as a public signal to the waiting client as well as a hindrance to victim identification. And most of all, it helped to divert the police by convincing them a psychosexual serial killer was operating instead of a unique and profitable business. If the dismemberment didn't do it, surely the phallic broomstick stakes forced up through the vaginal and womb walls, or the rectum, would.

At first there was no emotional reaction to using the sharpened broomstick stakes. But soon he'd become fascinated by the homemade stakes and began taking great care in their selection and transformation in his skillful hands. The sharpening, sanding, and oiling became tremendously important to him. Somehow extremely personal. It made using the broomstick stakes easier.

It made doing business easier. That part of the business.

Then slowly, without him being aware of it, he began to enjoy more than the preparation. He began to enjoy using the stakes.

That wasn't like him. Not at all. He was Victor the businessman, not Victor the Impaler.

He glanced over at his bookshelves, at the Vlad the Impaler books. When he'd seen them in the biography section at Barnes & Noble he had to have them. That really was when he first suspected the presence of a demon in him, a sickness, and his uneasy suspicions were confirmed when he read more and more eagerly about the sadistic despot and warlord.

Good Christ! He and the long-dead Vlad had something in common.

They were kindred spirits.

Victor wasn't pleased by this. He went into the kitchen and poured some Johnnie Walker Black into a water glass. The liquor felt hot going down; maybe it would jolt him out of his depression, his reluctance to accept what he'd done, what he was.

It was Gloria who'd suggested using the broomstick stakes. Maybe she was the one who'd infected him. And she was the one who'd suggested that Charlotte's penetration be anal, like that of the man. Victor remembered what he'd immediately thought when she'd suggested that. It was the way Vlad had impaled his victims. He'd agreed to Gloria's suggestion without argument, as if it was all business with him so it made no difference. But he knew by the smile in her hard, dark eyes that she was aware of this new side of him, or old side that had always been there as a secret even from himself. He and Gloria could have few secrets from each other.

Victor continued to pace. He simply couldn't sit down and be still.

He knew why he couldn't sit and be still, the real reason. What had happened wasn't Vlad the Impaler's fault, or Gloria's. The decision had been his.

He'd make the same decision again.

He took another generous swallow of scotch, nailing down the admission that hadn't come easily, and that somehow made him feel marginally better.

This time when his mind began replaying Charlotte's squirming and soft screaming on the hood of the car, he didn't immediately deflect his thoughts, the muted pleas for mercy and the violent images. He found his courage and welcomed them into his consciousness, into his new being.

Victor the Impaler.

Another swig of scotch.

I enjoy my work. Why shouldn't I?

33

"Why are we going the wrong way up a one-way street?" Jill asked.

Quinn steered the big Lincoln to swerve around a bus stopped for passengers and smiled over at her. "The pesky press, dear. They want to know what's going on all the time."

Jill winced as the Lincoln's right front fender barely missed the bus. "Isn't that their job?"

"Sure is. Right now, it's my job to see that they don't know about you. Because if they know, the killer will know." *If he doesn't already.*

Quinn figured that if Jill's story was accurate it was possible that the phony Madeline had related the elevator encounter to E-Bliss.org. Jill might already be in danger. A lot depended on whether the woman who'd been found dead in the subway tunnel was the woman in her story.

Of course, if Jill didn't identify the woman in the morgue as the real Madeline, that was no guarantee the real Madeline was still alive. At any given time, there was more than one undiscovered corpse somewhere in New York.

Horns blasted as Quinn steered the Lincoln onto Second

Avenue, headed the right direction now with the flow of traffic.

"I think we shook them," he said.

"Driving with you is an adventure," Jill told him. There was a curious elation in her voice, as if motion and risk had temporarily taken her mind off her more ominous troubles.

"Life's an adventure, dear."

"Sometimes a fatal one," Jill said gloomily.

Back in her doomsday mood.

Maria Sanchez thought she might be going crazy. She had no money problems, but three years ago she'd made a mistake Jorge didn't know about. She'd violated his strict rule of dealing drugs, not using them, and become a user. Now she was trying to quit.

She didn't think of it quite that way. Maria regarded herself as being in the process of quitting. She still had part of the stash she'd brought with her when she'd flown in to La-Guardia. Smuggling it in had been easy enough; arrangements had been made. Even if anyone had found the drugs in her possession, it probably wouldn't have proved a problem. Money had been laid down. People who counted knew who she was.

Who she wasn't anymore.

She scratched at her bare arms, stood up from the sofa, and paced back and forth across the living room of the apartment that was feeling more and more like a prison cell. Over the past several months she'd shortened up on her daily lines of cocaine, cut her usage almost in half. It wasn't as if she had any choice. Maria had always been the exception to the rule. What others were afraid or unable to do, she could accomplish. Her drug usage wouldn't be any different. Other people got hooked for life—not Maria.

Cutting back had been difficult at times, was difficult

now, but well within the scope of her will and physical ability to deny herself. Confidence was bred in her. She'd been sure she'd be able to quit entirely when the time came.

Now she was beginning to wonder.

So far, the trip to the morgue wasn't as bad as Jill had imagined. She was told she didn't have to view the actual body. They sat her down in a red plastic chair in an anteroom and would show her close-ups of the dead woman on a television monitor.

Quinn stood behind her and to the side with his hand resting gently on her shoulder. "There are worse things on cable television," he said. "The medical channel."

Jill didn't know if there actually was a medical channel, but his words did lend her courage.

Still, she drew in her breath as the first image took form on the monitor.

Quinn said nothing, but tightened his grip almost imperceptibly on her shoulder.

"Madeline," she said simply, her voice almost too soft to hear.

"You're sure?"

"Positive."

Jill turned her head to the side, away from the monitor. One photograph was enough. She knew it was Madeline and knew that was how she'd always remember Madeline. "Can we get out of here now?"

"Of course." As Quinn removed his hand he patted her shoulder, letting her know she'd done well and he was still concerned about her, looking out for her. "Are you all right?"

Jill nodded as she stood up. "Fine."

Outside in the warm sunlight, she felt slightly nauseous and swallowed. She felt better after drawing a few deep breaths through her mouth.

"Tummy okay?"

He must have known exactly how she felt. "It's all right now. The most awful thing is the smell. It doesn't want to go away."

"Usually after a visit to the morgue, I smoke a cigar," he said.

"Feel free."

He drew a stubby, almost black cigar from his shirt pocket. Jill was surprised to see that it was half smoked. It wasn't badly damaged where it had been snuffed out. The charred tobacco had been evened out and tamped with care.

"It's Cuban," Quinn explained, seeing her staring at the cigar. "They're kind of precious." He dug into a pants pocket for paper matches, then struck one and fired up the cigar. "Would you like one?"

"No, thank you. Aren't Cuban cigars illegal?"

"No Cuban cigar has ever been convicted of anything," Quinn said. He drew on the cigar, rolled the smoke around in his mouth, then exhaled. He grinned at her. "Want a puff?"

"No. Smelling the secondhand smoke instead of the inside of the morgue is enough for me."

They walked on to where the Lincoln was illegally parked in a loading zone, an NYPD placard visible on its dash.

"For you," Quinn said, "I'll smoke in the car."

There was no reason to avoid the press as they drove away from the morgue. But just in case, Quinn ran a red light to make sure they weren't being followed.

"Still sure of the identification?" he asked when they were stopped in stalled traffic on First Avenue.

"It—she's Madeline. The real one."

Quinn unbuckled his safety belt so he could work his cell phone from his pocket and pecked out a number.

"Isn't that illegal, too?" Jill asked. "Driving in New York City while using a cell phone?"

"Not if you're also smoking a cigar," Quinn said.

*　*　*

When Quinn was finished telling Fedderman he had a lunch date, he called to set up his own lunch with Renz.

Renz already had a luncheon appointment, but when Quinn told him what he wanted to talk to him about, Renz broke it. They were sitting now in Puccini's, an Italian restaurant that played opera for background music, only a few blocks from where Quinn had hooked Jill up with Fedderman near a good fusion restaurant on Amsterdam. From this point on, Jill would need protection. She was in more danger than she knew.

When Quinn was finished telling Renz about his visit with Jill Clark, and their subsequent trip to the morgue, Renz sat silently staring at his rigatoni carbonara. He wasn't listening to *La Bohème.*

"This Jill is having lunch right now with Fedderman?" he asked, to make sure, not looking up from his plate.

"Right up the street," Quinn said.

"The woman pretending to be Madeline might have been suspicious of her. We've gotta protect her. Gotta keep her away from the media wolves."

"You believe her story?"

"It's all we've got." Now Renz did look up from his food. "What's your gut tell you?"

Quinn didn't take the question lightly. "Tells me it's probably true."

A soprano warbled up the scale to improbably high notes. Renz sat for a while considering everything Quinn had told him, including political ramifications. Maybe especially political ramifications. Quinn sipped the Heineken he'd ordered and didn't disturb Renz until what felt like five minutes had passed. Possibly Renz had zoned out with his eyes open.

"Harley?"

"Jesus H. Christ!"

"Leaving him out of it," Quinn said, "I need for you to check and see who's obviously disappeared or gone into deep cover the past year or so. People the law might be interested in. It has to be done without raising any curious eye-brows. We can't afford to spook E-Bliss."

"I can do that," Renz said. "E-Bliss. I hate this high-tech bullshit, especially when it mixes with serial murder."

"Clark said it was a New York–based company. We'll check it out carefully."

"What about Clark? We can't leave her hanging out there. If she goes down with us knowing this and keeping it from the media, I'll never do anything but pound a beat someplace where I'll probably get shot, not to mention that poor young woman."

"Not to mention," Quinn said. He took a long pull of beer. "What I think, Harley, is that Jill Clark needs a new friend living right in the same apartment building."

Renz smiled, catching right on. "A woman friend. A close one who'll keep an eye on her, and who'd sure as hell know if one day she was a few inches taller or shorter or her eyes were a different color. Pearl?"

Quinn nodded. "We'll call her something else, though. Pearl's photo's never been in the papers in connection with this case, but her name has a few times."

"Call her what?"

"I dunno. I'd better ask her about it."

"Make sure you do. If we choose something she's sure to bitch about it."

"This is gonna be a dangerous assignment," Quinn said.

"Pearl's a pain in the ass," Renz said, "but she doesn't lack for guts."

"It isn't that," Quinn said. "Pearl will be watching over Jill Clark. I want Pearl watched over, too."

Renz began forking in his rigatoni as if he'd just rediscov-ered it and didn't want it to get cold.

"Goesh without shaying," he said with his mouth full.

Quinn wasn't so sure.

34

It was easy enough to find the brick-and-mortar address of E-Bliss.org, though it wasn't on the matchmaking business's website. Links led to links, and within half an hour on her computer, Pearl had the location of the company's headquarters. She was fast becoming the computer whiz of the detective team.

The business name E-Bliss.org was properly registered with the state's Division of Corporations. The principals were Palmer F. Stone and Victor and Gloria Lamping. Besides the business address, Stone and the Lampings had listed three different New York addresses of residence. When Pearl checked, she found that they had all moved and left no forwarding addresses. The office of E-Bliss.org, on West Forty-fourth Street, had remained constant.

While Pearl did more computer homework on E-Bliss.org, Quinn and Fedderman went to check out the West Forty-fourth Street address. The day had stayed warm and grown more humid as it had turned gray. Now a mist hung in the air, too fine to require a raincoat or umbrella, but thick enough so that the Lincoln's wipers *thwacked* intermittently to smear the wide windshield. Quinn realized Pearl was right: in the dense, damp air, the car's interior did smell too strongly of cigar smoke. The odor did cling. Maybe he should get one of those little deodorizers that looked like miniature pine trees to hang from the rearview mirror. He put it low on his list of to-dos.

The E-Bliss.org offices turned out to be in an office building not far from the theater district. Letters engraved in stone above the entrance said it was the Western Commerce Building. Quinn guessed that was because it was on the West Side. He and Fedderman left the car parked by a fire hydrant on the opposite side of the street, then crossed over. Quinn's bum leg, from when he'd been shot in a holdup, was bothering him slightly, maybe because of the rain. He was careful not to slip on the wet pavement. They entered the lobby.

It smelled musty and had a lot of cracked marble and a yellowed tile floor. The walls had been recently painted a tinted cream color that leaned toward brown. There were pillars ending in a lot of scrollwork at a high ceiling bordered by fancy crown molding that was painted a shade darker than the walls. Light tumbling through a clear leaded-glass window kept the lobby from being depressingly dim. The Western Commerce Building was still respectable and had hung on long enough that it was becoming prime real estate, thanks to the vast improvement that had been made in the nearby theater district.

Quinn and Fedderman were the only ones in the lobby. They went to a glassed-over directory near the elevators and saw that there were in fact two theatrical agents in the building, along with law offices, a real estate agency, an insurance firm, a dental clinic, and more of the kinds of offices you'd expect to find in such a building. There were also several ambiguously named businesses, among which was E-Bliss.org. It shared the sixth floor with Cagely Imports and E. Rupert Hall, Investments.

"Think we should go up and have a talk with Palmer F. Stone?" Fedderman asked. "If there is a Palmer F. Stone. Sounds like a name made up by somebody running a con."

"With a name like that, you either go into politics or run a con," Quinn said.

"There's a difference?"

"I don't think we should show ourselves yet," Quinn said. "We spook these people and they might be out of here before we can turn around twice. You wait here while I go up to the sixth floor and scope things out. If somebody notices me I'll duck into E. Rupert Hall and invest some money."

"Commodities," Fedderman said. "I saw on the financial channel that commodities are hot."

"They won't be if I invest in them," Quinn said and headed for the elevators. Their doors were framed with fancy plaster scrollwork that probably matched the clutter around the tops of the pillars, but he didn't feel like looking up and checking.

The sixth floor was quiet. Quinn had stepped from the elevator into a small alcove and taken half a dozen steps to where the thinly carpeted hall ran in both directions. A small sign mounted on the wall featured an arrow pointing to the left, where E. Rupert Hall and Cagely Imports had offices. There was no arrow indicating anything was to the right.

Quinn decided that if anyone asked he was trying to find the dental office on the fifth floor. He turned right and walked down the narrow but well-lighted hall.

A single new-looking wood door near the end of the hall was lettered E-Bliss.org in fancy painted gold script edged in pink. Very artistic. There was no way to see what was inside. Apparently the dating service's office was conveniently isolated from the other two businesses on the sixth floor. Quinn smiled. Romance flourished best in privacy.

He stopped about five feet from the door and briefly thought about opening it.

Not yet, he told himself.

But someday soon.

He turned around and walked back the way he'd come, then passed the elevators and entered the office of E. Rupert Hall. He asked a gray-haired receptionist who'd been reading a book about fingernail art where the dental offices were. Just to cover himself in case someone in E-Bliss.org had somehow been observing him.

The woman directed him to the fifth floor and went back to her book. Quinn thanked her and left, thinking the book was about five hundred pages and it didn't seem there'd be that much to write about fingernail art. He guessed it must have a lot of illustrations.

When he got back to the lobby, he and Fedderman returned to the car and drove toward Jill Clark's apartment.

It was time to explain to her that she had a new friend in the building.

When Pearl and Jill first saw each other, Quinn introduced Pearl as Jewel. They wanted to get Jill thinking of her as Jewel right away.

"She'll be right above you, on the eighth floor," Quinn said. It was one of three vacant apartments in the building—the nearest to Jill's. Quinn had told the disinterested landlord the NYPD wanted to rent it for a few weeks to observe someone in the building across the street. They gave him a voucher and he gave them the key.

Jill nodded, still obviously trying to get used to the idea, and still obviously glad someone would be nearby to protect her. She couldn't believe what might be the truth about Tony. On the other hand, it was impossible for her to dismiss the possibility from her mind. And even now that she'd gone to Quinn and found help, she hadn't escaped her fear. It was like a malicious live thing in her stomach gnawing on her whenever she dared to forget about it.

This couldn't be happening. Not to her.

But the creature in Jill's stomach reminded her that it was indeed happening. And to her.

Jill knew Madeline must have thought the same thing once.

This couldn't be happening. Not to me.
Not-so-mad Madeline in the morgue.

"Do you have a date coming up with Tony?" Quinn asked.

"Not for a while. He's out of town for the next few days and will call me when he gets back. He'll probably want to go out right away. That's the way it usually is." She looked as if she wanted to say something else, then stuttered, "I can't believe—I mean, Tony—"

"I know," Quinn said. "That's the reason deceptions having to do with the heart usually work so well. They're based on undeserved trust. People are susceptible."

Pearl knew he was right. The heart was a fool.

"Invite him over when he calls," Quinn said. "Make sure Jewel is there. Or meet him someplace for lunch and bring Jewel along and introduce her. We want it to seem like you and she are fast becoming thick with each other. A close friend of the intended victim will present a real obstacle to E-Bliss."

"The intended victim . . . ," Jill said. "That's me. That's what I'm having such a hard time believing."

"Madeline didn't believe it at first either. And you didn't believe Madeline."

Jill started chewing her lower lip and looked as if she might begin to cry. Maybe she was reliving her visit to the morgue.

"My suitcase is upstairs," Pearl said, to get Jill's mind on something else, "but I think I'd better stay here with you for an hour or so." She smiled. "There's no reason we shouldn't actually become friends, so we don't have to pretend."

"Just remember to do what Jewel tells you," Quinn said to Jill. "Jewel is very good at what she does, and she has your best interest at heart. She's here to preserve your life."

"I know that. She's here to save me from Tony."

"From anyone, dear. Jewel doesn't discriminate."

Pearl wished he'd get the hell out of there. "Where's Feds?" she asked. Maybe hurry him along.

"He's watching the new Madeline's apartment. We don't want to approach her yet. We don't want to approach anyone prematurely and see a lot of people and evidence scatter and disappear."

Quinn glanced at his watch and stood up from the sofa. "Speaking of disappeared people, I'd better go see if Renz has found any." He smiled. "So to speak." He supposed that would be progress. But learning the identities of people who'd supposedly gone to ground wouldn't reveal whose identities they'd assumed, or that they'd assumed any other identities at all.

But then, sometimes progress was made when it didn't seem so. Sometimes progress fell into your lap. If your lap was in the right place.

"You'll be fine," he assured Jill, as he moved toward the door.

To Pearl: "Leave your cell on, Jewel."

"Always, these days," Pearl said.

35

Quinn and Renz met for lunch at Tavern on the Green, where Renz ate at least once a week, because he was in love with the crème brûlée. They had a table with a view out a window onto Central Park and an array of topiary. A tall shrub that Quinn assumed had been trimmed to resemble King Kong loomed over people negotiating a narrow walkway from a paved area where cabs were dropping off and picking up passengers. Quinn watched a woman in a thin summer dress hold the arm of a very old man in a brown suit as they approached the restaurant's entrance. They resembled each other enough that he figured they were father and daughter, and he wondered what his own daughter, Lauri, was doing right now in California.

"Four people in this area seem to have gone to ground, and for good reason," Renz said. "Of course there must be more, but these four are obvious."

"E-Bliss would want them obvious."

Renz drew a folded sheet of paper from his suit coat pocket. He smoothed it out and propped it on his water glass, keeping his distance so he could read it without his glasses. "Velma Grocci, the wife of mob boss Vin Grocci, cleaned out his bank accounts and ran out on him. Left him a note saying she was never coming back. Not that it would matter much. Vin's facing several life sentences for ordering various murders, including a hit on an undercover FBI agent. Velma's life wouldn't be worth much once hubby went behind the walls."

"Sounds right," Quinn said.

"Iris Klinger, suspected of embezzling half a million dollars from the insurance firm she worked for. She skipped bail and disappeared."

"With the money?"

"Looks that way. Then there's Marti Ogden, recently of the Upper East Side. Marti's a woman. Thirty-year-old daughter of Hart Ogden. She and dad fenced stolen diamonds. Somebody tried to double-cross dad and dad killed him. He's doing twenty-five to life at Elmira. The guy he killed had dangerous friends. We were about to close in on Marti and arrest her for handling stolen property, maybe save her life, when she flew off to Buenos Aires on a chartered flight. No way to know where she went from there, though, if anywhere. We found it odd that she used her real name for the charter. Not smart."

"Maybe," Quinn said.

"Number four is Jocko Lucci. Swindled millions from New Jersey casinos and washed the money here with a chain of pizza joints. Another bail jumper."

"A guy like that made bond?"

"He could afford it. His wife put it up. She died four days after he ran out on her and his bail bondsman. Jocko left a note saying he was leaving the country."

"The wife died how?"

"A bus ran over her on Second Avenue. Thing is, she had time after finding hubby's note to call the law and stop him from leaving, but she waited a whole day and he was gone."

"Or became somebody else," Quinn said.

"That would be the somebody we've got in the morgue, minus head, arms, and legs, and plus a broomstick."

The waiter arrived with crustless, quarter-cut tuna salad sandwiches, but Quinn knew they were only an unimportant prelude to the crème brûlée.

Renz dutifully took a bite of his sandwich. "There've gotta be dozens, maybe hundreds, of other people who've disappeared voluntarily, and the law doesn't get involved," he said, around a mouthful of tuna salad. "Why should it? Nothing illegal's been done. Private detectives are sometimes hired to find these folks, but not with much success. If you know what you're doing or have connections, and the whole wide world to get lost in, you can usually stay lost."

"Yeah, but the runners in this case would figure to be not only in trouble, but high profile, at least to the police or whoever else might search for them."

"We won't stop looking for Marti Ogden, and the Feds won't stop looking for the other three."

"Trouble is, they're somebody else now."

"Trouble is," Renz agreed. He pushed his plate with the sandwich away. He'd had two bites. The healthy part of his meal was over. Time for dessert, even though Quinn hadn't had a bite of his sandwich.

Renz sat up straighter and looked around for their waiter, but didn't see him. Turning his attention back to Quinn, he said, "We've got some information on Victor Lamping. He's thirty-six years old, was born in Baltimore, served in the army in Special Forces in Afghanistan, and was dishonorably discharged four years ago."

"Discharged for what reason?"

"We're working on that, but it's not easy to find out. Special Forces aren't like other military outfits. They've got their own set of rules and it looks like nobody's up to challenging them. Once we contacted the Military Record Center in St. Louis, everyone in the place clammed up. We couldn't even find out anything about Lamping from before he joined the military."

"Well, we know what he's doing these days."

The sun had tracked to a slightly different position. Renz was almost in silhouette now against the expanse of bright window looking out on the green lawn and King Kong. Quinn wished he'd brought his sunglasses in with him.

"How do you plan on playing E.Bliss.org?" Renz asked. "Should we shut them down?"

Quinn was aware that Renz knew better; the politician in Renz needed affirmation that the decision wasn't his alone.

"Not in my judgment," Quinn said. "When we nail them, I want them nailed hard and for good. So far, we don't have anything approaching actual proof. We'll keep watching them while we build our case. The last thing we want at this point is to spook them so they roll everything up and disappear themselves. Jill Clark figures to be their next victim, so we can play for time."

"Agreed," Renz said. "But we wouldn't want the media to discover what we know and when we found out. They'll think we shoulda broke into E-Bliss's offices like Eliot Ness and the Untouchables and gunned everybody down. Make sure you keep the media out of it. Cindy Sellers is all over me every day like chiggers."

"I'll do what I can," Quinn said. "We've been reasonably successful so far."

Renz sat high in his chair again. "Hey, there's our waiter."

He had his arm halfway up to summon the waiter when his cell phone beeped. He dug the phone out of a pocket, flipped it open, and pressed it to his ear and identified himself. His hound-dog expression became even graver as he went to a different pocket with his free hand and got out a black leather-bound notepad. He said, "Uh-huh," and then said it several more times while making notes. Renz thanked whoever had called. He flipped the phone closed so it made a loud snapping sound.

"We've got another victim," he said. "Female. What's left of her was found less than fifteen minutes ago on the Lower East Side."

He tore off the top sheet of paper containing the information from his notepad and handed it across the table to Quinn. He slipped the notepad back in his pocket, then settled down in his chair.

"Round up your team and go," he said. "I'm waiting for dessert."

36

Palmer Stone sat in his office at E-Bliss.org and looked across his desk at Victor Lamping. For the first time, he was worried about his business partner and longtime associate. It wasn't so much anything Victor had done. It was more his behavior. He seemed distant sometimes, distracted. This could be bad for business.

On a table near the office window, a small TV was tuned to local cable news. The volume was muted, but closed-caption lettering appeared at the bottom of the screen. It was all about politics, sports, celebrity name-calling, a man who'd set a hamburger-eating record.

"How do you explain it?" Palmer asked.

He wasn't yet aware that Charlotte Lowenstein's torso had been found. What was the delay? He'd expected the news on TV hours ago.

Victor knew what he was talking about. "I don't explain it," he said. "Gloria and I did our work, including placing the object where it was sure to be discovered. I wouldn't worry. It has to be found soon. It isn't the kind of thing people consciously step over."

Stone's desk chair was located where he could see his reflection in a small framed mirror. He glanced at the suave middle-aged man in the mirror and automatically adjusted his imported silk tie. He always dressed well, leaving his suit coat on in the office, though it was rare that a client or anyone else ever dropped in. Almost all of E-Bliss.org's business was done via the Internet.

His hand came away from the straightened tie knot as he saw the increasingly familiar faraway look transform Victor's eyes. That look seemed to occur off and on during the first few days after a client deletion. Where had Victor gone? He certainly wasn't in the office.

Daydreaming didn't suit Victor, who, like Stone, was a dedicated businessman who let nothing interfere with the pursuit of profit. What Victor and Gloria did in the course of their work for E-Bliss.org was for them simply part of the job. Or so Stone had thought. He hadn't seen Gloria since the Charlotte Lowenstein deletion, but he doubted there was anything different about her behavior. Victor seemed to be another matter.

Stone smiled, making him look like a kindly father on a TV sitcom. "Something bothering you, Victor?"

Victor's attentiveness returned like a lamp switching on. He was back in the here and now. "No. Why do you ask?"

Stone shrugged. "You seem preoccupied lately."

Victor, in some ways a younger version of Stone, smiled like the dutiful son in the same sitcom. "I'm fine, Palmer."

"And Gloria?"

"The same."

"The messy part of the work you two do, it's simply business, Victor. Like a medical procedure. The termination of life, the dissection, and the diversionary act—it's all about money, and nothing else. Of course, I can understand how you might form something like an affection for the deleted client."

"I guard against that from the beginning," Victor said.

"Of course you do. What about Gloria?"

"You'd have to ask her."

"Do you think she might have gotten more involved than she should have with the last client? Charlotte?"

Victor laughed. "Palmer, she's . . . Gloria." He placed his elbows on his knees, leaning forward. "What's bothering you, Palmer?"

"In the kind of work you and Gloria undertake, there are two dangers. One is developing a revulsion for what you must do. The other is getting to like that part of the job too much."

"There's no danger of either of those things happening," Victor said. "Not with me, and not with Gloria."

"Fine," Stone said, sitting back in his leather upholstered executive chair and beaming with satisfaction.

But he'd seen the change of light in Victor's eyes and knew Victor was lying. The question was, who had the problem? Was it Gloria, or Victor? And *what* was the problem—revulsion, or too much attraction?

"Ah!" Stone said.

He was staring at the TV. Local cable news was running the story about another Torso Murders victim. The torso of an unidentified woman had been found only hours ago on the Lower East Side. Palmer knew the police would soon note the similarities of the crime with the other Torso Murders, and they would match at least one of the two bullets removed from in or near the heart with the gun that had killed the previous victims.

Victor was also staring at the TV. "Feel better now, Palmer?"

"Infinitely," Stone said. "Nothing makes me happier than business as usual."

If only Victor were as usual.

37

Quinn decided that sex with Linda Chavesky was better each time. He knew it had to do with trust. They'd both entered the country of lovers cautiously, knowing now there was no turning back. But they were learning and were more at ease with each other every time.

Of course, there were adjustments for each of them to make. Right now, lying next to Linda in his bed, watching the dying light around the blinds indicate the sun was about to set, Quinn would have enjoyed smoking a cigar. He could imagine himself doing that with Linda propped up beside him smoking an after-sex cigarette. But he knew it was only a mental image and would never become reality. Hell, for all he knew, smoking a cigar in bed might have become illegal in New York when he wasn't paying attention.

It hadn't been that long ago when Pearl had lain there beside him in postcoital languor, but it seemed to have happened in another world. It wasn't so much time as it was events that turned life's pages.

Quinn did still think of Pearl as more than simply a colleague who happened to be his former lover. When Pearl had found out about Linda, he'd read something in her eyes. Suddenly, with their romantic relationship supplanted by another for him, a part of her wanted him back. But only a part of her.

Maybe it was always that way with ex-lovers, even after tempestuous relationships. A reflexive thing. The heart refusing to surrender completely a piece of its past. He did love Linda, but he wondered in an abstract way if a part of him wanted Pearl back.

"What are you thinking?" Linda asked.

"That the Yankees should trade for pitching."

"I thought maybe about the latest Torso Murder victim."

Images of corrupt flesh, exposed bone, dried blood, and fecal matter cascaded through Quinn's mind. He went quietly mad for a few seconds.

"I've learned to push that kind of stuff aside," he said.

"Are you happy?"

"About the Yankees?"

She laughed and poked a rigid forefinger between his ribs. It hurt quite a bit.

She nestled deeper in the bed, lying on her side next to him so she could look him in the eye over the arc of her pillow. "Nift is keeping a few things back about the latest torso victim," she said. "He's obviously decided to delay as long as possible before sending the postmortem information along to Renz."

"Then he's probably already sent it to somebody else."

"He has. To Deputy Chief Wes Nobbler."

Quinn knew Nobbler. He was deceptively ambitious and rumored to be bent. As with many such bureaucratic climbers, there was a cult of junior officers who'd hitched their wagons to his star. Nobbler wasn't someone to be taken lightly. "You sure?"

"Yes, but I couldn't prove it."

She fell silent but for the faint sound of her breathing.

Quinn waited, knowing when not to press. That trust

thing. Linda had already stuck her neck way out for him. Would she stick it out even further?

He felt her shift position again next to him on the bed, rustling the mussed sheets and causing the box springs to ping and the mattress to give. She might be stirring with her reluctance to say anything more. She was risking her career for Quinn.

"She wasn't dead when the broomstick stake was inserted," she said.

The images came again, like disjointed snapshots. *Push them aside. Stop the slide show.*

"And it wasn't the same as the last stake," Linda added. "It was like the other, earlier ones, furniture oil and all."

"Was the stake the cause of death?"

"No. She was alive for quite a while after it was inserted."

God! "Did the bullets match?"

"Uh-huh. No doubt they were fired from the same gun used on all the other victims. A twenty-two caliber. Two shots to the heart, but the heart had already stopped."

"The matching broomstick stake, along with the bullets, pretty much leaves out a copycat killer," Quinn said. "But then why the variation with the victim before last, who was penetrated with a different kind of stake?"

"Anal penetration," Linda said.

"I can understand that," Quinn said. "Had to be, because the victim was a man."

"No," Linda said. "I mean with this last victim, the woman, there was anal penetration."

Quinn was surprised. *Another deviation from the usual M.O. But* with *the usual kind of sharpened broomstick stake. And the usual gun.*

And what about the latest victim? The latest chunk of meat lying cold and unidentified in the morgue. Meat that had once been a woman. If Quinn and his team had immediately gone storming after E-Bliss.org, even without the necessary proof to convict, might she still be alive?

Quinn doubted it.

Or convinced himself that he doubted it. If Jill Clark's story was accurate all the way down the line, the machinery leading to the last victim's death had been in place for weeks or longer.

He lay on his back with his fingers laced behind his head staring at the ceiling and trying to make sense of these latest developments. Psychotic killers stricken by compulsion didn't follow the kind of interior script exhibited by the Torso Murderer in any way other than with strict repetition. But in this case there were anomalies. Not a lot of them, but they were significant. The question was, what did they mean?

Almost certainly this latest victim was slain by the same killer, and if accumulating evidence pointed the same way, E-Bliss.org was behind all the murders. Pearl's theory that the sexual mutilations were acts of misdirection, to dupe the police into searching for a standard compulsive psychosexual serial killer, continued to prove out. *Pearl and her canny insights.*

On the other hand, the latest victims had been alive when the stakes penetrated them. They'd suffered long and terribly. The killer had committed acts of ritualistic sadism, exactly like those of a psychotic driven by compulsion. Not like the work of an E-Bliss.org employee, a stone-cold killer simply attending to business, grisly business though it might be.

Quinn had an idea where this latest development might be leading them.

He wished again he could smoke a cigar.

"Two killers acting as a team?" Linda asked.

"That would be my guess," Quinn said.

And that's all it is—a guess.

"I promise you we'll know for sure soon," he added.

Linda leaned over and kissed him on the lips.

"You're the detective."

38

It didn't take long for Pearl, as Jewel, to move into the vacant apartment on the eighth floor of Jill Clark's building. She was in 8G, not exactly above Jill's 7C unit, but close enough. She could get to the fire stairs in a hurry if she had to, and be downstairs and pounding on Jill's door, or kicking it in, within less than a minute. She made a mental note to tell Jill that. It would reassure her.

Pearl had brought everything she thought she'd need. It was packed in a twenty-six-inch rolling suitcase. Almost everything. The only thing not in the suitcase was the folding cot Quinn had given her. It was brand new from a discount store, still in the box. There should be instructions with it.

She unpacked the suitcase, then got the folding cot from its box and looked at it. She saw rolled green canvas, and what looked like aluminum tubes that must be legs. She withdrew one of the tubes and was surprised when another came with it. They were attached by a small metal plate of some kind run through with a bolt or rivet. She fumbled around and soon saw that the two tubes could be separated to form an X. Another of the metal tubes telescoped. Perhaps this was one of the side bars running down each edge of the cot. But how did you get the canvas on the damned thing? The canvas was what she was interested in, what she was going to sleep on. She played with the telescoping tube for a while, trying to figure out how it related to the canvas, until it pinched her finger painfully and she cursed and tossed it down on the rest of the cot's various parts sticking out of the box.

How had all those parts, along with the canvas, ever fit in the stupid box? It didn't seem possible. It *wasn't* possible. It was a trick, so the cot would be impossible to return.

Something white attracted her attention. Directions. She unfolded them and saw that they were in Spanish, also French and German, and some language she didn't recognize. Ah, there was the English part, on the back.

She studied the instructions. They confused her.

Quinn, she thought. Was he trying to mess with her mind, giving her something like this to sleep on? Or was it just his usual insensitivity? Either way, the cot was his idea, so let him put the damned thing together.

She'd go down and talk to Jill Clark. They were supposed to meet at her apartment in—Pearl glanced at her watch—ten minutes.

Without a backward look at the unassembled cot, Pearl headed for the door.

She had to descend only one floor, so she decided to take the stairs. That was the way she'd go if she had to get to Jill's apartment in a hurry, so she might as well familiarize herself with the route.

The stairwell wasn't air conditioned. There were two sets of wooden stairs with rubber treads, with a tiny landing in between so the steps could make their angled turn. Nothing she couldn't negotiate in a hurry. She opened the door to the seventh-floor hall and a noticeable movement of somewhat cooler air.

There was Jill Clark down the hall, in jeans and a yellow T-shirt, just stepping into the elevator.

"Jill!"

But the momentum of her step caused Jill to disappear into the elevator. Pearl wasn't sure if she'd heard.

Pearl hurried toward the elevator. "Jill! It's Jewel!"

The elevator door was closing.

It was almost all the way closed when Pearl looked in and saw Jill staring out at her.

"We were supposed to meet."

Jill looked startled and fumbled with the elevator's keypad to stop the door. Pearl tried to hold the closing door with her hand, but mechanics had taken over and wouldn't be denied. Pearl yanked her hand out of there before she got a finger pressed in the rubber seal.

As the door growled shut, Jill looked out at Pearl with a helpless smile and shrugged. "I'll be right back up."

The indicator above the elevator doors said the elevator was dropping.

Pearl was alone in the hall. She didn't have a key yet to Jill's apartment, so she decided to walk down and stand by the door.

She'd taken two steps when she heard the other elevator door softly rumble open behind her.

She turned around and saw Jill step out into the hall.

Pearl stepped toward her and realized suddenly that this was impossible. There was no way Jill could have ridden the elevator down to the lobby, and then returned on the second elevator. And why would she have taken a different elevator back up?

And why was she wearing different clothes?

Her hair was the same color as that of the woman in the other elevator, and worn in the same style. Her face . . . It wasn't exactly the same, Pearl realized. The first Jill had somewhat broader features, and something about her neck and jaw wasn't quite the same.

Pearl called up the image of the other Jill, commanding

her mind to re-create the woman in fine detail. She was sure the other Jill, smiling helplessly out at her as she seemingly tried to stop the elevator's closing door, but was probably holding in the button to close it, had the same light pattern of freckles along and above the bridge of her nose. Nothing you'd call a flaw. A minor distinguishing feature only a cop would notice.

My God! Even the freckles!

"I saw her," Pearl said.

Jill looked confused. "Saw who?"

"The other you. She was riding the elevator down to the lobby while you were coming up. You had to have passed each other. She must have been in your apartment and seen you approach out the window. Or maybe somebody called from outside and warned her."

Pearl dug her cell phone out of her blazer pocket, then put it back. Too much time had passed. The other Jill would be out of the building and putting distance between it and her. She'd be blocks away within minutes.

Jill had gone pale and was leaning with an arm against the wall.

Pearl steadied her. "It's okay. It was quite a shock to me too, and I'm not even you."

"She must have been learning about me, seeing what was in my refrigerator, my bedroom drawers, maybe trying on my clothes. . . ."

"Maybe stealing some of your clothes."

"I don't think it would be the first time." Jill stood away from the wall and Pearl released her hold on her arm. "A week ago I blamed the dry cleaners for something they lost, something I couldn't find the receipt for. And there've been a few other items, even some jewelry, that seem to have disappeared." She gave Pearl a wan smile. "At least you believe me now."

"Oh, we believe you," Pearl said.

Jill looked around as if suddenly realizing they were in the hall. "C'mon, Jewel. Somebody's liable to overhear us and think we're nuts."

At first Pearl didn't know who Jill was talking to. She almost glanced around. Then she realized she was Jewel and followed Jill down the hall to her apartment.

The door was unlocked.

"She must have left in a hurry," Jill said. "Maybe somebody did call and warn her."

Pearl edged in front of Jill. "Let me go in first."

Jill seemed to resist at first, then moved aside.

Pearl drew her 9mm Glock from its belt holster and used her free hand to push the door almost closed. She motioned for Jill to stay in the hall, and then Pearl was inside.

She was in a modestly decorated living room with cheap or old eclectic furniture. Covering most of the hardwood floor was a threadbare fake Persian rug that was mostly maroon. The blinds on one of the street-side twin windows were angled down, as if someone had been peering between the wooden slats keeping an eye on the street. The blinds on the window next to it were slanted to admit light from above. Sunbeams stenciled angled shadows over everything.

The apartment was quiet. It *felt* empty. But Pearl knew that could be deceptive. People who knew how to hide could be as silent and still as the furniture. With the gun pressed against her thigh, she made her way past a small galley kitchen on her right, then the opened door to a bathroom with chipped gray tile and old but clean white fixtures. There was a bunched plastic shower curtain, pulled all the way open to the faucet side of the claw-foot tub. Nowhere to hide in the bathroom. Pearl continued down the hall to the bedroom.

It was surprisingly large, with a double bed covered with a blue and gray duvet. On the wall near the foot of the bed was a tall chest with some of the wood veneer starting to peel. There was a small TV on a table near the chest. On another wall was a dresser with a mismatched framed mirror. A bench by the windows. The blinds were both half open to admit yellow sunlight. The room was bright. Pearl saw that the closet door was hanging open. A light beige dress, maybe something you'd wear someplace nice, was carefully spread out on the bed.

Pearl approached the closet cautiously, gun at the ready, then parted the clothes.

No one was hiding behind them.

She checked under the bed, the only other place in the room someone might find concealment, and saw only a few dust bunnies. The floor was bare wood in here, too, like the living room floor under the faux Persian rug, only in here there were throw rugs scattered about. Throw rugs. The most dangerous things in a house or an apartment—usually.

Still holding the gun against her thigh, she returned to the living room.

Jill had of course disobeyed her instructions and was standing just inside the door.

"I didn't hear anything," Jill said. "I thought something might have happened to you."

"And you came in so it could happen to you too?"

"It was dumb," Jill said. "I'm sorry." She hung her head like a kid who'd just been admonished.

"Well, that's one reason I'm here, to teach you how not to take risks," Pearl said.

"I'll learn," Jill assured her. "Really I will."

"Did you leave a dress on the bed when you walked out of here? Beige, lacy neckline, sexy?"

"No. I wouldn't have. I'm sure I didn't."

"But it *is* your dress?"

"It sounds like one of mine."

Pearl led her back to the bedroom and showed her the dress spread out on the bed, the closet door hanging open.

"It's mine, all right." She glanced around, angry and scared. "I didn't leave things like this," she said. "She's been here, handling my stuff, wearing my clothes."

"We might have gotten here just in time to save your dress," Pearl said wryly.

"Why would she steal my clothes?"

"Easier to be you if she has some of your clothes. And maybe she wants to hang around the building, even the neighborhood, and let people glimpse her wearing them. Getting people used to seeing her as you. Safe enough, unless you and the other Jill are in the same place at the same time. The people we're after are no doubt careful about that not happening."

Jill sat down on the edge of the bed, just missing the hem of the dress, and slumped staring at the floor. She looked as if she might start crying. Pearl didn't want that, didn't want to waste time with it.

"They're even stealing my clothes," Jill said. "They're stealing *me*. Madeline said I was halfway to nothing already. She was right."

"No, we can change that."

Jill looked up at her with moist eyes. "I believe you. I have to. These people might follow me anywhere. You're the only chance I've got."

"It's not just me, Quinn, and Fedderman," Pearl reminded her. "There'll be undercover cops looking after you every step of the way, Jill. You've got a whole brigade of guardian angels on your side. Angels who know their jobs. Angels with guns."

Jill stared again at the worn hardwood floor. "The only chance I've got," she repeated in a soft and lonesome voice.

Pearl thought she had it about right.

For the next several hours, Pearl stayed with Jill in her apartment and went over instructions Jill was to follow until the case was resolved and she was again safe. Jill was to inform Tony Lake that Jewel, who lived just upstairs, had become her friend. After that, Jewel would be hanging around Jill most of the time when Tony showed up. Maybe Jill would even invite her new friend to dine with her and Tony. The best way for Jill to be safe was for her to get Tony to think she and Jewel had become a pair, the way it was sometimes with women who were best friends. If he suspected anything, let him suspect they were lovers. That would make it even more problematic for E-Bliss.org to murder Jill and try to pass off another woman as Jill Clark. New best friend Jewel would almost certainly notice the differences in the imposter. Short of murdering both women, which would be way too risky, E-Bliss.org would have no choice but to delay the substitution.

That was what Quinn and his team were counting on—delay while they gathered evidence. While they built their case brick by brick into a wall that would fall on and crush E-Bliss.org in a court of law.

It was only when Pearl finally left Jill, to return to her apartment on the floor above, that it struck her.

Which of the two Jills she'd met today was the original?

39

Deputy Chief Harley Renz, potbelly straining the buttons of his white shirt, sat behind his desk looking like an angry Buddha with a basset-hound face. If he kept putting on weight, he'd soon catch up with Nobbler.

Quinn had filled Renz in on the latest developments in the Torso Murders case, and while Renz was reasonably pleased by the progress they'd made, he was seriously ticked off about Wes Nobbler and the leaks from the medical examiner's office.

Renz's office was too warm this morning, reflecting his mood. Sunlight fairly roared through the window, heating up Quinn's vinyl chair, his right arm and shoulder, and one side of his face. The same sunlight was also harsh on Renz's face, emphasizing his mottled, flushed complexion.

There was a lot of dust in the sunlight, as if Renz had just finished beating a carpet. Quinn had to control his breathing to keep from sneezing.

"I expected Nobbler to be a political animal and put the knife in my back," Renz said. "Nobbler's an asshole. But he's a player. What's that little prick Nift doing messing in

Homicide's business? He's a physician, for God's sake! What's he got to gain?"

"Aside from enjoying examining dead women," Quinn said, "he figures to move higher in the bureaucracy. Maybe be the city's chief medical examiner someday."

"He's probably the one dumping information on that Cindy Sellers bitch. Damned woman's a bottom-feeder."

"You're her source," Quinn reminded him.

"It started out that way; then she turned on us."

"But you're still talking to her."

Renz waved a hand dismissively. "I use her, she uses me, and we try to stay ahead of each other."

He leaned back, moving his mottled face out of the sunlight, and took a few deep breaths. Quinn thought he might pop a pill next. If he wasn't taking something for his blood pressure, maybe he should. Renz looked like the definition of an impending heart attack.

"The same gun, different kind of broomstick, vaginal, anal . . . Somebody's screwing with our minds, Quinn."

"That's how Pearl sees it. I think she might have a point. I also think we might have two killers."

Renz wearily rubbed his fleshy features, leaving marks beneath both eyes. "Serial killers don't usually come in pairs."

"But it happens," Quinn said. "A leader-follower kind of relationship. Together they're capable of what neither of them might do individually. And considering E-Bliss, the switch in M.O.s might be part of a diversion to lead us to the assumption that we're looking for a garden-variety psychosexual serial killer."

"I don't see where it'd make much difference to whoever's killing these people whether we're looking for one or two psychos. The murders are part of a business plan, if what this Jill Clark says is true."

"It's true," Quinn said. He told Renz about Pearl coming

face-to-face with the other Jill Clark yesterday in Jill's apartment building.

Renz dry washed his face again with his blunt-fingered hands. "Sometimes I think there are two of everybody," he said.

Quinn didn't know what he meant by that. Probably another reference to two-faced backstabbers in the NYPD. He should know they could be found wherever there was rampant ambition, which was just about everywhere.

"You sure you're set up well enough to protect the real Jill Clark?" Renz asked.

"She's safe as we can make her. Protection around the clock, and Pearl's staying on the floor above, playing the new best friend. We need more information. And we need to link Tony Lake and E-Bliss with the Torso Murders without Jill Clark becoming a victim."

"Sounds like she's ripe for it," Renz said, "considering what you told me about Pearl bumping into the other Jill yesterday."

Quinn heard a series of soft pops. Renz was absently cracking his knuckles. It was a new habit that could soon get on Quinn's nerves. *People do change their habits, sometimes their M.O.s. Maybe this is another Renz.*

"What the hell're you smiling about?" Renz asked.

Quinn hadn't been aware of the slight smile on his face. "Nothing. Nervous reaction, I guess."

Pop, pop went the knuckles.

"What would flush them out," Renz said, "is if they made a play for Jill." Quinn knew that was what he was secretly hoping for. "Unsuccessful, of course. But we need for something to happen before the media learn everything. That'd blow the investigation and we'd all get fed to the wolves."

"Maybe there's a way to hold the wolves at bay," Quinn said.

Renz sat forward again, subjecting himself to the hot sunlight. *Pop, pop.* "Are you about to show me your devious side, Quinn?"

"That's why you hired me."

"One reason," Renz admitted. "Takes one to catch one."

"And know one. Let's give the media a suspect."

Renz's face fell in disappointment. "Hell, I thought of that. Standard operating procedure. Trouble is, we don't have anyone to give them."

"All the better. That way they won't be able to nail anything down. If it's somebody we can't find, they won't be able to find him either and eliminate him as a suspect. It might also lull the real Torso killer into thinking we've gone off on a tangent."

Renz stopped unconsciously cracking his knuckles. "You've obviously given this some thought."

"Uh-huh."

Quinn watched Renz's expression, the Swiss-watch mechanism behind the sad eyes. Renz was figuring the odds and risks and rewards of what Quinn was suggesting, and what it might mean to his career, his relentless climb up the slippery ladder. It took him only seconds to grasp it all. He was shrewd as well as ambitious. It struck Quinn, as it had many times, that Renz was a great politician in a small way.

Renz smiled. "Who've you got in mind? Nift?"

"I wish," Quinn said. "I'm thinking Tom Coulter."

Coulter was a burglar and rapist who had allegedly murdered a single mother and her three young children a month ago in New Jersey. He'd used a kitchen knife on them, leaving his fingerprints on its handle and in the blood of the victims. There was virtually no doubt of his guilt. When police located him and approached with a warrant for his arrest, he shot at them and sped away in a stolen SUV. Neither he nor the vehicle had been seen since.

With the victims in their graves, and the disappearance of the killer, Coulter had pretty much dropped out of the news.

He'd reportedly been spotted here and there, but none of the leads went anywhere.

"Leak to the media that Coulter's suspected of committing the Torso Murders," Quinn said.

Renz began chewing the inside of his cheek, thinking it over. "Think there's enough similarity in M.O.s for them to buy into it?"

"Slash killings in this area—that's all they'll need because they'll be hungry for the story. They'll make Coulter a viable suspect. Rumor will build on rumor. The media will furnish the facts and the credibility."

"We've seen them do that before," Renz said.

"It might shake Coulter loose somehow so we can pick him up, but that'd only be a bonus. The main thing is, it'll generate endless ink and TV babble and take media minds off the real investigation."

"A diversion," Renz said in a pleased voice. "Like the diversion created by E-Bliss."

"Something like that," Quinn said.

"Raw meat thrown to the media wolves so they'll gorge on it and slow down. Chew on each other in their blood feast."

"More like that."

"I like it," Renz said, closing his eyelids and showing some REM movement, as if enjoying the imagery. "In fact, I'll enjoy it."

Thinking no doubt of Cindy Sellers.

40

Victor walked back and forth along Sutton Place, his untucked shirt whipped by the breeze off the East River, his thumbs hooked into the side pockets of his designer jeans. He knew he hadn't actually gone for a pleasant walk, as he'd assured himself. He was pacing. Trying to work off tension that had been building for days.

There were certain thoughts Victor couldn't shake, dreams he couldn't forget. Most of the dreams were about Charlotte Lowenstein. What he and Gloria had done to the poor woman was sick and depraved, but it had, for a while, provided some relief.

Still, Charlotte's death was disturbing to Victor in a way that wouldn't give him peace. He'd never been one to believe the hogwash that dealing out death somehow diminished the dealer. Especially if there was a sound business reason for killing. War, for instance. That was usually a business reason, and we made heroes of people who killed efficiently and in great numbers. The reality was simple. For some people to flourish, others had to die.

That rationale had worked for all of the victims but Charlotte.

As relief, then satiation, was gradually supplanted by reawakening desire, the dreams and dark yearnings returned. It was becoming more and more difficult for Victor to regard Charlotte's death as merely part of a business plan.

But why shouldn't he regard it that way? That was what it was. Victor told himself that repeatedly. One way or another, the E-Bliss.org victim clients were expendable. It was the computer that had decided that. This was the new age of technology, and in a way the dead clients were among the earliest victims of the new technology society. They had to be deleted. What practical difference did it make if he enjoyed ending their lives?

The lion that killed the antelope felt nothing beyond hunger, but did the antelope not suffer and die? What went on in the minds of slayer and slain was irrelevant. That was how the world worked. It was teeming with predators and prey animals, with nothing in between. Only people had their choice. They could become one or the other. Victor had long ago made his choice.

Conscience didn't enter into it.

That was exactly how Victor saw it when it came to the earlier victims, the ones for whom he'd felt little compassion or anything close to sadistic arousal. He was the lion, and they were the antelopes. The world in its turning. The lion did not regret. The lion did not worry.

Still, Charlotte worried Victor. Charlotte in her dying and death was causing him distress. She was the one victim he—and Gloria—had intended to enjoy.

And, God, we did enjoy her!

Gloria deceived her, but we both enjoyed her.

A gray Mercedes sedan turning off East Fifty-sixth onto Sutton Place honked at him, jolting him out of his gloomy self-recrimination.

He waved at the driver in apology for almost stepping off the curb into the car's path, then continued his restless walking.

This isn't like me, what I did to Charlotte, what I'm thinking. It's something I have to shake off or it will control me. And I can shake it off. It isn't me. Not the real me. It isn't.

Victor drew comfort from the fact that he, more than most people, possessed iron self-control.

If only I could sleep without the dreams. . . .

But in truth he knew there was only one thing that would enable him to sleep soundly through the night. It was the one thing that would chase the deep desires roaring through the core of him when he awoke from terrible nightmares in his sweat-drenched bed. That would free him from the persistent thoughts that claimed his daylight hours and prompted him to almost step in front of moving cars. That might someday cause him to make a critical mistake in his work.

Resist though he might, he needed another Charlotte.

Tom Coulter lay on his back in bed in his room at the Clover Motel, ten miles southwest of Hard Oak, Texas. He was a gangly man with raggedly cut black hair and bad teeth. He wore dirt-crusted jeans with a hole in one knee, expensive boots that needed polish, and a shirt unbuttoned to reveal scraggly dark chest hair and prominent ribs. He was perspiring heavily from the heat. He was breathing hard from the heat, too, not to mention the sour smell of his own body, but he was too tired right now to get undressed and shower. He had to rest. He closed his eyes, drew a deep breath, and sighed. Until he'd exhaled, his ribs looked as if they might break through his pale flesh.

In the Clover's gravel parking lot was the dusty green Volvo station wagon he'd stolen in Charmont, Illinois. Its license plate was stolen from a Chevy in a shopping mall in Morristown, Tennessee. Tom had parked it several doors down from his room; if the law came for him, he might have precious seconds to get away.

His jangled nerves made it impossible for him to sleep.

He opened his eyes and watched a fly bumping over and over against the dirt-smeared window, buzzing around and trying to find a way out to the light and freedom. He could identify with that fly. Most likely it wouldn't be alive much longer, but there it was, struggling to break through an invisible barrier like the barrier of lousy luck that had always plagued Coulter and blocked his progress. He would have swatted the fly and put it out of its hopeless misery, only it was too much trouble.

He absently reached to the bedside table and used the remote to turn on the TV. But after a glance at the screen he left the volume low and didn't listen to it. Some kind of commercial about an arthritis drug was on, so what did he care? His mind was still fixed on how he'd gotten here. It was like what he'd heard somebody on TV call a loop, where the same tape kept playing over and over.

None of what happened was really his fault. It was just that his luck had turned bad, and then it was one thing after another.

He'd been surprised in the kitchen by the woman in the house in New Jersey, but the opportunistic Coulter, figuring the shapely woman's presence was part of what the world owed him, simply smiled and told her the facts. He was a professional burglar, and now that she'd disturbed him at his work, it was time for her to undress. It was only fair, he'd explained to her.

She started to unbutton her blouse, started to cry, and that's when her two kids came in. Little bastards; he hadn't heard them at all, so they must have arrived with her and come in through the front door instead of the garage.

That was when his luck began to sour.

He turned around and told the kids to go to their rooms. It wasn't as if he had a gun or any other kind of weapon, so they didn't obey him. Instead they started to cry and looked to their mother for directions. Fat chance there. The bitch was crying too hard to be able to give them the word.

Coulter made a threatening jump toward the kids, yelling for them to shoo, so he could have some brief fun with their mother, then be on his way. Why didn't they move? He had no desire to hurt anyone. Well, mom, a little bit.

That's when everything really went haywire, and in ways he couldn't foresee. Simply shitty luck. It sure as hell hadn't been his fault.

When he moved to give the biggest kid a shove, the kid kind of sidestepped and Coulter stumbled and fell to his knees. The heel of his left hand landed on cookie crumbs or something that was brittle and dug into his flesh so that his hand stung. If it hadn't been for that, he might have noticed what mom was up to.

He was standing up when he heard her, in a new, confident voice, order him to get out—now, and fast. When he looked she was holding a gun she'd got from somewhere, a big blue steel semiautomatic. It made her a different woman. He sure didn't like the look in her eyes. He figured it meant he'd better not mess with her in any way at all.

Coulter was going to leave, and that would have been that. But he'd been too shocked to move. His feet were glued to the floor.

Mom started pulling the trigger, over and over. Coulter was horrified at first, then angry. She had no right to do that. She hadn't given him time to obey her command. He didn't have a chance. He sure as hell would have gotten out of there in a hurry if she'd given him the opportunity. He was a professional burglar and wanted nothing to do with guns. Nothing to do with violence of any kind. Whatever happened from here on out, it was on her and not him.

It was a good thing the gun was old and kept jamming.

He figured it wouldn't be long before it did go off, the way she kept pulling on the trigger; not squeezing, like you were supposed to, just clenching the thing tight and pulling so her bent forefinger went white on the unmoving trigger. Something seemed to be blocking it from moving. Maybe the safety was on. Maybe she'd figure it out any second and blow his brains out.

Maybe it wasn't too late to get out and away. He ran for the door, but he had to pass close to the woman to get there. When he pushed her aside, she must have thought he was attacking her. Bad luck again, for both of them.

She started hitting him with the gun, a couple of times on the side of the head, really hurting him. Retaliating in a way that any *fair* judge or jury would say was self-defense, he wrapped an arm around her neck and wrestled her to the ground, trying to get the gun away from her.

Then damned if the two kids didn't jump on him. He figured they must not have liked him attacking their mother, not knowing *she'd* attacked *him*. Coulter guessed you couldn't blame them.

The biggest kid, a boy about eleven, found a full can of root beer somewhere and started slamming it into the back of Coulter's neck. That distracted Coulter enough so that mom managed to get out from under him and grab a drawer handle so she could pull herself up.

But the drawer slid all the way out of the cabinet. Crash and clatter, and there were knives all over the floor.

Coulter snatched one up before anyone else could and started hacking and slicing away, yelling as if he'd lost his mind, which he guessed he had, for a while. But he was fighting for his life. He had no choice, and there were three of them and only one of him. Not a fair fight.

Then he was standing there holding the big, wood-handled kitchen knife he'd picked up with blood all over him, all over the floor. All over mom and the kids. It was the most unreal thing Coulter had ever seen.

Everything stopped. Time crawled, like in a bad dream. Nobody was moving, not even Coulter.

He noticed that he was the only one not dead.

The kids had so much blood on them he couldn't tell

where they were cut or stabbed. Mom had a deep gash from ear to ear. The way her eyes and mouth were wide open, it looked as if the knife blade had surprised her. Or maybe she'd died struggling to breathe.

The knife slipped from his hand and bounced on the floor.

Real time again:

Move! Move! Move!

Coulter got out of there, leaving the bloody knife behind.

Coulter had made it home to his apartment, back in the city, and showered and cleaned up. It was still almost like a dream. But he knew he had to move and keep moving, get far away, sort things out.

Coulter was wrestling his big suitcase out of the closet, so he could pack a lot of things in a hurry, when the police showed up.

He knew exactly what to do. Coulter never lived anywhere without a prepared exit route and a plan to go with it. He left everything as it was, set his bed on fire, and climbed the fire escape up to where he could reach the roof. From that roof he made it over a thick wood plank to the adjoining roof, let himself in through the service door, and took the elevator to the lobby. He already knew about the side exit.

Within five minutes of the knock on his door, he was making himself walk slowly toward where he'd parked the SUV he'd stolen for the trip he was planning.

He had to hand it to the cops. They'd spotted him somehow, but by that time the fire department had started to arrive with its equipment in response to the fire in his apartment. There was a lot of activity and confusion. After he pulled away in the SUV, a squad car followed him for a few blocks, but he shot at it, knowing there'd be no return fire on the crowded streets. He didn't know if he'd hit the driver, or maybe disabled the car, but it pulled to the curb. After turning the corner, Coulter drove a few more blocks, then ditched the SUV and lost himself in the mass of people in Manhattan.

After that, no problem. He stole another car—another big SUV, because he liked them—and was on his way out of town.

He'd overcome his bad luck.

There were lots of stories about Coulter after that, in the papers and all over TV. And not just New York papers and television.

He'd have kind of enjoyed the stories if they were true, only they made him out to be the bad guy. Still, he was famous. And for now he was free. He might even stay free, if only he could get to Mexico. That border had to be easy to cross in both directions, right? The government had never been able to stop the Mexicans from getting into the country, so he oughta be able to get out. When he got to Mexico, he could turn bad luck into good.

After a while, whenever he'd switched on the TV or bought a New York paper, there wasn't much being said or written about him. He had to admit he kind of resented that. He was supposed to be famous, right? What did it matter how he'd become a celebrity? You were one or you weren't.

He was one.

Not that he wanted any paparazzi around.

He didn't want to be a dead celebrity, or one spending his life in prison.

Now here he was at the Clover Motel, half watching a trapped fly at the window and half listening to a cheap little TV near the foot of the bed.

Mexico figured to be his best chance. He could even speak a little—

"... Tom Coulter, who murdered a suburban woman and her two children in New Jersey. In other news ..."

Huh?

He grabbed the remote from the bedside table and ran up the channels until he found another cable news network.

There he was! There was his photograph!

It was an old mug shot, one where the camera had caught him by surprise with his mouth open so you could see his bad teeth. His hair looked greasy and all messed up over one ear, too. *Like it was combed with an eggbeater,* his mother used to say. He wished they'd used another photo.

A voice from the TV said, "New York police confirmed today that wanted multiple murderer Thomas Coulter, who fled when police attempted to arrest him at his apartment, is suspected of being responsible for the Torso Murders that have terrorized the city and baffled law enforcement officials for weeks."

Holy Jesus!

How'd they come up with that? Was it some kind of trick?

No, he knew it wasn't a trick. He knew how the police worked, and it wasn't that way.

Of course, Coulter knew about the Torso Murders. They were national news.

And now I'm national news again.

The big stage.

The cops might have it wrong—big surprise. But I'm already wanted for three murders, so what's the difference? They sure as hell aren't gonna look for me any harder.

Cable news moved on to another story, then a commercial about some kind of vitamin supplement for dogs and cats.

Coulter was safe here, but he couldn't leave for a while, what with all the new publicity. Though he wasn't too worried about the photo, since it looked so little like him.

Sometimes a bad rap could have its advantages. Soon they'd be saying he was famous. Or infamous. Whatever. He knew there really wasn't any difference. His bad luck could be like good luck here.

Firmly back in the pantheon of celebrities, Coulter smiled.

His nerves were tingling too much for him to continue just lying there in bed, thinking wild thoughts and staring at a goddamned loser fly on the window. He should think of other things, give his mind a rest so his body could rest, too.

Why should dogs and cats need vitamin supplements? Wild animals never take them, and they do just fine.

You have to watch out for everything and everybody. Every goddamned thing in life is a racket.

The celebrity got up and paced.

Quinn and Fedderman entered the West Side brick building where Madeline had had her apartment. They did so separately, figuring someone other than the undercover cop at a well-concealed observation post across the street might be watching.

The undercover had reported there'd been no sign of the new Madeline for four days. During that time, the lights in her apartment windows never came on at night. And there still was no sign of anyone else observing the building, which of course might only mean that the somebody else was very skilled at his or her job.

Maybe the new Madeline was away on a visit somewhere, or maybe she'd moved out. Either way, Quinn figured it was time to take a look.

It would have been easy to see the super, flash their shields, and gain entry into the apartment, but there was always the possibility the super might talk.

Quinn and Fedderman met in the hall at the apartment door. Quinn, first in the building, had already tried to call up on the intercom from the lobby and hadn't gotten a reply. Still, they knocked and waited before going in.

Since the apartment was unoccupied, the door wouldn't be locked from the inside, and Fedderman was one of the best at using a lock pick. He had the door open and them in the apartment within three minutes.

Though the place was furnished, it was almost immediately obvious to a cop's eye that no one lived there. A thin layer of dust was visible on all the wood surfaces. It was hot, since the air conditioner wasn't running. There wasn't a sound that didn't filter in from outside, not even the refrigerator motor. The apartment even smelled empty.

Most of the furniture looked cheap, and what didn't look cheap was in some way damaged. There was a big pressed-wood combination bookcase, desk, and TV hutch along one wall. The books were all hardcovers without dust jackets and looked as if they'd been passed unread from tenant to tenant for years.

Quinn started with the living room. Fedderman began in the bedroom, and they worked toward each other. They looked in empty drawers and empty closets, in cabinets that held nothing other than roach traps, wadded rags, or empty cleaning or insecticide containers.

They searched for hiding places: inside light switch plates, the toilet tank, top closet shelves, beneath sofa and chair cushions, behind drapes, the outside backs of dresser drawers (a favorite place for people to tape envelopes and small packages that allowed the drawers to close all the way). They found nothing.

The refrigerator held very little: a few frozen dinners, an almost empty orange juice carton, and a withered tomato. A kitchen wastebasket, already emptied, yielded a week-old cash receipt from a deli in the neighborhood. It had been stuck to the bottom in something that had spilled there long ago. The receipt was for $9.63 and it wasn't itemized. Unhelpful.

When Quinn and Fedderman stood in the small galley kitchen, the final room of their search, Fedderman leaned back against the sink with his arms crossed and said what they both knew.

"The new Madeline's moved out."

"And moved clean," Quinn said. "This place might as well have been scrubbed by a pro."

"There'll be fingerprints," Fedderman said.

Quinn shook his head. "They won't do us much good. She wouldn't have been an E-Bliss client if her prints were on file."

"We should have had her tailed whenever she left here," Fedderman said.

Quinn shook his head again. "We've got only so much manpower, Feds."

"The same old story. We need one cop for every dishonest citizen."

"One honest cop," Quinn said.

"Renz is gonna be plenty pissed off."

"Like I am," Quinn said.

41

It seldom took Pearl long to become a pest, and here it was her job.

Tony Lake stood up from the corner table in Raissen's and showed his consternation for only a second when he saw Jill walk in with Pearl. Then his customary radiant smile flashed across the room to the two women.

The tuxedoed maitre d' spoke for a few seconds with Jill, then unnecessarily swept an arm to direct her and the other woman across the exclusive and isolated restaurant. Raissen's hadn't been open long. It occupied the entire top floor of a midtown office building. There were several color-coded rooms. This was the red room, open only for lunch. It had red tinted crystal chandeliers trailing oval rubies, was carpeted in deep red, and had white tablecloths edged in red. Dark red drapes framed a dazzling view of Manhattan Island and beyond. Like the other rooms in the restaurant, it featured genuine silver settings and cut crystal.

Supposedly just back in town, Tony was expecting only Jill, and he was planning on entertaining her and perhaps taking her back to his apartment while hers would be available for other purposes. The time of client substitution was fast approaching, and everything had seemed to be going smoothly, until just now.

"This is my good friend Jewel," Jill said, with a big grin. "We were supposed to meet for lunch today. I forgot all about it when you called. I didn't think you'd mind if I brought her along."

Good friend. Words Tony didn't like hearing.

He saw a short, slim-waisted woman in her late thirties or early forties with raven black hair and dark eyes. She was smiling at him with large, perfect teeth. It took some effort to keep his gaze from straying toward her prominent breasts, made more noticeable by the tight tan blouse she wore. It was fashioned of some kind of knit material and tucked into faded form-fitting designer jeans. Here was a woman, he thought, who was fully assembled.

Tony extended his hand and she shook it with a light, dry touch that somehow suggested considerable strength. She played sports, he figured, or worked out.

"Wouldn't want you to be stood up," Tony said amiably, motioning for Jewel to sit down. She sat on the opposite side of the table, leaving the chair directly across from Tony for Jill. Tony waited until they were both seated before settling down again in his chair and replacing the red napkin in his lap.

A waiter, wearing a tux with a red cummerbund, promptly came over and they ordered drinks. Tony stayed with the scotch and water he'd been sipping; Jill and Jewel both ordered sour apple martinis. Tony tried not to wince.

"So where'd you two meet?" he asked when the waiter had left.

"Would you believe the laundry room in my building?" Jill said.

"If you say it, I believe it."

"It's a creepy place," Jewel said. "Down in that dim basement. It wouldn't hurt if the super put some brighter bulbs down there."

"It would make it safer," Tony said.

Jewel gave a mock shiver and Tony couldn't help but glance at her breasts. "We were both down there at the same time doing a load of wash, so we were glad for each other's company. Jill—or maybe it was me—struck up a conversation, and we found out we have a lot in common."

"What would that be?" Tony asked. "Other than the obvious."

"Obvious?"

"That you're both beautiful."

Jill laughed a few seconds before Jewel. Tony didn't think Jewel seemed to feel as complimented. With her looks, she probably heard a lot of bullshit from a lot of men. She gave the impression she could handle it.

"Beauty aside," Jewel said, "we both came from the Midwest. And we haven't been very long in New York, so we don't know many people. Jill's promised to show me around, and maybe I'll sign up with Files and More so I can earn some money while I'm trying to land something permanent."

"It's a tough town at first," Tony said. "Then you learn to like it."

"Especially if you meet someone like Tony," Jill said.

Pearl had to admire that, especially the sincerity in Jill's voice. But she hoped Jill wouldn't do too much improvisation. This guy Tony didn't strike Pearl as dumb in the slightest.

The waiter came back carrying their drinks on a round silver tray. Talking was suspended while he placed the drinks around the table, as if talk might upset some delicate balance and liquid might slosh over a rim.

Tony knew the addition of Jewel as a new friend had considerably upset the replacement process. Jewel would have to be dealt with in some way. Apparently she'd already become a close friend and confidante, so she'd certainly realize any replacement Jill was a phony. Tony was sure Jewel was the only person in the building who'd had more than passing contact with Jill. Without Jewel, the game was on. Jewel was an obstacle.

Of course, something could happen to Jewel.

But wouldn't that put Jill's apartment building under police scrutiny? Either way, if the police suspected foul play they'd question Jill. Who might mention Tony.

It was a problem, all right.

Tony raised his scotch and water and suggested a toast.

"To the three of us," he said.

Their glasses clinked. They smiled at each other and drank.

Tony thinking something would have to be done to take Jewel out of the game.

Pearl settled into her new identity smoothly. It was made easier because she actually liked Jill Clark. Tony Lake, so far, hadn't proved difficult. He seemed obviously resentful of the women's close friendship, but no more so than any man whose lover had suddenly acquired a new best bud. One who was a rival for his time and turned up as an obstacle whenever he planned on getting intimate with the object of his love. Or with his target.

Jill, mostly running on instincts, also sometimes seemed actually resentful of Pearl's presence. Tony was good at his job; Pearl had to give him that. Jill knew who he was and what he was, but it was impossible sometimes to *feel* what he was. The Tony she saw on the surface could be disarming and deadly charming.

It seemed increasingly obvious to Pearl that Tony was not only wickedly intelligent but also had no scruples whatsoever. She wondered if, for strategic reasons, he might go behind Jill's back and make a pass at Jewel. Pearl, being Jewel, saw that as a potential problem.

Since she and Jill were spending so much time together, Pearl liked to keep Jill talking, thinking maybe some new piece of information might be mentioned that would aid in the investigation. Most of the time, when Tony wasn't around, Jill wound up talking about Madeline Scott. She was obviously still haunted by Madeline's death and maybe felt guilty that she hadn't believed Madeline's story at first. If she had, she might have been able to help in some way that would have prevented Madeline's death.

Pearl didn't think that was true, and whenever Jill began blaming herself, she talked her out of her depression. Madeline died because she knew too much. Nothing would have saved her. But something could still be done to save Jill, and a lot of women who'd follow, if E-Bliss.org could be shut down—and in a way that would prevent it from opening somewhere else under another name and resuming its chain of murders and ultimate identity thefts.

Maybe it was all the talk about Madeline that gave Pearl the idea of visiting Madeline's apartment. Jill had supposedly seen the new Madeline in the elevator, but in Jill's state of mind, that might not have been true. Pearl knew how the imagination could work. It could make you see what you expected to see. That was the problem with eyewitness accounts.

Like Jill's.

Jill had just gotten a temporary work assignment as a receptionist for a dental clinic, filling in for a vacation, so for at least a week she'd be away working every day. Jill would be protected there by the undercovers Renz had managed to get assigned to the investigation.

That would leave Pearl with not much to do other than hang around her apartment as Jewel. She had instructions not to go near Jill's apartment when Jill was out. Quinn wanted to make sure it was available for E-Bliss.org. It wouldn't do for its imposter to find Pearl there doing her Jewel act, and making up an implausible reason for her presence.

Pearl was going crazy with all the inaction, so why not make use of her time?

Wednesday morning, she left the apartment to hail a cab. A light summer drizzle was falling. It wasn't much of a rain, but enough to make the cabs go into hiding. Pearl walked in the direction she wanted to ride and soon ran across a side-walk vendor selling umbrellas for five dollars. She paid up and stayed reasonably dry while she walked another two blocks and finally managed to flag down a cab. She felt things going her way; less then ten minutes and she'd scored a double, ob-taining the two most precious items when it rained in Man-hattan: an umbrella and a cab.

Maybe she'd stay lucky. Though Madeline had moved out, there still might be something to be gained from looking over the vacant apartment again, and talking to the neigh-bors again.

She told the cabbie to drive her to an intersection that was within a block of Madeline's apartment.

"You think this Jewel is a cop?" Palmer Stone asked, star-ing out his office window at the light rain.

"It's possible, but I doubt it," Victor said. He was leaning back in the chair in front of Stone's desk, his legs straight out in front of him with his ankles crossed. "I think she's just a meddling bitch who turned up at the wrong time. She needed a friend, there was Jill Clark, and she attached her-self to Jill like a leech."

"Sounds kind of intense. You get the idea it might be wearing off? That Jill doesn't really like her around?"

"Sometimes. Especially when we want to screw. Jewel's timing seems to be perfect when it comes to preventing Jill and me from being alone together at a time or place where we might be intimate."

"Hmm. Some kind of lesbian thing, do you think?"

"That's the most likely explanation," Victor said. He prided himself on understanding women and he'd thought about this situation. "I'm sure Jill doesn't suspect it. Hell, maybe even Jewel doesn't realize it. You know how it works, Palmer. Latent sexual attraction neither woman wants to admit. I don't think it'd ever get to the point where they'd get it on together. The two of them might be shocked if they figured it out."

"You might tell Jill about it. Suggest that this Jewel has intimate plans for her."

"Not a good idea, Palmer. She probably wouldn't believe it, and we'd be risking turning both of them against me."

Stone sighed, dug his heels into the office carpet, and maneuvered his wheeled swivel chair away from the gloom outside the window. "Well, you're the expert on that part of the business."

As he had often lately, Victor found himself thinking about what he could do with Jewel if he had her like Charlotte. How she'd struggle against the tape that bound and silenced her, how she'd try to scream, how her dark eyes would widen when she saw the stake, how she'd—

"We might simply have to make Jewel expendable," Stone said, as if reading his thoughts. "If she might swing both ways, maybe we should introduce her to Gloria."

"No, not that," Victor said. "It'd be bad business. Anything that happens to Jewel might lead the police to Jill. Maybe even, later on, to the new Jill."

Stone turned his swivel chair back toward the gray rain. The usually silent rotating mechanism squealed softly, maybe because of the humidity. "I see the problem, but we're running out of time."

"Don't worry," Victor said. "I'll think of something."

Palmer Stone smiled at his business partner's blurred reflection in the window.

"You always do, Victor. You have imagination."

42

Renz was pacing his office grinning. Quinn wasn't sure he liked seeing the commissioner so pleased. It usually meant trouble. A steady drizzle from a leaden sky obviously wasn't the reason for Renz's good humor. The diffused light from the wet window, along with the pale glow of the desk lamp, gave Renz's sagging features a grayish cast. Now and then the long shadows from the raindrops crawling down the glass pane made him appear to be crying, his grin a grimace.

Quinn sat casually in one of the upholstered chairs near the desk and watched and waited.

"The media sure as hell bought into it," Renz was saying. "Every time you turn on the TV news, every time you pick up a newspaper, you see that shit-heel Coulter. He's on CNN, FOX News, everywhere."

"He oughta be getting nervous," Quinn said.

"It's bought us some time, just like you said." Renz suddenly looking serious, stopped pacing, and turned to face Quinn. "Now we've gotta make use of that time. What are our alternatives?"

So Renz is in his officious mood this gray morning.

Quinn knew how to deal with that. "Alternatives are several," he said. "My belief is that our best bet is to continue with Pearl playing Jill Clark's new friend Jewel, maybe force E-Bliss's hand."

"It's a damned dangerous game," Renz said.

Quinn wondered whether Renz remembered that he, Renz, had approved the strategy. "Everything about this case is dangerous."

Renz crossed his arms and nodded, as if approving of Quinn's answer. Then he said, "It could backfire. If either Pearl or Jill is killed."

"Or both of them," Quinn said.

"Christ! If that happened the media'd blame us for their deaths. They'd bury us. Don't doubt that for a moment."

Quinn didn't. "The way it works," he reminded Renz, "is it would be too dangerous for E-Bliss to kill both of them, and too dangerous to kill Jill with Pearl still around as Jewel. And it would be senseless to kill Jewel first, because it might draw suspicion if they later killed Jill."

"Sounds complicated," Renz said.

Quinn couldn't deny it. "It's like bombers flying in formation so enemy fighters can't attack one without drawing fire from the others."

Renz stood still and thought about that one. Quinn knew he watched hours and hours of old World War Two documentaries on the History Channel.

"I guess it makes sense, when you put it that way, but I still get the feeling we oughta move while we can nail some of these jokers."

"We still don't have much in the way of hard evidence," Quinn reminded him. "No identifiable victims, no solid connections between E-Bliss and their clients who've been killed—mainly because we don't know the identities that have been stolen. Surely E-Bliss has washed their files of any hint that they did business with the murdered women. Madeline Scott's the only name we've got, but now she's disappeared."

" '*She* being the new Madeline Scott?"

Quinn nodded, wishing Renz would stop playing the executive cop.

"All that client information's gotta be in their computers," Renz said. "They're a high-tech outfit."

"If everything incriminating hasn't been deleted yet, it will be at the first sign of trouble. And like you said, they're a high-tech outfit. They'd know how to actually destroy the evidence."

"What if we busted in there fast and confiscated everything?"

"Even if we could get a warrant, which I doubt, the computers might be set up to delete on seizure. There are lots of possibilities for built-in safeguards: destruction of files if the wrong password is used or the wrong fingerprint ID, or if the location of the computer is changed, or if a code number has to be fed in every so many hours so the files won't automatically be destroyed, or Stone might be able to send a signal some way we haven't thought of."

"Who knows what we'd find if we were successful, though," Renz said, undeterred by mention of all the potential tech catastrophes.

"I'm more afraid of what we wouldn't find. If nothing incriminating turned up, they'd know we were after them and every piece of potential evidence and everyone involved with E-Bliss would disappear. Then we'd be left with Jill Clark's unlikely story that she heard from a woman now dead, some unidentifiable torsos, and suspects who are on the wind. Nothing times three." Quinn said. Then he added, "Jill's all we have that could turn into something solid. They're not suspicious yet. They'll make some kind of play, some kind of mistake. Jill and Pearl put us in position to take advantage of it."

"You forgot to mention the new Madeline. She could be the key to this."

"If we could find her," Quinn said.

* * *

It had stopped raining by the time Pearl climbed out of the cab less than a block away from Madeline's apartment. This was the same unit the new Madeline had taken over after the death of the real Madeline Scott, and then recently abandoned.

Pearl watched the cab drive away down West Seventy-second Street, then stop near the next corner and pick up a man waving his half-closed umbrella like a signal flag. She stood for a moment getting her bearings and setting straight in her mind what she planned to do.

She decided to have the super let her into the vacant apartment. After looking it over, she'd talk to some of the neighbors. Since the new Madeline was gone from the building, she could identify herself as NYPD and maybe open some minds.

Quinn and Fedderman had gone over the place, as well as a CSU team, but Pearl knew it wouldn't hurt to look again. If nothing else, it might make this whole thing seem more real. The truth was, sometimes when she saw Jill and Tony Lake together, how devoted and seemingly enchanted Tony seemed, the horror that was behind it all was damned hard to accept.

But isn't that the way confidence artists work? Haven't I seen it over and over again?

It's real, all right, and doubting it can cost Jill Clark her life. Can cost me my life.

She breathed in warm, humid air that smelled fresh after the rain; held the still-folded umbrella in her right hand; and strode down Seventy-second toward the apartment building.

As she walked, she pulled her cell phone from her pocket and called Jill at her temporary job. Since going undercover as Jewel, Pearl had a different cell phone and number, registered to a Jewel Karsdan. Lies within lies. Like life itself.

Seeing Pearl's number on her cell phone display, Jill answered immediately. "Jewel? Is everything okay?"

"That's what I called to ask you," Pearl said.

"Yes, everything's normal here. Other than the job's boring as hell."

"Boredom we like," Pearl said.

"If you say so."

"Let me know if you leave early."

"I will, but it doesn't seem likely."

"Remember, your guardian angels are around, even if you don't see them."

"I appreciate that, really." A beat. "It's so hard to believe all this. I feel like a character in some kind of mystery novel."

"Tell me about it," Pearl said and broke the connection.

She was almost to the building entrance when she saw a blond woman wearing a lightweight white raincoat emerge and trot gracefully down the shallow steps to the street. She was clutching a large black leather purse tight to her side. There was something familiar about her, but only vaguely.

She turned and walked toward Pearl.

As the woman drew closer, Pearl's flesh began to crawl. She'd seen the sketches and the morgue photos of Madeline Scott.

When they were twenty feet apart, Pearl knew.

This woman *was* Madeline Scott.

Pearl put on her poker face and hoped her heart wouldn't hammer its way out of her chest. She and the woman exchanged the briefest of glances as they passed each other. Pearl didn't break stride as she listened to the receding *tap, tap* of the new Madeline's high heels on the damp pavement.

The sound faded.

One thousand, two thousand, three thousand . . .

Pearl casually turned around and began to follow the woman.

Victor graciously lent the woman his umbrella. Of course, Victor went with it.

He and the woman shared the large black umbrella until the cool drizzle that had been falling all morning became a fine mist and then stopped altogether.

"We're here," he said, folding his umbrella and smiling at the woman. Not that they'd had a common destination.

They and the rain had happened to stop simultaneously near a Village restaurant that had outside tables beneath a canvas awning. The metal tables and chairs were dry. Only a few of them were occupied.

The woman, a theatrical costume designer named Ruth Malpass, smoothed back her bouncy short brown hairdo, now limp from the rain and humidity, and took a closer look at the man with the umbrella. He appeared to be somewhere in his thirties and had regular, handsome features, eyes of an almost indeterminate color that seemed to reflect surrounding hues, and was nicely dressed in obviously expensive pleated brown slacks and a lighter tan pullover shirt with a collar. His medium-length brown hair was neatly combed. His wristwatch, she noticed, was a stylish and expensive Movado, and his shoes were rich-looking brown loafers.

Look at their wristwatch and shoes. That's what Ruth's mother had always told her. That was the way to judge a man's wealth and style.

Ruth had taken the advice to heart and it had served her well during her year in New York. A small, slender woman with large brown eyes and a long neck, she looked like a scaled-down high-fashion model. Ruth attracted plenty of men, and she preferred them to be at least solvent. If their watch and shoes were of good quality, usually so was their bank account. Not that Ruth was in it only for the money. But there were so many men to choose from, why not make money one of the criteria?

"Two of you?" a smiling waiter with a towel over one arm and a pad and pencil was asking.

"Definitely," the handsome man said. He really did have a charming smile.

"Why not?" Ruth said, trying to match the smile.

The waiter ushered them to a table near the black iron railing that defined the outdoor section of the café and took their drink orders. Handsome asked for a Jack Daniel's on the rocks. It was early for alcohol, but Ruth again asked herself, why not? She ordered a whiskey sour.

"I'm Vlad Novak," Victor said, offering his hand.

Ruth noticed the gold ring (not a wedding ring) and manicured nails. She shook his hand and smiled. "Ruth," she said.

"Got a last name?"

"We'll see."

The charming smile again. She had to admit it got to her. The light was such that she could see her twin reflections in his eyes.

"Vlad's an unusual name," she said.

"Short for Vladimir. It's an old family name, from when my grandfather emigrated here from Yugoslavia."

"Isn't there a baseball player named Vladimir?"

"There is," Vlad said. "And a good one. Vladimir Guerrero."

The waiter arrived with their drinks, and two vastly oversized menus in black leather folders.

"It's not too early," Vlad said. "Should we make it lunch?"

"We'll see," Ruth said again. Trying to hit the right note and not sound too coy. She didn't want to signal any kind of a turnoff here. *Testing, testing.* She fully intended to have lunch with this prize that had fallen into her lap.

The waiter glanced at Vlad.

"Leave the menus," Vlad told him.

Ruth's heart grew a few sizes.

"I'll give you time to decide," the waiter said. He laid the menus on the table and retreated. Ruth got the definite impression he was rooting for Vlad.

Vlad lifted his glass, and Ruth mirrored his action.

They drank. Smiled at each other.

Ruth found herself flushed with a desire she hoped didn't show. She searched uneasily for words. "Funny how things can just happen. I mean, you politely offered the use of your umbrella, and here we are."

"Into each life . . . ," Vlad said.

". . . A little rain must fall," she finished.

Vlad widened his smile.

"And then," he said, "the sunshine."

43

Pearl followed the new Madeline toward Columbus Avenue. The clouds that had produced rain were in the distance now, and the sun shone brightly. The day was beginning to heat up to summer intensity, New York becoming a concrete kiln.

Keeping well back from the figure ahead in the white raincoat, Pearl dug her cell phone from her pocket as she walked. She felt rather than looked at the keypad as she punched out Quinn's number.

He answered after the third ring. "Yeah, Pearl?"

"I'm following the new Madeline along West Eighty-third Street, headed west toward Columbus."

"Say again."

"You heard me."

"How'd that come to be?" Quinn asked.

"Long story. Short version is I was on my way to her apartment to look around then check again with the neighbors. I saw her coming out of the building, and I'm on her."

"She see you?"

"Not since I started following her; we passed on the sidewalk before I turned around and began the tail."

"Since she's seen you once, she might make you," Quinn said. "We can't have that. I'll get Feds to take up the tail."

"She's wearing a long white raincoat made out of some kind of lightweight material. Got on white jogging shoes, fairly new looking."

"Hold on a minute."

Pearl continued walking, the cell phone still in her hand, keeping her gaze fixed on the figure in white half a block ahead. The new Madeline had slowed to a relaxed kind of saunter. Pearl, who usually walked fast, had to make herself slow to the pace. Still, with her eyes and her mind trained on the woman ahead, she tended to graze people coming from the other direction if they didn't veer away from her.

She bumped into a woman who said "Scuse you." Pearl didn't bother to answer. No time for smart-asses.

The white raincoat slowed, then broke away from the cluster of pedestrians it had been moving with along the sidewalk. The new Madeline entered a building with a white-trimmed green canopy shielding stalls of what looked like bunches of cut flowers.

Pearl crossed the street to get a better angle of vision, then drifted down the block about a hundred feet and stood near the doorway of an electronics shop. She saw that there was produce as well as flowers in the stalls across the street. The new Madeline had entered a deli. It was two doors up from the corner, and it didn't look as if there'd be a side door she might slip out of unseen.

Pearl realized she was sweating heavily, from the rising temperature and from the tension of tailing the new Madeline.

Some business. Not like guarding a bank that was last robbed sixteen years ago.

She raised her cell phone to her ear.

"She just went into a deli on West Eighty-third near Columbus," Pearl said.

"Stay on her," Quinn's voice said on the phone. "Feds is

on the way. If she stays in the deli a while, maybe he can pick her up there."

Pearl moved back a few feet and leaned against a show window displaying various kinds of DVD players on sale. She began to breathe easier.

"Pearl?" Quinn's voice came over the phone.

"Yeah?"

"Stay on the phone."

" 'Kay."

Within a few minutes, the figure in white emerged from the deli. The new Madeline fidgeted with an object held in both hands, then tossed something small into a trash receptacle and raised whatever she was holding to her mouth. It was obviously a container of some kind of drink.

After two sips, the new Madeline began to walk.

"She's moving," Pearl said. "Still west toward Columbus. Looks like she bought some sort of drink. She's sipping as she goes. Not walking nearly as fast." Watching the woman she was tailing take another drink, Pearl realized she was thirsty herself.

"Stay on her. Be careful."

"I've got both those things going," Pearl said.

"She must have been visiting her old apartment," Quinn said. "Maybe she forgot something."

"Whatever," Pearl said. "Let's hope she's going to where she lives now."

"She will sooner or later," Quinn said.

The new Madeline began to slow and gaze into shop windows as she sipped her drink. Pearl swallowed dryly and dropped farther back. She didn't want to be glimpsed as a reflection in a window.

"Uh-oh," Pearl said.

"What?" Quinn's voice.

"She just went into a jewelry shop. Doesn't look like the kind of place that'd have another exit, but maybe I should get closer."

"If you—"

"No. Wait. She's out. She's moving. I guess she just ducked in to check on the price of something that caught her eye."

"Just make sure what catches her eye isn't you," Quinn said.

Pearl kept the cell phone stuck to her ear, but neither she nor Quinn spoke for the next few minutes.

Then Quinn said, "Feds just called on the landline. He's got her. Get out of there and go back to being Jewel."

" 'Kay." Pearl broke the connection and slid the phone back into her pocket. She didn't see Fedderman anywhere around and didn't expect to. She turned around and headed back the way she'd come.

Pearl knew that if the new Madeline stayed on the move for any length of time, an undercover cop would take Fedderman's place as her tail. Or they would tail her in twos. Whenever and wherever the new Madeline finally lighted, someone would be there to watch her.

Pearl decided to walk to a nearby subway stop, return to her apartment in Jill's building, and resume being Jewel, as Quinn had instructed.

So intent had she been on following the new Madeline, she hadn't noticed that she herself was being followed.

Ruth Malpass regretted drinking the second whiskey sour with the sandwiches they'd ordered. Vlad seemed unaffected by his drinks, but Ruth knew she was on the verge of slurring her words. She was sure she was thinking okay, and making sensible if somewhat flighty conversation, but she needed another fifteen minutes or so and some strong black coffee before she wanted to get up from her chair and try to walk steadily.

The rain seemed to be finished for the day. The sun brightened the street, but where Ruth and Vlad sat, at one of the metal tables beneath the restaurant's green awning, they were in shade. A set of steel wind chimes dangled about ten feet away, near where the awning met the brick wall. A slight summer breeze roused the chimes from time to time to gentle notes that sounded almost like the lazy strumming of a harp.

"You mentioned you were on your way home," Vlad said. "Do you live nearby?"

"No, I was going to take the subway. I came down here to shop at the stalls on Canal Street."

Victor knew where she was talking about, several blocks of stalls, mostly run by Chinese merchants, that sold knockoffs of famous brand names in clothing, jewelry, and other accessories. It was a teeming cauldron of commerce, where for ten dollars tourists could buy hundred-dollar items worth five.

"I was going to buy a knockoff designer purse there for my cousin in Michigan," Ruth said. "I never got there because of the rain."

"Isn't that illegal?"

"Technically, I guess so. You're not a cop, are you?"

"No, but I try to stay on the right side of the law." Vlad flashed her a mischievous grin. "But I'm probably no more legal than you are. You still want to go to Canal Street?"

She smiled. "No. I think I'm out of the mood now." She came down hard on her consonants, enunciating quite clearly. Few people would guess she was on the verge of having drunk a little too much.

"Shame you came all that way for nothing."

"It isn't that far," Ruth said. "Besides, I like to ride the subway. And I wouldn't say it was for nothing. You're hardly that. If I'd happened to buy an umbrella before you showed up with yours, we wouldn't have met."

"Destiny in the rain."

"Sounds like a romantic novel."

"Maybe it is."

Ruth felt her heart race. "Might we have some coffee in the rain's aftermath?"

Now I'm *talking like we're in a romantic novel.*

Vlad grinned. "I appreciate the invitation, Ruth. But we won't have to ride the subway. I can drive us to your place."

Ruth tried to clear her mind. It was hard to keep ahead of this guy. "I didn't exactly mean . . ."

"Oh? Now you're disinviting me?" He was smiling earnestly. He reached across the table and touched her hand.

She shook her head. "Vlad—"

"I'm joking, of course. I wouldn't presume. But we can have some coffee, and then I'll drive you home so you won't have to take the subway."

"I didn't notice you had a car."

"It's parked up the street from where we met. I was running some errands, but nothing that can't wait. I'd rather drive you home anytime."

Before she could say anything more, he summoned the waiter and ordered two coffees.

"There, it's settled," he said when the waiter had gone.

Ruth didn't really want to argue with him. She debated with herself as to whether she should invite him in when they got to her apartment. The place was a mess, with dirty dishes in the sink and her bed unmade. Better to wait for some other time. Neaten up the place and make a good impression. But it would be nice to ride uptown and not battle the subway. It wasn't true that she enjoyed the subway. That had been only a convenient lie. She wondered if he'd told her any lies.

She valued honesty in a relationship, and this looked as if it might become a relationship. She hoped.

"Malpass," she said.

"Pardon?"

"That's my name. Ruth Malpass."

He raised his coffee cup in her direction. "My great pleasure, Ruth Malpass."

When they'd finished their coffees, Ruth was confident she could walk a straight line. In fact, she felt confident about everything right now.

Perhaps sensing some unsteadiness, Vlad took her arm as they left the restaurant. She didn't in the slightest resist. During the ten-minute walk to where his car was parked, she laughed at something he said and squeezed his arm, letting him know they'd reached the point in their brief relationship where casual touching was okay. *Step by step.* Something about him. He'd been around. She was sure he knew the ritual, and where it would lead.

He hadn't mentioned his car was a newer model black Chrysler with darkly tinted windows. Beaded raindrops glistened in the sun like fine crystal on its waxed roof and long hood.

"Very impressive wheels," she said.

"It's a company car."

She decided not to ask him what kind of company, what he did for a living, or where he worked. She'd find out eventually.

He unlocked the car with his key fob and held open the passenger-side door for Ruth. When she was seated, he closed the heavy door and hurried around the front of the car to get in on the driver's side.

He was already seated behind the steering wheel fastening his seat belt when Ruth heard a soft sound behind her, glanced over her shoulder, and gasped.

Because of the tinted windows, and her attention fixed on Vlad striding around the front of the car, she hadn't noticed the black-haired woman sitting on the wide backseat. She had a severe hairdo and penetrating dark eyes. She was grinning.

Vlad laughed and patted Ruth's knee.

"Sorry to startle you," he said. "I should have said something. This is my sister, Ivana. We have to drop her someplace; then we'll be on our way."

44

She was a snap to follow. Fedderman stayed back about half a block behind the new Madeline, sometimes crossing to the other side of the street in case she might glance behind her. But she never did. It seemed not to have entered her mind that she might be followed. Either that or she was damned good at looking unsuspecting. Fedderman had seen it both ways. He thought she was simply unaware.

It had been twenty minutes since Fedderman had seen Pearl reverse direction and get off the new Madeline's tail, just after Quinn's phone call to her after Fedderman had talked to him. Fedderman didn't think Pearl had spotted him, either. That pleased him. He'd thought Florida might have spoiled him, that he might be out of practice at being invisible, but tailing, once learned, you didn't forget. It was like riding a bicycle but not like hitting a golf ball.

Fedderman was getting uncomfortably warm in the hot sticky air that followed the rain. Feeling the dampness under his arms, he took off his suit coat and slung it over his shoulder. It wasn't that he had to work hard to keep up with the woman in the white raincoat. She walked slowly, and she liked to window shop. Every now and then she'd enter one of the shops, but usually she didn't stay long. *Fickle*, Fedderman thought.

She turned the corner at West Eighty-fifth and walked a while, then went up the concrete steps of one of a row of three six-story brownstones that were in disrepair. The middle building looked vacant and had scaffolding along its front, but there was no sign of anyone working. The new Madeline entered through the oversized, green-enameled wood door of the third building.

Fedderman thought the way she'd taken the steps, kind of bounding up them, suggested she was a young woman, or in damned good condition.

He waited five minutes, then crossed the street, side-stepped around pigeon shit, and entered the building. He found himself in a small vestibule with yellow-stained green tile walls and a painted gray concrete floor. The place was stifling and smelled strongly of bleach overpowered by the acrid scent of urine. There were bits of tinfoil on the floor. They looked like Hershey's Kisses wrappers.

Fedderman glanced around and saw no sign of an elevator. The building was a walk-up. A TV was playing loudly in one of the units, tuned to the financial channel. He heard a man's voice proclaim that the bulls were in charge.

That'll be the day.

He stepped over to the row of six mailboxes that were painted the same yellowed green as the wall. The slot above one of the end boxes had a card in it on which *M. Scott, 6A* was printed in pencil. Top floor. *Good thing the new Madeline is in shape.* Fedderman was glad there was no reason why he should have to ascend the stairs and verify that indeed unit 6A was up there. It was too hot to climb the steep wooden steps. And a bad idea anyway to clomp up them and maybe alert the new Madeline that she might have been followed.

Fedderman pushed open the heavy wood street door and left the building, glad to get away from the heat and the stench of urine.

He walked half a block before he pulled his cell phone from his pocket and called Quinn.

They had the new Madeline's address. Progress.

Ten minutes after leaving Fedderman to take her place tailing the new Madeline, Pearl realized she was being followed. It was only an uneasy feeling on the edge of her consciousness, but one a longtime cop didn't ignore.

She began stealing glances behind her and caught just a glimpse of a figure quickly moving away on the periphery of her vision. After another block, she pretended to turn slightly and excuse herself for bumping into a man with a briefcase and saw the same sudden movement. This time whoever it was had ducked into a Duane Reade drugstore. A big one that Pearl knew had a downstairs, so it wouldn't do to enter it and try to find whoever was tailing her. There might be fifty customers inside. She and her tail would simply be playing cat and mouse up and down the aisles.

She told herself not to get excited. Her shadower might simply be some guy who liked short women with black hair and big boobs. Easy enough to understand. But she was curious.

One way to find out.

She decided first to put him at ease and end any of his suspicions that he might have been spotted. Without once more checking to see if he was there, she abruptly went down the concrete steps to a subway stop. She joined a crowd of people hurrying toward the turnstiles. The air was unnaturally still and heavy, as if an underground thunderstorm were due. Maybe someday New York would have one. As an escalator carried her even deeper belowground, she could hear the mournful, echoing notes of someone playing a harmonica not very well.

Not bothering to look up or down the platform, she waited about five minutes, then boarded a train.

She emerged aboveground from another stop four blocks from Jill's—and Jewel's—apartment building and strolled toward it. The sun was bright on the tinted windows of traffic headed past her at a crawl going the opposite direction, painting reflections of the street and sidewalk. When a large truck hissed its air brakes and slowly passed, she angled her stride slightly, moving toward the curb, so the reflection in its big side window gave her a brief but panoramic view of the block behind her.

She glimpsed the reflection she thought she might.

You're still there.

If some guy was following her simply because he liked her looks and was working up the nerve to approach her, he was going to a lot of trouble.

Not that I'm not worth it.

Her cell phone vibrated in her pocket. Great!

Quinn, maybe.

Pearl unobtrusively pulled the buzzing phone from her pocket and saw the number of Golden Sunset. She didn't want to talk to her mother now. She slid the phone back in her pocket.

It continued to vibrate. Pause. Vibrate.

After eight or ten steps she knew the phone was going to drive her nuts. She was sure her mother would let it vibrate ninety times before giving up and breaking the connection. Pearl could set the phone to kick over to voice mail, but she knew her mother would simply call back, maybe ninety times.

Not breaking stride, she removed the phone from her pocket again and flipped it open.

"Hello, Mom."

"Pearl?"

"Who else would it be? You just called me."

"Really? I thought I'd dialed the number of my friend Mrs. Kahn." Pearl knew this was a lie. Her mother pressed on: "Where were you, on the commode? Never mind. But speaking of Mrs. Kahn, how is your relationship going with her nephew Milton? I should say *Doctor* Milton Kahn. A girl could do worse—and here I know I get personal but why shouldn't I with my only daughter—than marry a successful dermatologist. And judging by my conversations with Mrs. Kahn, the aunt, Milton, the nephew, is successful in ways monetary as well as professional. She said he spent his early years in practice doing charitable work—which bespeaks a good heart, though we both know he has that—but now has a thriving practice with patients who pay. Has marriage so much as come up in a conversational manner? I think enough time has passed since your first meeting together that it would at the very least have been at some time a topic of casual conversation."

"Do I get a turn to talk?" Pearl asked.

"That's what I've been asking you to do, dear. Tell me about the status of your relationship with *Doctor* Milton Kahn. Since it was I who, you might say, arranged—along with Mrs. Kahn, the aunt, of course—that you two lovebirds meet, I feel I have some right to ask the question. That is, about the status of your relationship in regards to matrimony."

"I think Milt's a nice guy. That's where we're at."

"You've said that before."

"Well, it's still true. Mom, I'm—"

"I'm inquiring about the relationship not so much on a platonic plane. Where has it progressed to on—and here I attempt delicacy—more of a physical plane? In a successful relationship the line between the platonic and the physical isn't so noticeable as time and love work their—"

"Mom, I'm working."

"Exactly my point, dear. Is that necessary? I mean, this pertains to my still unanswered question, wouldn't you agree?"

"No." Pearl thought shock therapy might work. "I'm being followed by a man with a gun."

"Would it be likely in the slightest that the wife of *Doctor* Milton Kahn, renowned dermatologist, would even in this crazy world be followed by a man with a gun?"

"No," Pearl had to admit. "But I'm not anyone's wife, and I'm working, and you must understand that I don't have time to talk."

"People are judged by the time they take to—"

Pearl broke the connection and switched off the phone.

Still without a glance behind her, Pearl briskly took the steps of the apartment building's entrance and pushed through the front door. There was no one in the outer lobby, no one in sight through the windowed door to the inner lobby that would show anyone about to exit the building.

She counted to five slowly, then spun on her heel and burst back out through the door and down the two concrete steps onto the sidewalk.

And came face-to-face with Ed Greeve.

45

Pearl hadn't seen Greeve in over a year, but recognized him immediately. He hadn't changed. Same narrow, stooped build; same black suit; same lugubrious expression. A born mortician who'd somehow become a cop. She knew his nickname, *"The Ghost,"* and felt briefly proud that she'd been able to spot him on her tail.

He was puffing slightly as if he'd been running and had just skidded to a stop. She moved in close to him, catching a whiff of cheap cologne that reminded her of formaldehyde.

"Why are you following me?" She almost snarled the question.

Greeve didn't change expression, but he backed away a step. "I just happened to see you on the street a few blocks back and wanted to say hello. You're a fast walker. I tried to catch up without breaking into a run."

Pearl gave him a vicious grin that made it perfectly clear she knew he was talking bullshit.

That seemed to be okay with Greeve. There was no way for her to know for sure if he'd been deliberately tailing her. Certainly no way to prove it. He wasn't about to let this pint-sized pit bull take charge here.

He smiled and motioned toward the building. "So who lives in there?"

"A friend."

"Jill Clark?"

Pearl understood Greeve was letting her know that he'd followed her before, and that she was being observed. Trying to make her lose her temper so he could get on top in the conversation.

She didn't bite. "Yes. Jill's an old friend. If she's home, you can meet her." Letting Greeve know Jill wasn't home, or she wouldn't have extended the invitation.

He gave her his undertaker's smile—*someday you'll be mine*—and made a motion as if tipping his hat. "Thanks anyway. Maybe some other time."

"I don't want to catch you following me again," Pearl said.

"You won't."

He walked away without saying good-bye.

Pearl went back inside the building and became Jewel. She rode the elevator up to the eighth floor and her half-assed, barely habitable apartment.

The first thing she wanted to do was call Quinn, but almost as soon as she'd shut the door her cell phone began to buzz and vibrate in her pocket.

She took it out, flipped it open, and saw the phone number of Golden Sunset. Her mother again.

She tossed the phone, unanswered, onto the cot and then crossed the room to the landline phone.

Picked up the receiver.

Lowered it back in its cradle.

If Greeve, and by extension Wes Nobbler, knew that Jill Clark lived in the building, they might also know Pearl was staying there as Jewel. The line to this apartment might be tapped.

Probably not, but maybe.

Pearl returned to the cell phone on the cot.

It was wedged between the blankets and had stopped vibrating.

Quickly she snatched it up and pecked out Quinn's number. If her mother called again, she'd get a busy signal.

Maybe she'd even think Pearl was busy.

Ruth stopped believing anything they told her as the big Chrysler slowly pulled in beneath the steel overhead door that was still rumbling open above them, like thunder portending a storm.

As the car braked to an abrupt stop, the lean but muscular arm of the woman in the backseat snaked around Ruth's neck, and Vlad leaned over and held her arms pinned to her sides. Behind the car, the door was already clanking and rattling closed. The outside light faded with its descent.

The arm around Ruth's neck tightened, making her attempted scream a strangled screech no louder than the cawing of a crow. As Ruth fought for breath, she thought she could hear and feel the cartilage in her throat cracking.

There was an increasing pressure in her head, as if her skull were full of expanding gas, and the dimness of wherever they were became total blackness as suddenly as if someone had yanked down a shade.

Ruth gained consciousness before she opened her eyes. *Think!*

She realized she was breathing through her nose. Her lips felt bruised. She explored with the tip of her tongue, wedging it between her lips with effort. Something tacky, some kind of tape, had been fastened across her mouth. She tried to move her hands, but could only wriggle her fingers. Her arms were bent behind her back, her forearms tightly taped together and immovable. *Tight* seemed to be the operative word.

There was the certain knowledge without memory that time had passed, and she'd missed it.

Think!

Memory rushed in. Her mind quickly put together the pieces of what had happened since she'd gotten in the big dark car.

Ruth began to panic but quickly brought herself under control. She might be a costume designer now, but there was a time when she'd been a soldier, when she'd learned to organize and do difficult things right. She'd served in the U.S. Army in Kuwait, as a sergeant in a supply depot. She hadn't seen action but she might have, and now her training took over. It was as if she were five years younger, thinking as she had back then. This was a tough spot; that was for damned sure. But she kept her head.

Don't panic. Assess your situation. Plan.

Here was the situation: Supply Sergeant Ruth Malpass was lying nude on her stomach on a flat metal surface, her feet off the ground. *Has to be the car's hood.* It was still warm, bare flesh against heated, ticking steel. *Legs not bound. I can still kick.*

Plan!

While you're planning, act!

But when she attempted to kick, she realized how widely her legs were parted. Her calves and feet flailed frantically, contacting nothing but air. She couldn't put her legs together.

She stopped kicking and moved her legs slightly in a soft pincers motion to feel the obstruction. Someone was standing between her thighs, up close to her crotch so her knees were far apart.

She lay still then with her eyes closed, thinking her leg movement might be taken as automatic reaction to being bound and gagged. Her captors might assume she was still unconscious.

"She's awake," a man's voice said immediately. Vlad.

Bastard Vlad.

There was no sense in playing possum now. They knew she'd regained consciousness.

Ruth opened her eyes.

She was in a basement garage of some sort. As soon as she saw it, she could smell it, the faint scent of oil and gasoline. She had a headache and was squinting. She couldn't see the source of the light, but it was harsh and shone from above, probably from bare fixtures. There were stark shadows along the walls.

Don't give up! Plan!

Her neck was twisted and she was being held fast against the car so her left cheek was splayed against the hood. She saw the woman who'd been in the car—Vlad's sister, Ivana—walk around the hood of the car. Heard something that might be soft plastic rustling beneath her feet with each step.

Something on the floor. Covering it.

Supply Sergeant Malpass could find nothing there that might be used to her advantage. But she could guess the waterproof plastic sheet's purpose. Her captors wanted to contain any mess they might make.

Ivana was nude, her breasts small and pointed, her ribs prominent. Her black hair was still combed severely back into a tight bun. Her dark eyes still burned. She was holding something with both hands. A mop? A broom? She reminded Ruth of a witch—the narrow, hard features; the black hair and intense eyes; the broom. An evil witch.

She raised the broomstick and Ruth saw that she was wearing white rubber gloves. When she held the broomstick still higher, Ruth saw that it wasn't as long as she'd assumed. It might have once been attached to a broom, but it had been sawed off well above the bristles. It was about three feet long, and sharpened to a fine point.

"I wanted you to see this," the woman said, grinning as she had when Ruth first saw her in the car.

Ruth felt the bulk of the figure between her legs move in

tighter, felt strong hands on her knees, the thumbs digging into the soft, sensitive flesh behind them, pressing harder and painfully, causing her to go limp as he forced her thighs further and further apart. Then her left leg was pinned tight against the car by the heavy weight of a body, and the powerful hand released its unnecessary grip on that knee.

The witch moved back around the car, out of sight behind Ruth, and Ruth felt more hands on the backs of her legs, up high, higher, forcing her buttocks apart.

"Are you still with us, sweetheart?" the witch who called herself Ivana asked.

"She's more conscious than she's ever been," Vlad said calmly.

"We'll do this very slowly," the witch said.

Ruth made a final, frantic, and futile effort to break free. Vlad laughed, bearing his weight down on her hard so she grunted in pain and stopped struggling.

She knew now that all the planning in the world wouldn't change a thing. She surrendered entirely. All she wanted now was for this to please be over. It was the end of plans. Everything ended sometime. Everything. This must end soon.

It must!

She screamed over and over soundlessly into the thick layers of duct tape, praying for unconsciousness and oblivion, a refuge from an agony she'd have thought impossible. It was there, almost within reach. She could sense it. A vast blackness without pain or dread knowledge.

"I brought smelling salts," she heard the witch say in a faraway voice.

"You plan for everything," her brother said.

46

"It happened two days ago," Linda said. "That's about as close to a time of death as we're going to get."

They were in Quinn's bed, sated by good food, good wine, and good sex. Quinn was lying on his back looking up at Linda, who was sitting propped on her pillow, which she'd wedged against the headboard. He knew she'd deliberately waited before telling him this. He understood and was glad, because he thought he knew where it was going and it figured to make him mad as hell.

Linda had just told him about a woman found dead in a landfill outside Newark, New Jersey. Found pretty much by luck, actually, because a bulldozer operator happened to notice a human foot protruding from the dozer's scoop as he was about to drop a load into a valley of varied trash that would soon be filled over with earth.

"Let me guess," Quinn said. "Wes Nobbler got this from the Newark police and is keeping it secret for now."

"Good guess. Nift hasn't mentioned it to anyone, either. But they'll both have to soon, even though their position is that the dead woman's simply another homicide victim and has nothing to do with the Torso Murders."

"If she was found in Newark, how come we have her body here in New York?" Quinn asked.

"Nift and Nobbler pushed hard, told Newark there's a possible tie-in with the Torso Murders."

"And Newark's keeping this quiet."

"For now. Nobody wants to screw up catching this guy."

"But that's exactly what Nobbler and Nift are doing."

"I agree. But that wouldn't be their spin."

Quinn felt his anger rise. "They're going to get away with this shit?"

"For a while," Linda said. She seemed to have given this a lot of thought and become resigned to it. "It seems there's only one thing that links this one to the Torso Murders. She died of massive internal bleeding from injuries caused by the insertion of a sharpened broomstick stake."

"Quite a link, I'd say."

"Yes and no."

"Renz isn't aware of any of this?"

"He knows about the homicide victim. Not about the broomstick." Linda reached over for her warm can of Diet Pepsi. It was leaving a damp ring on a magazine lying on the table on her side of the bed. She took a long swig, made a face, and put the can back down. "More importantly, he doesn't know what they found out yesterday, that the broomstick's the same kind used in most of the Torso Murders. Nift is keeping it from his media mistress, too, but he'll have to tell her soon or she'll know he stalled on it. He wouldn't want to get Cindy Sellers pissed off at him."

"For damned sure." Quinn found himself again longing for a cigar. Here, in his own bedroom, smoking one wasn't even remotely possible. *Women and cigars.* "No bullet wounds in this one?"

"None," Linda said. "And she's still got her head and all her limbs. There's a positive ID, too. Ruth Margaret Malpass, address on the East Side. It didn't take long for her to be missed. She was a costume designer working on an off-

Broadway play, *Major Mary,* scheduled to open in the fall. Two assistants from work went by to check on her when she didn't come in to her studio. Not like her, they said. They got the building super and her neighbors in on the hunt. When they and no one else were able to locate her, they called the police. It was too early for her to be officially missing, but her description matched the woman found in the landfill. She was positively identified almost immediately through her fingerprints. She'd been in the army, and they were on file through her military records."

"So the sharpened broomstick is the only connection," Quinn said.

"It was inserted anally, like in the latest Torso Murders."

"Something else similar." Quinn said.

"And it was inserted when she was alive," Linda said. "Continuing on the killer's new variation on his M.O."

"God help us." Quinn said.

"He didn't help Ruth Malpass," Linda said. "I hope He doesn't help Nobbler and Nift."

"Nobbler's counting on all the *dis*similarities to keep him out of trouble, but you're right, he can't play dumb much longer."

"He's got a defense," Linda said. "There are no prints on the broomstick, the victim is whole and easily identifiable, and she lived quite a while in New York, even went to art school here, and seems to have had plenty of acquaintances and connections. Something else. I used my home computer to check out E-Bliss's database. They don't have a Ruth Malpass as a client."

"How'd you get to their client list?" Quinn asked.

"Easy," Linda said. "I joined it."

Quinn didn't wait until morning. It was eleven-fifteen. Renz might still be awake. If he wasn't, Quinn would take care of that.

He phoned from where he was, in bed next to Linda. Though he was seething inside, he might as well be physically comfortable.

Renz picked up on the second ring, sounding angry.

Quinn began relating what Linda had just told him, but Renz interrupted.

"I already know," he said. "It's breaking news, all over TV, all over the damned country, but not in my office."

"Nobbler must have gotten nervous and released it."

"Or Cindy Sellers learned it somehow. I'll bet *City Beat* already has a special edition all over town."

"Was it on TV news about the broomstick stake?"

"Second from the lead. First thing I saw was one of Tom Coulter's old mug shots, then a news anchor holding up a sawed-off broomstick explaining what happened to the poor Malpass woman. The news sees a tie-in because Coulter killed his victims in New Jersey. They think he might have come home."

"Maybe he did," Quinn said. "This could be a copycat killing."

"That's what Nobbler's going to say, a copycat job."

"It's possible, considering what *wasn't* done to the victim."

"Don't even go there," Renz said. "I don't want to think we might be responsible for Coulter figuring he was going down for the Torso Murders anyway and joining the party."

"I doubt it was Coulter," Quinn said. "He's basically a professional burglar that killed in a panic."

"Once they get a taste . . ."

"Yeah, sometimes. But I still don't like Coulter for it. The media's on him because we gave him to them. If we hadn't, they wouldn't even be mentioning his name."

"That's true," Renz said, after a pause. "Meat to the wolves. Tell me something else reassuring, Quinn. Like what we do next."

"You have a press conference as soon as possible," Quinn

said. "Emphasize the differences between the Malpass murder and the Torso Murders. Hint that we have good reason to believe Malpass wasn't murdered by the same person, that we know something the public and the killer don't know. Say we have no reason to believe there's any connection."

"Play dumber than Nobbler?"

"Dumber faster. You can do it. I know you can."

"Hmm."

"It takes a fox to play a rabbit," Quinn said.

"Have I told you lately that I like your style?"

"It's why you hired me."

When Quinn clicked off his cell phone and laid it back on the nightstand, Linda sat up straighter in bed, drawing up her knees and hugging them. She'd been listening to Quinn's end of the conversation.

"Do you think it's possible this one is Coulter's?" she asked.

"No. The balls to commit burglary and the balls to commit murder are two different things."

"Four," she said.

Quinn did half a sit-up and kissed one of her knees, then settled back down.

"Do you think Ruth Malpass's death is connected to E-Bliss?" she asked.

"I don't think there's a chance in hell it isn't the same killer," he said.

Linda frowned, puzzled. "If Malpass wasn't an E-Bliss client, why would the Torso Killer murder her? I don't see anything to gain. She was outside the circle. Where's the motive?"

"Think about it."

Linda did, for about five seconds.

"My God!" she said.

"It started out strictly business," Quinn said. "Now he enjoys it."

47

Palmer Stone had the morning *Post* lying open on his desk. He'd invited Gloria to read it, but she told him she already had.

Stone had called her in for a morning confab. Gloria, alone, not with Victor. So here she was, wearing a white tunic, black slacks, and black boots, with her red silk scarf knotted loosely at her neck.

Stone was in his big swivel chair behind his desk, his head not moving as he stared at Gloria, but his body inching this way and that in the chair. Nervous.

"If you already read the paper," he said in his usual modulated voice, "you know this dead woman they found in New Jersey was impaled with a sharpened broomstick."

"Kinda shit happens," Gloria said.

"I don't like it happening right in our backyard. It makes me wonder."

"The cops'll probably wrap it up soon. The guy they suspect's photo's right there on the front page." Gloria motioned with her head toward the newspaper on the desk. "They even have his name. Tom whatever."

"Tom Coulter. He's a house burglar who had a job go bad and killed some people."

"In New Jersey. Where this woman's body was found."

"Awful close to New York."

Gloria tilted her head and stared at Stone with an expression of disbelief.

"Jesus, Palmer! This New Jersey thing has nothing to do with us. They didn't find just her torso. And they identified her immediately. If the press is tying it in with the Torso Murders, they're wrong."

"I'd like to agree with you, but I'm having a tough time." Stone puffed up his cheeks, blew out some air. "The three of us have worked together for a lot of years."

"So let's stop gassing to each other about what we both already know. I'd ask what's bothering you, Palmer, because you're obviously bothered, but I can guess what it is. I know why you wanted to see me this morning."

"Don't bother to guess," Stone said. "I've got an inkling of a suspicion your brother killed this woman."

"Victor? Don't believe it, Palmer."

"I didn't say I believed it."

"But you're tilting in that direction."

"Why shouldn't I be? He's been acting strange lately, and the way the woman—Ruth somebody—died, it sure put me in mind of Victor."

"Was Ruth a client, Palmer?"

"You know she wasn't."

"Then what would be Victor's motivation? Why would he do one off the books?"

"I can't answer that for sure, Gloria. But speaking of books, I've been to Victor's apartment and seen his. I noticed some new additions. Brand-new-looking books on Vlad the Impaler. You know who he was?"

"Of course. I'm not ignorant, Palmer. He lived during the Middle Ages, I think. Bad guy. Terrorized his enemies by impaling people and hoisting them up on poles driven into the ground. Weird guy. Sick."

"Your brother seems awfully interested in him."

"Victor's always been into history and biography. What's that got to do with motive?"

"I'm wondering," Stone said, "if maybe Victor's come to enjoy that aspect of his work so much that he's moonlighting—not for pay, just for pleasure."

"You're suggesting my brother's some kind of sick sadist." Gloria fixed her onyx eyes on him. He couldn't look away. "Listen to me close, Palmer. Victor didn't kill that woman."

"Then who did?"

"Tom Coulter."

"I kind of doubt it."

"Then maybe it was someone who's read about the Torso Murders or followed them on TV. Some guy who leaned toward sadism to begin with and decided to get in on the act. Only for him, there was no reason to sever the head and limbs. He didn't care if the body was identified."

"He didn't expect the body to be found," Stone pointed out.

Gloria didn't change expression. It was true that she and Victor hadn't expected the body to be found. Acres and acres of trash, every kind of refuse, and Ruth Malpass had been five feet down in it, waiting to be shoved into a vast pit of trash. It was a fluke that she was found.

Gloria crossed her arms and spread her feet wide, becoming angry, and glared at Stone. "If you really suspect Victor of killing this woman, I can put your mind at ease. During the time the police say she was killed, he was with me. We were in his apartment. We take turns preparing each other a gourmet dinner once a week. Last time, it was Victor's turn. We were enjoying lobster lasagna and a good wine when that woman was killed."

"Victor never left your sight?"

"Not for more than five minutes, if that long. And I stayed until almost midnight."

"Why so late?"

"We got to talking about business and lost track of time. I know it was close to midnight because I looked at my watch and told him how late it was."

Stone sighed, making Gloria wonder if he might be feigning relief. You could never tell for sure with Palmer. The discovery of Ruth's body had complicated things.

"Do me a favor," Stone said. "Even if you don't take what I'm saying seriously, keep an eye on your brother. We don't really know people, even the ones closest to us."

"I know Victor," Gloria said. "He's like me. We're business-people first and foremost. As you are, Palmer. We're not sadists or devil worshipers. We pray to profit and to the good Lord."

"In that order?"

She flashed a crooked grin. " 'Fraid so."

"People can change, even the best people. I don't want Victor doing anything dangerous, either for him or for the company."

"He isn't, I'm sure."

"Still, will you watch him? If there are any changes, you might be the first to notice."

Gloria uncrossed her arms and loosened her stance. She was no longer intractable. Her expression suggested that, however unlikely, Stone might have a point. She had to concede him that. "I'll watch him, Palmer. If he starts behaving strangely, I'll let you know."

Stone stood up behind his desk wearing the smile she knew so well, the inclusive, reassuring one that lulled the marks.

"I'm counting on you, Gloria."

"You've always been able to do that, Palmer. Nothing's changed."

As she left the office she was smiling, too. Her smile was nothing like Palmer Stone's.

She was thinking about Ruth Malpass.

48

Tom Coulter sat straight up in bed.

Even though it was three a.m. he'd been sleeping lightly in his room at the Tumble Onn Inn Motel. Maybe he'd been dreaming, or maybe he'd been waking up and his imagination had gone on a romp. Either way, he was scared. He made an effort to control his breathing. He'd been waking up like this lately, feeling all tight inside, out of breath.

He tried his version of mental discipline to ease his tension, getting tough with himself.

What the hell are you afraid of, you big pussy, except every cop in the country wants to kill you?

Didn't work.

He fell back on the bed, his eyes wide open.

The Tumble Onn Inn was just outside of Burback, Louisiana. It was where Coulter's flight from the law had left him, this ramshackle clapboard building constructed in a U around a swimming pool full of algae. The outside walls had once been white but were now a dull gray mottled with mold. There were rust-colored vertical stains where the gutters leaked.

At least it wasn't the kind of place where the staff was curious about the guests. The old guy at the desk wore rimless glasses held together by black electricians' tape and looked as if he'd been hired especially for the motel to give it local color. He hadn't raised an eyebrow when Coulter paid cash. He was used to guests who didn't qualify for credit cards. Coulter didn't worry much about him.

On the other hand, the old bastard probably watched TV, and Coulter's name and image were all over the damned news channels. They kept using the photo he hated, the one with his hair all messed up and with his bad teeth showing. Damned thing made him look ignorant. Made him look like a criminal.

The rattling old air conditioner had stopped working since Coulter had gone to bed and fallen into an uneasy sleep hastened by cheap vodka. Either that or the power was off again. It was close and hot in the cruddy little room. There was no sound except for the insects buzzing outside in the darkness.

Coulter was breathing okay now. He tried to relax, even though he was sure *something* had awoken him. He told himself it might have been anything. A cat, or maybe even some kind of wild animal, making a noise. A possum. There had to be plenty of them around. There seemed to be a dead one every two or three miles of road.

He was wearing only his jockey shorts, trying to keep as cool as possible, but his body was coated with oily perspiration. *Too close to the damned swamp.* Something soft, probably a moth, brushed his forehead, and he swiped at it with his right hand, not really expecting to make contact.

This wasn't how he'd foreseen things. His notoriety had overwhelmed him. Not that he didn't still enjoy being a genuine celebrity. But no matter where he went he could be sure people had heard or read about him and probably seen his photo. It was always a worry. That kind of thing could be damned wearying if the law was itching to hang a string of murder raps around your neck. The irony was, he'd never set out to kill anyone. He wasn't that sort of guy. This had all been done *to* him, a series of bad breaks, most of them brought on by mistakes made by other people. All he'd done was react to a shitload of bad luck. Another example of how unfair life was to him.

Nothing had changed from the time he'd jolted awake and sat up on the sagging mattress. No sound. No movement of light or shadow. No stirring of air. Beads of sweat continued to form and trickle down his bare neck and arms.

He made himself relax and let the weariness close in on him again.

Everything's gonna be okay, at least for a while. Go back to sleep. . . .

His eyes flew open.

No doubt about it this time. Very faintly in the night, the unmistakable crunching sound of tires rolling slowly over packed gravel.

Something had driven into the parking area outside the rooms.

Coulter slid out of bed and went to the window. He crouched down and parted the blinds and peered out into almost total blackness. A sliver of moon provided the only light. He gave his eyes a minute or so to adjust, and then figured, hell, they didn't need it, since he'd been sitting like a mushroom in a dark room.

He saw nothing out there but the same six cars that had been parked in front of rooms when he'd pulled in earlier that evening. They were all older models, one of them a vintage '98 Olds with a flat front tire. Coulter liked and knew about cars. He'd stolen a lot of them in his younger days and figured the Olds would have been a collector's item if it weren't such a rust bucket.

Staying in a low crouch, he shifted his weight and glanced in the other direction over the sill. Parked two spaces down from his room was the late-model black Ford F-100 pickup he'd stolen two days ago. Faint moonlight glimmered off its fender. It looked like a gigantic toy on drastically oversized tires. Which was maybe what it was.

Another sound!

It might have been a car door shutting as quietly as possible, pulled closed, and latched.

Something's going on out there, all right.

Coulter backpedaled away from the window to where his Levi's were wadded on a chair. He hurriedly slipped into them, then yanked a T-shirt over his head. He thought about going barefoot, then changed his mind and took the time to work his feet, sockless, into his boots. Sweat was pouring off him, stinging the corners of his eyes.

He picked up the .38 handgun from the nightstand by the bed and held it in his left hand while he dug the truck keys from his pants pocket with his right. The gun was a blue steel semiautomatic with a checkered wood grip. He'd stolen it in Baton Rouge and had never fired it. Didn't even know for sure if it worked. He thumbed the safety off. Then he moved to the door.

Coulter rotated the knob with a trembling hand and slowly opened the door a few inches.

Sultry night air flowed in, carrying the fetid stench of the nearby swamp. He could see nothing outside but the dark parking lot, the shadowy bulks of cars nosed into spaces outside the identical rooms. He glanced to his right. The big Ford pickup, resting high on its huge knobby tires, looked tantalizingly close.

No movement out there. No sound other than the drone of insects. Not even a car passing on the state road, not at three in the morning. And the big trucks didn't use this narrow, meandering road, with the interstate only about ten miles away running almost parallel to it.

Coulter felt his confidence returning. Maybe all he'd heard was some guy going out to his car because he'd forgotten his cigarettes. Something like that. Nervous as Coulter was, maybe he'd gotten himself all in a dither over nothing.

Maybe not.

Either way, I ain't goin' back to sleep. I'm outta here.

He stepped all the way outside, moving cautiously in his cowboy boots. His crunching footfalls were barely audible in the still night as he made his way toward the truck. The ignition key was tight between his fingers, ready to insert and twist. He was squeezing it so hard he felt it cutting into his flesh. In his left hand, he still carried the gun.

Maybe I should switch. Can't shoot good left-handed.

Too late for that.

He made it to within ten feet of the truck, then used the key fob to unlock the doors. A dim light came on inside the truck's cab. He straightened up and moved faster, not worrying now about the noise, and opened the driver's-side door and swung himself up behind the steering wheel.

Wham!

A blinding light hit him in the face like something solid. He reeled back even as he reached forward. Amazingly, the ignition key found its slot. Red and blue flashing lights were all around him now, and sirens began to yowl.

Ignoring the maelstrom of light and noise, he slammed the shift selector into reverse, twisted the steering wheel as he stomped on the gas. Gravel flew as the truck did a 180-degree spin. The truck had stopped, but was still rocking as he rammed the selector into drive, and headed hell for leather for the driveway leading to the state road.

The truck's big engine roared with power as Coulter laid the gun on the seat beside him and hunched over the steering wheel. He was gripping the wheel with both slippery hands. Something made a loud crack behind his right ear. Glass breaking. Like a rock had been hurled through it. Only he knew it hadn't been a rock.

Shooting at me! Jesus!

His right foot mashed down on the accelerator even

harder. Gravel, dirt, large rocks were hurled into the air off the knobby tires as the truck lurched forward. *Sonuvabitch has got power,* he thought, as he felt himself pressed backward in his seat. There was a bump that made him rise off the seat cushion, and the steering wheel writhed in his hand. The truck leaned left and he yanked the wheel right.

Then he was out of the motel's parking lot and picking up speed on the paved road. The flashing colored lights, the yowling sirens, were still there, flitting this way and that in the darkness, but they were behind him now. There was nothing ahead but black road, and a faint yellow line snaking away into the night, leading toward freedom.

The truck cab got brighter. He glanced in his right outside mirror and was almost blinded by headlights that had slid in close behind him. The mirror exploded as a bullet caught it. He mashed down harder on the accelerator, putting distance between him and the headlights.

Coulter thought he should shoot back. He owed it to himself. And maybe it'd make the State Patrol or whoever the hell they were let up some on the gas. Gripping the wheel tight with his left hand, he picked up the gun with his right.

Shootin' hand. Look out now!

This was going to be awkward. He made sure the truck was aimed straight ahead, held on to the steering wheel with his left hand, and twisted his body so he could get his right arm out the window and shoot behind him.

The gun worked okay. He managed to get off a shot but had no way of knowing if it had hit anything. The car hit a bump just as he was about to squeeze the trigger again, and the sudden jolt made him bump his wrist against the hard window frame, knocking the gun from his grasp. It dropped down and away onto the pavement.

In the shitpot now!

He turned back so he was sitting straight, staring out through the windshield and steering with both hands. Whoever was chasing him had gotten close again. The lights in the rearview mirror were blinding, even though the mirror was set for nighttime vision. He reached up and twisted it so the light was deflected. No need to look behind him. He knew they were there.

Just drive, goddamnit. Forget about the gun. You wasn't gonna hit anything anyway.

Drive!

Coulter saw a county road intersecting with the state road, made up his mind in an instant, and swung left. This road was narrower than the one he'd been on, and bumpier. He knew what he had to find. The kind of turnoff where the big four-wheel-drive truck could go and low-slung police cars made for highway pursuit couldn't follow. That was his only real chance to escape the shitstorm his bad luck had put him in.

If I can just make it into the swamp I can . . . think of something. . . .

The headlights were still back there. The road began to wind. A bullet sparked off the already damaged outside mirror, startling Coulter. But he didn't lose control of the truck. He kept his head. He was learning all about himself, and he liked it. He had the balls for more than breaking and entering. He was a goddamned Jesse James.

As the truck roared and sped along, the swamp seemed to move in closer on either side. Within half a mile he saw what he needed, a crude wooden sign indicating a turnoff ahead. As he flashed past it, he couldn't even read what it said, but he put light pressure on the brake pedal, getting ready.

Then there it was on his left, an opening in the swamp. It wasn't much more than flattened grass, but enough of a road to provide access for the big truck. Just enough.

Luck from shit to gold!

As Coulter yanked the steering wheel to the left, the truck leaned hard and went up on two wheels. Then it dropped back and tracked perfectly onto the narrow, grassy road. As soon as he straightened it out, it flew up in the air, and Coulter felt the top of his head hit the headliner. As he plopped back down in his seat, he fumbled and found a firm grip on the steering wheel. He clenched his teeth and followed the truck's headlight beams into the swamp.

This was goddamned working. This was what he wanted. There was another, smaller bump, then rooster tails of water rose high and away from the front wheels and the truck rocked to a dead stop.

Coulter's heart stopped with it.

Here was his lousy luck again. He should have expected it. It was his role in life to have the rug yanked out from under him. God had had it in for him from the beginning.

He jammed the selector into a lower gear and played the gas pedal. Mud and rocks slammed against the insides of the fenders, but the truck didn't budge. Wasn't this thing supposed to have four-wheel drive?

Don't let me down now! Please! C'mon! C'mon!

If God wouldn't help him, maybe the devil would. Or the all-powerful God of Trucks and Fools. The big engine roared. The oversized tires spun free and threw more mud, found traction, and the truck lurched forward and picked up speed.

Coulter gleefully stomped the accelerator. The truck responded as if it were alive and born for the challenge.

Small branches whipped and scratched against the truck's steel sides. Welcome sounds. They meant the swamp was opening its arms for him and freedom could be had. He drove like a maniac. More dark water splashed from time to time, some of it splattering on the windshield.

Coulter used the truck's wipers and forged on. The road had become a narrow, muddy tunnel through the swamp. That was fine with him. The bumpier and muddier the better. This was exactly the kind of place that would soon bog down a low-slung car.

After a while, Coulter chanced a glance in the rearview mirror and saw through the trees a glimmer of headlights, far behind. A few seconds later he looked again and saw only blackness.

He backed off a bit on the accelerator, driving more carefully. His breathing was ragged and his heart was pounding as if it might break a rib. He knew he wasn't out of the woods yet, literally, but he couldn't help letting out a loud whoop. He'd shaken them.

Desperado on the run!

Goddamn he was something! He'd shaken them!

For now.

49

Wes Nobbler and Greeve had gotten to Ruth Malpass's apartment first and confiscated her notebook computer. After that, it was seconds for Quinn and his team. When they requested the laptop, they were informed that Nobbler and Greeve were the real NYPD, but that they'd share.

Quinn informed Renz of this, and Renz promptly phoned and gave Nobbler one of his better ass-chewings and made it clear who was working the Torso Murders case.

It wasn't Nobbler.

Nobbler had reluctantly given Quinn's team a copy of the hard drive of Malpass's computer's, made after Pearl and an NYPD computer whiz observed the transfer of the files to make sure it was complete.

The drive revealed no sign of E-Bliss.org. Pearl had gone over it and found some e-mail messages and addresses to follow up on, but nothing promising. The computer's Internet history was also unrevealing. Ruth had read several newspapers online and regularly visited a few show-business sites and gossip blogs. Pearl had reported that Ruth had bought lots of shoes over the Internet. That meant nothing other than that Pearl had new sources of shoes.

Today Pearl and Fedderman were getting follow-up statements from Ruth's neighbors, who were telling them what a fine woman Ruth was. That had been the report from two of the actors and the producer of *Major Mary,* the musical she'd been costuming.

Quinn got a key from the super and entered Ruth's apartment. It was pretty much what he expected except for the scent; there was a sachet or something like one somewhere giving off a faint whiff of cinnamon. The apartment was a functionally furnished loft, with a southern exposure and shelves of art books and pottery and sculpture. There was a shiny steel framework on one wall that held clothes. At first Quinn thought they were Ruth's and simply didn't fit in the big oak wardrobe, but then he realized they must be part of her work.

Near a window was a wooden drafting board with a large pad of paper on it. The top sheet was curled back over the high end of the slanted board. There was no chair nearby. Ruth must have stood while she worked.

"Hello?"

Quinn was startled by the voice. He turned and saw a short woman with no waist and a lot of frizzy blond hair. She was wearing loosely cut jeans and a sleeveless white blouse. Her incredibly large blue eyes were the sort that didn't blink much. They looked frightened.

"I'm Hettie Crane from downstairs," she said, "a neighbor and good friend of Ruth's. When I heard what happened to her . . ."

Whatever else she'd been about to say was choked off by emotion.

"I know," Quinn told her gently. He introduced himself, showing her his shield.

Hettie only glanced at it, but wouldn't have been able to see it well anyway from as far away as she was. She stood stiff legged where she'd stopped just inside the door, as if she might be invading Ruth's privacy if she ventured farther into the apartment. The way her friend died had obviously shaken Hettie's world.

"You all right, dear?"

Hettie nodded. She lifted her chin slightly and tried to smile, but her facial muscles wouldn't cooperate.

"It always smelled so good in here," she said. "Ruth burned scented candles." Her eyes became moist. She swallowed.

Quinn smiled at her and decided to give her time to wrestle some more with her new reality. Her juicy blue gaze followed him as he walked over to the drafting board.

The top sheet of paper was filled with skillfully rendered sketches of what looked like military uniforms, male and female. Quinn flipped the raised sheet of paper and saw more of the same.

"These mean anything to you?" he asked Hettie, keeping his tone casual.

She reluctantly came over to stand next to him where she could see Ruth's drawings.

"They're costume concepts for *Major Mary*," she said. "I know because I'm directing the play. It was set to open in a couple of months." She moved closer and looked again at the sketches. "It'll still open. We'll use Ruth's costuming ideas. These sketches. They're far enough along, and she would have wanted it that way." She looked up at Quinn. Her eyes were still teary. "It'll be at the Marlborough Theater in the Village. It's a musical comedy."

"Good luck with it," Quinn said, and meant it. "Did you know Ruth well?"

"Very well. She's the one who recommended me for my apartment. This building rents to a lot of theater people."

"So you had mutual friends."

"Quite a few," Hettie said.

"Was Ruth involved with anyone?"

"Romantically? Sexually?"

"Either one," Quinn said, smiling.

"She broke off about four months ago with this guy she'd been seeing. Buddy Erb. He's an actor."

"Know where he can be found?"

"In L.A. He does the voice-over in that commercial where the frog recommends an insurance company and then drives an SUV off a cliff. You know the one?"

"Sure."

"Buddy does a great frog."

"Got that kinda voice," Quinn said. "They fight or anything when they broke up?"

"No, they just got tired of each other. It was pretty much over when Buddy got the job offer."

"The frog?"

"Yeah. Which meant he had to move to the West Coast."

"Yuck," Quinn said. "All that sun and surf."

Hettie gave him a look. She knew what he was doing, loosening her up, getting her to talk so maybe she'd yield a nugget of information. It was okay with her. She wanted the big, homely-handsome cop to catch the animal who had killed her friend.

The guy has an interesting face, Hettie thought. Rugged and memorable. And so, so trustworthy. He should have been an actor. Leading man. Not that he wasn't way too old for her . . .

Not that he wasn't an actor, in his own way.

"I know Buddy pretty well," she said. "He's an actor, not a killer. And from what I hear, his sexual needs are standard issue. If you check, I'm sure you'll find he was on the other side of the continent when Ruth was killed."

"We'll check. You know how we are." Quinn ran his fingertips over the sketch pad, as if trying to gain some knowledge about the sketches' creator. "Ruth date a lot?" he asked.

"Some. She liked men, but she was busy much of the time. Especially lately, what with *Major Mary*."

"You recall her mentioning anyone?"

"Since Buddy? No."

"Since Buddy, did she ever use a dating service?"

"I doubt it. Ruth was great to look at. Men liked her. If she wanted to go out, there was always somebody there."

"I don't want to sound like a TV cop—"

"You'd make a great TV cop."

"But did Ruth have any enemies whom you know of?"

"Everybody loved Ruth." Hettie gave him a sad grin. "More TV dialogue, but it happens to be true. She was a terrific and talented person. Even the sicko who killed her must have loved her in his own twisted way."

"How so?"

"He chose *her*, didn't he?"

50

Hettie had left, and Quinn was standing in the center of Ruth Malpass's apartment, slowly looking around, when Pearl came in.

"Anything from the neighbors?" he asked.

"Nothing useful. They all liked Ruth. She'd been seen coming and going with a man now and then. Nobody steady. Nobody lately. She was friendly—I heard the word *sweet* a lot—but pretty much kept to herself." Pearl glanced around the apartment. "Anything here?"

"Nothing unusual or helpful. Just like on her computer."

"Nobbler had it first. You think we saw everything that was on it?"

"You watched the file transfer. The tech whiz seem okay?"

"Yeah. Seemed."

"Then we probably got it all," Quinn said. "Nobbler'd be taking a hell of a risk tampering with that kind of evidence. And it'd take somebody who really knew computers to be sure whatever was deleted was really and truly gone from the disk for good. You know how it works."

"Yeah. E-mail is forever."

They both turned when they heard the door open.

Fedderman. He looked tired, and his brown suit was even more wrinkled than usual. He'd canvassed the top floors, while Pearl had worked the ones below. He didn't look happy.

"Any luck?" Quinn asked.

Fedderman shook his head.

"Probably not except maybe for the woman living right in the next unit, a loft apartment just like this one. Name's Emma McKenna. Real nice. Pretty enough to be an actress."

"She probably is an actress," Quinn said. "What did you learn from her."

"She was a good friend of Ruth's. According to her, they kind of looked out for one another. She said Ruth phoned her on what must have been the day she died and left a message on her machine. Said it probably wouldn't happen, but if a guy named Vlad came around looking for her, tell him he just missed her and get his phone number." Fedderman shrugged. "Emma didn't know anyone named Vlad and said Ruth never mentioned a Vlad before the phone message. So it probably means nothing."

Pearl said, "Holy Christ!"

Fedderman looked at her in surprise. "Huh?"

Quinn and Pearl both stared at him.

"What?" Fedderman asked.

Quinn said, "Don't you watch The History Channel?"

After explaining to Fedderman about Vlad the Impaler, they set to work doing a search of the names Vlad and Vladimir, using phone directories at first, then moving on to their computers.

In the five boroughs of New York City, there were a surprising number of Vlads and Vladimirs. The Vlads who showed up in the various criminal databases were for one reason or another unlikely suspects. One, who'd at first seemed a possibility, was in the Russian Mafia and had been killed last year in New Jersey.

Almost certainly the killer—if Vlad was the killer—wouldn't have used his real name. Still it was something that should be checked. Every ten years or so, something like this paid off. The drudge work of detection. Renz assigned a young cop named Nevins, fresh out of the academy, to do more extensive checking. He seemed enthusiastic.

Pearl stayed behind and helped Nevins, out of pity, while Quinn and Fedderman left the office to look over the vacant apartment Pearl had seen the new Madeline leaving.

Just in case she hadn't found what she might have gone there to retrieve.

"Happy hunting," Nevins said, as they went out the door.

Pearl rolled her eyes.

51

A white van with the peel-off magnetic sign of a painting company was parked in front of the building the new Madeline had lived in. Peel-off signs. Sometimes Quinn thought they'd been invented especially for the convenience of criminals.

Quinn and Fedderman decided not to bother with the super. They entered the building, pushed the elevator's "up" button, and didn't see a soul on their ascent to Madeline's floor.

They'd guessed right. The door down the hall that was propped open was to the new Madeline's unit. Quinn went in first. A rug-sized canvas drop cloth covered most of the living room floor. A guy in paint-splattered white coveralls was perched on the next-to-top step of an aluminum stepladder, using a brush to apply paint where ceiling and wall met. There was a pleasant but nose-tingling smell emanating from whatever kind of paint he was using. The new color was peach. Quinn would have preferred the previous white.

"Help you?" a woman's voice asked.

A young woman wearing white coveralls and a painter's cap stuck on top of a lot of carrot-colored hair came in from the kitchen. She was carrying a plastic bucket of spackling compound and a small trowel that looked as if it'd had a lot of use.

Quinn and Fedderman showed both painters their shields. They seemed satisfied. The one on the ladder set back to work. The woman was probably the boss.

"We want to take another look around the apartment," Quinn said.

"For clues?" Carrot top couldn't say it without smiling.

"Before you paint over them," Fedderman said.

She raised red eyebrows. "Was a crime committed here?"

"We don't know for sure where the murder took place," Quinn said. "That's what the clues would be about." There was no point in telling her the crime didn't occur in the apartment. Let her be impressed.

She didn't seem impressed.

"Did somebody say murder?" the painter on the ladder asked. Apparently he wasn't up on the news.

"We're from Homicide," Fedderman said. "Murder it is."

"Oh, great!" the man said. "I hope we didn't paint over any fingerprints."

"Not to worry," Quinn told him. "That part of the investigation's already been done."

"By the crime scene unit?"

"You must watch TV," Fedderman said.

"Law & Order," the man said.

"We're for that," Quinn said.

"Well, you're in luck," the woman said. "We just got started. This is the only room we've worked in. That shouldn't matter much, should it? I mean, aren't most murders committed in the bedroom or kitchen? Nobody ever gets killed in the living room."

"Depends on what's on TV," Fedderman said.

"Football," the woman said. "Football on TV brings out the violence in men."

"Oprah, too, sometimes," Fedderman said.

The woman laughed. "You gotta be jesting. Everybody likes Oprah. Like with Raymond."

"You must sniff a lotta paint fumes," Fedderman said.

"We'll take a look around," Quinn said. "Thanks." He thought the redheaded woman might be about to get genuinely angry at Fedderman. He'd seen it before with Oprah.

The apartment was small, so there wasn't much to look at, especially considering they'd been there before. Quinn took the bathroom, while Fedderman began in the bedroom.

The medicine chest had been cleaned out, as had the small closet built into the wall, where towels and other bathroom supplies had been stored. Even the old tub looked as if it had been cleaned. The plastic plates were removed from the switches and sockets. The painters had been there, preparing. A clear plastic shower curtain lay neatly folded beneath the washbasin. Quinn used it to pad his knee as he knelt down and craned his neck so he could look at the underside of the porcelain basin.

Nothing there but plumbing.

He took a last look around, then went into the bedroom to join Fedderman.

It had been cleaned out, like the bathroom. Whatever the new Madeline had left behind had been either sold, stolen, or hauled away. The bed had been stripped down to the mattress and box springs.

"Look under the bed, Feds?"

"I always peek under the bed," Fedderman said. "Even at home."

Fedderman walked over to the closet and opened the door. It was as empty as they'd seen it last time. The two or three tangled wire hangers seemed to be dangling in the same pattern as before, like a wire mobile. Cops remembered things like that. Patterns.

Fedderman started to close the closet door.

"Wait a minute," Quinn said, staring into the empty closet.

The painted, thin piece of plywood on the closet's back

wall, maybe eighteen inches square, that allowed access to the bathroom plumbing behind the tub didn't look quite the same. Something . . .

"Was that access panel slightly crooked like that?" Quinn asked.

Fedderman stared at it. "No." An ancient line of paint was even visible halfway along one edge. "Somebody's been in there and didn't put the panel back quite straight. Maybe because they were in a hurry."

"Or maybe we got us a careless plumber," Quinn said.

He bent down, listening to the cartilage in his knees crackle. There was a fine dusting of white powder on the closet's bare wood floor near the access panel. Some of the powder had gone down into the cracks between the boards.

Fedderman leaned close and looked over Quinn's shoulder.

"Wanna bet what that is?" he said. Plumbing access panels were a common place for drug addicts to conceal their stash. They didn't seem to know that's where narcs looked immediately after examining the inside of the toilet tank.

Quinn traced his fingertip through the film of powder, then touched his finger to his tongue, ran it across his gums beneath his lower front teeth.

"Coke," he said. "High quality."

Fedderman straightened up. "So the new Madeline is a user. She must have left her stash when she moved out, then came back for it."

"Maybe because she had help moving," Quinn said.

"And vacated the place in a hurry. When she got feeling needy, she had to come back for her stash. Got careless, somehow punctured a Baggie or dropped some of the product while she was snorting."

"In a hurry and shaky," Quinn said, picturing it.

"Or maybe we've got it wrong," Fedderman said. "Maybe she came back to hide something behind the panel."

Quinn didn't think that was likely, but it was possible.

Most of these old access panels stayed just as they were for years.

While he was kneeling, he took a closer look at the wooden access panel. It was fastened to the wall by large screws at each corner. There was no paint in the slots, and the screws looked loose. A few flakes of paint lay on the floor beneath them. Obviously somebody had been at the panel recently.

"Go see if you can borrow a screwdriver from the painters, Feds."

"On my way."

When Fedderman had left the bedroom, Quinn gathered his strength and stood up on his noisy, wobbly knees. The leg that had taken a bullet didn't feel any more unsteady than the other leg. Time had healed. He felt light-headed for a moment. *Feeling my age. Nothing good about that.*

"Regular or Phillips?" Fedderman called from the living room.

"Bring both," Quinn called back.

He didn't feel like kneeling again to reexamine the screws.

The new Madeline hadn't hidden anything behind the access panel in the back closet wall. When Quinn removed the plywood panel he found only the bathtub plumbing, and some more white powder on the floor. The spaces between the floorboards were wider there, and quite a bit of the powder had fallen down into them.

It was easy to see what had happened. There was a bent nail sticking out of the right side of the access opening. It was sharply pointed and had traces of white powder on it. Quinn pointed it out to Fedderman.

"She must have snagged the plastic pouch her coke was in and spilled some of it."

"You can see where she tried to scoop it up and put it back in the bag. A lot of it went down into the floor."

"Better than up her nose," Quinn said.

Quinn held the panel flat against the wall and began replacing the screws.

When he straightened up and backed awkwardly out of the closet, he said, "We know she's a user. And since she lost a lot of her stash here, she'll probably need more soon."

"Narcotics is liable to pick her up."

"We don't want that," Quinn said.

"So we gotta make sure she doesn't get nailed on a drug charge." Fedderman shook his head. "Some police work. The new Madeline is a pain in the ass."

"If we think she is," Quinn said, "imagine what a pain in the ass she must be to E-Bliss. It can't have been part of their plan to supply one of their new identities to a cocaine addict."

"Maybe they don't know she's a user."

"Maybe not yet," Quinn said.

"But we know it," Fedderman said. "Now we gotta figure out some way to use what we know."

"Or avoid getting hurt by it," Quinn said, closing the closet door.

They returned the painters' screwdrivers, pointed out where they'd missed a spot, and left the apartment.

52

Her skin was itching on the inside. Maria Sanchez, the new Madeline, was having difficulty sitting still. If Jorge could see her now he'd be disgusted. He had been so disdainful of people in the business who got hooked on the product. She wondered what his reaction would have been if he'd known she'd become a user, then a cokehead. And she knew that was what she'd become—a cokehead. Knew it now, this minute, more than ever.

She felt trapped in the apartment E-Bliss.org had moved her into after they'd hustled her out of the one the old Madeline had occupied. Once they'd decided she should move, they'd watched over her every step, so there'd be no mistakes, nothing traceable left behind. She hadn't even been alone long enough to sneak her stash out from behind the bathroom plumbing access panel on the back wall of her bedroom closet. Which meant she'd have to return.

And she did return to get what was hers, before anyone else had a chance to move in.

In a rush, already shaking because she'd waited too long, she snagged the plastic Baggie on a nail and ripped it open as she withdrew it from behind the plywood panel.

Shit!

At least half the high-quality cocaine spilled from the bag. Some of it she managed to scoop up, but the rest was a loss. It had sifted down in the cracks between the floorboards.

Like my crappy life.

Gonna be lots of wired cockroaches.

A giggle burst from her at the thought. Then the image intruded and she decided it wasn't funny. Wasn't funny at all.

She replaced the panel and got out of there fast, certain that no one had noticed her, and returned to her new apartment.

The cocaine had carried Maria for a while, and then it was gone and the waiting had begun. She'd seen it enough times with other cokeheads and knew how it was going to feel.

It started sooner than she'd expected, and it worsened fast.

She sat with her legs drawn up in a corner of the threadbare sofa. She'd been trembling, and now she was hot. Perspiring. The temperature was always off one way or another in this goddamned rat hole. This wasn't the kind of environment she was used to. Palmer Stone had promised to move her yet again, into an apartment where the water didn't run brown. It couldn't happen too soon for Maria.

She stood up and began to pace, had to move, had to keep moving. Something she'd read somewhere returned to her:

"All the trouble in the world is caused by people who can't sit still when they find themselves alone in a room."

Wasn't that the truth? And most of the trouble they caused was for themselves.

The part of her stash Maria had saved had gone so fast it had surprised her. And disturbed her. She hadn't realized how much stuff she was using, and with increasing frequency, increasing need. She hadn't suspected how deep into the trick bag she'd fallen.

Stone had warned her to be cautious, especially for the first six months. *Six months!* He had no idea what he was asking. She was going absolutely, undeniably insane.

She began to scratch her arms, her neck, leaving tracks from her gnawed fingernails. Maria knew she'd soon become a quaking mess if she didn't make a connection and get a fix. She'd seen people like that, users colliding with reality. How pathetic she'd thought they were. How weak and contemptible. Maria wasn't sure she'd changed her opinion of them now that she was one of them. She felt weak and contemptible.

She had to take the chance soon, or it would be too late. Once the nausea began—and it soon would—she'd be such a wreck nobody would trust her enough to sell to her. It would be impossible to score any kind of drug, and if she did happen to connect with a dealer, her desperation would be so obvious she'd be robbed of everything she had. The pathetic thing was that she knew she'd turn it over willingly, even eagerly, for the smallest sample of whatever would help her. She couldn't let it reach that point, where she'd do anything for salvation for an hour.

Maria decided the smart thing, the cautious thing, would be to act before it became too late. If she explained it to Palmer Stone, she was sure he'd understand. If only he'd take the time to listen and think about it.

She sat back down, got back up, paced some more.

Without recalling how she got there, she found herself in the kitchen. She opened the freezer door of the refrigerator and got out the bottle of vodka she kept there. It was only half empty. It wasn't what she needed, but it would help. For a while, anyway.

She removed the cap from the bottle and let some of the cold vodka slide down her throat. The alcohol content kept

the vodka from quite freezing, increasing its viscosity without lessening its effect. It would help her to stave off the
need and agony.

Buying time. That's what she was doing, buying time and
passing time and going mad.

The time she was buying was worth less by the minute.

She picked up the remote and switched on the TV. The
news was on, some hick sheriff's deputy or something from
someplace down South being interviewed by a woman in a
tight sweater and bad hairdo. The volume was too low to
hear, but the crawl across the bottom of the screen said the
alleged Torso Killer, Tom Coulter, had been spotted and almost caught in Louisiana.

Maria laughed. It sounded slightly maniacal even to her.
She switched off the TV and tossed the remote over on the
couch.

Crazy world! Crazy!

She walked from room to room, carrying the bottle, tracking the same path of her despair along worn carpet and sagging wood floor.

Maybe Stone wouldn't understand. Or care. He was a lot
of talk, Palmer Stone. A lot of bullshit.

She knew Stone's type all too well. She couldn't count on
him, and she didn't have to. The only person she could count
on in this insane and unfair world was herself. She had to
make a connection somehow, and soon.

Soon, God, soon!

She wanted to sit down but couldn't. Something in her
wouldn't allow it.

All the trouble in the world . . .

They were in the office on West Seventy-ninth Street. The
window air conditioner was noisy and fickle, being ornery.
Right now it was too warm in the office. Pearl, in an unchar-
acteristic burst of domesticity, had gotten them all coffee

and delivered the cups to the desks on round cork coasters she'd found somewhere. The coasters featured ads for some kind of ale Quinn had never heard of. In the warmth created by the malfunctioning air conditioner, neither Quinn nor Fedderman really wanted the steaming coffee, but they took sips from time to time so Pearl wouldn't get mad.

"The new Madeline must have E-Bliss spooked," Quinn said. "They had the initial problem when the real Madeline Scott somehow escaped when they tried to kill her. Then the new Madeline must have picked up on something from when Pearl spotted her in the elevator, so they moved her out of the building. Thanks to Pearl—" he glanced toward where she was perched on the front edge of her desk—"we know where she's living now."

"And we know she needs coke," Fedderman said.

"We'll keep a watch on her," Quinn said. "Except for Pearl, whom she's already seen. When the time comes, the new Madeline will make a hell of a witness for the prosecution."

"We've got leverage on her," Fedderman said. "Major drug rap. She'll cut a deal and cooperate."

"If they don't kill her," Pearl said.

She understood why she wouldn't be included in the watch on the new Madeline. Not only would she be a familiar face, but she'd be too busy elsewhere playing Jewel and looking after Jill Clark. And she could still *feel* Greeve following her, even though there was no sign of him. He wasn't nicknamed "The Ghost" for nothing. If he didn't know about the new Madeline, there was no point in leading him to her.

"We'll watch her partly to protect her," Quinn said, "and partly to see where she goes. Apparently she's still in contact with E-Bliss from time to time."

"We looking at her as bait?" Pearl asked. She knew it would be a coup to nail Tony Lake, or Vlad, or whatever name he was using, or maybe even Palmer Stone, in the act of trying to kill the new Madeline. And they might feel she had to be killed if they found out she was into drugs and vulnerable. She had to be a danger to them.

"We'll play this close," Quinn said. "Renz will give us some undercover help we can trust not to leak anything. And I'll bring in Nancy Weaver to fill in for Pearl. We've used Weaver before. She's good, and we can trust her, especially if there's a possibility of promotion in it for her. Between us, we'll keep a close tail on the new Madeline."

"Starting when?" Fedderman asked.

"Renz has already got an undercover outside her apartment. One of us will relieve him this evening. Word is, she stays cooped up, keeps the blinds closed."

"Scared," Fedderman said. "That's good."

"What's left of her stash might be running out," Quinn said.

"Also good."

"But pure hell for her."

"She took the elevator down," Fedderman said. "Far as we know, nobody forced her to get in."

"Meanwhile, let's go over the murder book on Ruth Malpass," Quinn said. "See if between us we can spot something useful, especially if it makes a closer connection to E-Bliss."

"Weaver?" Pearl said. "Weaver filling in for me?"

It wasn't out of the blue. Quinn had been expecting it.

"Weaver," he confirmed. He tried to use a tone of voice that would discourage Pearl from making a drama out of it.

Pearl wasn't crazy about seeing Officer Nancy Weaver brought in on the case. The two women didn't like each other, maybe because similarity bred contempt. And competition. Weaver and Pearl shared the same relentless approach to their work, as well as the same tendency to raise hackles. Weaver didn't have Pearl's short fuse, though. Quinn had to give her that.

"Weaver's back in uniform," Pearl said. "Got some shithole assignment over in Brooklyn. She got caught fooling around with a married lieutenant on the vice squad."

"Seems the place to do it," Fedderman said. "What the vice squad's all about."

Quinn wished Fedderman would take it easy. There was no point in detonating Pearl.

"That woman put the 'cop' in copulate," Pearl said.

"But she's good at what she does," Fedderman said. "Being a cop, I mean." He tried but failed to take a sip of his searingly hot coffee. "Almost at the boiling point," he said, looking at Pearl and not his coffee.

"All Weaver wants is to be promoted," Pearl said.

"I want her promoted, too," Quinn said, "if it's for helping us break this case. Weaver's got her flaws, but she's also smart and resourceful. Renz will put her back in plain clothes for this, and she'll work herself to the nub to stay there."

Pearl made a sniffing sound. "It's hard for Weaver to stay in any kind of clothes."

Fedderman gave her a pained look. "Give the woman a break, Pearl."

"Just don't give her any trouble," Quinn said in the voice he used to warn people. No mistaking it. Like God laying down the law from on high.

"You know me," Pearl said.

53

Some ringing phones are better left unanswered.

Victor had been alone in the offices of E-Bliss.org and fielded Maria Sanchez's phone call.

He was still pale and obviously angry when Palmer Stone walked in wearing one of his Armani suits and carrying his Hansom and Coach leather briefcase. Palmer was also wearing his usual handsome and benign expression, that of the kind sitcom father who'd never once raised hand nor voice to his make-believe wife and children.

"Something the matter, Victor?" he asked, with a concerned frown, as he set the briefcase alongside his desk and settled into his leather swivel chair. Victor might well have been his troubled son.

Victor, slumped on the sofa, stopped gnawing on his lower lip. "The Sanchez bitch phoned here a while ago, talked like she was crazy. Didn't even use her Madeline Scott name, called herself Maria. As if Maria Sanchez still actually existed somewhere."

The concerned frown, genuine now, stayed glued to Stone's symmetrical features. "I didn't expect to hear from her again. She seemed to understand the rules, and why they're necessary."

Once the new identity was assumed, there was *no* reason ever to contact E-Bliss.org again. It didn't exist anymore. The old identity no longer existed except here and there on paper or in obscure databases. Each special client was made to understand that that was the entire idea, to draw a line between an old and a new reality. Madeline Scott (Stone no longer allowed himself to think of her as Maria Sanchez) seemed smart enough to comprehend that. Seemed safe as a special client. Apparently she hadn't come as advertised. Stone felt himself getting disturbed and pushed the heat of his anger aside. Anger was an emotion he couldn't allow. Only one letter away from *danger,* he reminded himself. Bad for business in so many ways, anger.

Victor, Stone observed, seemed to still be angry over the phone call. Victor, who might himself be a potential problem. Stone wondered, would Gloria, if he asked, be able to deal with Victor?

A problem for another day. Here was Stone, worried about Victor's anger today.

"What did our troublesome special client want?" he asked Victor

"Said she wants the better apartment we promised her. She wants money. She wants us to live up to our end of the arrangement. She wants things to change. She wants, wants, wants!"

Stone smiled. "She wants quite a lot."

"No, I think she wants one thing," Victor said. "A fix."

Stone thought for a moment, then shook his head no. "Maria Sanchez couldn't be a drug addict. She was around the stuff, but not a user. Somebody like that, in her position, she wouldn't survive long if she even started to use."

"If it became a problem."

"It always becomes a problem," Stone said. "Or often

enough that no chances are taken. People in the business know that going in."

"Maybe it was a problem that hadn't had time to develop enough to be noticeable."

Stone said nothing. That *was* a possibility. An unsettling one. The company might have inherited a nascent problem, only just beginning to become a monster.

"I know the signs, Palmer. I know how cokeheads talk, especially when they get desperate. The bitch was unhinged."

"I still say it's unlikely that drugs are the problem," Stone said.

"If she's not a head that hit the wall, she sure sounded like one. You should've heard her, Palmer. She was ranting like she was nuts. She had to be crazy to phone here in the first place."

Stone thought back to the poised young woman he himself had interviewed, to the background file reaching into her childhood. She'd been something of a revolutionary as a young girl, but a smart one. Near the top of her college class when she met her husband. Stone even knew her IQ, which was in the superior range. He remembered her correct and concise replies to his questions, the calm and appraising intelligence in her cool blue eyes.

Palmer Stone knew breeding and quality when he saw it. Maria Sanchez qualified.

"I'll phone and discuss things rationally with her," he said. "Don't worry, Victor, I can calm her down."

Victor thought about the surest way to quiet the nutcase new Madeline Scott, a way he'd relish and she wouldn't. But he said nothing and with effort turned his mind away from possibilities already stirring in the core of him. The new Victor would think about the new Madeline Scott later, but he wouldn't act on his imaginings. Not in any way involving her. It wouldn't be worth the risk. She was business and would stay business.

He knew this was the kind of situation that called for

bullshit, and nobody was better at it than Palmer Stone. He was built of the stuff.

Victor stood up from the sofa, stretched, and nodded.

"Whatever you say, Palmer."

Jill could see that Tony was getting tired of it. And maybe a little puzzled.

He'd dropped in unexpectedly this evening, and two minutes later Jewel had turned up at the door. Jewel the pest and barrier to the bed. Jewel was talky, and downright pushy sometimes. She didn't take a hint and she didn't scare away. Tony and Jill were stuck with her. Jill played it that way, raising her eyebrows and making a what-are-you-gonna-do face at Tony when Jewel wasn't looking.

Jill had been barefoot tonight when Tony arrived. As soon as Jewel showed up, on had gone the shoes. Obviously, Tony saw that as a bad sign.

"Let's go out someplace and grab a bite to eat," he suggested, standing up from where he'd been sitting on the sofa.

"Great idea!" Jewel said.

Tony glanced at Jill. "I mean't—"

"The three of us," Jill interrupted.

He stared at her, not even caring now if Jewel saw the look he was giving her. *Why did you say that? What the hell's the matter with you?*

No doubt Jill saw Jewel as a friend as well as a pest and didn't want to hurt her feelings. Not that Jewel seemed to have any.

Tony bet she could be made to feel. He found himself looking at her from time to time, sizing her up. Small woman with a great body, if she'd quit trying to conceal it. Slender waist, big boobs and ass. Sometimes he wondered what she'd look like nude. Jill had caught him looking at Jewel like that, and he had to think fast and make it all seem innocent. Jill wasn't difficult to deceive. Tony didn't think many women were. They only thought they were clever, which made them all the easier to fool.

"We can go back to that pizza place," Jewel said. The three of them had eaten several times at a pizza joint down the block.

"Sounds great." Jill looked at Tony.

"Sounds good," was all he could muster.

The three of them started toward the door. Jill hung back and let Jewel go out first.

In the hall, when Jewel was half a dozen steps ahead of them, Jill raised her head and whispered in Tony's ear, "She's my friend. I don't want to be rude to her."

She could feel the tension in Tony, hear it in his breathing. How long could this charade last without him becoming suspicious? And if he did suspect, what would he do? She was beginning to think this might be the evening when she was going to find out.

Then his face broke into his beautiful smile. Easygoing Tony. The Tony she knew.

He bent over as they approached the elevator and whispered back to her, still smiling, "Hey, I understand. What're you gonna do?" He kissed her ear.

Despite herself, she felt something in her melt.

He's a killer.

Sometimes it was so hard to remember that.

He reached over and squeezed her hand gently, lovingly, assuring her he did indeed understand her predicament with Jewel.

"Don't worry, darling," he said patiently. "We'll be alone sooner or later. Just the two of us. I'll see to it."

Something with a thousand legs walked up Jill's spine.

54

Tom Coulter stationed himself at the small wooden table where he'd sat drinking last night in Rodney's Roadhouse. The mingled odors of stale beer and stale sweat were in the air, along with tobacco smoke. Nobody in Rodney's was afraid to inhale.

The place was narrow but long, with a bar to the right of the entrance, tables to the left, a few of them back beyond the bar where the light wasn't so good. Most of the light was provided by illuminated signs advertising beer: a hunter holding up a bottle, label out, posed near a dead buck; a girl in a skimpy bikini casually sipping brew while water-skiing; a famous baseball player, retired and free of contractual constraints, regarding a half-empty frosty mug and grinning with a foam mustache. Mixed in with the beer signs were a few advertising cigarettes. Like Rodney's itself, most of the ads seemed to date back about twenty years.

Coulter's table had old initials carved in it, worn almost smooth with the grain. It was the farthest table from the bar, near a short hall leading to the back exit, which was a screen door poked full of holes. From where he sat he could sip his beer and observe everything going on in Rodney's, and at the same time get out in a hurry if it became necessary. Beyond the back entrance was the swamp, where Coulter had lost himself before and could again. City boy that he was, he had come to regard the swamp as a reliable friend on call to lend him shelter.

Rodney himself, a guy about fifty, built like a potato sack with a lumpy face to match, wandered back now and then to see that Coulter had enough beer in his bottle. It wasn't the kind of place that furnished glasses. It took two of those trips before Coulter noticed that Rodney had an artificial right eye that didn't match his left. Or was it the other way around?

It was getting to be evening, and the roadhouse regulars were filtering in. Half a dozen guys who looked like construction laborers were at the bar. Two homely women in jeans and sleeveless T-shirts perched on the last two stools at the end of the bar near the entrance. Coulter had figured it out on the first night that they were whores working the place. One of them, Cathy Lee, chunky and obviously proud of her generous cleavage, had approached him. She had a tangle of blond hair, wore way too much rose-scented perfume, and had a sweet twenty-year-old's face with forty-year-old eyes. He'd bought her a drink and strung her along, but not so much that she hadn't deserted him for a more likely prospect.

Cathy Lee sensed he was watching her and turned her head and nodded, smiling. She wasn't coming over, though. She figured sooner or later they'd get together. Coulter thought that under ordinary circumstances she'd be right. Cathy Lee might have been his going-away present to himself, only there wasn't the time. He had other ideas for tonight.

About half the tables had people sitting at them now. The air wasn't good. It was humid from the swamp, as well as heavy with the unpleasant smells trying to crowd one another out. Conversation and laughter were getting louder, and speakers mounted high on the walls were playing a lament by some country singer about a man who'd shot at his wife's lover and accidentally killed the wife. *A guy with my kind of luck,* Coulter thought.

He was particularly interested in two rough-looking guys at one of the tables. One was about Coulter's height but even skinnier and had a scraggly red beard, though the hair on his head was brown. The other guy was short but broad and had his head shaved. Had—guess what—a strand of barbed wire tattooed around both oversized biceps.

Swamp turkeys, Coulter thought. Every once in a while someone would approach the two men. What looked like money would change hands; backs would be slapped; high fives would be given; smiles would be exchanged. Coulter eared in and made out that the tall skinny guy's name was Joe Ray. The short, broad one was called Juan, though he didn't look as if he had a drop of Latin blood in him.

Coulter figured they were dealing drugs, most likely meth. He'd fallen behind lately on the news, but he knew this part of *Looziana* was meth country. There'd been an explosion that had killed two guys cooking the stuff in a house trailer not far down the state road, and the sheriff had promised action in shutting down meth labs. Coulter smiled. *A sheriff. Wild West. And the hayseeds don't know the biggest desperado in the country's sitting right here among them drinking draft Bud.*

They'd crap in their drawers if they did know, and that I'm sitting here with a plan.

Coulter hadn't been lounging around wasting time in Rodney's. He'd been watching and waiting, figuring things out.

He knew he wouldn't be safe around here much longer. He couldn't afford to stay anywhere very long. He'd stashed the big F-150 truck back in the swamp and had been more or less living out of it. He knew he shouldn't move it around much. Its description and plate number must have been broadcast all over the country.

Joe Ray and Juan, the meth guys, had a truck. A beat-to-shit old Dodge pickup nobody'd look twice at in swamp country, mostly rust and dents, but with a legal license. And they were bound to have drug money stashed wherever they lived.

Coulter had the F-150 out in the gravel parking lot tonight, parked way back near the trees. Black swamp mud was artfully packed on its license plate so you couldn't read most of the numbers and letters, in case anyone got curious. This model of truck, being so popular, was one of several F-150s on the lot, so Coulter felt pretty safe about leaving it there.

When the meth guys left Rodney's tonight, he'd follow them to wherever it was they slept, hold them up at gunpoint, and trade trucks with them. He'd have to explain to the dumb jerkoffs how things worked. They wouldn't report their truck being stolen, because if caught with it, Coulter would blow the whistle on their illegal meth operation. The F-100 they could paint, and then maybe arrange for a junkyard title and drive it as long as they wanted. Guys like them had the connections. Yokels were into trucks.

Coulter figured that when the two meth guys thought about it, they'd be glad for the deal. Sure they'd lose some cash, but they'd be gaining an expensive new truck in exchange for their rolling piece of crap. Some trading up.

The other thing about his plan, before he drove away in their junker and with all their cash, was that he would be sure to let them know they'd been held up by the most wanted fugitive in the country. Couple of hicks, it'd probably be the biggest thing in their lives. But they wouldn't tell anyone. They couldn't. They'd have an interest in him not being caught. Not with their rust-bucket truck, anyway. Also, they'd probably secretly be on his side. Underdogs stuck together tight, just like the smelly swamp mud around this place.

Pleased with himself, Coulter sipped his beer and through half-closed eyes observed money changing hands.

Money that would soon be in his hands.

55

She had to do *something*!

Had to *move*!

Maria Sanchez decided to walk off some of the energy that was building up in her like a nuclear device about to reach critical mass.

She left her shit-hole apartment, and when she got outside the building took a deep breath and turned right. The evening air was cooler than the heat of the day, but not by much. The city's concrete still radiated heat from today's bright sun.

She strode along the sidewalk almost at a run, but after a few blocks, when she realized how hard she was breathing, she slowed down.

Maria hadn't set off with any particular destination in mind, but since she was walking toward Columbus Circle she decided to go there. If the scream that was like an itch in her throat had gone away by then, she'd walk back to the apartment and see if she could make it a while longer before going out and taking the risk of trying to make a buy.

Columbus Circle, then back. Then, if the need returned . . .

At least she had a plan.

Plan or go mad!

Maybe, once she made it back, she wouldn't go out again at all tonight. She could drink some booze—not at all her drug of choice—and watch some crummy TV on the lousy little set in the corner of the living room until she was tired enough to sleep. She knew Palmer Stone was right, that the smart thing, the only thing that made sense, was for her to bide her time and keep a low profile.

But Palmer Stone wasn't the one with the scream caught in his throat.

What the hell was she up to?

Nancy Weaver, who'd been watching the new Madeline's apartment building from across the street, saw her leave the building, dressed casually in brown slacks, white joggers, and a red tunic gathered at the waist by a thick brown belt with an oversized buckle. On the opposite side of the street, Weaver began to shadow her.

After only a few strides she knew it wasn't going to be easy. The woman was damned near running.

Weaver was the shorter of the two women and was wearing clunky black cop's shoes instead of joggers. Every once in a while she'd have to take a few skips to keep pace with Madeline; otherwise she'd have to break into a jog. She wasn't dressed for jogging, what with the leather shoes and the skirt and blazer. She'd attract a lot of attention. Some of it might be Madeline's.

Finally, on Broadway, Madeline slowed down.

Weaver stayed well back, huffing and puffing and wiping sweat from her brow with the back of her wrist. She didn't want to screw up this temporary assignment. Quinn believed in her, and he was about the only one left. She knew if things went right he'd put in a word for her. He was a tough guy and a real cop, and he recognized her talent for being a detective. And he had pull. He could get her back in plain clothes permanently. She could take it from there. Sure, she'd been dumb before and gotten herself all jammed up and back in uniform. It wouldn't happen again, though. She'd make sure of that.

Madeline had slowed down even more and was kind of ambling. It was almost as if she'd been trying to get away from something and had finally found some relief. Working off tension. Weaver had been there herself and understood. She just wished Madeline didn't have those long legs. Wished *she* had those long legs. A cop with legs like that could get herself promoted.

Following Madeline became progressively easier at this slower pace. Weaver fell into the other woman's rhythm. It was almost as if she were inside Madeline's mind and knew ahead of time what she was going to do, where she was going.

They were almost to Columbus Circle.

Gloria hadn't had much trouble keeping up with Maria Sanchez, a.k.a. Madeline Scott. She was glad, though, that the bitch had finally slowed down. They were almost at Columbus Circle. That would be good. Plenty of traffic. Rush hour. Everybody in a hurry. Careless.

Gloria had shoved the first Madeline off the subway platform just as the train was roaring in. Even if someone in the crowd edging toward the train had noticed, it would have seemed only a slight, accidental nudge. They wouldn't have guessed the technique and power in it.

Not a subway this time, Gloria had decided. A street vehicle. Preferably a cab, but an ordinary car or truck would do. A bus might work well. She was confident Maria Sanchez's stay on this earth was fast coming to an end.

If Gloria didn't have the opportunity this time, she'd wait for another chance. It would come. She had patience. God would provide.

After Victor had related to her his conversation with Palmer about Maria's phone call, Gloria knew something had to be done, and she had to be the one to do it. Victor and Palmer would agree that Maria had to be deleted, she was sure, only not soon enough. They were men, and this bitch knew how to string men along. For the safety of all of them, for the company, Maria had to go soon, before she did damage they couldn't control.

Watching the woman striding ahead of her—the erect posture; long legs; slender hips; and tight, round ass—Gloria momentarily considered doing things the slow way. But she soon reconsidered. This was business and nothing to play with, however enjoyable it might be. It needed to be fast, and look like an accident.

No problem. Gloria smiled, remembering not only the first Madeline, who'd been too breathless and shocked to scream, disappearing beneath the speeding subway train, but also the many hits she'd made for a long-ago insurance scam. She could make this work. Bringing about other people's accidental deaths used to be her specialty, and it was a skill you never forgot.

Weaver saw Madeline slow down near the traffic circus of Columbus Circle. Cars, trucks, buses coming fast and from odd angles as traffic lights signaled in the dying light. A person had to be careful crossing the street here, but even with care, things happened.

Madeline stopped at the curb among a knot of about a dozen people waiting for the light to change. Several more pedestrians joined the crowd, edging in tight, closer to each other. Some of them leaned slightly forward, as if the traffic light would signal the beginning of a race.

Weaver slowed her pace. She didn't want to reach the intersection too soon. Better to keep some distance between herself and Madeline.

She felt a tingling pain in her right calf, and her left foot was sore from her shoe being a little too tight. All that high-speed walking had taken its toll. And apparently it had all been for nothing. It wasn't as if Madeline was late for an appointment. Weaver felt a twinge of aggravation with this woman who was taller, more attractive, and irritatingly blond. And with those legs.

The light changed, and waiting parallel traffic roared and sprang forward. The charge was led by a gleaming white stretch limo. Pedestrians could cross now in the direction of the flowing traffic, but they had to wait for right-turning vehicles to give them a break. This being New York, right-turning vehicles didn't.

Gloria was standing directly behind Maria Sanchez when the signal changed. She could smell her shampoo and perspiration, feel the heat emanating from her lean body.

Exhaust fumes suddenly overpowered all other smells. A bus. That would be perfect!

Gloria had both fists bunched, ready to plant them between Maria's shoulder blades and give a short but powerful shove. But the man next to Maria for some reason glanced over at Gloria. Gloria kept a poker face and let the bus rumble around the corner.

The man was looking forward again, concentrating on the traffic.

Gloria waited, mentally ticking off the seconds, aware of everything around her, knowing she had to synthesize time, movement, and her target's inattention so that it all added up to sudden death.

Her meat.

Here came a cab.

* * *

Weaver picked up her pace and moved toward the intersection, knowing there'd soon be a break in the flow of right-turning traffic and the pedestrians straining to go would step down off the curb and claim their territory between the white lines.

She heard the screech of rubber on blacktop. There was a flurry of movement ahead as people waiting at the curb surged across, moving around something. Most of them kept walking, glancing behind them and down, as if at an object they'd dropped that wasn't valuable enough to stop for and retrieve. Several were looking deliberately *away* from something.

Uh-oh!

Weaver could see the yellow roof of a stopped cab with its service light glowing.

She stood on tiptoe and saw Madeline well ahead of her, among the throng of people striding across the street. *Damn!* Weaver would have to hustle to catch up.

As she stepped off the curb to make her way around the cab, she saw what everyone was staring at. A dark-haired woman wearing a red scarf lay in front of the cab. There was a pool of blood beneath her head.

Weaver couldn't stop. She had to hurry to keep pace with Madeline. She made her way through the stalled traffic as drivers rubbernecked at the downed woman. As she walked, she fumbled in her pocket for her cell phone so she could call and get the woman some help, but a siren whooped nearby and she saw a radio car on the other side of the street. It was making its way toward the scene of the accident. She slid the phone back into her pocket.

Whatever had been compelling Madeline to walk must have worn off. Weaver followed her down the concrete steps to the subway stop at Columbus Circle.

They rode in a stifling, crowded car back to within a few blocks of Madeline's apartment. Madeline, looking despondent and exhausted, sat between a scowling black youth wearing dreadlocks and a black leather jacket despite the heat, and a bearded man studying a tabloid newspaper printed in some language Weaver didn't recognize. Weaver stood gripping a steel pole for support, looking everywhere but at Madeline.

With Madeline safe inside the building, Weaver took up her observation position in the doorway of a closed tailor shop diagonally across the street.

She leaned her back against the heavy plate-glass door, crossed her arms, and let herself relax. The new Madeline was in her apartment, tired, and unlikely to go out again soon. Weaver figured everything was under control. At least for a while, the excitement was over.

The lettering above her head on the inside of the door read RIPS AND TEARS OUR SPECIALTY.

56

Tom Coulter climbed up into the F-150 and followed the two meth guys, Joe Ray and Juan, from Rodney's Roadhouse. They drove a couple of miles back into the swamp, over rutted, muddy roads sometimes so narrow that leaves brushed the windshield. Coulter thought it was creepy and saw no reason why anyone would choose to live like this. The heat and humidity made you sick, and the damned weird-looking bugs were bigger than the roaches in New York.

The Dodge pickup slowed and made a right onto a narrow dirt road that turned out to be a driveway. Coulter stopped before following it and looked the place over.

No big surprise where a couple of swamp turkeys like Joe Ray and Juan lived. It was a flat-roofed, clapboard house that looked as if it had never been painted. Vines grew up the front wall and much of the side wall that Coulter could see. A sagging gutter ran across the front of the house, its drainpipe disappearing into a wooden barrel. About a hundred feet off to the side was an outbuilding more rickety than the house. Coulter figured that was where they had their meth lab.

He waited until they'd gone inside the house, then rolled the F-150 up the drive, pulled it close behind their rusty Dodge, and gunned the engine and tapped the horn a few times. He wanted to get them out of the shack so they could see the difference in the two trucks. They were dealing big-time here, not junk vehicles and money under the mattress.

The two of them came ambling out the front, Joe Ray first, and let the screen door slam behind them. They stood on the porch, looking surprised and wary. Coulter was getting a kick out of it. Neither man displayed a weapon. Pair of yokels against a genuine desperado. His confidence soared. This should be easy.

Coulter got out of the truck and walked over there, then he casually reached behind him and drew the Glock out from where it was tucked in his belt at the small of his back. *Whoaho!* The two meth guys came hyperalert. Their eyes darted this way and that, making Coulter think of trapped animals. There was no direction they could move without Coulter bringing them both down. He wouldn't have drawn the Glock otherwise. He smiled inwardly. Organization was the key to success.

Then the two of them, seeing the hopelessness of their situation, seemed to calm down.

"What the hell you want?" Joe Ray asked, showing a little bravado.

"He wants to get hisself killed," Juan said.

"My, my," Coulter said and moved the gun barrel over to point at Juan. Juan looked scared, but held his ground. What else could the dumb schmuck do?

"It ain't love makes the world go round," Coulter said. "It's business. We're all businessmen. I want to talk a deal."

"What kinda business you in?" Joe Ray asked.

"Right now, far as you're concerned, the truck business." Coulter almost giggled. "And I guess you could say the travel business."

The meth guys said nothing.

"We're gonna trade trucks," Coulter said. "Your bucket of rust for my almost-new Ford F-150."

Joe Ray looked off to the side and spat. "Now why am I thinkin' that ain't your truck?"

" 'Cause it ain't. That's my problem. But you got a problem, too."

"Which is?"

"Me. And I got the solution for both of us."

"You're one smart asshole," Juan said.

Coulter grinned. "Maybe I should shoot you in the knee."

Juan went pale.

Joe Ray said, "Let's all ease up here." He looked with wary, level eyes at Coulter. Maybe a spark of helpless anger in those eyes. "Let's quit jerkin' each other off. Say plain what you come here to say."

"I'll take your truck with its legal license plate. You keep the Ford, paint it up, get yourselves a salvage VIN and a legal license, and you're way ahead of the game. You boys smart enough to follow that?"

"We follow," Joe Ray said. "We ain't sure we like where it might lead."

"Cops lookin' for that truck?" Juan asked. He was staring with longing at the sleek black Ford with its oversized tires. Even dusty as it was, the bruiser of a vehicle was obviously a quantum leap trade-up.

Coulter gave them his best desperado grin. "Let's say the rightful owner would like to have it back. I guarantee you he's in another state and won't be a problem for you. Me, I need transportation. I drive outta here in the junk Dodge, and I won't be a problem for you, either."

"Way you tell it, we part company and nobody's got a problem."

"Congratulations. You finally caught on."

Juan glanced at Joe Ray. "It don't sound like a bad deal."

"Don't shit yourself," Joe Ray said, staring at Coulter.

"Well, there is one more thing," Coulter said. "I want the meth money you've been raking in at Rodney's."

"What the hell is meth?" Joe Ray asked.

"What I can smell coming from that outbuilding over there, where you cook the stuff." Coulter shifted his weight. The Glock was getting heavy. "It still ain't a bad deal for you. That's a thirty-thousand-dollar truck, easy. You got that much meth money?"

The two men exchanged a sly look.

Coulter smiled. "I guess you do."

"I don't like the deal," Joe Ray said.

"Doesn't matter a bit. I drive away with rusty and the money; you stay here with your new truck. You call the law on me, they pick me up, and you're toast. Same thing the other way around. So we're both safe. That's the beauty of the proposition. We got no choice but to trust each another."

"You musta gave this a lotta thought," Juan said.

"Thinking happens to be my specialty," Coulter said. "That's why this deal's gonna work. Now, next thing happens is you two yokels lead me to where you got the money stashed."

"Ain't likely," said a woman's voice.

Coulter looked to where Cathy Lee from Rodney's Roadhouse was standing hip-shot near the corner of the shack. She must have come out a back door. She had on a stained gray robe, was barefoot, and her frizzy blond hair was flattened on one side as if she'd been sleeping on it. Her boobs were hanging halfway out, and she was holding a double-barreled shotgun. The effect was alarming.

"You boys don't watch the news," she said, motioning with her head toward a small satellite dish on the corner of the shack's tarpaper roof. "This is the guy killed all them people in New York."

"Killed people?" Juan said, looking at Coulter with new respect.

"The Torso Killer. He's probably the most wanted man in

the country." Cathy Lee smiled at Coulter. "Ain't you just proud of yourself?"

Coulter couldn't stop staring at the shotgun.

"There'd be a reward out for him," Juan said. "Prob'ly a big one."

"I ain't interested in no reward," Joe Ray said. "What I'm interested in is burying him."

The shotgun wavered. It was a long gun. Heavy, for a woman. Coulter wondered, how strong and quick could she be, little country whore? And her eyes looked all red and swollen. She might have been napping and could still be half asleep.

She was holding the shotgun low now, its barrels at a forty-five-degree angle to the ground.

Her mistake. Coulter's only chance.

He'd barely started to bring the Glock to bear on Cathy Lee when the shotgun came up astoundingly fast and she fired.

He was on his back in the mud. The pain in his chest made him gasp. His heart started banging irregularly, like an engine running crazy on empty just before it quits.

Everything went spinning, and then everything went dark.

They say the last thing that goes when someone's dying is his hearing. Coulter heard distinctly the sucking sound of a boot sole in the mud, very near his head. Joe Ray's voice from high above:

"Both barrels. You surely made a mess here, Cathy Lee."

"My bad," Cathy Lee said.

Joe Ray, Juan, and Cathy Lee studied on it for a while, then decided not to bury Coulter nearby. He was, after all, the most wanted man in America. If the police traced him to the area, they'd eventually find the body. On the other hand, the meth guys and Cathy Lee sure couldn't say they'd killed him and try to claim any kind of reward. The farther away Joe Ray, Juan, and Cathy Lee stayed from the law, the better for them.

They decided to drive Coulter off some distance and dump his body, make it look like he was shot on the side of the road. Could be the law would think he was hitchhiking and some mean bastard drilled him for sport. That's if he was found before some gator dragged him off.

The Ford truck was another matter. You could tell that under all that dust and caked mud it was a cherry. They could have it painted another color. Joe Ray knew where he could get a "ghost truck" VIN from a similar-F-150 that was wrecked and in a salvage yard, and have the truck retitled. The truck wouldn't be legal, but it would be close.

Coulter they wanted no part of, but the truck was worth the risk.

57

The first thing in the morning, Victor drove the Chrysler over to a parking garage off Broadway. From there he walked the crowded, sunlit sidewalks to the offices of E-Bliss.org.

Now and then someone gave him a second glance. He needed a shave. He'd slept with his clothes on, on Gloria's sofa, and his usually razor-creased suit pants were wrinkled. The matching coat, which he'd draped over a chair back, was still neatly pressed. The effect was that the pants looked even baggier. That and the black stubble on his face made him look like a homeless person who'd rolled a rich banker after first getting him to remove his coat. This wasn't at all like Victor, not to care about his appearance.

Palmer Stone glanced up from the E-Bliss applications he was studying when Victor gave a perfunctory knock and walked into his office. Stone was working at his desk with his suit coat on, as was his custom, and was impeccably groomed. Always when someone walked into his office he looked like a captain of commerce interrupted in an important task involving world affairs. This morning, he was quite a contrast to Victor.

Stone laid down the printout he'd been holding. It was

John Lutz

rife with information about a lonely, middle-aged widow in Queens.

"Victor! What on earth happened to you?"

"I tried to get in touch with Gloria yesterday afternoon and evening," Victor said, driving to the point, "and I couldn't. I spent the night in her apartment. She never came home."

Stone appeared alarmed at first, then thoughtful. "It isn't the first time, Victor."

"It is without me knowing where she was. We always knew—know—where the other one is. We've got this extra sense like we pick up each other's radio waves, and Palmer, she's not broadcasting."

"Victor, it's a little premature to think she's . . . gone."

"I've got a bad feeling, Palmer."

Stone swiveled to the side and leaned back in his chair, facing the window but obviously not looking outside. Victor and Gloria. He knew both of them well, but there were some aspects of their relationship that still puzzled him, made him wonder. But then, he never had a sister.

"You know Gloria," he said. "She's probably off on some adventure."

"She would've stayed in touch. When I called her cell number, her phone was turned off."

"Maybe she simply didn't want to be disturbed."

Victor started to pace, raking his fingers through his hair with each step. "I told you, Palmer, Gloria and I are on what you might say is the same wavelength. I've really got a hunch something's happened to her."

"Could be you're being an alarmist."

Stone didn't like what he was seeing here. More indication of instability in Victor. Gloria hadn't seemed upset when Stone had talked to her about her brother. On the other hand, she hadn't seemed surprised. There seemed no reason for Victor's consternation. He did know his sister was a lesbian with an active sex life, so why couldn't he accept the fact that she might right now be sleeping late in some lady-love's warm bed?

Victor clenched and unclenched his fists. "Listen, Palmer—"

But Stone raised a manicured forefinger for quiet as his phone rang. He snatched up the receiver.

Gloria, he hoped.

Victor paced and watched while the caller did most of the talking. Stone's mature, handsome features grew more and more set and pale.

Something was obviously very wrong.

Victor stopped pacing and collapsed on the black leather sofa facing the desk.

Stone hung up the phone and swiveled his chair to look directly at him with an expression of fatherly concern.

"Gloria was struck by a cab yesterday near Columbus Circle," he said. "They tried to get in touch with someone, but couldn't."

"She doesn't have a landline phone," Victor said.

Stone nodded gravely. "The people at the hospital finally figured out how to look in her cell phone log. The last call she'd made was to here."

Victor sat up straight. "Hospital?"

"She's at St. Luke's–Roosevelt, in critical condition. Her skull's been fractured and her hip and left leg are broken."

"Jesus! But at least she's alive."

"The cab hit her when she stepped off the curb. That's what witnesses said. An accident."

"What the hell was she doing—"

"Who knows, Victor? Gloria's her own woman." *That's for damned sure.* Stone swiveled his chair toward the window again. He tilted back. "You'd better drive over there and see her, Victor. See if she's conscious, talking. Maybe she's under the influence of sedatives. You understand what I mean?"

But when Stone swiveled around for an answer to his question, Victor was gone.

Stone combed through both the *Times* and the *Post*, but neither of the papers made mention of Gloria's accident. That didn't surprise Stone, but it relieved him. News was news. Gloria wasn't remotely famous, which meant the media would probably ignore the story tomorrow morning, too. That meant her name wouldn't be in the papers or mentioned on television or radio. Stone much preferred it that way. Less of a threat to the business.

A little after one o'clock, Stone's phone rang as he was rifling through a middle file cabinet drawer. Without standing up, he rolled his chair over to the desk and picked up.

Victor, calling from the hospital.

"She looks terrible, Palmer," Victor said plaintively. "Her head's all bandaged and her face is so swollen you wouldn't know it was her."

"Is she conscious?" Stone asked.

Drugged up? Talking?

"There's no way to be sure if she knows what's going on around her."

"What do you mean, Victor?"

"She's in a coma, Palmer. The doctors say they don't know how long it will last, or even"—Victor's voice broke—"if she'll ever come out of it."

Stone was surprised to find his own throat tightening. The three of them had been together in one scam or another for a lot of years. He did feel for Victor. And for Gloria. Emotions were doing that more and more lately, catching Palmer by surprise.

"Is there anything I can do, Victor?"

"I don't think so, Palmer. I don't think there's anything anyone can do."

"I'm sorry, Victor. I really am."

"I know that, Palmer."

After hanging up the phone, Stone sat back and assessed the situation. Gloria was obviously out of commission. Judging by what Victor had said, she wasn't about to say anything that might attract suspicion as to what she . . . did for a living. And someone being struck and seriously injured by a vehicle was a common occurrence in New York. There was nothing about Gloria's accident that would attract undue attention.

Stone sighed and smiled.

Any danger to the company had been narrowly averted.

The question now was, how would what happened to Gloria affect Victor? Stone had been suffering doubts about him before Gloria's accident. Gloria had gone a long way toward assuaging those doubts, but not all the way.

Now this.

Palmer wondered, could Victor still do his job?

58

Jill watched Tony's eyes follow Jewel as she wove her way through a maze of red-clothed tables toward the restroom. He wasn't the only one watching. Half the men in the restaurant at least sneaked a glance at Jewel. She was quite the temptress when she wasn't dressed like a cop.

She wasn't dressed like one now, in her tight black dress with the low neckline, her three-inch heels. Jill knew that Jewel wanted to look like anything but a cop.

They were in Dominick's Italiano, a new gourmet restaurant on the West Side. Tony had raved about the extensive wine list in order to talk Jill into going there with him, and naturally Jewel had invited herself along. Jill, of course, hadn't resisted and had given Tony the evil eye when he had begun to voice his objections.

"Did you ever think," Tony now asked Jill, as he still watched Jewel, "that she's a little *too* friendly with you?"

Jill saw Jewel veer left and disappear into a hallway, walking none too steadily, as if maybe she'd had too much wine with her dinner. But then, Jewel—or Pearl—was a pretty good actress.

"What do you mean?" Jill asked. "*Too* friendly?" He was giving her a crooked little smile.

Then she realized what Tony meant. "Jesus, Tony! Jewel and me? Are you kidding?"

The crooked smile turned sad, as if gravity had suddenly claimed it. "Not Jewel and *you*. Just Jewel. I mean, the way she looks at you sometimes."

"Get off it, Tony. Jewel's no lesbian."

He shrugged.

Jill started to take a sip of her coffee, then changed her mind and sipped from the half-full wineglass the waiter had left. "Tony, neither one of us is in romantic love with the other."

"I'm in love with you."

"You know what I mean. Jewel and me in some kind of sexual relationship. It's absurd."

"Not absurd at all."

"Well, I think so."

"It happens," he said.

"Of course it does. That's the way the world works. I'm not homophobic or passing any kind of moral judgment."

Tony reached across the table and squeezed her hand. "I know you're not, hon. I know you better than that. But do me a favor, will you, and just pay closer attention. I mean, the way she hangs around you all the time doesn't seem to me like the usual platonic relationship."

Jill felt her face flush with embarrassment and anger.

Tony had gone too far. He seemed to know it. He sat back abruptly in his chair, which was on rollers, and the force carried him a few feet from the table. When he tried a smile it didn't quite work. He rolled back to the table. Most of the dishes had been cleared and they were waiting for dessert, some kind of chocolate-iced cream puffs the *Post* food editor had raved about.

Jewel arrived at the same time as the cream puffs. She

looked neater than when she'd left the table. Her hair had been combed and her freshened makeup made her features even more vivid. She sat down with some difficulty in the tight dress and replaced her napkin in her lap. "Some restroom," she said. "You oughta see how clean and modern it is. Everything automatic." She smiled at Jill. "You should've come with me."

Tony and Jill exchanged glances. Jewel gave no indication that she'd noticed. She smiled at the waiter and asked for two of the miniature cream puffs from the pyramidal display on a tray.

No one spoke until the waiter was finished serving dessert and had poured the coffee and departed.

"You okay, Tony?" Jewel asked. "You seem kind of . . . I don't know, out of sorts."

He frowned. " 'Out of sorts.' What's that mean?"

"On the edge of being grouchy," Jill cut in, tempering her words with a smile.

Tony sighed. "I guess I am on edge. I'm sorry. Somebody at work I like a lot had an accident and he's badly injured."

"That's too bad," Jill said, wondering why Tony hadn't mentioned this to her earlier.

"Hospitalized?" Jewel asked.

"Yeah. Poor guy was hit by a car."

"Damned shame," Jewel said.

"He's going to be okay, isn't he?" Jill asked.

"I sure hope so. He's one of those guys everybody likes."

"Things like that always happen to the wrong people," Jewel said.

Tony might not have heard her. He was twisting his red cloth napkin, staring hard at it.

But Jewel knew he had heard.

"These cream puffs are delicious," Jill said. She swallowed a bite and licked chocolate icing from her finger.

"They sure are, hon," Tony said, though he hadn't yet

taken a bite of his. He came out of his distraction for a few seconds to glare at Jewel.

Jill finished her second cream puff. "Mmmm! These are sinful."

"Dangerous," Jewel agreed, thinking things couldn't go on much longer as they were. Tony was one of the sharper knives in the drawer. He was getting suspicious and might make some kind of move.

She made a mental note to get on the Internet, check and see how many double murders occurred every year in New York City.

A lot, she bet.

59

Both of them knew the other was awake.

Quinn lay beside Linda in his bed, listening to the nearness of her breathing. He knew the breathing of complete relaxation from the breathing of sleep. So did she, he was sure.

He watched the morning sun brighten the rectangular outline around the tightly closed blinds, then send lances of light to lie in narrow rhomboids on the rug and the sheets near the foot of the bed. Faint traffic sounds were building up outside, in another world. Jackhammers, the urban equivalent of woodpeckers, clattered away in the far, far distance.

"What are you thinking?" Linda asked. Her words seemed to linger with effort in the still room.

"Honestly?"

"Sure. What else? Even if it's something as prosaic as wishing you didn't have to get up and relieve the pressure on your bladder."

"You talk a lot like a doctor," Quinn said.

"Act like one, too, I'm sure." The sheets rustled and a bedspring *poinged* as she shifted position beside him. "Is that a turnoff?"

"Turn-on."

"Really?" She sounded genuinely amazed.

"Men pay money to have women dress up as nurses and have sex with them," Quinn said. "So why not doctors?"

"Some of the men probably *are* doctors."

"You know what I mean." He tried to give her bottom a gentle slap, but she wasn't where he'd thought.

"Doctors like Nift," she said.

"Nift's got a wife."

Linda made a slight huffing sound. "Like that stops men from paying prostitutes."

Quinn looked over at her. "You know something about Nift?"

"More than I'd like."

"Most anyone who knows him would say that."

"He isn't normal, the way he moons over female corpses."

"I guess it is out of the ordinary." Quinn sat up in bed and worked himself sideways, feeling the cool hardwood floor on the bare soles of his feet where the carpet ended. "I thought he might only do that at crime scenes. He acts the same way at the morgue?"

"He's almost always good for an insensitive remark or two."

"Could be he's just like the rest of us, trying to stay sane."

"Or it could be he's just got a nasty mind and can't help expressing himself."

"What about during the actual autopsies?"

"To be honest, he's very professional then. Despite what I say about the guy, he's a skilled physician. But if we have an attractive dead female not yet on the table, he can't seem to control himself. Other than that, he's all business."

"Other than that."

"When he's not ratting somebody out."

"That's business, too," Quinn said. He stood up.

"Where you going?"

"What I'm thinking right now is—"

"Never mind," Linda said.

* * *

Victor watched the nurse outside Gloria's critical care unit trade whispers with a doctor so they wouldn't be overheard. With a backward glance at Victor, the nurse scurried away down the hall. The doctor, a tall, blond, shambling man in baggy green scrubs, headed in the general direction of where Victor sat in the furnished alcove that served as one of the hospital's waiting areas. He was one of those very tall men with a perpetual forward lean, as if he'd adapted to low ceilings.

In the waiting area, there were a sofa, a couple of matching black herringbone wing chairs, and a wall-mounted TV playing a rerun of *Who Wants to Be a Millionaire?* Regis was blue on blue on blue in this one. Victor thought, *who wants to be monochromatic?*

Victor had assumed the doctor was going to walk past; he seemed preoccupied. Then he appeared to snap back to reality and made a sudden turn toward Victor, holding out his hand.

Victor stood up from the sofa and shook the cool, dry hand.

"You're the patient's brother?" he asked Victor, with a concerned expression. He had a pale complexion, red-rimmed blue eyes.

Victor said he was.

"I'm Dr. Polanski. The nurse said you've been asking for an update on your sister's condition."

"Nobody wants to tell me anything," Victor said.

Dr. Polanski nodded, as if he'd heard the complaint many times before. "She's still in a coma," he said. "Her hip and leg injuries are serious but under control and pose her no danger. It's the head injury we have to keep an eye on."

"But she's going to be okay?"

Dr. Polanski took a deep breath. "She should be. It's difficult to know for sure with this kind of head injury. There's still significant hemorrhaging, causing blood seepage between the skull and the membrane covering the brain. This is causing pressure that has to be relieved. As of now, there's no way to know for sure whether that pressure's done damage to the brain itself."

"She looks calm. Is she suffering?"

"No, she's sedated, and we're going to keep her in an induced coma for at least another few days."

"Induced? You mean you've deliberately put her in a coma?"

"It's what we do in cases like this, Mr. . . . ?"

"Lamping. Victor Lamping."

"Your sister has no other family?"

"I'm afraid not."

"I'll tell the nurses to keep you informed," Dr. Polanski said. "And to notify you when your sister is conscious and you can visit her."

He extended his hand again, and Victor shook it.

"With a little luck," Dr. Polanski said, "your sister's going to be okay."

Victor watched the doctor stride swiftly down the hall and disappear through two wide swinging doors that parted for him automatically, seeming to hurry themselves because they knew he wasn't going to slow down. They leisurely closed behind him so that their NO ADMITTANCE message was again on display.

After checking the nurses' station to make sure they had his cell number, Victor left the hospital and took a cab to the offices of E-Bliss.org.

Seated behind his desk, wearing flower-patterned suspenders over a white shirt today, Palmer Stone looked properly concerned as Victor filled him in on Gloria's condition.

"So the coma's induced," he said thoughtfully when Victor was finished.

"I've told the nurses I want to be there when they bring her out of it," Victor said. He let himself fall back into the leather sofa, making air swish from the cushions like a sympathetic sigh. "I've never trusted nurses."

"Nor I," Stone said. The air from the cushions caused a stirring that brought a whiff of Stone's expensive cologne to Victor. Stone laced his fingers on the desktop. "How are things progressing in the Jill Clark matter?"

"Not well," Victor said. "Her upstairs neighbor and new best friend—that bitch Jewel—is complicating things. She's on Jill like a spandex suit. Sometimes I think she's hot for her; other times I think she wants a ménage à trois."

Stone calmly regarded Victor. "That hardly seems likely."

"Yeah, I guess you're right. It's just that the two women have become so close I can never get Jill alone. And when and if we are out of Jill's apartment, we can't get our client in without worrying about Jewel showing up. I think Jill gave her a key to the place."

"Hmm. They *are* close friends. That could be problematic."

"One thing's for sure," Victor said. "Jewel's never gonna buy into a new Jill. No way to fool her when they're like sisters. And we can't delete both of them without making the cops suspicious."

"There might come a time," Stone said, "when we simply might have to take the risk."

"If it weren't such a risk," Victor said, "it would be a pleasure."

"We're not in this for pleasure, Victor. We're in it for profit."

"Yeah. You're right, Palmer. I was just ruminating. No harm in that."

"None," Stone agreed. "I do it myself." He sat back and opened a drawer, then laid some file folders on his desk. "I hate to cut our visit short, Victor, but I've got to get to these."

He picked up a ballpoint pen from where it lay on the desk. "Keep me apprised of Gloria's condition."

"Of course I will," Victor said, standing up from the sofa. He shook his head. "Problems always come in bunches."

"They can be solved in bunches, too," Stone said.

"I'll try to keep that in mind."

Stone wasn't sure if Victor was being sarcastic. That was what made Stone uneasy about him, the recent *unevenness* that seemed to have seeped into his personality. It made him unpredictable.

Stone watched him walk from the office and softly close the door behind him. Victor had missed a patch of stubble when he shaved this morning, and his expensive dress boots didn't glisten with the usual shine. It was difficult for Stone not to be concerned. Maybe the changes in Victor could be attributed to Gloria's condition. On the other hand, Victor had begun to worry Stone well before Gloria was struck by a cab.

Stone laid the pen back on the desk and leaned back in his chair. He ruminated.

It seemed that things were coming unraveled. Maybe it was time for him to disappear. He had an exit plan that Gloria and Victor didn't know about. He thought of it simply as Plan B. Gloria and Victor were friends as well as business associates, and he owed them some loyalty, but a man had to take care of himself. He wasn't quite ready to act on his plan, but he'd continue giving it some thought.

After a few minutes, he went over and picked up the morning *Times* from where it lay on a table near the sofa. The paper was still folded. Stone hadn't so much as glanced at it.

When he opened the paper and saw the headline, he had to smile: TORSO MURDERER FOUND DEAD IN LOUISIANA.

This would certainly reduce the pressure. However it figured in the mix, it was a plus for the company and a minus for the police.

Stone felt relief move through him, easing a tension in his stomach he hadn't even realized was there. For now, all thoughts of Plan B faded away.

Still smiling, he carried the paper over to his desk and sat back down to read the details.

Making sure the devil wasn't in them.

60

"We've lost our decoy," Renz said, in a voice that suggested a close relative had died.

Quinn and Renz were in Renz's office. Renz looked terrible in the harsh morning sunlight. His bloodhound eyes were encircled by saggy flesh that was even darker than usual. Before him on his desk lay this morning's *Times*. Quinn thought that was enough to explain Renz's appearance.

"Not quite yet," Quinn said. He'd read the paper over breakfast and given the Coulter story some thought. "As far as the media are concerned, Coulter's still the Torso Murderer."

"Until another torso turns up and the shit hits the fan again, and then us."

Quinn knew that by "us" Renz meant "me."

"Look at the bright side, Harley."

"I am. I see a fire about to consume us."

"You have a point about the real killer taking another victim, and establishing that Coulter wasn't our man. But the killer's probably thinking right along with you. He stays pretty much in the clear until he murders again. That might make him wait a while. Meanwhile, Coulter's dead and can't provide alibis for the times of some of the Torso Murders."

That last seemed to cheer Renz somewhat. His bleary eyes opened wider and he looked thoughtful. "That's true enough."

"What about Nobbler?"

It took Renz a few seconds to understand what Quinn meant. "Yeah, it might settle him down, too. Far as we know he bought the story about Coulter being our prime suspect. Maybe he'll pull in his horns."

Quinn didn't disagree. But he knew that when Nobbler saw that Renz wasn't pulling in any horns, he'd realize Coulter had only been a decoy. That was if he didn't realize it already. Nobbler was smart and had his sources within the NYPD.

"The other thing Coulter's death does for us," Quinn said, "is put E-Bliss off their guard. They're thinking the pressure's off them, as long as everyone's assuming the Torso Murderer died when Coulter died."

Renz bit on his flabby lower lip and nodded. "It might make them careless."

"When you hold your press conference," Quinn said, "emphasize that the case against Coulter is still being made, even though he's dead. We aren't jumping to any conclusions. We want to be absolutely sure of his guilt."

"I like that," Renz said. "Cover our asses for when the real killer leaves us another grisly present."

"The idea is to nail the killer before then," Quinn said. "We do that, and none of the stuff about Coulter will matter."

"You got that right," Renz said. "The public wants this prick stopped, and whoever does it will be a hero. Or heroes." He placed his hands behind his neck, leaned back in his chair, stretched, and stared up at the ceiling while flexing his muscles so that his biceps jumped around beneath the taut material of his shirt. "Who do you suppose shotgunned

Coulter? I mean, nobody's stepped forward to take a bow and be an instant celebrity."

"Let the Louisiana cops worry about it," Quinn said. "We've got our own worries."

Renz sat forward, picked up the *Times,* and tossed it to the side of his desk.

"Fill me in on some of those worries," he said, "so I can worry some more."

Maria Sanchez absently scratched at her arms, paced five steps this way, five steps back. This was getting unbearable. She had to get out and risk scoring some coke. It was either that or go mad.

She walked to the window and glanced outside.

It was still morning. Not even goddamned noon. It felt as though she'd been awake for ten hours after finally dropping into an uneasy sleep about dawn. New York was bright and hot out there. A city strange to her. And ominous. It wouldn't work, trying to make a buy during daylight. She needed the night. She needed the people who came out at night.

She needed.

She would have to wait for darkness. Then she would act.

She needed.

61

The evening brought showers, lightning flashes, and thunder rolling like artillery volleys above the stone and glass towers along the avenues. Then, with a humid hot breeze off the East River, the rain stopped falling, the lightning ceased, and night dropped like a curtain in a darkened theater over the city.

The new Madeline, Maria Sanchez, stood before the cracked full-length mirror mounted on the bedroom door and gave her image a final appraisal. Teased-out blond hair, tight red sleeveless T-shirt that emphasized her breasts, form-fitting black skirt that hugged her lean hips and came to just above her knees, fishnet black stockings, and killer four-inch red high heels. Makeup definitely on the heavy side, with black false eyelashes, too much eyeliner, and bright wet-look lip gloss. Lots of paste jewelry that looked as cheap as she wanted to look. She winked at herself and ran her tongue along her lower lip. She was satisfied. She looked like a whore.

To make the kind of buy she had in mind, she had to pass for a poor dumb working girl who needed a fix and had recently turned enough tricks to afford one. She had to be trusted by people who had trust in nothing other than money or power. Dressed as obviously as she was, there was always the chance they might think she was an undercover narc; but she could sense when that might happen and do something even an undercover cop wouldn't do to prove her dishonest intentions. When it came to survival, the new Madeline was like her preceding persona and had few inhibitions.

In Mexico, and during trips with Jorge to San Francisco, she used to feel above the kind of people she was now about to move among. She was the wife of a drug king, making her a drug queen, a superior creature with both money and power. It showed on her even when Jorge wasn't present. She'd inspired respect and fear among the addicted and the lower echelons of dealers. Now she had to pass as one of them.

Maybe I am *one of them!*

Trying to ignore her stab of panic, Maria turned away from the mirror. She went to the window and gazed out at the streetlights below. They were starred in the damp air, but the rain had stopped.

It was time to go out.

Before leaving, she added one more accessory to her outfit: a small black beaded purse. It contained a comb, some Kleenex, and a mace bomb she'd bought at a flea market. Supposedly, one whiff of the stuff and whoever might want to harm her would collapse helpless in a coughing fit. She didn't even know if the thing worked, but carrying it made her feel better.

At the door she considered taking an umbrella, then almost laughed out loud. The woman she'd been assessing in the mirror wasn't the sort who'd carry an umbrella if it wasn't raining. Being caught in the rain would be the least of the chances she'd routinely take. Tonight, Maria was that woman.

* * *

At first it was difficult to walk in the stiletto-heeled shoes. Maria took a cab south on Broadway until she was in a neighborhood that met her needs. The cabbie, who'd swerved to the curb immediately to pick her up, seemed to know what part of town she wanted to go to before she told him. Image could be everything in this world.

On foot again, it took her a few blocks to stop wobbling. She was almost surely working up a blister on her left big toe, but the hell with it. Blisters she could deal with later.

Now that the rain had stopped, there were plenty of people back out on the sidewalks. Maria ignored the stares she drew, and the occasional remarks. She went to clubs in the Village that looked like places where drug buys might be made. Her clothes were working their magic. Men propositioned her in ways bold and subtle, suave and crude. One place turned out to be a lesbian bar, and she was asked by a butch-looking woman wearing what looked like a leisure jacket to dance to an old sixties rock tune. Had to say no twice. She noticed everyone was dressed as if it were the sixties and realized that maybe she was, too. Women in her ostensive profession were in many ways a constant.

A sign made of pink paper letters strung together and draped on the mirror behind the bar declared that it was NOSTALGIA NIGHT and exhorted everyone to HAVE FUN! Maria had never regarded nostalgia as fun, merely weakness.

She thought about dancing for a while to work off the tension that was building in her, but she was worried she might sprain an ankle in her four-inch heels. A bald woman wearing a baggy tie-dyed T-shirt and huge gold hoop earrings grinned and waved a handful of bills at her, beckoning her to come back. She mouthed, "Don't leave," but Maria pushed through half a dozen women just entering and went back out into the warm night.

The fourth place she tried was Billie G's, in a crumbling brick building just off Christopher Street. It occupied the entire first floor, a vast space with a bar so long four bartenders were working it. There was a good-sized parquet dance floor, a neat rectangle running parallel to the bar. On the other side of the crowded dance floor were tables. The clientele seemed to be of both genders and every sexual orientation. The dancers moved jerkily to a rhythmic, relentless pounding sound that Maria suspected was an amplified heartbeat.

She took a table along a wall and ordered an economical well drink, bourbon and water on the rocks. The waitress, an emaciated woman with one eye made up to look blackened, didn't give her a second look. *My kind of place,* Maria thought.

Putting on a pointedly disinterested act whenever someone approached her table, she studied the crowd. If she was a prostitute, she was a particular one. Knowing what to look for, Maria sipped her drink and kept to herself.

Near the end of the bar up near the door were some black-boots-and-leather types. Tough-looking guys who might be bikers, or might be daytime worker drones from the financial district, out of their Brooks Brothers garb and playing a role.

Farther down the bar were more traditional types, wearing everything from jeans to suits and ties, drinking everything from beer and straight booze to Cosmopolitans.

As people entered Billy G's, some of them paused near the leather guys, then walked on. It was quick, it was deft, but Maria's practiced eye saw money and small items change possession. A geek in low-rider pants, and with his lacquered hair combed into five-inch spikes, was definitely not running with the leather crowd, yet he, too, paused at the end of the bar and made an almost unnoticeable exchange.

Maria sat and watched, becoming optimistic, thinking maybe she wouldn't have to finish her piss-and-water drink.

Within about ten minutes one of the leather guys, a big one with a graying beard, slid off his bar stool and made his way along the edge of the dance floor toward the restrooms. He was shirtless beneath a black leather vest with chains dangling from it. His muscular arms were adorned with tattoos, and when one of the dancers accidentally bumped into him, he gave the man a casual but vicious swipe with his elbow. The injured dancer, bent over in pain but still moving to the beat, glared at him, but didn't try to retaliate.

Maria had watched people going and coming from the restrooms, keeping track. It was possible that the bearded leather guy would be alone in the men's room.

This is why you came here. Do it!

She stood up from her table and moved among the dancers to catch up with him.

The restrooms were at the end of a long hall and down a flight of dimly lit, steep concrete steps. The stiletto heels were a problem here, too. Maria had to be careful as she descended the steps. The stairwell was narrow, and the closer she got to the bottom, the more the stench of stale urine and pine disinfectant confirmed what was at the base of the steps. Urine was definitely winning the battle with the disinfectant.

She edged around an enthusiastic couple necking in the stairwell, the woman pressed tight against the wall and making soft mewing sounds. Maria heard a door open and close—someone exiting a restroom—and a slim figure began climbing the steps toward her.

When the figure got closer, she saw that it was that of a man in an unbuttoned and flapping sport jacket.

Good. One down. All the more likely that the beard's alone.

At the base of the stairs were two gray-enameled flimsy wood doors identical in every way. Each had international skirt- and pants-clad figures stenciled on it, indicating the restroom was for both men and women. *Cute.*

Maria took a deep breath before remembering the ammonia stench of urine, then quickly exhaled and pushed open the nearest door.

Oddly, the air was better in the restroom. Maybe more disinfectant. There was a urinal mounted on the wall to the left. On the right was a stall. Its door was closed, and Maria could see a pair of definitely female ankles above dainty feet wearing low-heeled pumps.

She backed out and went to the other door.

This time, when she entered the restroom she glanced to her left, where she figured that with a flip plan the stall would be. Its metal door was open and it was unoccupied.

Standing to her right, at the urinal, was the bearded leather guy taking a piss.

Polite to a fault, Maria stood and waited for him to finish and turn around.

He zipped his jeans and turned at the same time. She saw the surprise in his eyes. He'd assumed another man was behind him, waiting to use the urinal.

He looked her up and down and smiled at her with rotten teeth. "If you're gonna stand an' pee, I hope you don't mind if I watch."

She returned the smile. "You know, I wouldn't mind at all."

His flesh-padded blue eyes darted this way and that, confirming that they were alone. He was obviously curious. "What's your play?"

"I'm looking for something to play *with*."

"You look more like *you're* somethin' to play with, if a man's got the cash."

"Some men did have the cash. Now I've got it."

"And now you're lookin' to spend it?"

"Isn't that what it's for?"

"Depends on what you wanna buy."

"White powder, not for a baby's ass."

He grinned and breathed out loudly and slowly, signifying that he was thinking. She could smell his foul breath, even from three feet away.

"You a cop?" he asked.

"If I am, I sure as hell got a sore anatomy from raising the cash for a score."

"You must be pretty confident I ain't a cop."

"Yeah, I bet tourists come up and ask you directions all the time."

He laughed. "You sure as shit ain't no workin' girl. You wear that outfit like it's some kinda costume. And maybe it is."

"I don't wanna pass a fashion test. I'm here to buy some coke."

"Thing is, there's a rumor there might be a raid on Billy G's tonight."

"Don't you hear that rumor every night?"

"Just about," he admitted.

"Listen, I sat upstairs and watched you deal to other people. From local jerkoffs to geeks from the burbs who drove their father's car into the city. My money's good, too. And to tell you the truth, I'm kinda desperate."

"Now, that I believe. But desperate to score some coke, or to make an arrest?"

"Oh, get serious." She lifted her T-shirt to expose her bare breasts, then squeezed them together, aiming her nipples at him. "Would a cop do this?"

He kept his eyes trained on her breasts until she lowered the shirt.

His hand went to a pocket in his leather vest and came out with a small tin container that had held breath mints. Maria wondered where he'd got it; he sure hadn't bought it and used all the mints. She inched her right hand into her unzipped purse.

"This has got high-grade stuff in it," he said.

She reached for the tin and he drew it back away from her outstretched left hand. "You don't trust me?"

"I trust no one."

"Well, you gotta place your trust in reliable old me. It's not like you're Donald Trump and you got any kinda bargainin' position. Is the stuff real or is it talcum powder? That's a question it's gonna cost you to answer."

"I don't buy without a taste."

He shrugged massive shoulders beneath the black leather vest. "You say you been watchin' me doin' business. How the hell you think I *stay* in business if I ain't honest?"

In a perverse way, it was a reasonable question. "Okay. How much?"

"Whatever's on you." His gaze returned to her breasts. "An' then some. You can show me you're really a workin' girl, an' that play outfit you're about to take off ain't a costume."

She fought down her fear and revulsion, letting her anger lend her courage. "Maybe you didn't notice I already showed you. And us working girls get paid."

"Sometimes they just get screwed."

The door opened, and a man in dress slacks and a blue pullover looked in. The expression on his face went blank and he quickly backed out.

The leather guy shrugged his bull shoulders again. "All I'm askin's a bonus." He held up the tiny tin container. "An' by the way, it ain't talcum powder. Like you mentioned, that's for babies' asses. This is for your nose, sweetheart. I got a whole nother somethin' for your ass." He noticed her hand in her purse, and the perfect stillness of very dangerous men about to act came over him. "I really do hope you're reachin' for your money."

She pulled out the flea market mace bomb and aimed it at his face, extending her arm so it was only inches away, and mashed down hard on the plastic button with her thumb.

Work! Please work!

Nothing happened.

"*Oh, shit!*"

He was just beginning to break into a grin when the mace hissed out into his face. It caught him when he was inhaling, and he gasped and staggered backward, floundering on the slick tiles.

He went down hard, bonking his head on the porcelain urinal.

The tin container flew from his hand and slid beneath the stall door.

Maria tried to pick it up in time but missed, fell down herself, and crawled into the stall.

There it is! Behind the toilet bowl! There!

As her hand closed around the tin container, she felt the leather guy's hand close around her right ankle. He had the grip of a man who'd spent thousands of hours squeezing motorcycle handlebars.

Maria clasped the container with one hand, and the edge of the stall door with the other. She managed to haul herself up to a standing position, but he still had her ankle.

The leather guy was lying on his back and had his mace-burned eyes clenched closed. There were tears streaming down his beefy face. He wasn't about to let go of her. Maria was glad to know he couldn't see her. She had a fighting chance.

Maintaining her grip on the steel door so she wouldn't lose her balance, she raised her left foot high and came down on his hand with the four-inch stiletto heel.

No reaction.

Again! Harder!

He yelped and released his grip on her ankle. The narrow tip of the heel had penetrated the web of flesh between his thumb and forefinger so deep that when he'd yanked his hand back it had almost pulled off her shoe. He was holding his injured hand in tight to his body, as if trying to stanch the bleeding. Still lying on his back, he began kicking out blindly with both feet, hoping one of his heavy boots would find her.

Maria stayed in the stall out of range and chose precisely the right time to dash past him. One of his flailing legs barely missed her. He was screaming now, but probably no one could hear him upstairs over the din of voices and the loud thudding of the amplified heartbeat.

Her attacker was swiveling on the floor like a crazed

break-dancer, wasting his time now kicking at the opposite wall. She knew she'd made it. Edging from the restroom, she leaned down and said, "Asshole," between his screams. Making sure it was loud enough for him to hear.

Immediately he zeroed in on her voice and brought his huge body around on the tiles.

So graceful for such a big man.

As she left, he kicked the door shut after her.

62

She'd been down there too long. It was a worry.

Officer Nancy Weaver, seated at the bar in Billy G's, glanced at her watch. The new Madeline had been downstairs in the restroom for almost fifteen minutes. It wasn't the kind of place where anyone stayed a second longer than was necessary.

Weaver had made a trip to the restrooms herself and knew there was no way out of the building other than to come back upstairs. But no one had done that except for the somewhat alarmed-looking man who'd apparently gone downstairs and then immediately turned around and come back up.

Weaver knew there were a lot of things that could instantly repel someone from a restroom in a place like this. Still, the expression on the man's face stayed with her. Probably it had nothing to do with the new Madeline. Probably.

It was the long time Madeline was spending down there that bothered Weaver. She—

A commotion at the other end of the bar drew her attention. She heard the word *police* several times. She strained forward over her drink to see into the back bar mirror.

Great! Just what I need.

It looked like undercovers from the narcotics squad were making a collar. They had the guys in black leather lined up braced against the bar while they frisked them. One of the undercovers, a skinny guy with wildly spiked hair—who'd made an earlier buy Weaver had witnessed—had his 9mm stuck in one of the leather creeps' ear.

Movement caught her eye to the left. The new Madeline had just come back upstairs. She saw what was happening down the bar and froze at the top of the steps, looking terrified.

She had good reason. The expression on her face was already drawing attention. The way she was dressed was holding it.

Weaver had to make a decision. She knew it was one that could make or break a career.

It took her only a few seconds to decide that becoming identifiable to Madeline was preferable to Madeline being scooped up in a drug raid.

This had to be fast and smooth. One of the cops was already walking over to shut down the music. Everybody in the place would be subject to at least a cursory questioning or body search.

She slid down off her stool, noticing that Madeline's eyes were already exploring, looking for a way out. She'd never make it. At the least she'd be suspected of prostitution, possibly taken in. Weaver herself was dressed kind of sexy, taking advantage of her plainclothes role, and might be accosted and have to show her shield.

She approached Madeline and clutched her elbow. "I'm your friend. Follow me."

Madeline stared at her with surprisingly calm, appraising eyes.

"Like I've got a choice," she said.

Weaver led her diagonally across the dance floor toward the front exit, where a couple of uniforms were now standing. She kept her left hand on Madeline's elbow. Cupped in her right was her shield. She'd need a little luck, but she might be able to get clear of Billy G's without Madeline discovering she was a cop.

They made it past the leather types being braced. The two big uniforms at the door were both staring at them. Why wouldn't they? A couple of ladies dressed for heavy action about to walk out on a drug raid. If nothing else, they'd be fun to search. Weaver thought she knew one of the uniforms slightly and hoped he wouldn't recognize her right away.

He smiled, but not at her. "Couple of working girls trying to slip away," he said.

The other cop, who looked like a kid still, with his baby fat and trying to grow a mustache, stepped toward them.

Weaver shifted her body, holding her palm down near her hip and turning it out so the uniform could see the badge. He stopped, gave a hard look at the shield, then at Weaver. She gave him a hard look back and winked. No dummy, the child cop. He glanced at his partner, then moved toward him.

He was whispering to his partner as Weaver led Madeline out the door. The other cop, the one Weaver knew, was staring at her. She could see he recognized her now, but he said nothing.

She and Madeline were clear, out in the warm night, which felt cool after the body-packed Billy G's. Weaver held on to Madeline's elbow as they walked fast, Weaver leading. She could feel that she was stronger than the taller woman, and in better condition. Or maybe the difference was the wobbly high heels. Madeline was beginning to huff and puff.

A block down, Madeline suddenly yanked her elbow away and stopped.

"That was close," Weaver said, thinking Madeline would figure her for a hooker who thought she, Madeline, was a sister prostitute who'd been working the bar at Billy G's.

"Sure was," Madeline said. "Thanks for the help. We walked right past those dumb cops at the door."

"Took them by surprise," Weaver said, faking a giggle. "Stunned them with our beauty."

She thought maybe they'd share a good laugh together, two losers temporarily on top. Bond a bit. Now that Madeline had seen her and would recognize her, maybe it would be a good idea to gain her confidence. Quinn would understand why Weaver had to act fast and get Madeline out of the club; maybe he'd want to take advantage of what had happened in some way, though at the moment Weaver couldn't figure how. What she wanted was to turn a piece of bad luck into something good.

Madeline wasn't having any. Without cracking a smile, still breathing hard, she unzipped the little black purse she was clutching and reached into it. "Let me give you something."

Weaver thought she might be getting out money, offering her something for helping her out of Billy G's. "Listen, you don't have to do that, honey. Really."

"I insist. You saved my ass in there."

"Sisters gotta stick together."

Madeline drew from her purse a small cylinder and extended it toward Weaver's face. Her thumb was on top pressing down.

An instant after Weaver recognized it as a mace container the fine spray hit her in the eyes and blinded her. *Jesus!* She desperately swatted out with her right hand to knock the mace bomb away, but it was too late. Her fingertips barely brushed Madeline's stiffened arm and didn't move it. Weaver tried to breathe but couldn't. As she started to choke and swipe at her eyes, Madeline shoved her to the sidewalk.

Ouch! The back of her head bumped hard on concrete. Pain flared behind her eyes and she heard herself gasp.

The sudden involuntary intake of air at least cleared her nasal passages, but only temporarily. Her eyes were on fire.

I'll kill her! Kill the rotten bitch!

Not that she was in a position to kill anyone.

She experimented and found that she could breathe out without choking. In was harder.

Weaver started to get up but fell back. A pulsing ache began in her right knee. She must have landed on it before flipping onto her back.

Kill her . . .

Lying blinded and in pain on the damp concrete, coughing and wheezing, she distinctly heard the brittle *clack, clack, clack* of Madeline's ridiculous high-heeled shoes moving away.

Mace. Some goddamned gratitude!

She was still trying to breathe and knuckle the chemical from her burning eyes when she felt rather than heard someone step over her and hurry on.

63

Tonight was going to be different.

As he walked, Greeve thought about how tailing Weaver had paid off. Two days ago she'd led Greeve to the building where the woman he now knew as Madeline Scott lived. Greeve hadn't known her name at first, but it was simple enough to find out she was the reason why Weaver was watching the building. An hour had passed, and then Scott emerged and Weaver fell in behind her.

What to do but join in?

It was fun being the caboose on the train. Scott, Weaver, Greeve. He thought Weaver was pretty good at her work.

Scott returned carrying a newspaper and some magazines. Weaver was nowhere in sight. But Greeve knew she was there.

Same thing had happened the next evening; Scott emerged from her building and Weaver appeared from a doorway across the street and tailed her.

That time Greeve didn't follow them. He waited until they returned about half an hour later. It looked as if Scott had only gone down to the corner deli for some takeout food. Weaver took up her post again when Scott entered the building.

Greeve watched the windows to see which lights came on. Third floor east.

A later check of the mailboxes in the vestibule, when Weaver wasn't around, established that M. Scott was the tenant of that apartment. Greeve inserted a pen with a clip into the grilled front of the box and skillfully snagged a thin piece of mail and rolled it up on the pen. He withdrew it without damaging it. The piece of mail was an ad inviting Madeline Scott to open a free checking account at a nearby bank. Now he knew where M. Scott lived and knew her full name.

He inserted the undamaged mail back in the box and smiled.

Detective work. Greeve was so good at it, sometimes it amused him.

Tonight was different, all right. The usually sedately dressed Madeline Scott was something when she emerged from her apartment building. She was dressed like a hooker. Maybe she *was* a hooker. All Greeve really knew about her was that Quinn and his team were interested in her. And with those high heels, she had a helluva wiggle. He skillfully followed Weaver, who was tailing Madeline. Greeve loved this kind of thing.

After a short cab ride, Madeline walked from dive to dive, usually not spending much time inside. She seemed to be searching for someone. Or something. Greeve followed the two women into one of the clubs, an S&M place that was divided into cubicles. They were in there about ten minutes; then it was off again on the hunt.

He stayed outside of Billy G's. He'd been there before and knew the layout and figured the odds were too great that Weaver might notice him if he ventured inside.

From across the street, he watched the drug raid go down, wondering what that was all about, if it had anything to do with Madeline or Weaver. There was no way to know. A place like Billy G's might be raided frequently. He smiled, wondering if Madeline would be taken in as a prostitute. The way she was dressed, she shouldn't be surprised. He could imagine her being escorted to the police van parked down the block, and then climbing up into the back in that short skirt.

He was the one who was surprised when Weaver came out the door dragging Madeline along by the elbow.

What the hell's this all about?

At first he thought Weaver might be taking Madeline in. But they turned the wrong direction for that, away from the police van. He watched as the two women hurried down the block, and then he casually crossed the street to fall in behind them.

Behind them was a good place to be. It was something watching Madeline walk in those high heels. Weaver . . . she was worth watching, too.

They stopped, and Madeline yanked her arm free of Weaver's grip. They stood close to each other talking. The conversation seemed amiable, but the body language was all wrong. Greeve knew he was looking at two people who were wary of each other. Then Madeline reached into her purse and fished something out.

At first Greeve thought she might be drawing a gun, but it appeared that her fist was clenched around nothing—or something very small. She stuck her fist up close to the surprised Weaver's face, and instantly a fine mist became visible in the glow from a nearby streetlight.

Tear gas or mace.

Madeline used both hands to push Weaver to the sidewalk. Then she broke into a fast walk, clacking along in her high heels. After about ten feet she stumbled and almost fell. She bent gracefully and removed the stiletto-heeled shoes. With a quick glance back at Weaver, Madeline broke into a run, carrying her shoes as her nylon-stockinged feet hit the pavement. The whole thing had taken about ten seconds.

Shit!

Greeve didn't like anything resembling an outright pursuit, but he had to stay close to Madeline. He broke into a brisk jog, his gaze fixed on the pale action of Madeline's legs flashing in the shadows up ahead. She could really run, without those high heels. Thanks to the tight skirt inhibiting her leg movement, he thought he'd be able to stay with her.

When he reached where Weaver lay on the sidewalk, she was still gagging and coughing. Her eyes were swollen and unseeing. She hadn't had time to close them or turn away. She was clutching her gut and trying to catch her breath. Whatever she'd been sprayed with, tear gas or mace, she must have breathed in plenty of it.

He stepped over her and kept going.

64

After a couple of blocks, Madeline slowed to a walk, paused, and put her shoes back on, bending in that same graceful motion but this time brushing off the bottoms of her stockinged feet.

Must have been hell on the nylon, Greeve thought.

She resumed walking at a normal pace. Greeve was glad. He was starting to get winded. And overheated. He had his charcoal gray suit coat open. It was flapping as he walked. With his dark shirt and tie, he was sure he wouldn't be noticed even if Madeline glanced behind her.

It was a standard tail again. He breathed in and out hard, twice, and decided he was okay, practicing his trade and liking it. It felt good to fall into Madeline's rhythm, moving close to the buildings off his left shoulder so he could fade from sight if she did happen to glance back while he was near a streetlight or illuminated sign. They were on a dark block, mostly closed businesses, so there wasn't much chance he'd need to move to cover.

She surprised him. The rhythm and angle of the pale legs abruptly changed. Then she disappeared. She'd turned into a doorway, or a passageway between the buildings.

What the hell?

Whatever it was, he could handle it.

He didn't think he'd been spotted, but there was no way to be sure. He picked up his pace, then lengthened his stride to a run. For all he knew, she was running again, her shoes back in her hand.

Near the shadowed area where Madeline had disappeared, he slowed down and advanced more cautiously.

She'd apparently entered a dark passageway.

Odd, a woman alone . . .

Nothing to do but follow.

He moved forward, his left fingertips brushing the rough-textured brick and mortar as he slipped around the edge of the building into darkness.

He was shocked to see her standing directly in front of him.

His momentary astonishment cost him his life. He felt the knife blade enter his left side and slide upward to his heart. Actually *heard* the blade scrape against a rib. Through an electric wave of pain, he felt his wallet being removed roughly from his pants pocket, then his belt buckle being loosened. The night was becoming even darker.

His pain propelled him so he moved without any thought of direction. Then he saw a faint glimmer of distant light and staggered toward it. Light meant life.

The light became fainter and moved farther away as he fought his way toward it.

Farther . . .

His pants worked themselves lower and lower, bunching around his ankles, and he fell.

Officer Ben Murray was walking his beat with a slow relentlessness, rattling doorknobs and wondering if he'd ever make it through to the end of his shift. It was a boring job, foot patrol in this part of the Village. And that was what made it dangerous. Boredom bred carelessness, and that could get you hurt or killed.

His wife, Milly, had been concerned about him getting hurt lately, not exactly nagging at him, but letting him know she was worried. She'd been getting to him. Causing Murray to think too much. Not just about the danger, but about the things you saw, things you'd never forget. He hadn't told Mil, but he'd been considering getting some other job, one where there wouldn't be so much risk, so much cynicism, so many indelible memories.

He tried the knob on the entrance to a closed erotic-book shop. No give. He peered through the windows at the racks of paperbacks and magazines and saw nothing suspicious, so he turned to move on to the next door. The bookshop had been burglarized twice in the last month. Maybe he could talk the owner into slipping him a key, so he could stay in there at length some nights and guard the place, maybe read some of the magazines. Several of the merchants on this beat were glad to—

Huh?

There was a guy with his pants down staggering along the sidewalk. Finally the puddled trousers tripped him and he fell hard. The way he dropped, without trying to protect his head or face, made Murray sure he was dead or unconscious. He unsnapped the flap on his 9mm's holster and ran toward the man.

Murray was immediately aware of the yawning black passageway alongside him, but for the moment he ignored it and tended to the fallen man.

The guy's suit coat had twisted around and Murray saw the distinctive brown strap of a shoulder holster. Murray used two fingers to pull up the leather folder in the man's shirt pocket. It contained the blue and gold shield of an NYPD detective.

Jesus, a cop!

There was blood on the guy's shirt, on the sidewalk, on Murray's hand.

It was then that Murray became aware of a sweet and subtle scent wafting from the dark passageway. He snapped his head around and saw that the passageway was empty.

But somebody wearing too much perfume had been there recently.

Something tugged at his shirt. The guy, the detective, not dead, one hand plucking at the material so Murray would lean closer. The guy's lips were moving as he tried to speak but couldn't. *Dying words. Christ!* Murray put his ear close to the man's mouth.

What the guy said was soft but distinct: "Whore . . ."

That was it.

Murray felt for a pulse and found only still flesh.

65

Quinn entered Renz's office and paused briefly, nothing showing on Quinn's face. He hadn't known Nobbler was in there, but he'd heard loud voices. He wondered why Renz had called him in with Nobbler present. Maybe he wanted a witness, just in case. Or a referee.

Deputy Chief Wes Nobbler's face was crimson as he paced Renz's overheated, humid office. Renz was obviously trying to show some compassion for him; after all, Nobbler's best friend and coconspirator, Ed Greeve, had been knifed to death last night. Quinn wondered how much compassion Renz actually felt. He'd been plenty pissed off on the phone when he'd called and told Quinn how Greeve had gotten himself killed. Pissed off at Nobbler.

Nobbler stopped and whirled to face Renz, who was seated behind his desk and looking calm in a way that portended a storm.

"You've got a hell of a nerve," Nobbler said, "working in goddamned secret and setting up an undercover cop to tail Madeline Scott."

Renz, maybe thinking staying seated would help him remain calm, didn't move. His voice was tight. "Greeve wouldn't even have known about Madeline Scott if he hadn't been following Weaver."

"So what? Greeve's—Greeve *was* a cop. He was supposed to follow people."

"Not other cops."

"He was following that Scott bitch when he was killed. I know because he phoned me on his cell from outside Billy G's just before he started the tail."

"Following both women, you mean."

"It doesn't matter."

"Doesn't *matter*?" Renz rested both palms flat on the desk, as if it might float away on Nobbler's sea of senselessness if he didn't hold it down. "Like hell it doesn't matter. You're interfering in my case. If I've got a cop following my cop following a suspect, I oughta goddamned know about it. What was Greeve doing tailing Weaver, anyway?"

"He thought it might advance the investigation."

"*My* investigation. And Weaver had lost Scott when Greeve was killed. Greeve was following Weaver, so he probably lost Scott when she did. There's no reason to suspect Scott killed him."

"Who else *but* Scott?" Nobbler asked. "You knew Greeve. Do you honestly think he was killed by some other, *real* prostitute he was about to bonk?"

"He had his pants down around his ankles," Renz pointed out. "And according to Officer Murray, Greeve's last word was *whore*."

"That's all the friggin' media in this town cares about. It's all over the papers and TV—how a police detective was killed by a prostitute. One of the headlines is even COP CAUGHT WITH PANTS DOWN."

"They're usually not so precise."

Nobbler turned a deeper shade of red. "Don't give me that kinda shit. You know Greeve wasn't killed by some ordinary whore who caught him—"

"With his pants down. You can't blame the media. They're saying it because that's where the evidence points."

"Do you believe it?" Nobbler asked, actually vibrating while trying to maintain self-control.

"Frankly, no."

"But we wouldn't believe it if it had actually happened that way," Quinn said.

Both men stared at him, as if noticing him in the room for the first time.

"Fact is," Quinn said, "we don't know it *didn't* happen that way."

Nobbler glared at him as if he wanted to rip out his throat.

"He's right, Wes," Renz said. He puffed up his saggy cheeks and blew out a long breath. "Nobody likes it, but he's right."

"Everybody's human," Quinn said. "Greeve was vulnerable just like the rest of us. He might have gotten mixed up with a prostitute, and then things got out of control. It could've happened even with Greeve, with the right woman, whether she was a saint or a whore."

"That's right," Renz said. "Remember Bernie—"

"Yeah, yeah!"

Nobbler jammed his fists deep into his pants pockets and strode to stare out the window. Some of his anger seemed to have leached out of him. "Why are you so interested in Madeline Scott?" he asked, not turning around.

"She has the same name as a homeless woman who was killed by a subway train," Quinn said.

If Nobbler was already aware of that, he gave no indication. "So what?"

"Coincidence?" Quinn asked.

"Maybe. They do happen, or the word wouldn't be in the dictionary."

"It's not in my dictionary," Quinn said.

"You think Greeve being knifed while he was following

Scott might have something to do with the Torso Murders?"
Nobbler asked.

"We don't know. We can't even be sure Greeve was still
tailing Scott when he was knifed."

"Coulter's been killed down in Louisiana," Nobbler said.
"The Torso Murder case is gonna be shut down. Neither of
us solved it," he added almost absently.

"I thought only one of us was trying," Renz said.

Nobbler ignored him, continuing to gaze outside at the
summer glare. "The Torso Murderer was already on the run,
taking both of us pretty much out of the game. Maybe nobody in law enforcement is gonna get credit for his death.
Hell, Coulter mighta been shot so somebody could rob him.
Or maybe it was a hunting accident."

"Likely was," Quinn said.

Nobbler turned around. "So Coulter being shot is the
kind of coincidence you believe in."

Quinn smiled.

"We're trying to solve crimes here," Nobbler said. "We
shouldn't set up separate squads and not share information."

"Information like autopsy reports?" Quinn asked.

A big vein in Nobbler's forehead began throbbing as if it
were a fire hose about to burst and start spewing all over the
place. He started to reply, then bit down hard on his lower lip
and stalked from the office, slamming the door behind him.

"He took that well," Renz said.

"He's got no right to be pissed at us," Quinn said.

"You think it mighta been the new Madeline who knifed
Greeve?"

"I don't know. It doesn't sit right."

"So many things about this case don't," Renz said. "It's
not gonna be long before the media wolves get on to us. It's
hard for me to believe. We set up a killer already on the run
as a suspect to divert them, just picked the guy out of a hat,
and damned if he isn't shot to death down in Louisiana."

"His photo was all over the country."

"Still . . ."

"Could actually have been a coincidence."

"Jesus, Quinn."

"Maybe we oughta test it by setting up another wanted killer who's somewhere out there on the wind. We mighta stumbled onto something here."

Renz covered his face with his hands for a moment, then removed them and looked up at Quinn.

"I'm thinking about Ed Greeve," he said solemnly.

"He wasn't a bad guy," Quinn said. "And he was a hell of a cop. He deserved better. When's the funeral?"

"I didn't mean that," Renz said. "I was wondering why anyone would stick him."

"The logical answer is he cheated a whore and she took offense."

"Screw logic. It's caused a lotta trouble in my life."

"Mine, too," Quinn said with genuine sadness. "It's what we live by and love, and it's frightening where it can take us."

"Like real love," Renz said.

66

"I talked to a neighbor in the same building," Victor said. "She told me she saw Madeline Scott go out alone right after dark dressed like a hooker."

They were in Palmer Stone's cool, ordered office at E-Bliss.org. Victor's shirt was wrinkled and he needed a shave. Possibly he was growing a beard. Stone had never liked beards around a place of business.

"What time did she come home?" Stone asked, from behind his desk.

"She didn't. Not all night. I gave up watching for her about six this morning."

"That's bad," Stone said. "Maybe she's on the run."

"Why would that be?"

"A cop was stabbed to death in the Village last night."

"I don't see the connection," Victor said. "My guess is she really was hooking and spent the night with a client."

"She doesn't need the money," Stone said.

"Maybe she needs the sex," Victor said. "Some people like it too much."

Stone stood up from his chair and ran his hands through his meticulously styled gray hair, considering a nymphomaniacal Maria—Madeline Scott. His hair miraculously fell back into place. "I suppose it's possible."

"Drugs and sex. Maybe even something else."

"I don't even want to think about the something else," Stone said.

"What with the cops thinking the Torso Murders are stopped, maybe we should take Maria Sanchez out," Victor said.

Stone knew he didn't mean out on a date. "Delete her?"

"If you'd rather put it that way."

Stone would rather. He didn't like altering the nomenclature of their business. "Let me think on it."

"She's a loose cannon, Palmer."

"I don't want to take any unnecessary chances."

"Madeline Scott will have a fatal accident. Who the hell cares about her enough to even notice? Hardly anyone in New York even knows who she is. And you know she's dangerous. She's getting more and more unstable, and she runs off at the mouth. I mean, with Maria, the transformation was never completed. She's not like our other special clients. She never really *became* Madeline Scott."

Stone thought Victor was making a pretty good case against Maria Sanchez–Madeline Scott. And with the police assuming the late and unlucky Tom Coulter was responsible for the Torso Murders, there wouldn't seem to be any connection between them and her death. Not as long as Sanchez-Scott's death was thought to be accidental.

Stone wished Gloria was out of the hospital and well. She was the expert on accidental death. Victor . . . Well, the changes in Victor lately had to be taken into consideration. His increasingly sloppy appearance. His apparent streak of sadism. Emotion shouldn't be mixed with business. And of course there was the stress of Gloria's serious injury. More emotion. Would Stone be sending a loose cannon to delete a loose cannon?

"Let me think on it," Stone said again.

Victor shrugged. "You're the boss."

Lately Stone had been wondering about that.

Two days later, Victor was back in Palmer Stone's office. He was more neatly dressed this time, in a medium blue suit made from some kind of light material that gave it a graceful drape. And he no longer needed a shave. The scraggly beginnings of his beard were history. Stone liked him much better this way.

"Remember our conversation about Maria Sanchez?" Victor asked.

"Let's refer to her as Madeline Scott," Stone said.

"Okay. Whichever she is, I've been watching her."

Stone wasn't really surprised. "Why?"

"You said you were thinking about deleting her. I thought it would be a good idea to make some preliminary plans."

"And now you want to know my decision," Stone said.

"No, I don't think we should go near her."

"Really?" Stone had been leaning in exactly the opposite direction. Victor had convinced him. He just hadn't been sure Victor was the man for the job.

"I found out the police are watching her. And around the clock."

"Question is," Stone asked, "were the police watching you while you were watching Madeline Scott?"

"Not a chance. I'm sure about that, Palmer. I'm a pro."

"So are the police. Especially Quinn."

"We're okay on this," Victor said. "When the cops lose interest in her, then maybe we should delete her."

"Maybe," Stone agreed.

"I know," Victor said, with a smile. "You'll think about it."

But what Palmer Stone was actually thinking about was the police surveillance of Madeline Scott. How long had she been under observation? Why would they be watching her?

What did it mean?

67

"Som'un's out there," Cathy Lee said sleepily.

It was a warm, muggy Louisiana morning, and the drone of swamp insects was almost louder than the sound of the car rolling over muddy ruts to park outside the ramshackle house.

Cathy Lee looked over at Joe Ray, who was snoring lightly, lying on his stomach with his face half buried in his pillow. Juan was in the other bedroom, quiet for a change. Usually he snored loud enough to rattle the leaves on the trees, which was why Cathy Lee had her and Joe Ray's door shut.

Cathy Lee crawled out of bed, crossed the bare plank floor, and peeked out the window.

Her heart gave a jump.

A sheriff's department car was parked out there in the shade of the big willow tree. She knew there was enough incriminating evidence in the meth lab to get all three of them locked up for years. She glanced behind her. Maybe she could slip out the back, run out on Joe Ray and Juan. She was sure they wouldn't hesitate to run out on her. The truck was parked out in back of the house, and she could get in and drive away.

But the big engine turning over would make a lot of noise. Somebody would surely hear it. And the sheriff's car might give chase.

She watched the car door open and a tall, broad-shouldered sheriff's deputy got out and looked around. It was hot, and he'd left his Smokey hat in the car. A young guy with a buzz cut, real good-looking. Kathy decided maybe she could handle him, go out and see what he wanted (not that she didn't know), and divert him from looking in the outbuilding.

Careful not to wake Joe Ray, she put on her white terry-cloth robe, making sure it was open enough to reveal cleavage. Then she did what she could with her hair and sidled out onto the porch without slamming the door.

The deputy looked at her and smiled. It made him look ten years younger. Maybe this would be easy.

"Mornin', ma'am," he said. "I'm Sheriff's Deputy O. E. Simmons."

"Mornin' to you, Sheriff's Deputy O. E. Simmons. I'm Cathy Lee Aiken, an' I'm at your service." She almost smiled and saluted, but figured that might be too much.

He didn't respond as she thought he would. His smile stayed stuck on but dimmed, and she realized he simply had one of those faces, was one of those people who smiled through everything because that was the way their features were set. And on second glance, he didn't look so young. Not if you paid attention to his eyes.

"Anybody else in the house?" he asked.

She was looking at the big 9mm handgun perched on his hip. The eyes and the gun. Best not to lie to this man. "Two fellas. Joe Ray an' Juan."

"That's three."

"No, sir. Joe Ray is one fella."

"Uh-hum." He moved in closer to her. There were crow's-feet at the corners of his eyes, as if he'd squinted into the sun too much.

He didn't react as she took the three sagging wood steps

down off the porch to meet him, letting the robe part to reveal a lot of leg. His eyes told her he wasn't interested in her in the way she wanted. Out of the shade of the porch roof, she was the one squinting into the sun, at him. *Are you gay, Deputy O. E. Simmons?*

"You come here to see one of 'em?" she asked.

"If one or both of 'em might own the truck we found out in the swamp."

Cathy Lee breathed easier. When they'd gotten the F-150 retitled and painted a dark blue (her favorite color), Joe Ray and Juan had ditched the rusty old Dodge off the road in the swamp about a mile from the house. That shoulda been the end of it. Something given up to the swamp you could put out of your mind as gone for good. She guessed there hadn't been enough time for the saw grass to grow up where the truck had mashed it down, and somebody'd spotted the old hulk and reported it to the state police.

"We got a problem?" a voice asked.

Joe Ray had awakened and stumbled sleepy eyed out onto the porch. He was shirtless and barefoot but had pulled on his old jeans. There was a rip in one leg, revealing a dirty knee.

"It's about the old Dodge truck we left in the swamp," Cathy Lee said. She looked at the deputy. "Have we broken some kinda law?"

Simmons looked puzzled, still with the smile that wasn't a smile. "This wasn't a Dodge. It was a near-brand-new Ford."

Joe Ray had started down the porch stairs and almost fell. He looked panicky for a moment. Cathy Lee realized she was standing with her mouth hanging open.

"Somethin' wrong?" the deputy asked.

"We got that truck all legal," Joe Ray said too defensively.

Simmons narrowed his eyes. These two were acting as if he'd happened onto a Mafia meeting. "You the one left it stuck out there in the mud?"

"I don't know nothin' about it. My friend Juan was drivin' it last night."

"Where would he be?"

"In the house, fast asleep. Musta had a late night."

The deputy rested his right palm on the top of his black leather holster and glanced off to the side.

"What's in that outbuilding?"

"Gardenin' tools. That kinda stuff," Joe Ray said.

"I never noticed any plantin' around here when I drove in."

"I hear somethin' about a truck?" Juan asked. He'd come out onto the porch. He was barefoot, like Joe Ray, but wearing a white T-shirt with his jeans.

"The Ford truck," Joe Ray said. "You know."

"I was on my way home from Rodney's Roadhouse last night," Juan said, "an' got it stuck in the mud. Woulda thought that was impossible with that big Ford, it havin' four-wheel drive an' all, but I missed a turn an' drove it well off the road. I gave up after tryin' to get it out an' walked the rest of the way here. Truck's still where I left it, I guess."

"Yeah, I saw it," the trooper said. "Need a tractor or somethin' with a winch to pull it out."

"You got that right."

"You have a snootful when you left Rodney's?"

"Two beers, is all. You can ask Rodney."

"I've always trusted Rodney. Weren't drinkin' behind the wheel, were you?"

Juan's smile was sheepish. He hadn't been high on booze last night, but on something else. "I can honestly say no, officer."

"I don't know a damned thing about that truck," Cathy Lee said.

Anger flashed in Joe Ray's eyes. "You rode in it enough. You even got yourself—"

"Best not go there, Joe Ray," Cathy Lee said.

"We can show you where we left the old Dodge," Juan

said, tumbling to what might be a dangerous development. Showing a little cooperation and changing the subject. Maybe they should invite the cop inside, where he or Joe Ray could get close to a gun. Not that they wanted to kill a sheriff's deputy, but if it came down to that . . .

"Uh-hm." Simmons looked from one of them to the other. "Forget the Dodge. I gotta say I'm curious about the Ford truck. Big F-150."

"It ain't stole," Joe Ray said. "You can check."

"Already did. I wonder if we looked in the cab, we'd find some beer cans or liquor bottles. Maybe even some illegal substance."

"Not on your life," Juan said, using a forefinger to cross his heart.

"Truck's not very far from here," the deputy said. "Let's go see."

Juan shrugged. Joe Ray looked worried.

"Seemed far enough when I was walkin' it last night," Juan said.

"You can stay here, ma'am," the deputy said to Cathy Lee. "We' won't be more'n fifteen, twenty minutes." He looked at Juan and Joe Ray. "I'll drive, since you've got no vehicle. I apologize, but you two'll have to sit in back, where we usually transport prisoners." Without averting his gaze from them, he walked over to the car and opened a rear door.

Joe Ray and Juan glanced at Cathy Lee and ambled over to get in the backseat. They both had their thumbs tucked in their front jeans pockets. Joe Ray, leaning over to enter the car first, got a look at the steel grille separating the front and back of the interior, and the absence of inside door handles. There was a control for the window to go up and down, but he knew it would be dead.

Halfway into the car, he hesitated and turned and looked back at Deputy Simmons. "This ain't a trick, is it?"

"No kinda trick I know of," Simmons said. "Just regulations, sir. We got passengers, there's where they gotta sit."

Joe Ray nodded and disappeared into the back of the car. Juan followed.

As the deputy walked around to get in behind the steering wheel, he glanced over at Cathy Lee. His smile seemed genuine again. And at this distance, he was youthful again.

"This is just a formality. We won't be long, ma'am."

"I'll make some coffee," she said.

When the sheriff's deputy's car reached the spot where the F-150 was bogged down off the road, Simmons steered slightly onto what passed for a shoulder and braked to a halt. The back of the blue truck's bed was visible through lush green foliage. Flattened-out grass and some sheared-off small saplings showed where the big Ford had gone in. The road had curved, and the truck had gone straight and just missed some good-sized cypress tree trunks, one on each side. It hadn't missed their lower branches.

"Looks like you broke some wood goin' in," Simmons said over his shoulder.

"Tell you the truth, I mighta fell asleep at the wheel," Juan said. "I got sleep watchamacallit—a sleep disorder—so I'm tired most of when I'm awake, doze off unexpectedly at the darnedest times."

"Sleep apnea," the deputy said. "Doctor can treat that for you."

"I don't wanna wear one of them breathin' apparatus things when I sleep," Juan said. "Looks to me like they'd suffocate you."

"Cure your sleep apnea," Joe Ray said.

"I'll be right back," the deputy said and climbed out of the car and shut the door before they could answer.

Deputy Simmons didn't look back at them as he approached the truck. Morning sunlight slanted in low through the trees, and the F-150's bulbous blue tailgate gleamed like an Easter egg badly hidden among the greenery.

When he was as close to the vehicle as he'd been last time, Simmons rolled up his uniform pants and waded into shallow, brackish water. He thought about removing his shoes, but it wasn't worth the risk of stepping on something. Or getting bitten by something. Besides, the sheriff's department would compensate him for a pair of regulation shoes ruined in the performance of his duties. He hoped. There was no other, dry way to reach the damned truck.

He felt the cool water rise on his bare legs, then spill into his leather shoes. His socks were soaked within seconds.

All in the job.

When he got to the mired truck, he attempted to open the driver's-side door and found it locked. He could see across the cab that the opposite door was also locked.

Laugh's on me.

In part so he wouldn't look foolish to the two men confined in the rear of the cruiser, he began a slow, sloshing circuit of the truck, making a show of examining its exterior.

When the one called Juan had driven it into the swamp, the branches had scratched it considerably. One deep gouge in the right front fender revealed black paint beneath the blue.

Black.

Simmons was pretty sure the truck hadn't been manufactured with black primer paint. This vehicle had been repainted. It was awfully new for a repaint, unless it had been in an accident.

Standing and staring at where black paint showed through some other, smaller scratches, the deputy suddenly remembered it hadn't been that long ago when every lawman in the South was looking for a black Ford F-150. It had been stolen by that Coulter guy who'd been found dead and full of shotgun pellets about ten miles down the state road. This truck had a different license plate number, but that was no surprise.

Sheriff's Deputy O. E. Simmons decided to leave the two

men locked in the backseat of his car for a while. Wading back toward the car, he was surprised to realize he was excited. Somebody had sure as hell shot Coulter, the Torso Murderer, and left his dead body on the side of the road. Maybe it was the two assholes in the back of the patrol car. A couple of killers. Wouldn't that be some collar? Maybe get him elected sheriff someday.

Slow down, slow down. . . . Don't jump to conclusions, get ahead of yourself, and screw up royally.

Simmons played it casual and acted like there was nothing wrong as he drove the two men back to the ramshackle house. He parked where he had last time, in the shade of a big willow.

Cathy Lee Aiken was nowhere in sight outside.

"Any guns in the house?" Simmons asked the two men behind him, making it a casual, routine question.

"Not as I know of," Juan said.

"Not a one," Joe Ray said. "I got an old shotgun, but it's back in the truck. Broke down proper an' outta sight behind the seat back."

Leaving the two men confined in back, Simmons locked the car and left it. He went up on the plank porch with his gun drawn. Knocked. Got no answer. Knocked again. Same result. He could feel the hot sun on the back of his neck.

"Ma'am?"

Silence.

He tried the knob and found the door unlocked.

When he glanced back at the patrol car, he saw the two men staring at him intently through the back side window. The skinny one, Joe Ray, actually had his nose pressed to the glass.

The deputy hurled the door open and went into the house fast, gun level and held before him with both hands. Keeping his arms rigid, he swept the barrel from side to side.

The living room was unoccupied.

With his heart lodged low in his throat, he checked out

the two bedrooms and found them also unoccupied. A ceiling fan was turning slowly in the bedroom with the double bed. There was a used condom on the floor. There was also a double-barreled shotgun leaning in a corner.

So much for no guns in the house.

As he entered the tiny, unoccupied kitchen, he smelled it. He relaxed and holstered his gun.

The coffee was on, but Cathy Lee was gone.

68

Sometimes love was grand.

Linda had brought some take-out Chinese to Quinn's apartment, and they were eating lunch at the tiny table in the kitchen. It was comfortably cool despite the outside temperature of almost ninety. Quinn was having orange-flavored chicken; Linda, moo goo gai pan. They shared egg rolls and a large foam container of white rice. Quinn had gotten some bottled water from the refrigerator to drink and put it in tumblers with ice so it would stay plenty cold..

The kitchen smelled good with the aroma of food and soy seasoning. Quinn thought it remarkable that he didn't feel strange sitting here sharing a meal in this kitchen, at this table, with a woman other than May or their daughter, Lauri. So many years in the apartment with May, with Lauri growing up. Then the divorce, and Lauri coming back to live briefly with Quinn, while May stayed in California with her new husband.

Now they were both in California, May and Lauri, and here was Quinn in the apartment with a woman named Linda. A stranger to them, and sometimes to him.

It was almost as if the apartment and its contents were

different in some strange, unidentifiable way. Quinn remembered the comedian who'd claimed someone had stolen everything in his apartment and replaced it with identical duplicates. That was how Quinn felt, as if he were playing himself in a dream of his life. And in that context, everything seemed normal. *Pass the rice, please, whoever you are.* Quinn wondered if Linda ever felt the same strange detachment and alienation. Would it ever pass?

They ate for a while in slow silence while the world moved at its own pace outside the kitchen.

"Nift's got a bean up his nose about something," Linda said, dipping her egg roll into sweet-and-sour sauce.

"Could be my fault," Quinn said. He took a sip of water. "I'm afraid I made him aware that Renz knows he's had someone in the medical examiner's office sitting on postmortem information."

"That gonna be looked into? An official investigation?"

"It's unlikely, but Nift doesn't know that."

"No wonder he's been nervous lately." Linda chewed and swallowed her bite of egg roll. Quinn loved to watch her throat work. "The little twit deserves whatever they do to him."

"He's not the only informer in the medical examiner's office."

Linda looked alarmed, then smiled. "Well, sure, there's me. But that's different."

"Because you're on the side of the good guys?"

"Damned right."

Quinn grinned at her. "You are *so* different from Nift."

"God, I hope so!"

He sipped from his condensation-slippery glass of water and appraised her. "When we're finished with lunch—"

"I'll go back to work," she interrupted. "And aren't you supposed to be out trying to catch the bad guys?"

"Haven't you heard? The Torso Murderer was shot to death down South."

"Must have hurt like hell, being shot down south."

Did she believe me?

"You sound skeptical," he said.

"More like realistic. How long do you think that far-fetched Tom Coulter story's gonna hold up?"

"Maybe Coulter really *was* the Torso Murderer. Now and then we get lucky."

"The cops down in Dixie are gonna start tracing his actions over the past few weeks, and when they try to square times and places with him being here in New York committing murders and dismembering the bodies, it isn't going to work."

"They won't be very eager to backtrack on Coulter," Quinn said, "considering he's dead." He reached across the table and touched the back of her hand. "Everything's gonna be okay."

"Sure it is. You only need to fool the media. Media wolves are relentless, Quinn, and the E-Bliss folks strike me as smart and have sure as hell known all along that Thomas Coulter wasn't the Torso Murderer. Assuming we've got this figured right."

"We do," he said.

"And you think it's gonna all hold up?"

"I didn't exactly say that."

"I love confidence in a man."

Linda finished her iced water, then picked up her purse from the floor and stood up. She was wearing a brown pantsuit with a white blouse, low-heeled brown shoes, no jewelry other than a silver bracelet. All very demure and businesslike, yet somehow sexy as hell in a way he didn't quite understand. She wasn't his type, really, so how could this have happened? A month ago, Quinn wouldn't have dreamed he could fall in love again. If that had happened, what other surprises might life throw at him?

"You're going?"

"Back to the morgue," she said. "Nift needs me."

"So do I."

She came around the table and rested a hand on his shoulder. "I hope you always feel that way. Sometimes I'm bad luck for men."

"Not this time."

"We have no control over that." She realized that if Wes Nobbler knew Renz and Quinn had been aware of Nift hiding or delaying information, Nobbler also knew somebody must have ratted Nift out. Renz must have his own informer in the medical examiner's office. It shouldn't take Nobbler and his cronies long to figure out it might be Quinn's lover.

Linda understood how it worked. Nobbler would need her on his side, and he'd squeeze hard. She'd be forced to choose between her career and Quinn.

"You're trying to tell me something," Quinn said.

She leaned down and kissed him on the forehead. Her lips were cool and dry.

"Telling you to be careful," she said and moved toward the door.

"Because you love me?"

"Because I love you," she said, and then left the apartment.

Quinn finished his orange-flavored chicken and started in on some of what was left of Linda's white rice. It needed seasoning, but he decided not to bother.

He knew Linda was right about the Coulter story unraveling soon. That was pretty much all he knew about what she thought. She was a mystery.

Maybe that was the thing about her that made him hers.

Palmer Stone's desk was clear, its surface polished. The cleaning woman hadn't been in for a while; Stone was responsible for the strong scent of Lemon Pledge in his office. Everything, in fact, was gleamingly clean, squared away, and in its proper place. Business profits, Stone sometimes said, were often the result of appearances. Perception had a way of becoming reality. Sometimes there was opportunity in perception. Like now.

"While the law thinks the Torso Murderer is dead," Stone said, "maybe we should get back to business."

Victor appeared surprised. "But Gloria—"

"How is she?" Stone asked.

"The same. Now and then you can see her pupils moving under her closed eyelids, but that's all that moves." The muscles in his face tightened and his eyes became moist. "I tell you, Palmer, it tears your heart out."

"I do sympathize," Stone said. "I wish there were something I could do."

"I know. . . . It's so goddamned rough."

"It is," Stone said. "Nevertheless, we'll have to tend to business without Gloria. She would approve of that, I'm sure."

Victor looked over at him. "We talking about deleting Maria Sanchez?"

"No, we decided there was too much risk in deleting her. But we should be able to delete Jill Clark, despite the almost constant presence of her friend Jewel. If Jill disappears leaving a note saying she's left New York, who's there to question it?"

"Jewel."

"Jewel will ask Tony Lake about it. He'll be heartbroken, unable to understand why Jill left him."

"I can play that role," Victor said. "I have before. But Jewel's no dumb bimbo."

"I know, Victor. But I'm sure Jewel will buy into it, especially since she has no choice."

"What about our special client?" Victor asked. "The one waiting to become Jill Clark?"

"We can't leave a torso to be found as a signal that she can take over Jill's identity and move in. That would let the police know Coulter wasn't the Torso Murderer. We'll simply alter procedure and talk to her, make it clear it will be the only contact—ever—between us. She can be Jill for a while somewhere else, and then move back to New York, if that's where she wants to be."

Victor ran his fingers lightly over a chin that Stone was glad to see cleanly shaven today. "I don't know, Palmer. Jewel's a persistent pain in the ass. She might not accept my story. She might go to the police."

Stone made a dismissive motion with his manicured right hand. "If she does, so what? Jill decided to leave New York, like countless other young women who grew tired of the struggle. And there's always the note." Stone sat forward. "You *can* persuade Jill to write the good-bye note, can't you?"

"Of course. She's no problem. I can persuade her to do anything." Victor began rubbing his chin harder, as if trying to sand it smooth. "Once I—"

"Never mind that."

"Weak stomach?"

"My stomach doesn't factor into it," Stone said. "You're tasked to do something, you do it, and I handle my end of the business. We decided early that, in everyone's best interests, compartmentalization would be our business model."

"Yeah, we did." Victor thought he might have to remind Palmer of that in the near future.

"Listen, Victor, I know Jewel's a hindrance, but Jill must be deleted because of her link to the old Madeline Scott. And don't forget she's gotten at least a glimpse of the new Madeline."

Victor stopped with the chin rubbing. It had become so vigorous that it had left a red mark. "Okay, Palmer. It makes sense. You're right, as usual."

Just the kind of talk Stone wanted to hear. "It's a business decision, Victor, pure and simple. It best serves our select client, and it best serves the company. Think of it that way, and it's our only reasonable option. It's important, of course, that Jill Clark never be found."

"There's a place in New Jersey."

"I don't want to know about it. That's your department, and I trust you can manage it as well as you always have."

Stone deliberately hadn't mentioned Gloria again. Victor would be acting on his own.

"When do you want it done?" Victor asked.

"Soon," Stone said.

"How?"

"That's totally up to you."

Victor smiled.

69

The old man behind the desk at the Tumble Onn Inn watched the Louisiana state patrol car pull into the lot with its lights out. That made four cars.

"What're you waiting for?" he asked one of the troopers in the motel office.

There were two troopers in the office, making it feel half as big as it was. It seemed the only space to move around a little was behind the desk. That was where the old man, whose name was Ike, sat on a high stool that had a low but rigid bentwood back. He hauled his scrawny body up onto the stool now and then to ease his perpetually aching spine. It was better than standing and trying to make nice with the guests. Or with the cops. Ike had suffered in his life at the hands of the police and was wary of them.

Neither of the troopers bothered answering Ike. They were polite enough when they chose to speak. It was just that they didn't seem to think of him as someone worth answering.

Ike had misplaced his glasses, which made the two troopers look almost exactly alike. Burly six-footers with dark, flat-topped military haircuts and aggressive chins. One of the troopers had on some kind of cologne or aftershave that made Ike feel like sneezing.

Ike persisted. "She's just one woman alone, an' she probably ain't the one you're lookin' for anyways."

"*You* called *us*," one of the troopers reminded Ike.

"Well, I figured she wasn't right somehow, the way she flew off the handle when I told her no."

The other trooper smiled.

"Imagine a woman like that," Ike said, "offerin' to sell sex to an old guy like me. Hell, testosterwhatever's just a memory to me. These days, the only part of me that *ain't* stiff—"

"Don't tell us," the trooper who'd smiled said.

"You might not believe it to look at me, but I'm eighty-six years old. And she just up an' bold as you please said she didn't have the money to pay for her room these past two days, an' would I take a—"

"We don't need to know that part," the same trooper said. "We only need to know if it's the woman we're looking for. The description you gave on the phone makes us suspect she is."

"Lookin' for her for what?" Ike asked, raising his thick gray eyebrows, making his cadaverous face seem even thinner. "You two guys want a—"

"Hey!" the other trooper said, raising a cautioning forefinger.

"I don't understand you guys," Ike said. "Hell, I just thought a patrol car'd swing by here and you'd take her in for vagrancy or tryin' to peddle her ass. Who is she, Bonnie Parker?" He fixed his bleary eyes on them. "You two even know who Bonnie Parker was?"

"Owned a diner outside Slidell, if memory serves," the trooper on the right said. "Big redheaded woman, loud voice."

"Different Bonnie Parker," Ike said, eyeing the trooper with contempt. "I guess you ain't heard of Bonnie and Clyde."

"We know a lot of Clydes," the other trooper said.

"John Dillinger?"

"He had something to do with Enron, right?"

"Christ on a stick! You call yourselves law enforcement officers?"

The troopers were both grinning. Ike, knowing he'd been had, glared at them and shifted position on his stool. "They stayed here once, the real Bonnie and Clyde. Room number eighteen."

Both troopers were staring dead eyed at him, not buying it.

One of them turned at the soft sound of gravel crunching out in the driveway. Another car arriving. This one had its lights off, too, but Ike could see it out the window and it wasn't a state police car. It was a sheriff's department car from nearby Pool County.

"That's him," one of the troopers said.

"Who?" Ike asked.

He didn't think they were going to answer him. Then the nearest trooper said, "The only one of us here other'n you who's seen Mary Smith."

"An' she offered me a—"

"Forget that part of it," said the trooper farthest away.

The other trooper winked. "Excuse my partner. He's kind of a prude. And we don't think the woman really is Mary Smith."

"Don't make me no never mind," Ike said. "That's the name she signed in under. Said her husband'd be here the end of the week with some money, an' she'd pay me cash when she checked out."

"That before or after you got that offer of sex?"

"After. She went to cryin' when I turned her down. Then she gave me the husband story."

"And you believed her, even though she signed in as Mary Smith?"

"I pretended to. She's a sweetie. An' she seemed all frazzled an' I felt sorry for her. Thought she might have some kinda mental or drug problem an' she should be in the hands of the authorities. Anyways, I seen more Smiths sign in here than you can imagine."

"I can imagine a lot of Smiths," said the trooper farthest from the desk.

"Let's go," said his partner. To Ike: "Just sit tight here, old fella, and we'll finish our business and you can go back to that girlie magazine you've been reading."

Ike started. He'd thought he'd concealed *Bizarre Desires* under *People* on the table behind the desk. Now he saw that *People* had been knocked sideways and *Bizarre Desires* was plainly visible. He must have brushed up against the table.

"Hell, I got no idea where that came from. I used to read *Playboy* years ago."

But the troopers were gone. It was amazing how quickly and quietly they'd moved, for such big men. They hadn't let the screen door slam behind them. Ike hadn't even heard the stretched-out spring squeal the way it usually did when the door opened and closed. They were here; they were gone.

Ike went back to his magazine, but he couldn't read it or even focus on the photographs.

Too much going on outside.

70

Outside, the two troopers walked to a line of trees at the edge of the parking lot opposite the room where Mary Smith presumably lay sleeping. The room's lights were out, anyway.

A knot of their fellow troopers was already there, along with Lieutenant Floyd Balamore from headquarters up the highway. A young, tan-uniformed guy who must be Simmons, the Pool County sheriff's deputy, was standing beside the lieutenant.

Simmons shifted his weight and the moonlight touched his face, and all of a sudden he didn't look so young.

"We've got the back covered in case there's some way out we don't know about," Lieutenant Balamore said to Simmons. Balamore was African American, big, smart, and very ambitious. He had sparkling dark eyes and wore a tiny brush mustache that was always impeccably trimmed and made him look as if he'd just sucked a lemon and, hey, it'd tasted okay.

"We're gonna advance in a semicircle," Balamore said, "with weapons drawn, and two men are gonna knock on the door and identify themselves as police. One of them's gonna be looking back at you, Deputy Simmons. When you're positive this is the Aiken woman, you give us the nod."

Simmons, who'd seen and talked with Cathy Lee Aiken back at the swamp shack and was 90 percent sure she was also "Mary Smith," nodded.

"Like that," Lieutenant Balamore said, "but not yet." His smile was thin beneath the twitchy little mustache. A comedian too dry for those under his command, he felt unappreciated. Simmons, he figured, was as humorless as the rest of them.

Balamore turned to his somber troopers. "Let's do this thing. And remember, the subject might be armed and dangerous."

They spread out, just as he'd instructed, and slowly advanced across the dark parking lot toward the end room that presumably contained the woman registered as Mary Smith, and whose description matched that of the woman they sought, Cathy Lee Aiken. Armed and dangerous as a woman named Cathy Lee could be.

The two troopers at the motel room door stood well on either side of it, concerned that a fusillade of bullets might smash through it at any second. The one on the left leaned in, knocked three times, and loudly proclaimed he was police. The one on the left had his gun raised and held with both hands. His head was turned and he was looking at Simmons, who was off to the side of the door and about twenty feet away.

Having met Cathy Lee, Simmons didn't think all these precautions were necessary, but he had his gun out so as not to be the only one not ready to blast away. There was enough firepower here to take on an armed battalion. Nobody even knew if Cathy Lee Aiken—assuming the woman in the motel room *was* Cathy Lee Aiken—actually had a gun.

The motel room door slowly opened, and the form of a woman in a white robe appeared. At first she stood motionless. Then she moved forward, leaning out into the moonlight, and Simmons saw her face as well as her cleavage.

She was Cathy Lee, all right. He nodded in an exaggerated way, so there would be no mistake.

No sooner had he done that then Cathy Lee suddenly bolted straight out the door and past the two nearest troopers. She stopped ten feet beyond them and pulled a large revolver from beneath her robe, causing the robe to flap open and reveal her otherwise naked body. She began turning in a tight circle, taking in the entire scene with wide eyes while affording everyone an entire view of what was beneath the robe.

There was no contingency plan for this. The startled troopers who'd been at the door froze when they saw her. The troopers lined in the lot couldn't fire for fear of hitting their comrades behind Cathy Lee. The troopers behind her couldn't fire without risking hitting one of those standing out in the lot. And of course there was the fact that in every demonstrable way she was a woman, and that gave men with guns pause.

Cathy Lee raised the revolver with both hands and began squeezing the trigger. The big revolver roared again and again. One bullet slammed into a car parked fifty feet to her left. Three went twenty feet up and lodged in some tree limbs. One went away into the night over a bean field. The last struck the side of a tractor trailer driving past on the state highway, hauling tires north to Atlanta. The driver wasn't even aware the trailer had taken a bullet, one that was now probably bouncing around inside a tire.

Cathy Lee pulled the empty gun's trigger several more times, then sat down on the ground and began to cry.

71

Palmer Stone had showered and was shaving, preparing to leave for the office, when he noticed the news was on the small-screen TV in his bathroom. A beautiful and sincere blond anchorwoman was talking about a woman who'd been arrested in Louisiana, and was thought to be the confederate of the two men who'd been charged with murdering Tom Coulter and with possession and distribution of methamphetamine.

Because of Coulter's fortunate death and the assumption that he'd been the Torso Murderer, Stone had been following the news reports on him with some interest. He'd read about the woman who'd been with the two men charged with murdering Coulter, and knew something about her. A woman like that knew how to take care of herself. Stone thought she'd gotten away clean. Well, not clean, but away.

Obviously, she hadn't.

The mug shot of a distraught-looking woman with scraggly brown hair was shown on the tiny flat-panel screen. She had dark and desperate eyes, attractive features, and was staring at the screen with her lips parted as if she were about to speak. Stone thought there was something about her reminiscent of trailer parks, cheap beauty shops, and tattoos in unmentionable places.

"Twenty-year-old Cathy Lee Aiken resisted arrest," the anchorwoman was saying, "and after a fierce gun battle with police, in which, thankfully, no one was killed or injured, she was taken kicking and screaming into custody. Police regard her as a valuable source of information about the recent whereabouts of fugitive Tom Coulter, the alleged Torso Murderer, and what led to the murder of Coulter himself by suspects Joe Ray Jeffers and Juan Adamson, allegedly. It's reported that Aiken had been living with the two alleged killers in what some people are said to be describing as a ménage à trois." She lowered her gaze and flipped a page that had been invisible until she lifted it to camera level, then looked back up and smiled. "They say dogs can't talk, but in Spangler, Idaho—"

Stone used the remote to switch off the TV and stood holding the remote for a while, still aimed like a gun at the blank screen.

The Aiken woman might know something about Coulter that would preclude him from being the Torso Murderer. Maybe she and Coulter were lovers, and he'd been with her in some sleazy motel, or wherever she might live, at the times of some E-Bliss.org clients' deaths and virtual rebirths. The torsos that so confounded the police couldn't be attributed to him.

Stone laid down the remote, which had a dab of shaving cream on it, and resumed leveling his sideburns. He was uneasy about the arrest of the woman in Louisiana. The threat wasn't yet clearly defined, but it was there, all right. She looked terrified in her mug shot. She looked like the sort who might scare, who might talk and talk.

On the other hand, Cathy Lee Aiken's credibility wasn't the best. She was a prostitute—or at least a woman of questionable morality—and an accessory to murder. Not to mention her probable involvement in an illegal methamphetamine operation. Why should anything she say be taken as gospel?

The law demanded facts, not the frantic babbling of a woman in custody and charged with committing serious crimes herself.

But the image of Cathy Lee Aiken was still in his mind.

Cheap whore! No one will believe you. You'll lump the truth in with your lies, and after a while no one will listen.

Still, when she talked, it would mean the police would double their efforts to solve the Torso Murders, an investigation that might lead to the company—his company—that he'd raised from an idea into a profit machine not even yet running at full speed and power. Stone felt the added pressure like a wedge of lead in his gut.

He nicked himself and winced in the mirror. He was shaving sloppily. As Victor had been shaving recently.

Stress could do that to a person.

Quinn and Renz were in Renz's office at One Police Plaza. It was too warm in the office. These days it almost always was. Quinn was beginning to think Renz liked it that way. Renz was taking medication for his blood pressure. Maybe that had something to do with it. And there was a stronger than usual smell of cigar smoke. Renz's secret vice. Something he and Quinn had in common.

"This woman the Louisiana cops have in custody," Renz said. "They say she's talking up a storm. Nailing those yokels who killed Coulter to the cross."

"Was she in on it?" Quinn asked.

"Looks that way. That's why she's running off at the mouth. I talked by phone to a state police lieutenant down there a couple of hours ago. He says they can't shut her up."

"They get that way sometimes when they're both scared and guilty," Quinn said.

"That one's both. And she opened fire with a revolver on a bunch of state police. That's enough to put her behind walls where they don't make cupcakes. I say let her blab. I love a motormouth suspect."

"She say Coulter was murdered for that stolen truck he was driving?"

"No," Renz said. "He actually wanted to leave them the newer truck and take their old rust bucket because it wouldn't draw attention and it'd be harder to trace. And of course the yokels wouldn't report it as stolen. That mighta worked, but he also demanded money. The two yokels were dealing meth. Coulter tried to hold them up. Made out like he was Jesse James or something, she said. The yokels didn't like it. She said one of them shot Coulter, and then later they drove him to a spot near the highway and dumped his body. They kept the truck, though, had it repainted and got it a junkyard title."

"That truck's movements are gonna be traced back to when Coulter stole it," Quinn said. "People will remember it and Coulter. Maybe think they remember, whether they saw them or not. Coulter will have an alibi for at least one, and probably more, of the Torso Murders."

"Aiken woman's already saying he spent time hanging around some roadhouse in Louisiana. It places him down there at the time of the most recent Torso killing." Renz pressed his temples with his forefingers, as if he had a bad headache. "Media pricks aren't gonna like it that we put them on the wrong road."

"They had fun while it lasted," Quinn said.

"Puts the pressure back on E-Bliss, too," Renz said. "That could be good or bad."

Quinn knew he was right. Once it got out that Coulter couldn't be the Torso Murderer, E-Bliss.org had nothing to lose by resuming operations. The company would also know that the investigation into the Torso Murders would heat up again. He made a mental note to call Pearl and tell her to stick as close as possible to Jill Clark.

Renz's phone line blinked and he picked up. Someone calling on his direct line. He swiveled his chair so his back was to Quinn. Not that Quinn couldn't hear him. And not that it mattered, because the caller did most of the talking.

When Renz had finished the conversation and swiveled around to face Quinn again, he hung up the phone and said, "That was my new best friend, Lieutenant Balamore, in Louisiana. He tells me all three suspects are talking now, accusing each other of every crime ever committed. It's a feast of information. Don't they have sense enough to lawyer up?"

"I don't know. What's Balamore say?"

"He says they don't. They don't have an average IQ between the three of them. But in this day and age, with *Law & Order* reruns playing around the clock on TV, how can anybody not know to lawyer up?"

Quinn simply shook his head.

"Law and order," Renz said. "As if they go together."

But Quinn did sense a cosmic mechanism beginning to shift at the core of events. An old cop's instinct feeling imbalance and movement without yet quite knowing what it all meant, where the momentum would take them.

It was often that way before the dominoes started to fall.

Stone worked late in his office. Not that he actually had work to do. He thought that probably the stress was getting to him. Or was it that he actually felt more at home here, in his place of business?

More and more lately, his office seemed a sanctuary from the encroaching menace of Quinn and his detectives. He'd never met Quinn, but he'd met other Quinns, men who simply wouldn't quit, who in another era would have been hunters of the most dangerous game. Who were, in fact, in this era hunters of the most dangerous game. But Palmer Stone didn't feel dangerous. He was no predator. He felt more like prey being run to ground.

Never for a second had Quinn believed Coulter was the Torso Murderer.

Stone sat behind his desk and passed his fingertips over the fine mahogany finish. Wood, the warmth and solidity of it, was reassuring. Here behind his desk he used to feel as if he could solve any problem, surmount any obstacle. It was different now. Quinn had made it different.

He used the remote to switch on his flat-panel TV mounted on the opposite wall. It was tuned to the financial channel. He switched it to the news.

There was the now familiar mug shot of Cathy Lee Aiken.

The TV went to split screen and in contrast to the disheveled and frantic-looking Cathy Lee was the same impeccably groomed blond anchorwoman who had first broken the news to Stone about the confederate of Coulter's killers being apprehended.

"Authorities say Cathy Lee Aiken is talking," the anchorwoman proclaimed, as Stone turned up the volume. "And talking and talking and talking. Her two partners in crime, allegedly, are also said to be cooperating with police. More and more doubt is accumulating about the late Tom Coulter actually being the man who committed the Torso Murders." The camera zoomed in on perfect pale features grown suddenly appalled. "Which means, of course—"

Stone pressed the red button on the remote and watched the beautiful bearer of bad news fade with her voice into nothingness.

Right now, nothingness seemed like a welcome state of being.

Palmer Stone was alone again in his office. Alone with his thoughts and not liking them.

The police, Quinn and his minions, were relentlessly tightening the noose. Despite the daily security sweep Stone conducted in his office, he couldn't be sure it wasn't bugged. Technology these days quickly overwhelmed technology, like a beast that kept devouring itself.

Technology, the science that made E-Bliss.org possible, had turned against Stone.

Victor was on his assignment to delete Jill Clark. But despite Stone's reassurances to Victor, Stone knew the Clark woman's cloying best friend, Jewel, might pose a problem.

The new Madeline Scott, Maria Sanchez, was like a hand grenade waiting to explode. Should she also be deleted? She was a special case, a grave danger. But E-Bliss.org had never, ever, deleted a special client. It was a violation of Stone's business ethics.

Then there was Victor. Another worry. Victor, who seemed to be sinking into some kind of degeneracy and sadism. His collection of literature on Vlad the Impaler, his apparent state of nervousness that always lay just beneath the surface. It was all very disturbing. And Gloria was no longer around to control Victor. For all Stone knew, Gloria might never come out of her coma.

And if she did regain consciousness, would she have all her mental faculties? Would she know what *not* to say if authorities questioned her?

The business, Stone's precious business, was unraveling like the people who were at its heart.

It was all so hopeless, so out of control. Stone did feel like a cornered prey animal docilely waiting for the predator's jaws to close.

He buried his face in his hands, his fingers slowly becoming claws leaving red indentations on his forehead and around his eyes.

He began to sob.

When finally he stopped and was calm again, his expression was blank. He had obviously made up his mind about something.

He opened a bottom desk drawer and reached inside.

72

Quinn was having dinner with Linda at a Vietnamese restaurant in her neighborhood when his cell phone vibrated in his pocket.

Linda, about to take a sip of her tea, paused and watched him pull out the phone, flip it open, and press it to his ear. He'd only glanced at the caller ID.

"Go," he said, then listened.

They were near the door to the kitchen, and pungent spices were thick in the warm air. The buzz of conversation around them was no concern; they'd automatically asked for an isolated table, knowing Quinn might receive a call.

After about thirty seconds, he said, "Make sure that's where he's going; then wait outside her building. Be sure and let me know if anything else develops."

Quinn broke the connection and immediately used his forefinger to peck another number into the phone. He glanced meaningfully at Linda. She nodded her understanding of his polite apology for the interruption of their evening. No words needed between them. *Getting familiar.*

"Was that Pearl?" she asked while Quinn waited for his call to be answered.

"Weaver," he said.

"Who are you calling now?"

"Fedderman."

Fedderman apparently answered. Linda could see Quinn's attention turn away from her a moment before he spoke.

"Feds, Weaver just called. I've had her watching E-Bliss's offices. She said she tailed Victor Lamping from there to his apartment, and he left about an hour later to go shopping. He bought a broom."

Linda stiffened as she looked at Quinn.

Quinn met her eyes and quickly looked away. "Right," he said. "Then he returned home. A while later he went out again in his car. Weaver thinks he might be headed for Jill Clark's apartment. Yeah. I'm across town. 'Kay. See you there."

He snapped the phone closed and slid it back into his pocket, then gazed beseechingly at Linda. She thought he looked like a small boy eager to go out and play rather than finish dinner. Kick the can. Hide-and-seek.

Is that all we are, people playing a grown-up game? A serious game, lives at stake, but a game nonetheless?

Of course it's a game. And someone has to play it. If that person thrives on it, all the better for the rest of us.

Quinn thrived on it. He was a hunter, a predator. If she doubted it before, she didn't now, looking into his intense green stare. Now it seemed not so much like the eager stare of a beseeching child. It was the eye of a tiger. She'd always laughed at the expression. She understood now what it meant, and she almost felt sorry for Victor Lamping.

Then she remembered Quinn's words: *He bought a broom.*

She knew that no matter what she said, Quinn was leaving her to play the game.

"I'll stay here and finish my dinner," she said, "and you can call me when you get a chance."

"Linda—"

"Go," she said. "It's your job."

It's your life.

He stood up, leaned across the table, and kissed her cheek. Then he laid some bills next to her plate and hurried toward the door.

He'd left his car parked in a garage, and they'd walked to the restaurant from her apartment. She watched him through the length of the restaurant and out the glass door, watched as he hailed a cab. Watched the cab drive away.

Watching through glass.

This is what it's like to be a cop's wife.

She finally took that sip of tea.

After ten minutes in the cab, Quinn's cell phone vibrated again. He picked up.

Weaver's voice. "Damn it, I lost him, Quinn."

Quinn was surprised. It wasn't like Weaver to lose someone she was tailing. "Where and how?"

"In heavy traffic near Times Square. He's driving that big black Chrysler sedan. We were in the theater district, and it was almost curtain time. Big black cars were all over the damned place. I just a minute ago realized I got mixed up and started following the wrong one."

"You sure of that?"

"Oh, yeah. The car I was following pulled up to valet parking in front of a restaurant. Two women and a guy who looked to be about a hundred got out and went inside."

"Where are you now?"

"Way uptown on Broadway. Long way from Jill Clark's apartment. If that's where Lamping was going."

"It's where he was going. He's on his way there. I feel it."

"So do I," Weaver said honestly. "And with that god-damned broomstick."

"And a twenty-two pistol."

"What about Pearl? Is she guarding Jill?"

"She's there."

"So should Victor be, about now," Weaver said in a sad and frustrated voice. She would beat herself up over this for months. If it turned out the way it might, maybe all her remaining years.

The cab slowed, then stopped in heavy traffic. Horns began to blare. Their varied, urgent tones echoed in discord among the tall buildings. Everyone in the city of dreams and doom was frustrated. Quinn leaned to the side and squinted out the window up at a street sign near the corner. He still had blocks to go. "I'll never get there in time."

"What about Fedderman?"

"He was home when I called. He won't make it, either."

"Better call Pearl," Weaver said. "Or get a radio car over to Jill's apartment."

But Quinn had already closed the phone lid, ending the conversation.

Traffic moved and the cab broke loose and picked up speed. Slowed, stopped, crept forward.

Quinn sat staring at the phone. If he called and had a radio car sent to Jill's apartment, the siren or the sight of uniformed police might well scare Victor away.

If he called Pearl rather than the police dispatcher, Victor would walk into a trap. Wasn't that why they were using Jill? For bait?

And there was always the slight chance that Quinn might reach Jill's apartment in time to apprehend Victor before he had the opportunity to use his weapons of choice. If he had a sharpened broomstick with him, and the gun that had fired bullets into the hearts of the Torso Murder victims, Victor would be nailed solid and as good as convicted.

A slight chance.

Quinn leaned forward and tapped on the Plexiglas divider across the back of the front seat. When the cabbie turned, Quinn held his shield up so the man would see it.

"Drive faster," Quinn said loud enough to be heard on the

other side of the Plexiglas. "Put a wheel up on the curb if you have to, but just get there."

The driver did exactly as Quinn instructed, bumping his cab's left-side tires over the curb and onto the sidewalk. Quinn slid sideways in the seat.

They passed half a dozen stopped cars that way. Then, at the intersection, they were stalled in gridlock.

The driver looked back over his shoulder and gave an exaggerated shrug.

The cab sat motionless.

Quinn held the phone in the glow from a streetlight and pecked out Pearl's cell phone number.

Fedderman thought he had a chance to get to Jill Clark's apartment in time. He had the unmarked and was using the flashing lights behind the grill. Vehicles in New York seldom got out of the way as they should have when their drivers saw flashing lights, maybe because they had no place to go. Fedderman would give them a short, deafening blast of siren, and they'd find a way to let him pass. He was doing okay.

Near Fifth Avenue, brake lights suddenly flared on the delivery van he'd been tailgating.

Both vehicles had been building speed and were doing around thirty. As Fedderman stood on the brake pedal and yanked hard on the steering wheel, the unmarked's right front fender clipped the van. The steering wheel came alive and spun in Fedderman's hands.

He managed to gain control and avoid hitting a man walking a dog. While his attention was diverted, the car's right front tire caught on a curbstone sticking a few inches into the street. A hubcap went spinning out in front and crossed the street in a graceful glittering arc, causing a lot of rubber screeching and horn blaring. Then both the unmarked's right-side tires shredded their sidewalls along the edge of the curb.

"Shit!" Fedderman said just before the car jolted over a storm drain and his head bounced hard off the side window.

The car shuddered and bucked before coming to a stop near a NO PARKING HERE TO CORNER sign.

Fedderman sat dazed for a while.

When he came around he saw concerned and curious faces peering in at him through the car windows, saw beyond them people running toward where he sat in the crippled vehicle.

He thought he'd better call Quinn, then abandon the unmarked and commandeer a cab.

It was after business hours. The midtown building where E-Bliss.org had its offices was almost completely unoccupied. The windows facing the street were dark.

All but one, where a faint light filtered through closed drapes.

The inside of the building was quiet. Peaceful. The nighttime janitor service wouldn't show up for hours. The corridors were silent and empty, their waxed floors flat and gleaming dully like perfectly still waters.

There was no one around to hear the sharp, single shot.

It might as well have been a domino falling.

73

Victor had figured out a way to follow Palmer Stone's instructions, and make Jill Clark's death look like an accident. Gloria, the expert on accidental death, would be proud.

He parked the Chrysler a block down from Jill Clark's building and walked back. He was wearing khaki pants and a blue pullover shirt, well-worn jogging shoes. On his head was a Mets cap, not cocked at an angle like a younger man might wear it, but square on his head like someone trying to be unrecognizable on security tape would. People passing on the sidewalk didn't give him a second glance. If asked later to pick him out of a lineup, they'd have a problem. He didn't want to make a memorable impression tonight except on Jill Clark, and she'd remember him for the rest of her life.

In his right hand was a navy blue duffel bag with a Nike swoosh and a web handle. Mr. Average, possibly returning home from a workout at the gym. The bag contained two rolls of duct tape, pruning shears, dental floss, and a package of single-edged razor blades. Protruding from its almost zipped opening was the blunt end of a wooden broomstick, redolent of the way tennis racket handles jutted out of club bags. The other end of the yard-long length of broomstick, inside the bag, was carved and sanded to a point. Not too sharp a point; Victor had learned not to create immediate extensive internal bleeding, so his subject's agony would be prolonged.

As he strolled, he smiled. Jill would cooperate rather than die right away. Everyone scratched every way they could for those last precious seconds of life, for something as opposed to nothing.

Nothing was forever.

Jill would write her good-bye note within the first ten minutes, and then the real fun would begin. Victor had to concentrate on Gloria and her tragic state in order not to have an erection and attract attention.

After he was finished with Jill, Victor would pour cleaning solvent over her, which he knew was stored beneath her sink. Then he'd extinguish the pilot light on her old gas stove and turn on all the burners.

Before leaving, he'd set Jill, and then the draperies, on fire.

Within minutes of his exiting the building, the blaze should be steady and strong. The gas would continue to seep until it, too, was ignited. By the time the fire department arrived, the apartment would be an inferno.

He'd take the broomstick with him. With a fire, you never could tell what might not burn completely—and where the broomstick would be, it might not burn at all.

Victor didn't have a full erection, but he was tumescent as he entered Jill's building. He hoped that if anyone did happen to see him, they wouldn't notice.

Gloria! . . .

Pearl's cell phone in her purse played the first four notes of the old theme from *Dragnet*. Although it was muted, she still heard it and removed the phone, saw that it was Quinn calling.

"Everything okay there, Pearl?" he asked.

"Just another night in paradise," Pearl said. "I'm in the bedroom trying not to be a pest."

"And Jill?" There was an unexpected concern in Quinn's voice.

"She's in the living room watching TV. Some sitcom rerun about a bunch of neurotic misfits living in an apartment in New York."

"You don't like it?"

"I've seen the episode four times and don't want to see it again."

"Victor Lamping is on his way over there," Quinn said.

"He's probably coming as Tony Lake. Nothing new there. He'll be tickled to see me."

"He was seen buying a wood-handled broom earlier today," Quinn said.

"Oh. . . . Who's on him?"

"Weaver was. She lost him. Listen, Pearl. Feds and I might not be able to get there in time to help you."

"Weaver *lost* him?"

"Don't be catty, Pearl."

"Could be he's just coming over to try again to bed Jill. Poor bastard's balls have probably turned blue from trying and failing."

"A broom, Pearl. He's not going to be Tony Lake tonight."

"Maybe he just needed a broom. To sweep."

"Pearl . . ."

"I can handle things here, Quinn. You know I can." *Not like that screwup Weaver.*

"I can get some radio cars over there within minutes."

"And spook Victor after we've gone to all this trouble to lure him into our trap?"

Her reaction didn't surprise him. "There's that possibility."

"Probability, even if they arrive without lights or sirens."

Pearl unconsciously passed her hand over her Glock 9mm in

its belt holster. "I'll control things here and wait for you and Feds."

"You're taking a chance, Pearl. Sticking your neck way out."

"So are you, Quinn. It's the only way we can stop these assholes."

"I don't want—"

"Don't worry. Nobody's gonna do the slightest harm to Jill Clark."

"I was thinking about you, Pearl."

But you're letting me face one of the creepiest killers ever by myself.

"Don't worry about me, Quinn. I'll do my job. If you have to worry, make it about your friend Dr. Linda."

"Damn it, Pearl—"

She broke the connection.

Why did I say that? Why did I have to say it?

She heard the rasp of the intercom from the other side of the door, in the living room.

Heard Jill answer it and invite someone up.

Jill went to the mirror near the door and made sure her blouse was tucked tightly in her jeans, then fluffed her hair. It was an effort making herself look good for Tony Lake now that she knew what he might be capable of doing to her. What he might have done to those other women.

But even now, sometimes, he could be so charming it was—

There was a scuffing sound in the hall. She pressed her lips tightly together and rolled them to make sure her gloss was on evenly, then turned away from the mirror.

Two knocks on the door, firm and loud.

She gathered herself, then went to the door and opened it. Smiled big and broad.

"Tony!"

*   *   *

Quinn was three blocks from Jill's apartment, seething in the back of the cab. A block ahead, something was going on involving a tall van and some flashing yellow lights. Maybe a tow truck trying to handle more than it could manage. Whatever it was, it had traffic stalled to intermittent gains of ten or fifteen feet before brake lights flared again and the cab would come to a complete halt.

The driver's gunfighter eyes met Quinn's in the cocked rearview mirror. He swiveled in his seat to face Quinn and mouthed that he was sorry, there was nothing he could do to make better time.

Quinn squirmed and nodded. He understood, and he didn't see that things were going to change anytime soon.

He reached in his wallet and counted out what was on the meter, along with a generous tip, then tapped a knuckle on the clear divider and shoved the wad of bills on the steel swivel tray.

Then he was out of the cab and striding along the sidewalk in the direction of Jill's apartment. If the leg he'd been shot in months ago still ailed him, he didn't feel it. He resisted the urge to break into a run, knowing it would only exhaust him and might ultimately slow him down.

As he walked, brushing people aside, ignoring their hostile glares and remarks, he fished his cell phone from his pocket and pecked out Pearl's number.

What the hell was going on in Jill's apartment?

74

As Pearl moved toward the bedroom door, she heard her cell phone faintly playing *Dragnet* in her purse on the bed but ignored it. She knew it couldn't be heard from the living room.

She inched the door open. She could see across the living room to the small foyer and the hall door.

Tony, all right.

Jill was facing him, with her head raised as if expecting a kiss, playing her role.

As Tony pecked her cheek, he drew a small semiautomatic handgun from behind his back. It had a sound suppressor attached, dull gray and about six inches long with baffles. He began bending his elbow awkwardly so he could point the gun at Jill.

He's going to shoot her low in the side, to wound, and then . . .

Pearl didn't hesitate. She had her Glock out within seconds and snapped off a shot she knew would be wide of Tony but would certainly miss Jill. It wouldn't take him down, but it might startle him into forgetting for a few seconds about Jill.

Tony reacted fast. He shoved Jill away and swung the gun toward the sound of Pearl's shot, instantly saw her advancing down the hall toward him.

Pearl had a clear shot at him now. As she steadied her gun she saw a dulled muzzle flash and heard the silenced pistol spit at her. Tony's shot missed. So did her return shot. She knew he had a twenty-two. It was his weapon of choice, and even silenced it had sounded like a small-caliber gun. Pearl figured it would probably take several shots to stop her. Her powerful 9mm Glock could put Tony down with one shot.

If it hit home.

Pearl kept advancing down the hall, the Glock bucking and crashing in her hand. Tony wasn't retreating. *Grade A for guts. Kill the bastard!* She expected any moment to feel the sting of a bullet.

One of Tony's wild shots glanced off a framed print hanging in the hall just as Pearl came alongside it. Less than a foot from her face, the frame swung and dropped to the floor as the glass exploded into thin fragments. Pearl felt the right side of her face catch fire. She suddenly couldn't see from her right eye, realized it was closed, tried to open it but couldn't because of the pain.

Shit!

It only made her enraged. No time or room now for fear.

Through her watery left eye she took shaky aim and squeezed off another shot, knowing it would hit nothing but wall.

She saw a blurred figure dart to the side, turn, and disappear out the door to the hall.

Pearl staggered all the way into the living room and became aware that she wasn't headed toward the door. She was dizzy and had lost her bearings. She aimed her left eye at a huddled figure pressed back in a corner.

Jill.

Pearl started toward her and was suddenly nauseated. She looked down at her right arm and saw blood splatters on it.

There was something else wrong. Pain was taking her over, making it difficult to breathe. *Am I going into shock?*

No, damn it!

She took two steps backward and fell slumping into the sofa.

The figure huddled in the corner wasn't there anymore. Then she saw it. Jill was crawling across the room toward her.

"Jewel?"

Jill's voice sounded as if it had come from the next room. Only it hadn't. Jill, standing up now, was only a few feet in front of Pearl.

"Jewel? Jewel? My God! You okay?"

"My cell," Pearl said. "Go get my cell phone. In my purse in the bedroom."

"Jewel?"

"My cell, goddamnit!"

On foot, Quinn dashed against the traffic signal through speeding, blaring traffic. He didn't slow down once he set foot on the opposite curb.

He'd reached Jill's block and was almost to her building, running flat out now, heart pumping so fast and hard it hurt.

Maybe he'd make it.

Maybe he'd get there in time.

A horn blared close to him, startling him. A cab veered to the curb about twenty feet in front of him. A voice:

"Quinn! Quinn!"

Quinn stopped and saw Fedderman shouting out the lowered side window in the back of the cab.

"Quinn!"

The cab's rear door swung open wide, looking as if it might spring off its hinges. Fedderman was leaning out waving at him.

"Get in, Quinn! Get in!"

Quinn knew they could make better time than he was making on foot as long as traffic didn't bog down again. He ran toward the cab, stumbling and almost falling as he stepped off the curb. His ankle felt sprained, but not enough to slow him down.

Getting too old for this . . .

No, not yet!

Victor understood it now—Jewel was a cop. They'd been waiting for him to come after Jill.

And the bitch had shot him!

He knew it wasn't serious, but a bullet had grazed the side of his neck, fortunately missing that carotid artery. Still, blood was flowing down inside his collar, and he could feel the warm wetness down his back.

He couldn't be sure if he'd hit Jewel; he'd been was firing small-caliber rounds at a distance. Almost surely she was coming after him.

No time to wait for the elevator. He threw himself down the steps, managing to stay on his feet by gripping the banister and shoving off the walls at the landings. He thought he could hear Jewel's footsteps on the stairs above and made himself move faster. She might have a clear shot at him any second. And she'd probably called for backup. He had to get out of the building, reach the streets before more police came.

He was in the lobby, almost slipping and falling on the slick tiles. Still holding the silenced handgun, he thought about turning around and firing a snap shot up the stairwell to at least slow down Jewel if she was pursuing him.

No time even for that.

He bolted toward the heavy door to the street, hit it hard with his shoulder, and spun as he lurched outside.

* * *

The cab pulled to the curb. Fedderman shoved a wad of bills at the driver as Quinn, on the right side in back, opened the door and started to climb out.

"Hell is that?" he heard Fedderman say.

Stooped over and with one foot still in the cab, one on the curb, Quinn looked up and saw a man burst from the doorway of Jill's apartment building. He must have hit the door hard on the inside because he was spinning as he broke outside. Quinn saw something in his right hand. Identified it immediately.

"That's Victor!" Fedderman shouted.

Quinn very calmly but loudly shouted, "Gun!" He gripped the butt of his old police positive special and pulled the revolver smoothly from its leather shoulder holster.

The cab's window behind him starred as a bullet smacked into it. Victor was standing with his feet spread wide facing Quinn. He was holding his weapon with both hands aiming carefully. Quinn noticed it hadn't made any noise and saw the bulky silencer on the barrel.

No time even to seek shelter!

Quinn lowered himself to a kneeling position to present a smaller target and fired a shot at Victor. Another shot barked nearby. He glanced back across the interior of the cab and saw Fedderman's ample stomach paunch and wrinkled tie mashed against the outside of the opposite side window. Fedderman was standing and firing across the cab's roof.

Another shot, and a bullet snapped past over Quinn's head.

Outgoing.

Victor had decided to make his stand. He made no attempt to escape. A bullet zinged off the cab's hood. The cabbie had had enough. Quinn heard the engine roar and felt rather than saw the cab pull away fast from the curb.

Exposed now, Fedderman moved up so he was standing directly behind Quinn. Both men fired over and over at Victor. Quinn's ears rang from the din and he could smell cordite, see brass casings from Fedderman's 9mm bouncing around like loose coins on the sidewalk.

Victor seemed almost to melt as he fell.

He lay motionless with one leg twisted beneath him.

Quinn and Fedderman separated and approached the still body from different angles. Fedderman, his white shirt cuff flapping above his gun hand, reached it first and kicked the silenced .22 away from where it lay next to Victor's dead hand.

He stooped low and touched the base of Victor's neck lightly, feeling for a pulse, and then looked up at Quinn. "Gone."

"Let's get upstairs," Quinn said, breathing hard. "See how Pearl is."

75

Quinn and Fedderman saw the door to Jill's apartment hanging open. There was no way to know what was going on inside, or how many people were involved. Victor had probably been alone, but there was no way to be sure.

They entered cautiously, guns drawn.

Jill was sitting on the floor in front of the sofa, her face blank. She was obviously in shock. Pearl was slumped on the sofa. Her right eye was tightly closed and there was blood all over that side of her face and in spatter marks down her right arm.

She squinted at Quinn with her left eye.

"More blood than anything else," she said. "Bullet hit a picture on the wall. Blew it all to hell. Glass in my eye."

She seemed only mildly annoyed, rather than enraged or in any great pain. Must be in shock, like Jill, Quinn figured.

He turned to instruct Fedderman to call for EMS for both Pearl and Jill. Fedderman was already standing off to the side with his cell phone making the call.

"Don't need an ambulance," Pearl said. "You or Feds can drive me to the hospital. Or I can take a cab."

"Call Renz when you're done with that call," Quinn said to Fedderman. "Let him know what happened."

Then he sat down beside Pearl on the sofa and held her close.

As soon as Renz hung up after Fedderman's call, he phoned Cindy Sellers. She'd hear it and publish it first, even if the news hit TV before the next edition of *City Beat.*

Sellers was print media and should be used to getting scooped by TV or the Internet. But she'd get the jump on all the major New York papers. A deal was a deal. Besides, Renz would rather have Sellers as an ally than an enemy.

Her questions were brief and to the point. Renz's answers were the same. They both knew the rules. Renz kind of enjoyed the conversation. They were two ruthless and expert players who by chance and opportunity found themselves on the same side of the board.

When the conversation was over, Renz went to his office door and locked it. He was smiling.

Quinn had come through again. The Torso Murderer— the real one—lay dead on the sidewalk, and Renz's career was alive and well.

As planned.

He returned to his desk and fired up a celebratory cigar.

Pearl had done her job. Jill Clark was mentally shaken but otherwise unharmed. The paramedics tried to load Pearl onto a gurney to carry her to the ambulance. She was having none of it. The glass wasn't actually *in* her eye, so she demanded to be stitched up then and there. The paramedics said the best they could do on the spot were butterfly bandages to temporarily hold the deepest cuts together and stop the bleeding. Pearl told them that would do. Tough Pearl.

Thought she was staying on the job, going with Quinn and Fedderman.

"Not a chance," Quinn told her when he realized she expected to stay in the hunt. "You've done enough, Pearl. If you won't go to a hospital, stay here and rest. Or go up to your own apartment. Jewel's."

"That place is a rat hole," Pearl said.

"For a rodent that's lucky to be alive."

"You calling me a rat, Quinn?"

Quinn said, "Stay, Pearl!" As if she were a dog he was disciplining and taking no more shit from. Well, better than a rodent.

Pearl didn't like it, but she knew when not to argue. *Stubborn bastard!* She slumped down on the sofa, slouching so she was sitting on her spine. Like a spoiled brat unfairly denied.

Quinn was unmoved. He turned to Fedderman.

"Let's go see if Palmer Stone's working late tonight," he said, not looking back at Pearl as he moved toward the door.

Fedderman slid a fresh clip into his 9mm, glanced at Pearl, grinned, and said, "Hard ass." He hurried to catch up with Quinn.

Pearl stayed behind and fumed.

Quin and Fedderman commandeered one of the unmarked city cars that had arrived at the scene. Quinn drove it fast but not recklessly, staring straight ahead, thinking about Pearl and what had happened to Victor Lamping, and what he, Quinn, would like to do to Palmer Stone.

He double-parked outside Stone's office building and flipped down the sun visor to display the NYPD placard. Quinn and Fedderman were the only ones in the elevator as it rose to the floor where E-Bliss.org's offices were located.

Quinn knew Renz had probably tipped Cindy Sellers by now. All secrets were known. The news of Victor's death might already be on TV and radio.

As they entered the suite of offices, Quinn signaled Fedderman, and both men drew their weapons and held them tight against their thighs.

The small anteroom was empty. It had a still and desolate air about it. After enough years, cops could sense unoccupied premises. After enough years, they learned not to entirely trust their instincts.

Weapons raised and at the ready now, Quinn led the way, and they pushed through to Stone's office.

The offices of E-Bliss.org were occupied—in a way. Palmer Stone was at his desk, appropriately dressed in a dark business suit with white shirt and red silk tie. He was slumped forward with both arms and his head on the desk, as if he were taking a nap. There was a dark-rimmed, perfectly round hole in his temple. The gun that had created it was in his right hand. The bullet hadn't exited his head, so the desk had only a small pool of blood on it. Near Stone's left hand was a precisely folded suicide note. Everything about the scene was neat and orderly, considering. The live Palmer Stone would have approved.

The note was computer generated and had been printed out. It said simply, "I know when business hours are over." It was signed in blue ink, no doubt from the Montblanc pen lying uncapped on the desk.

Quinn replaced the note where he'd found it. He used his cell to contact Renz and tell him what had happened.

While they were waiting for the army of CSU techs and the M.E. and EMS, Quinn and Fedderman slipped evidence gloves on and began a cursory examination of Palmer Stone's files and the contents of his desk drawers.

Unsurprisingly, there was nothing incriminating. Merely the expected business letters and signed correspondence with suppliers and satisfied clients. Maybe the computers would yield more later.

Fedderman, who was near the office window, glanced outside and down at the street.

He turned to Quinn. "Troops're arriving."

Quinn took a deep breath, released it, and looked around the spare, neat office, then at the still body behind the desk.

"They can have it," he said and moved toward the door.

And stopped. Something made him not want to leave. Not just yet.

He walked over to the desk and stared at the shocked expression on Palmer Stone's face.

"We ever seen Stone before in the flesh?" he asked.

Fedderman shook his head no. "Seen his photo on the Internet. What's left here in his desk chair looks like the photo."

Quinn continued to stare at the dead man. He simply couldn't tell for sure, but he had to allow for possibilities.

"You notice anything about those files we went through?" he asked Fedderman.

"Nothing I wanted to notice."

"The signatures on the documents and the suicide note aren't the same."

Fedderman took a moment to think about that. "And Stone's business *was* providing doubles with new identities." He wiped his wrist across his mouth, then looked doubtful. "But if the dead guy at the desk isn't Stone, and the note's a phony, why wouldn't Stone have signed it?"

"He might have wanted only the dead man's prints on the pen and paper in case they might be lifted. He could've held the gun to the man's head and made him sign the note. I'll bet the gun's been wiped clean except for the dead man's prints. I'll bet the office has been wiped clean. And Stone's been clean, never been arrested or in the military. His prints aren't on file."

Fedderman leaned forward and stared hard at the dead man's face. "It sure looks like Stone."

"What if it isn't?" Quinn asked.

But he already knew the answer.

If Stone was alive but officially dead, what did he have to

lose by murdering the woman who'd destroyed his business and brought about his downfall?

Or women?

Jill Clark, who'd already barely escaped. And Pearl.

By cell phone, Quinn tried to contact Pearl, who was still having her injuries tended.

She'd managed to browbeat a second paramedic, who'd come for Jill, into applying stitches rather than the butterfly bandages. The grumpy paramedic answered her phone. Quinn told him the situation.

Pearl, listening to one side of the conversation, told the paramedic to tell Quinn that Weaver was with Jill, who was unhurt and had refused medical attention.

"She says to tell you—"

"Never mind," Quinn said. "Just take care of her. Make sure she's okay."

"What we do," the grumpy paramedic said.

"And tell her to get the hell out of there. Out of the building."

"With this one, telling her's not the same as her doing it."

"I know," Quinn said. "I'm an expert on the subject."

He broke the connection, then immediately called Renz and told him the situation at E-Bliss.org.

Renz didn't say anything for almost a minute, thinking about all the ramifications of maybe looking foolish if Quinn was wrong about Stone not being Stone. The consequences could be even worse than simply looking foolish. There were deep wells to fall into here. Even tiger pits.

But Renz was still more cop than bureaucrat or politician.

"Could be," he said. "Not likely, but could be." He paused. "You're on your own with this hypothesis, though. It's gotta be that way, Quinn." *Well, almost more cop than bureaucrat or politician.*

The Two Palmer Stones was Quinn's theory, Quinn's game, Quinn's risk—and if Quinn just happened to be right, Renz's glory. And if it turned out Quinn was wrong, no harm to Renz. Win-win.

"We're on our way to Jill's apartment," Quinn said.

"I'll call Weaver," Renz said, "and make sure she takes Jill somewhere safe." *No political risk there. Only upside.*

While Quinn was stuffing the cell phone back in his pocket, Fedderman said, "Pearl okay?"

"For Pearl," Quinn said. "For now."

They took the elevator down and Quinn gave directions to the CSU crew that had just entered the lobby. Then they were back in the unmarked bucking traffic and retracing their route. Ignoring potholes and blaring horns and angry shouts and traffic laws and traffic lights. Driving hard toward Jill Clark's apartment.

"Think he'll go there?" Fedderman asked.

Quinn concentrated on threading his way through traffic. "I think he might. That's enough."

"Should still be plenty of law there. Maybe they haven't even taken away Victor's body."

"That'll all be out in the street," Quinn said. "And if there's something going on there, all the better for Stone. It'll be easier for him to enter the building without attracting suspicion and confront Jill and Pearl."

"He's not stupid," Fedderman said. "He might think we could be on to him and he's got that figured in his plans."

Quinn smiled a smile Fedderman had seen before. It would never prompt anyone to smile back.

"We have our own plans," Quinn said.

76

Stone was there.

Quinn and Fedderman knew it almost as soon as they entered the building. They saw him first as a lower leg in richly tailored dress slacks and polished wing tips, for only a second as he rounded the corner and began climbing the stairs.

Neither Quinn nor Fedderman said anything as they quietly gave chase. They didn't want Stone to know they were there. Ideally, they'd come up behind him before he realized he wasn't alone and take him down alive. They needed him in court, as a defendant and as a witness.

As Stone began climbing the last flight of stairs to Jill's floor, he prepared to enter her apartment by drawing a small pearl-handled gun from his suit coat pocket.

As he did so, Quinn made the slightest noise on the creaking stairs.

Stone turned in surprise. It was as if the dead man back in the office had risen up and they'd startled him.

Quinn didn't hesitate. He couldn't. There was distance to cover.

He charged.

The wind rushed out of Stone as Quinn leveled a shoulder into his midsection. At the same time, Quinn's left hand found Stone's right, forcing the pearl-handled gun to point at the ceiling.

As the two men slid toward the floor, Quinn squeezed hard with his powerful left hand. Flesh and blood vessels compacted against bone as Stone's right wrist was crushed. The gun dropped like a child's surrendered toy and clattered onto the floor.

Stone wasn't the sort to put up a fight.

He sat down winded on the wooden steps, leaning forward and gripping his aching wrist. Saliva dripped from the corner of his mouth. He brushed away the drool, working hard to control his breathing, then gave a sad smile and shook his head.

Fedderman read him his rights, then leaned close to him so their faces were only inches apart. He studied Stone. "The dead guy sitting at your desk—"

"Isn't me," Stone finished for him. "Obviously."

"Your double," Quinn said. "Who thought he was going to move into your life and be well paid for it. Instead he was used to fake your suicide."

"Things had reached an impasse," Stone said. "Because of you, I might add."

"You're the one who shot the poor bastard," Quinn said, not posing it as a question. Just making conversation here. The idea was to get Stone to admit it in his own words.

Quinn held his silence. He waited, waited. . . .

"I killed him," Stone said. "I'm not averse to doing the wet work when I must." He managed to shrug. "Business is business."

Quinn whistled out a long breath in relief.

It was over. He and Fedderman exchanged a look. Quinn thought Fedderman might have smiled.

With Stone alive and an admitted killer, and with Jill's testimony, the case against E-Bliss.org was solid. And when they found the new Madeline Scott, she'd have little choice but to reveal her true identity and testify for the prosecution.

"I think," Stone said, "I won't say anything more until my attorney is present."

Which struck Quinn as odd, considering Stone had just confessed and confirmed that they had the right man.

Very odd.

He cuffed Stone's uninjured wrist to the banister.

Pearl had reluctantly taken Quinn's earlier advice and returned to Jewel's apartment. She wasn't sure where Jill was. Weaver might have taken her someplace safer.

After cleaning up as best she could, combing her hair without looking closely at the two-inch-square bandage on her right cheek near her eye, she decided to go downstairs and check on Jill, make sure she wasn't still in her apartment.

As she turned from the bathroom mirror, the light penetrating through the narrow window was like a lance in her right eye. She put on the black eye patch the paramedic had given her and then did assess her appearance carefully in the mirror.

She decided she looked like a pirate after a run-in with the Royal Navy.

Aargh! she almost said softly. Then she decided nothing was funny and looked away from the pathetic face in the mirror.

She went downstairs and knocked on the door to Jill's apartment.

The light behind the peephole in the door changed and she knew Jill—or someone—was there. Jill, probably, too shaken to immediately open the door to anyone's knock. After what had happened to her, Jill might not trust anyone for months.

"Me," Pearl called. "Jewel." The alias had become a secret password.

The light behind the peephole remained constant.

The man peering through the peephole sized up the woman at the door. She was small, didn't look like much of a threat, and seemed to have been in some kind of accident. She was wearing an eye patch and a glob of white bandage on her face.

If he waited her out, she might simply go away. He'd already searched the apartment, looked in all its hiding places, and knew Jill Clark wasn't home. She must have been placed somewhere else for her protection. This woman—Jewel, she'd said her name was—obviously knew Jill. Maybe she'd know where Jill was. She seemed to be alone.

He decided to make the woman tell him what he needed to know, then kill her. If he could somehow get to Jill, everything might still go as planned.

The cops hadn't left that long ago. There might still be some around. He'd have to move fast and noiselessly.

He holstered the gun he was holding and drew a knife.

77

The door suddenly opened and a dark-haired man with fierce brown eyes clutched Pearl's arm painfully and yanked her inside the apartment. She hadn't had time to think, much less offer any resistance.

I don't recognize him. What the hell have I gotten myself into?

Who the hell is he?

Now what?

He was showing her a knife, slowly revolving the blade in the air. Obviously displaying it for effect.

He grinned meanly as he held up the long-bladed knife, figuring terror would melt the woman into something he could easily handle. It had always amused him that women reacted that way when they saw a knife that might be used on them. Perhaps it was a natural fear of penetration. Something sexual. Whatever, it made them inert and helpless.

Pearl kicked him in the knee.

The man roared with pain and slashed out at her with the knife. Pearl stepped inside the arc of the swing and punched him in the stomach. He grunted and shoved her backward, almost making her lose her balance. When he came at her she sidestepped his charge, barely avoiding the flashing blade. She was terrified that he might slash at her from the other direction, her blind side.

Damned patch!

But she was afraid to tear the patch off now, afraid of sudden brilliance and pain that might be worse than vision with one eye.

She remembered a tacky glass vase on the table near the sofa, swiveled her head so she could see it through her left eye. Fixed its image in her mind. When the man charged her again with the knife, she avoided the blade and dodged left, toward the table.

He whirled and came at her low, using the knife underhand this time. It would be harder to avoid his upward slashes, more difficult to see them coming from below eye level. Pearl felt for the cheap vase, a florist's pressed-glass giveaway designed to hold one rose. She fumbled it, feeling it slide from her fingers.

Then she lowered her hand and caught the vase as it toppled. She got a good grip on it and slammed it into the man's face.

It didn't shatter. She swung it again and felt it make solid contact with the man's head.

The force of the blow made her lose her grip on the vase. It bounced on the floor and passed from her range of vision.

She no longer had the vase as a weapon, but it had bought her precious seconds. She knew how to use them. She bolted for the door.

Had her fingers wrapped around the knob.

Was pulling the door open.

But she knew she wouldn't be fast enough. She was trapped in one of those horrible slow-motion nightmares.

She was aware of the knife suddenly protruding from the door frame, near her face, where it had penetrated enameled wood after the man's desperate throw, his attempt to cut her on the run.

At least he isn't armed now.

Gunfire exploded behind her.

Oh, shit!

He's got a gun, too! And he's determined!

So was Pearl. She had the door open and was almost in the hall. If she could get around the corner, out of sight, she might make it to the stairs. Screw the elevator. No time. She felt the familiar smoothness and grit of the hall's tile floor under the sole of her left shoe.

Gonna make it!

A truck slammed into her back.

She knew she'd been shot. She stumbled forward, then seemed to strike an invisible wall and bounce off it. Her balance shifted, as if the floor tilted.

Pearl felt herself moving backward, back, back into the apartment on numbed legs. Exactly where she didn't want to go.

The impact of the second bullet was greater than that of the first. It flung her against the door, slamming it shut and trapping her inside with her assailant. Everything around her began to whirl, making her dizzy.

She was looking up at the door. It was square in her one-eyed vision and moving farther and farther away, getting smaller.

Odd . . . Am I floating . . . ?

She realized she was on the floor, her upper body on soft carpet, hardwood floor solid beneath her bare heels. Had the force of the shots knocked her out of her shoes? She'd seen it happen.

She looked again and found the door. It was standing wide open. There was more noise, banging sounds, but she could barely hear them, as if they were coming from far away.

Gunfire?

There was Quinn, crouched in the doorway in shooting stance, filling the doorway, blasting away with that antique revolver of his.

Quinn.

It was strange how calm she was now.

Quinn. Looking so serious. A serious man, Quinn. So simple and complex. A good man. Hard to find, hard to lose. She was going to miss him so. . . .

She thought she might have smiled at him.

78

"You with me, Pearl?

Quinn's voice. There was a horrible taste in Pearl's mouth, and her lips were glued together with dried mucus.

Yuk!

"Pearl?"

She didn't want to open her eyes, but she did.

There was Quinn, standing over her, looking serious.

It came back to her in a rush, the man in Jill's apartment, the struggle, the gunfire.

Jesus, I've been shot!

"Don't try to move, Pearl."

She felt her lips rip apart. "Wha' happened?"

"You were shot and spent five hours on the operating table. You've been unconscious for a while, and now you're back."

Mingled scents came to her: pine disinfectant, peppermint, fresh linen. She let her gaze roam, painfully and with one eye. Her vision was slightly blurred more than a few feet out, beyond a tray on which sat a green plastic glass and pitcher, a box of tissues. She was in a hospital bed.

"Unconscious? A while?"

"Three days," Quinn said.

Three days! Serious. Maybe critical.

"That qualify as a coma?"

"Sure," Quinn said.

"I'm gonna live?"

"Yeah, if from now on you do everything I say."

"Quinn . . ."

"I'm sorry. You're gonna be okay, Pearl. You're in Roosevelt Hospital. You were shot twice. One bullet broke your collarbone. Another entered your back near the shoulder blade and deflected downward and lodged near your liver. They've both been removed. You're gonna be fine."

"So I really will live?"

"You will." His smile came and went like a ghost. "You've got a lot of physical therapy ahead of you."

Pearl tried to move but found she was too weak. "My back, nothing hurts. Everything's numb."

"It's the drugs. It'll hurt later, Pearl."

"Good old Quinn, giving it to me straight."

"Few enough people will, in this screwed-up world."

"Don't I know it? When can I get out of here?"

"Maybe in two or three more days. They're gonna evaluate you again."

"Jill okay?"

"Fine."

"What the hell happened?"

"Feds and I caught up with Palmer Stone on the stairs of Jill's building, and he admitted faking his suicide, killing the man who had become his double and thought he was going to become Stone after the real Stone disappeared. We tried to get more out of him, but he went silent and asked for an attorney."

"He decided to lawyer up *after* admitting to murder?"

"Yeah. That's what struck Feds and me as wrong. We figured he had a reason, that he was maybe trying to delay us.

And we could think of only one reason why he'd want to keep us in the stairwell as long as possible."

"He didn't want you to go to Jill's apartment. He wanted you to think any danger to her was over."

"Right. He knew what was going to happen up there, because he knew who was waiting. But you went to see Jill. You found Jorge Sanchez instead."

The name didn't mean anything to Pearl for several seconds. Maybe because of the drugs. Then it came to her.

"The infamous drug lord? But he was killed in Mexico City."

"Not the real Sanchez. The man the Mexican police shot to death was one of Sanchez's several doubles, who was tricked into leaving the hotel Sanchez and his wife were in. The police took him for the real Sanchez and killed him. Even Sanchez's wife, Maria, thought Jorge was dead. She had to have been shocked to see him in the dark passageway when he stepped out of the shadows and killed Greeve."

"Greeve had been shocked, too," Pearl said. "He wasn't killed by any prostitute. They just made it look that way. He was trying to pronounce Jorge's name before he died."

"Right. Jorge is in the hospital now, and talking. But he isn't going to make it. He was planning to join his wife in New York after assuming the identity of an E-Bliss client himself. They were going to meet again as two other people and move out of town, away from the drug trade. And it might have worked out for them if Jorge could have killed Jill. She was the only one who could swear she saw both Madelines and could tie them in with E-Bliss. Jill was the link he had to destroy. But Jorge's plans went about as sour as Palmer Stone's."

"So Maria Sanchez was the new Madeline."

Quinn nodded.

"What about Tony Lake?"

"Victor Lamping?"

"Yeah."

Quinn was surprised she'd forgotten; he'd told her all about Lamping while holding her and waiting for the medics in Jill's living room. "He was dead before they got him to the hospital."

Pearl let her head sink back into her pillow and thought about that. About handsome, smiling, lying Tony Lake. Everything about him a lie.

"Good," she said.

Quinn said nothing.

"E-Bliss," Pearl said. "What a nightmare."

"Even more than you think," Quinn said. "Stone and Victor's sister, Gloria Lamping, whom Stone ratted out, are trying to outtalk each other, cutting deals that aren't going to happen. That's where I got much of my information. Gloria's still recovering from being run down by a cab. She knew about the killings. Stone says she even committed some of them."

"A woman doing that to another woman." Pearl managed to shake her head slightly on the pillow. "A nightmare," she said again.

"One that's over," Quinn said. "You're awake now, Pearl."

He touched her hand as gently as he'd ever touched her.

Quinn stayed with Pearl until almost midnight, then went home to his apartment and found Linda's note.

She'd thought things through, the note said, and she realized she could never be a cop's wife. She was also going to quit her job with the city. She felt there was no choice, after being exposed as an informant who'd chosen sides in an NYPD internal dispute. No one would trust her after that. And she didn't deserve Quinn's trust.

She'd signed her name under the word *good-bye.*

Quinn felt like sobbing, then like breaking up the furniture, but he did neither. He thought about trying to phone

Linda. But he didn't do that, either. He knew she'd made her decision, and he wouldn't be able to argue with the fatalistic logic in her note even if she did answer his call.

In truth, he was saddened but not surprised. He knew where she probably was now, someplace where they served booze. He cared but he understood that it was hopeless to try to help her. Some people you couldn't save. Some people you couldn't save from themselves.

Those were the ones who haunted you, because you could have tried harder even though you knew it was hopeless, because somehow or another, on the way out, they made others partners in their destruction. Even the people they loved. Maybe especially them.

He folded the note carefully, as if he might keep it.

Then he reconsidered, wadded it small and tight, and dropped it in the wastebasket.

79

A month later, Quinn was sitting at an outside table of a West Side restaurant nursing some kind of overpriced latte that was actually pretty good. An old woman sat at the table opposite his. She had three precisely aligned narrow gouges in her left cheek where her cat had clawed her. If that's what had happened. If the woman even owned a cat. Quinn never got tired of observing people in New York and trying to read them.

A signal changed and traffic streamed past in the street only ten feet away, raising the noise level and leaving a low-lying haze of exhaust fumes. Pedestrians hurried along the sidewalk, occasionally bumping and shoving at each other in the narrowed space between restaurant railing and curb.

Quinn smiled. He knew that sooner or later one of those pedestrians would be Pearl. She was supposed to meet him here in five minutes for lunch.

Pearl was doing well since her release from the hospital. Last week she'd even begun working again as a guard at the bank. She continued to attract and befuddle Quinn, and he knew she always would.

Quinn glanced at the *Times* folded on the table. In it he'd read with satisfaction that the latest polls showed Harley Renz was the most popular police commissioner in the city's history. There actually were rumors concerning a mayoral bid, most of them probably generated by Renz. Quinn figured Renz had come out of the Torso Murders case better than anyone.

Fedderman had also come out okay. He was back in Florida, continuing his uneasy retirement, waiting for another call from Quinn. From time to time he sent Quinn citrus fruit.

Palmer Stone and Gloria Lamping had lawyered up, but in truth they were helpless now. The system had them in its teeth, and the system would shake them and chew them to a fineness that was nothing.

Two weeks ago the dead body of Maria Sanchez had been discovered in a bathtub in a Tijuana motel. Her tongue had been cut out and her mouth stuffed with cocaine.

The Torso Murders had ceased.

Jill Clark had reclaimed her life.

Quinn noticed a bobbing, dark-haired head in the oncoming stream of pedestrians and stood up so he could be seen.

He grinned. Pearl was here.